CRIMES AGAINST MAGIC

CRIMES AGAINST MAGIC

STEVE McHugh

47NORTH

Text copyright © 2013 by Steve McHugh
First published in 2012 by Hidden Realms Publishing

Published by 47North
P.O. Box 400818
Las Vegas, NV 89140

ISBN-13: 9781477848081
ISBN-10: 1477848088
Library of Congress Catalog Number: 2013941256

Cover design by Eamon O'Donoghue

CRIMES AGAINST MAGIC

STEVE MCHUGH

47N⬤RTH

For Vanessa.

My better half in every sense of the word.

Thank you.

PROLOGUE

Soissons, France. 1414.

Rumors of how the French had murdered their own people reached me long before I'd arrived at Soissons. Even as an Englishman, and despite the never-ending conflicts between our countries, I couldn't accept that the French would do such a thing. But when I walked through the city's open gates and saw the multitude of bodies lying side by side, I believed.

The town had been ripped asunder in an act of exceptional brutality, the inhabitants torn to pieces—men murdered as they defended their families, women brutalized and raped until their captors tired of them and left them to die. Not even children were spared, killed alongside their friends and families. The carrion took over, desecrating the remains even further. A city of a few thousand people reduced to food for crows and rats.

It soon became apparent that there would be no survivors to the massacre. My search of the city only brought more dead, even more questions, and few answers. Most had obvious sword and axe wounds, or heads crushed by hammer, but some had claw marks across the throat and torso. Something far worse than simple armed soldiers stalked the city.

I stopped by a partially eaten body. The man's sword had fallen onto the path beside him. His abdomen was covered in bite marks. Whatever had attacked him had devoured his internal organs. The bite marks could have belonged to a large wolf, but I knew I wasn't going to be that lucky.

Dusk was beginning to settle. Birds flew home for the night, a brilliant red sky lighting their way. A low growl resonated from the end of a row of houses close by. I placed my hand on the hilt of my *jian*, drawing the Chinese sword a few inches out of its sheath as I continued toward the noise.

I reached the end of the houses and peered around the corner. The stench of death had hung in the air from the moment I entered the city, but it mixed with something else, something more animal than human.

In the center of a large courtyard, a beast sat hunched on muscular legs, its maw deep inside the stomach of a dead man, feasting loudly. Intestines had spilled out of the wound and now rested beside the body on the blood-slick ground. Several more dead men were littered around, none of whom appeared to have been devoured.

I looked up at the sky. "It's shit like this that makes me hate you." The man I worked for couldn't have heard me—there was an ocean separating the countries we were in—but it made me feel better to say it.

I stepped into view. The beast immediately stopped feeding and looked up at me. "Live food," it growled.

A sigh escaped my lips. "You don't have to do this."

The beast stood on two legs, stretching to its full height. It was over a head taller than me, and its muscular frame was covered in dark fur, now matted with blood. The beast's hands consisted of an elongated palm with long fingers, each tipped with a razor-sharp claw. I should know how sharp those bastards were—I'd fought enough werewolves in my time.

The werewolf lifted its nose and sniffed the air. "I can smell your blood, little man." It stepped forward and opened its mouth, showing me the dozens of wickedly dangerous teeth dripping with gore.

"That's very impressive," I said. "You know what I've got? This." I tapped the *guan dao* strapped to my back—a Chinese halberd, consisting of a one-and-a-half-meter-long wooden pole with a curved sword edge on one end and a sharp spike on the other.

The werewolf shrugged. "You're just a human. I can kill you before you even draw it."

"Maybe." I hurled a silver dagger into the throat of the beast. It dropped to its knees, desperately trying to remove the dagger as panic set in. Its long fingers were unable to get a good grip on the slick hilt, and it started to choke as blood filled its windpipe. The werewolf raised its eyes back to me, utterly afraid, as I covered the distance between us and drove my silver-laced *jian* into its chest, piercing the heart and killing it instantly.

I held onto the *jian's* hilt and placed one boot on the werewolf's chest, dragging the blade from the dead beast with a sucking sound. A loud thud accompanied it a second later as the sword came free and the corpse hit the ground. I retrieved and cleaned my dagger before checking on the five dead men lying about the courtyard. The huge muscles in their shoulders and arms made them appear almost deformed, and each one was missing his middle and index fingers. Deep claw gouges sat in their flesh, and one of them had lost his entire face when the werewolf had struck. Their uniforms showed that they'd been English archers, and they'd died in a horrific manner.

Then one of them opened his eyes. And screamed.

CHAPTER 1

Southampton, England. Now.

I *love this part.* The thought rattled around my brain. The first few minutes of a new job always started the same—excitement built in my fingers and toes, moved to my arms and legs, and then settled in my stomach just long enough to give me butterflies.

The feeling bubbled away as I passed my party invitation to one of three huge bouncers at the mansion's front door. It was an official invite, so I was unconcerned about being denied entrance. For the amount of money I'd bribed a staff member to get hold of the damn thing, it should have come in a solid gold envelope. A friend of mine had given me the job a few weeks earlier. Initially, I'd been reluctant to accept. Most jobs went through my partner, Holly, and she recommended the best ones to undertake. I was a thief, and a good one at that, but I'd stayed off most law enforcement radars because I never had any contact with my clients. It was all done electronically via Holly.

Saying yes to the job brought a whole new set of problems to deal with. My friend needed me to steal something from a house, despite the fact that he was fully aware of how much I hated breaking into homes. For a start, the occupants were much more likely to call the police and freak out to the media, but mostly

I hated them because the variables for a home break-in are astronomical. Anything can go wrong. There are neighbors and pets to consider. And children. Will the inhabitants wake up in the night for a drink? Does one of them work the late shift and get home just as I'm getting started? Even after researching the owners, I considered home jobs a damn minefield of crap, to be avoided like the plague. But my client was a good friend, and the pay was excellent. Besides, I owed him. And he's the sort of man who collected on his debts.

The bouncer waved me through, and a waiter offered me a glass of champagne. Personally, I've always hated the stuff, but as everyone in the huge room beyond had a glass of champagne in hand, I decided that blending in would make life easier, so I accepted the drink.

The hosts lived in one of Southampton's high-class neighborhoods, one of those frequented by footballers and others with too much money and not enough taste. Case in point, the massive foyer I found myself in had a large zebra skin rug on the marble floor. It lay miserably between two ornate staircases leading to an empty landing above. More bouncers stood at the top of each set of stairs, turning people away when they tried to get to the upper floor. I'd have put money that the owners of the house would use that area to address the crowd below, thanking everyone and looking down at them all from their lofty perch.

I walked through the house and noticed several small mahogany display cabinets. Each one contained a collection of bronzed statues of ancient Greek warriors and the occasional vase from the same time period. People congregated around them, pointing and talking about the host's acquisitions.

"Nice suit."

I turned to see a young woman, champagne flute in hand, running one perfectly manicured finger gently down the crystal stem. It was either a subconscious gesture of nerves or a conscious gesture of seduction. I hadn't decided.

"I've not seen you before," she continued. Her eyes were large and deep brown, with thick lashes, and her full red lips looked moist and inviting. A golden dress clung to her voluptuous body, leaving little to the imagination. She licked her bottom lip slowly, never taking her gaze from me. Okay, she knew exactly what she was doing.

"I haven't seen you either," I said.

"You know the birthday boy well?" She moved forward ever so slightly and brushed my shirt cuff. "A bit of fluff," she lied, using the distraction as an excuse to get a good look at my ring finger.

"Thank you," I said with a smile, ignoring her question. "I'm Nate."

"Jasmine." She moved again and her golden dress rode up perfectly toned thighs. Just a small amount, but it was enough to gain my attention. She caught me watching as she readjusted herself, and smiled. "So what do you do to afford such beautiful clothes? Footballer?"

If I'd been drinking the champagne, I probably would have ruined the moment by spraying it all over her immaculately made-up face. Instead, I just chuckled. "I've never kicked a football in my life. I'm a thief."

Jasmine raised her hand in front of her mouth to hide her smile. Most people would rather hear a reasonable lie than the fantastical truth.

"And what do you steal?" she asked. "Women's hearts? Their virginity?"

It was my turn to smile. "It's been a long time since I've stolen a woman's virginity. I was under the impression that virginal women no longer exist."

"And hearts?"

"You can't steal what is given freely."

Jasmine smiled again. It was a beautiful smile, and I regretted that I would never see it again once the job was over. I glanced past her at a clock hung high on the wall. Almost ten. The party had only been going on for a few hours, and it would be a while before it hit full swing.

"A lot of women turned to watch you as you walked in. As did their boyfriends. They don't like it when a new man enters the equation, especially one who turns their dates' heads."

I'd noticed a few of them moving between me and their girlfriends or wives. "So where's your boyfriend?"

"My boyfriend is an asshole who thinks that playing football gives him an excuse to cheat on me with that bitch in the corner over there."

I took a step to the side and followed Jasmine's gaze. At the end of a throng of people another stunning woman leaned against a faux Roman pillar, drink in hand, and pretended to be interested in the young muscular man who spoke to her. Every now and then she glanced briefly at the expensive watch on the man's wrist. "He why you're flirting with me?"

"He was to begin with. But now I'm enjoying myself." Jasmine blushed slightly, downed her champagne in one motion, and picked up a second flute as a waiter walked past. "Maybe if I had fake tits I wouldn't have been left here all alone."

"You don't need to change a single thing. If he can't see that, then he's a fool."

I moved back to my original position, facing Jasmine, who looked pleased.

"Yet I stay with *him*. What does that make me?"

I hadn't counted on being a relationship counselor. "You want to go for a walk?" I asked out of a desire to get her off topic.

She watched her boyfriend for a few seconds. "Yeah, let's go outside."

Jasmine took my arm as we threaded past dozens of people, most of whom appeared as fake as the woman with Jasmine's boyfriend. A few of the men, obviously friends of theirs, gave me evil glares, but no one stopped us.

We walked past a huge swimming pool and down to some secluded benches. I turned back to get a good view of the bedrooms on the top floor. *This might be easier than I'd imagined.*

Jasmine sat on the bench and crossed her legs, allowing the skirt to move up her thighs again. We continued to flirt, and eventually she asked, "So, Mr. Thief, what are you really doing here?"

I leaned up against a giant stone gargoyle, its face a permanent snarl that not even a mother could love. "I'm going to steal a book."

She laughed. "A book? *Really*? Is it expensive or important?"

Her tone of disbelief was almost identical to the one I'd used when told what I was stealing. I shook my head. "No idea. I've been asked to steal it, and I intend to go through with it."

"So what about me?"

"You're a...*complication*." I smiled.

Jasmine returned the smile and shook her head before looking around the garden. "Are you planning on ravishing me in the darkness?"

I glanced at my watch. Eleven p.m. I wanted to get this job finished sooner rather than later. "Do you want me to?"

She nodded and took a deep breath. "God, yes." Her voice was raspy. She moved back slightly, uncrossing her legs. "I know how to get into the bedrooms upstairs without going past those idiots on the staircase."

"Lead the way."

Jasmine led me up to the house and through a side door, where steps led down into some sort of game room. A pool table and dart board occupied one side, a huge TV and several leather couches on the other.

We passed through the room and walked down a dark corridor. Jasmine stopped me at the foot of a set of stairs and looked around the corner before dragging me past them to a lift. She shoved me inside and hit the button for the top floor. She pushed herself against me and kissed me hard.

"I've only just met you," she whispered.

"Does that matter?"

Jasmine shook her head. The lift began to ascend and she moved away from me. "It's been so long since anyone's made me feel like this," she sighed and kissed me once more. A small moan escaped her lips as she started to kiss my neck as my hands roamed her body.

I stared up at the ceiling of the lift and silently wondered whom I'd pissed off in a previous life. Having to upset a beautiful young lady who wanted to do unspeakable things to me was not going to make me happy.

The lift stopped and the doors opened with only a tiny squeak. Jasmine grabbed my hand and led me quickly across the hallway and through a set of double doors. As we dove into the room I caught a glimpse of the bouncers at the top of the stairs, their eyes never wavering from the front door.

The bedroom was huge, with a four-poster bed to one side, an ornate dressing table next to it. Another huge TV hung from the cream-colored wall opposite the bed. Everything was white, cream, or a variation. Even the bed's wood had been dyed cream. It was vaguely disturbing, like the room had been covered in milk.

"Is this the master bedroom?" I asked as I looked through the large windows down onto the back garden.

"Yeah," Jasmine said, followed by the click of the door locking.

I turned around to discover that she'd removed her dress, letting it fall freely to the floor as she walked toward me. She rubbed her hands over her exposed breasts, squeezed them slightly and smiled as I watched. She definitely didn't need work done. Stunning was too timid a word to use. "You like?" she asked.

I nodded and walked toward her. "I want you to know something."

"*Now*?" she asked as she played with one of her nipples.

"You can do better than your boyfriend. Not all men are assholes, and you deserve to find one who isn't."

"Are *you* an asshole?" Jasmine licked her finger and ran it down her body to her pierced bellybutton.

I tried not to watch her move—I didn't want to let my own desire to overtake me. "You need to know something about me."

Concern flickered over her face. "If you're married, I won't do that."

"No, nothing like that." I raised my hand, so that the back faced Jasmine. She stared in shock as lines of brilliant white crisscrossed my skin. If I'd been shirtless she would have seen it continue up my arms and across my chest and back.

Wonder changed to panic as Jasmine fought for breath. "I'm sorry," I said as she passed out into my arms. "I'm a sorcerer," I whispered as I laid her on the bed and pulled the covers over her body.

I don't like to do violence when on a job. I've always thought it sloppy and unprofessional to hurt people just to make your life a little easier, and while Jasmine would wake up after twenty minutes with a headache, that was the extent of the damage I'd done by removing all the oxygen from her lungs.

I made my way over to a large painting opposite the bed. It depicted the party hosts in some sort of regal pose. A small dog sat in the woman's arms. The whole thing looked ridiculous.

I pulled the painting off the wall, placed it gently on the floor, and turned back to the now-exposed safe. The steel was cold as I placed my palm against it. A moment later the white, spider web pattern re-emerged across the back of my hand and wrist. After a few seconds of concentration the steel began to buckle and warp. Soon after, the air pressure I'd created was enough to bend the safe's door, snapping it free of its hinges. I tossed the metal door with ease onto a thickly padded armchair nearby, where it landed with a soft thud.

Inside the safe was a large quantity of money, some jewelry, and a small black box, just big enough for a paperback book. I ignored the money and jewelry and removed the box, opening it to reveal the leather-bound book inside. The pages looked old and worn, and the leather appeared singed in places. It seemed like a complete waste of vast quantities of money. But then it wasn't my money that had purchased it.

I dropped the box back into the safe and placed the book inside a satin pouch I'd brought with me. I slipped it into my jacket's inside pocket before replacing the painting and hiding the ruined safe door behind a chest of drawers. It would give me some time before anyone noticed something was wrong.

One last glance at the still unconscious Jasmine and I left the room, taking the key with me. Once in the hallway, I locked the door and pushed the key back into the room through the crack between the door and carpet, allowing Jasmine to let herself out when she was ready. I wasn't worried about her telling everyone she'd seen me—eyewitness reports were notoriously unreliable, and besides, she'd probably be so embarrassed to wake up naked in her friend's bed that mentioning what had happened would have been the last thing on her mind.

I was going to use the lift and make my exit through the back garden, but one of the bouncers at the top of the stairs was arguing with a few guests who wanted to go upstairs. I used the opportunity to walk past undisturbed and continued down into the foyer and out the front door. The cacophony from the party guests followed me down the drive and past five 4X4 BMWs that had probably never seen an off-road path in their lives. The noise faded when I reached my car on the street.

I climbed into the black Audi TT I'd stolen earlier and felt a twang of guilt over Jasmine. Hopefully she wouldn't get into any trouble for what I'd done. I pushed the emotion aside and removed the book from my pocket, holding it up to the car's interior light. A smile broke across my face and a thought entered my mind.

I love my job.

CHAPTER 2

After finishing the previous night's job in Southampton, I'd driven to London and stayed at a prebooked hotel room, ditching the Audi on a nearby road. As it was only seven in the morning, I had plenty of time before I needed to meet Holly. She lived in London, not too far from St Paul's Cathedral, giving her amazing views of one of the most beautiful buildings I'd ever seen. Granted, I only remembered ten years back, but it would have probably been pretty high up the list of impressive structures even with full recall.

Holly had arranged to meet me near her place. There were a lot of restaurants and bars close by, and we regularly used them to meet after a job. It was easy to blend in with all the business workers and lawyers constantly having meetings. My hotel was close to Tottenham Court Road, so it only took five minutes at most to get there on the tube. In fact, it took longer to get through the tube stations than to actually use the train.

I took the Northern line to Embankment, crossed to the District line, and took another tube to Whitechapel. Whitechapel is famous for one reason—Jack the Ripper. Mention the place to almost anyone on earth and their first thoughts will be those six murders back in late 1888. In a sea of death and horror at the time, people remember only those six. It was probably because he was never caught, but giving publicity to brutal murders and the perpetrator felt…wrong. After a hundred years, the line between murderer and celebrity blurred to the point of nonexistence.

I made my way past the start of the Jack the Ripper tour, where a large group of people were all waiting for their chance to walk in the steps of history. I continued on to an alley about halfway down the street. At the end of the alley stood a large, barrel-chested man in a dark suit.

"He know you're coming?" he asked in a deep voice.

"No, I thought I'd just pop in. It's been a while since I've last had a good girlie chat."

"Don't piss about, Nate. You know he gets shitty if I don't ask."

"Yes, Jerry, he knows I'm coming." I glanced at my watch. "Although I'm about two hours early."

"Ah, fucking hell, he doesn't like that." Jerry rubbed the dark goatee that was a few inches long, cut to a point to resemble a hairy spear tip. The cogs turned as he thought what might happen if I went in early. "Okay, you can go in, but if he complains, I'll say you threatened me."

I stared at the almost seven-foot-tall, three-hundred-pound frame of the mountain in front of me. If I threatened him, I'd better do it from behind a tank. "Say I used mind control on you," I suggested.

Jerry smiled and moved aside, showing the door he'd been hiding. He pulled back the steel gate with a nasty creak and nodded as I opened the thick wooden door and stepped inside.

On my first trip to Jerry's boss many years previous, I'd expected the door to lead to a small office or shop. Instead, it led to a tiny room with dingy white tiles on all the walls. You could go from one end to the other in about three steps. But Jerry certainly wasn't trying to stop anyone from gaining entrance to a tiny, dirty hole. His presence was to stop people from using the stairs it contained.

Easily the length of the longest tube station escalators, the stairs started in the tiny room and led down. I followed them as the lights on the stairs flared to life, illuminating the same dingy white tiles lining the walls.

After a few steps the door behind me slammed shut. A rush of air flew over the back of my neck and I sighed.

"You know the whole *creepy* vibe doesn't really work well when I've been here dozens of times before." I continued to the bottom of the stairs and out onto an abandoned subway station. It was so old that no one knew its original name. I'd heard that it wasn't even on any of the old Underground maps. A nice little hidey-hole, tucked away for use only by a select few.

At one end of the small station platform was an archway, which led to the portion between where I was and an identical platform on the other side of the station. It contained a makeshift shop with dozens of items all set out on dark wooden shelves and benches. More items hung from metal hooks welded to a large metallic grate next to an arch identical to the one I'd walked under. A middle-aged man sat behind a large metal desk. He was examining a pocket watch through an eyepiece. His other eye was covered with a black patch.

He looked up at me. "You're early." He brushed his long gray hair off his shoulders, revealing a deep scar along one cheek.

I glanced at the huge man sitting in the corner, his arms crossed over his gargantuan chest. He nodded at me once and went back to pretending to be invisible.

"Robert will never speak to you, Nathanial," the middle-aged man said.

"Too well trained," I said. "And the name is Nate, or Nathan. You know this."

Francis smiled and gestured toward the silent bodyguard, who opened his mouth to show a stub where his tongue should have been. "You see, someone cut it off a long time ago. He cannot talk."

For all the times I'd been to see Francis, his bodyguard's lack of tongue had never come up before. I just thought he was quiet. "I'm sorry," I said to Robert. His shrug suggested he'd gotten used to it long ago.

"And why do you care what I call you? Do you even know if Nathan is your real name?"

"No matter what I may have been called, I'm now Nate. That's real enough for me."

Francis waved away my concerns. "So, *Nate*, did you bring it?"

A small smile spread across my lips. "Of course I brought it. You hire me and I deliver."

I removed the satin pouch from my pocket and placed it on the shining counter by Francis. He hungrily spilled the contents onto a velvet cloth.

"I take it that little book is exactly what you wanted."

Francis carefully turned the leather-bound book over and over in his hands, a smile of glee across his lips. "Do you have any idea what this is?"

"It's a book. I assume an old, expensive one."

"It's a *very old* copy of the *Iliad*."

"Someone wanted a copy of Homer's *Iliad*? Couldn't they get one from the library?"

"A client requested that I find her a copy. A very specific copy, in fact."

"Why that copy?"

Francis shrugged, causing his hair to spill over his shoulders. "No idea. But she paid quarter of a million for it. And for that I don't ask too many questions."

I couldn't help but smile. "Oh yeah, getting paid that much money for an old book is perfectly normal."

The noise from the man in the corner almost sounded like a chuckle. Francis didn't seem to find the humor in it. "I did check her out, *Nathanial*," he said tersely. "But this book is nearly two thousand years old. The amount of money I was paid for this is but a fraction of its true value."

I knew Francis was exaggerating, but I decided it was best just to take his point and let him live in his moment of happiness. "So do I get paid then?"

Francis carefully inserted the book back into the pouch and placed it on the counter, which he reached under and withdrew a small black bag. "Fifty grand," he said. "And more important, you no longer owe me any favors."

I had no concerns that he was going to steal it back from me or that he'd have his men attack me. That wouldn't be good for business. Contrary to popular belief, there is honor amongst thieves. It just comes in a monetary form.

A decade previous, I'd woken up in an abandoned warehouse with no memory of anyone or anything, including myself.

Beside me was a Heckler and Koch USP compact, with a full magazine of silver bullets. Along with the gun, there had been a wooden cane with a sword inside and a piece of paper with the name Nathan Garrett on it, which I discovered was in my own handwriting.

It's hard to explain how it feels to know nothing about yourself, but there's a lot of fear involved. Fear at the unknown, fear that there are people who know exactly who you are but that you may never meet them, and, at least for me, an all-consuming fear that you're not safe. That something was terribly wrong. It was a horrible experience, which is probably why a few minutes after panicking about my predicament, I used magic for the first time.

The windows on the warehouse exploded out, embedding the glass deep in the nearest tree trunk a few dozen feet away from where I sat. Originally, I thought I'd gone mad, but over the next few days I used magic over and over again. Just a little here and there, but eventually I started to hear voices. They told me to keep using magic, to let it flow out of me. That shook me enough to stop using it altogether as I started my search for who, and what, I was.

Francis had been the man to not only tell me about the world I live in—and I couldn't possibly thank him enough—but also make me aware of exactly what I was, a sorcerer.

He explained that a sorcerer's magic is bound to two different schools. The first is Elemental—water, earth, fire, and air. Most users of magic start in this school; the magic I'd used in my target's bedroom was air, hence the white glyphs, which crossed over my arms. Each type of magic corresponds to a different color glyph—white for air, orange for fire, green for earth, and blue for water.

Sorcerers start by learning one form of magic in the Elemental school. But over time, anywhere from decades to centuries, they can learn a second. In my case, the second element I had control over is fire, meaning I was a lot older than my early thirties appearance suggested. This second form can never be the opposite to one already learned, so I could never learn earth or water magic, no matter how much I tried.

The second school of magic is called Omega magic. This magic is too powerful to be wielded by a novice. For this reason, any sorcerer wishing to use Omega magic is usually millennia old at least. It consists of mind, matter, shadow, and light. As with the Elemental school, each magic corresponds to a different color, although I wasn't powerful enough to use any of the four types.

Over the years, I'd heard rumors of a third school. Blood magic. But I'd never found anyone willing or knowledgeable enough to talk about it at length. The only thing I did learn—it scares the shit out of people.

Without Francis, I'd probably still be living on the streets, using just enough magic to keep myself alive. But even after the discovery of what I was, I'm wary of using too much magic; the idea of having the feeling of being able to do anything with magic was not one I wished to repeat.

"The robbery isn't on the news yet," he said, bringing me out of the memory of his teachings. "How did it go?"

I stuffed the money in my backpack. "Easily. Footballers have too much money."

Francis chuckled. "Do you have any other jobs on?"

I shook my head. "I plan on relaxing for a few weeks."

"When you need more work let me know. I can always find something for you to...*acquire* for me."

"Enjoy the book," I told Francis, who hurried away to make a phone call. I said my good-byes and left the station, opening the main entrance door and nodding to Jerry as I stepped back outside into the daylight.

The cold, crisp air was a bit of a shock to the system after the heated Underground, but I soon warmed up once I'd made my way back to the tube station.

As I descended the steps, deep in thought about the possibility of some time off, an attractive young blonde woman bumped into me, brushing her hand against mine. I was about to apologize when suddenly my world started to spin. I steadied myself against the side of the stairwell as a noise rang in my ears. By the time I'd recovered, I'd noticed that the mystery woman hadn't even paused. She'd continued on her journey up out of the mouth of the tube entrance, vanishing into the increasing crowds above. I darted up the stairs after her, but searching produced no results. I rubbed my hand where she'd touched it and wondered what had just happened. I wasn't poisoned, I was certain of that, and the noise and dizziness had left me as suddenly as it had arrived. Maybe I was tired, or maybe my memories were beginning to come back. Either way, I felt normal once again, so I shook my head and continued on my journey.

CHAPTER 3

My mobile rang the second I stepped out of the tube at Bank. My mind still pondered the blonde woman from a few minutes earlier. Something about her seemed familiar, although I couldn't place what. Maybe a memory, stagnant in time, was finally coming loose. Or maybe she looked like someone I'd seen on the TV. It was hard to tell where the memories came from sometimes.

"Hey, Holly," I said as I started my walk toward St. Paul's Cathedral. It was coming up to lunch time, and the tube would get busy again. I didn't like crowds. You never knew who was in them.

"We're at a sushi restaurant near the cathedral. It's called Zen. My dad's just gone to get some drinks."

I crossed a busy road, running the last few feet to avoid a barreling truck. "I'll be about twenty minutes," I said after giving the driver a look at my middle finger.

"Did you see Francis?" Holly was just over thirty years old, and despite her family—who, if you were feeling generous, could be described as having loose morals—was unaccustomed to the criminal life of constantly looking over your shoulder and trusting as few people as possible.

Her father, a man I'd worked for before meeting Holly, had told me that she was smart as a whip, but her sense of danger was often overridden by her sense of adventure and excitement. It was a fair description, but I made sure to keep her out of anything that might cause her problems. It was why she had as little to do with Francis as possible. Some of his jobs were on the... *dangerous* side.

I didn't want to start discussing Francis, or Holly's payment, out in the open. "I'll see you soon." I hung up and continued on my walk, as the sounds of midday London washed around me. I sometimes wondered how anyone ever got a moment's peace in a city the size of London. It would have certainly driven me insane to live with the constant noise. Visiting is one thing, but I preferred a slightly less cluttered place to live.

By the time I'd reached the cathedral, lunch was in full force. All the lawyers and business graduates tried to look as important as possible in their impressive suits as they ate overpriced sandwiches and discussed things that would bore most people into a permanent coma.

The sushi bar was easy enough to find. A huge yellow sign outside made sure I was unlikely to get the wrong place. From the front entrance, I spotted Holly reading a book at a four-person table toward the rear of the restaurant.

The restaurant hostess, a young Asian woman, came over. I explained that I was looking for my friend, but she stared at me, slightly confused. It was only then that I realized I'd not spoken to her in English, but Japanese, a language I didn't even know I could speak. I hastily repeated myself in English and she smiled slightly and she passed me a menu before allowing me to walk over to Holly.

"Nice choice of restaurant," I said once I stood beside her.

Holly put the book down and beamed. Her shoulder-length blonde hair was tied back, showing the tip of a tattoo just below her hairline. She'd gotten the angel a few years previous. It covered her back, with the wings creeping up slightly on either side of her neck.

Holly stood and embraced me. "It's good to see you again."

"You too," I said and sat opposite her. Holly and I spoke every few days, but we only saw each other once or twice every few months. Any more than that and it would increase risks for both her and me. But less than that and I would…miss her. She was always so full of life and energy, it was hard not to get sucked in. "I thought you were with your dad?" I motioned toward the book.

"He's popped out for a few minutes, which probably means an hour or so. Figured I might as well catch up on my reading until one of you arrived."

"Hope you weren't waiting too long." My stomach audibly rumbled. "Guess I should order."

"Already ordered you some duck futomaki and sashimi. I know you don't like salmon, so I had them make it with tuna instead."

I bowed my head slightly. "Thank you."

"You must be the only person in the world who hates salmon but likes other fish."

"Then I'm the only person with working taste buds."

Holly chuckled for a second before I caught the movement of her eyes as she spotted someone by the restaurant's entrance. "Your dad back?" I asked as a waitress placed my food in front of me. The smell made my stomach rumble once again.

Holly nodded. "See for yourself."

After dunking one of the small tuna rolls into some wasabi and soy sauce, and taking a bite, I turned to watch Holly's dad make his way into the restaurant. Mark O'Hara wasn't a large man. Physically, he was only a few inches taller than me, so less than six feet, and could never be considered muscular. But he was wiry and capable of horrific violence on those who have wronged him. He ran his family, and by extension those who worked for him, with an iron fist. If you stepped out of line, he'd let you know, and it probably wasn't a good idea to do it again.

"Nate," he said, the word rolled in a thick Irish accent.

I stood to shake his hand. "Good to see you. Nice shaved head. Not at all intimidating."

Mark smiled and rubbed his newly bald head with one hand. "My wife seems to like it, and it's nice to be able to worry people without ever having to do anything." He motioned for me to sit back down before sitting on the chair next to me. "I found someone when I was on the phone outside."

Holly's smile disappeared when she glanced back over to the entrance again. Mark didn't notice the concern on his daughter's face, he was too busy reading the menu, but I certainly did and knew who that expression was meant for. At the entrance stood another man, arrogance seeping out of him like an aroma. He sneered at a patron who made the mistake of bumping into him. For a brief moment I thought he was going to attack the innocent customer. But instead he looked up at us and found something else to hate—me.

The man was Lee, Holly's younger brother by about eighteen months, and Mark's youngest son. He's a psychotic prick who likes to get his hands dirty, usually with someone else's blood. He strolled toward us, an unwavering gaze of anger aimed at me,

despite the smile on his lips. He too had shaved his head, probably to make himself appear more like his dad. But unlike Mark,
Lee had grown a goatee to go along with it.

"Holly," he said warmly and waited for her to hug him.
When seated, he removed his leather jacket to show off his
figure-hugging t-shirt. The green top was tight around his muscular arms. Black tribal tattoos snaked out from under them and
stopped at each wrist, on one of which sat an expensive gold
watch. He'd taken it from a man he almost beat to death outside
a nightclub a few years back.

The assault had gone to trial, but no one wanted to speak out
against him. Lee instills either fear or admiration in most of those
he meets. Which, as I'd shown him neither, was the reason for
his distain of me.

"So what's with the family reunion?" Holly's voice couldn't
hide her nervousness. In all the time I'd known her; Holly had
never liked or trusted her younger brother and had as little to do
with him as possible. She told me it had to do with something
that happened when she was younger, but she'd appeared upset
just remembering it, so I hadn't pushed further.

Mark lowered the menu onto the table, and an aura of seriousness settled over him. "Holly, I wanted to let you know that
Lee will be taking over more duties. He's been doing the fights
with me for a few years, but I've decided to pass the whole enter-
prise over to him."

By *fights*, Mark meant those of the illegal variety. The family
had managed them for years. With Mark overseeing everything,
they'd always been done as fairly and respectfully as possible,
and they'd managed it without any trouble. It helped that in all
his years no fighter had ever died. They'd been hospitalized,

and although most had probably taken one too many shots to the head and couldn't remember what had happened, everyone lived. I wasn't so confident that Lee would be able to lay claim to that statement after a few months of fights under his tutelage.

"That's great news," Holly lied as she gave her brother a hug. "But are you sure, Dad? I know how much you love them."

Mark grinned. "I'm not getting any younger. And besides, I need to let my boy stand on his own feet more often. He's nearly twenty-nine; he'll do just fine." Apart from being a career criminal, murderer, thief, and general nuisance for the police, Mark had one massive fault. And that was his inability to see any fault in his youngest son. Or any of his four kids for that matter. It made him a great father on many occasions, and a crappy one on others.

Mark and Lee ordered sushi and we all ate in silence. Every now and again I noticed Lee watching me. I came close to asking him if he had a problem, but that would probably cause one, and I didn't want to make a scene in the middle of a crowded restaurant.

"Holly, we need to have a chat," Mark said as he finished his plate of salmon wraps.

Holly glanced at me with a look of *are you okay?* I nodded and watched her leave the restaurant with her father and then picked up the book she'd been reading. I didn't fancy sitting in uncomfortable silence for ten minutes.

Apparently neither did Lee. "You're a real cunt, you know that?"

I sighed and placed the book next to my plate. "As the authority on all such things, I'll take your word for it." I had no idea where that last sentence had come from, and found myself surprised that I'd said it. Normally, my way of dealing with Lee was to ignore him or remove myself from the situation. Apparently my brain thought differently.

Lee's expression hardened and he flexed his head from side to side, cracking his vertebrae in the process. "The rest of my family might think the sun shines out of your ass, but I know different. You're just a thief who thinks he's above his station."

"And you're just a thug with a powerful daddy."

Redness crept up his neck—apparently I'd hit a sore point. "Once I'm in charge of everything," Lee menaced, "I'll show you the error of what you've just said."

"Well, luckily for me that's not going to happen anytime soon, now is it?" I leaned back in my chair and watched anger bubble away behind Lee's eyes. "Next time you threaten me, do it when you can follow through. It'll make you look like less of a little bitch." The words just kept coming, like a waterfall of speech designed to piss off the utter psychopath who was sat in front of me. But instead of feeling concerned, I was perfectly comfortable with his growing anger.

Lee was a few steps over the line that made you evil, but thankfully even he wouldn't have picked a fight in the middle of a crowded restaurant during the day. Instead, he continued to shoot daggers at me until Mark and Holly returned.

"We need to go." Mark placed some notes on the table to pay for everyone's lunch. "Business waits for no man." He shook my hand again. "Keep my little girl safe."

"Always," I said. Holly shook her head slightly in mock indignation.

"I fucking hate him," Holly whispered once her family had left.

A young couple sat next to us with a small child in tow. "I think we need to go to a more...*secluded* setting for this conversation."

"You coming back to my place then?" Holly asked, unhappiness evaporating with a smile.

I smiled. "Sure, why not. I've got a few hours to kill."

On the walk back to Holly's place, we decided to take a shortcut. We were about halfway down the empty alley when something told me we were being followed. I turned and found Lee standing in the mouth of the alley, a look of villainous intent on his face.

"What do you want, Lee?" Holly called to her brother, the fear in her voice easy to distinguish.

He strode toward us, menace evident in his body language. "Your boyfriend and I need to have a chat."

"Oh, for fuck's sake," Holly shouted. "Grow up. You're not a child anymore."

"It's okay," I said and turned to glance at Holly, taking my eye off her brother.

When I turned back, he hit me in the jaw, knocking me sideways, and followed up with a kick to my ribs that took me off my feet and dumped me on the cold, wet ground.

Lee shoved Holly aside, and for the first time I noticed the chain wrapped around his fist. He tore my rucksack from my back and tossed it across the alley, and a second later he dove on me, throwing punch after punch at my stomach and head. Blood flowed from my forehead into my eye, and when Lee had finally had enough, he stood back up and started stomping and kicking me.

I tried to avoid as much as I could, twisting my body to kick back out at him, but one massive kick to my head made my vision go dark. I'd never used magic in a fight before, never wanted or needed to. Hell, I wasn't even sure if I could, but I was damned if I was going to be kicked to death in a London alley.

Lee stopped kicking me and dragged me back to my feet. "Still feel like being a smart mouth?" he asked and punched me in the stomach hard enough to double me up as my oxygen rushed out of me.

For the first time I realized that Holly was screaming at Lee to stop. She tried pulling him off me, but he just pushed her away and hit me again.

"Stop it, you fucking nutcase," Holly shouted.

Lee's gaze tore away from me and settled on his older sister. I'd never seen Holly afraid before, but right then she visibly shrank away from him. "Mind your fucking tongue," Lee snapped and slapped Holly with the back of his hand, knocking her to the ground.

Something in me changed. As I watched Lee threaten his sister, I contemplated a few dozen ways to kill or maim him. And all of those methods would take only a few seconds. It was like trying to find a tiny crack on a vase and suddenly noticing dozens of flaws present. Flaws I could take advantage of.

I exploded up from my knees toward Lee, dodged a punch, and slammed my elbow into his ribs. He staggered back and raised his hands in boxer's stance, a sadistic smile spread across his lips.

"I thought this wasn't going to be fun," he said.

Lee threw a powerful left hook, which I deflected aside. I struck him in his kidney with the heel of my palm. He winced with pain, and I followed up with a punch to his ribs and finished with a heavy shot to his chin as his guard slipped. Lee's head snapped to one side. He put his hands out to stop himself falling face first onto the cold concrete.

"You have one chance to run," I said, although it really didn't sound like something I'd say, but the flick of the blade in his hand gave me his answer. He shot up, swinging it toward me. When Lee was inches away, I slammed one open palm into his wrist and the other into the back of his hand, snapping his wrist and forcing him to let go of the knife. My second and third strikes hit him in his ribs once more. This time, the force of the blows broke bones.

He was no longer in any position to fight, but he'd hit Holly and tried to kill me. This was no longer about winning.

Lee cradled his arm against his chest, his breathing fast and pained, and looked down at the knife, which had fallen to the ground. I kicked it close to him. "Pick it up," I said.

He watched me for a moment and then bent over to retrieve it. His eyes never left my face. He weighed it in his good hand before dashing forward and swiping it in an arc toward me. I stepped inside the attack and smashed my elbow into his jaw. His head snapped back once again, and I followed with a knee to his gut. Lee dropped the knife and doubled over in pain, collapsing to his knees.

"I want you to remember what happened here," I said. Lee reached for the knife again. One quick and powerful knee to his face not only ended those dreams but also shattered his nose and knocked him out cold.

I picked up the knife and stood over Lee. Blood streamed down his face and onto the pavement. It would have been easy to kill him. One quick slice and the world would have lost one psychotic asshole.

"Nate," Holly said from behind me. "You okay?"

I turned to see concern on her face, mixed with fear. And I wasn't convinced that her fear was aimed solely at her brother. I tossed the knife onto the floor. "Yeah, I guess. Let's get you home."

As we walked away, Holly never looked back once, leaving Lee to bleed on the pavement. I glanced behind me for a final time and tried not to think about how easy it would have been for me to kill Lee. I hadn't been in a fight like that in ten years, but it felt...normal. And that should have terrified me. But it didn't.

Just what the fuck did I used to do for a living?

CHAPTER 4

Soissons, France. 1414.

The English archer's screams continued intermittently for the better part of the day. They were blood curdling, full of pain and fear, but I doubted he knew what he was doing. The deep gouges in his leg and ribs were responsible for his massive blood loss. He was either really lucky or, as his moans of pain suggested, unlucky.

An empty house, close to the pile of corpses, served as our short-term refuge. I dragged the archer inside and placed him on a bed of straw. I cleaned his wounds with fresh rain water, which made him scream out, before wrapping them in clean cloth I'd found inside the house. Then it was a matter of waiting. Hopefully, he would have some answers as to why werewolves were in the ruined city. Or why everyone here had been killed.

Initially, I was concerned that the noise would bring more surprises my way, but nothing came. If anything else was inside the city walls, it was obviously accustomed to the sounds of pain and suffering.

As night fell, the archer stirred. I watched the young man and when he moved, I unsheathed my *jian* and placed it next to me, hand on hilt, in case my fears of what had happened to him were realized.

It took a long time until he fully woke. "Where am I?" he asked weakly.

I crossed the small room, sword in hand, and held a bowl of water to his lips. The rainfall had been steady and the bowl I'd placed just outside had filled quickly. It had saved me travelling farther into the city to get more fresh water. The archer sucked down the cool liquid with eagerness. "More?" he asked.

I shook my head and placed the bowl back outside—the rain was heavier now. "Not for a few minutes."

"Hungry too."

That was a surprise, and not a good one. "Let me check your wounds." He held his breath as I slowly removed the bloody cloth, but I found no wound beneath it. My fears had been right all along. But he still had a chance. I had to allow him that. Even so, I kept the sword unsheathed. "What do you remember?"

"I was on the city walls. We were betrayed by some of the English. The French came...they killed...killed so many."

"Betrayed? By whom?"

The archer tried to shrug but couldn't quite manage it. "They came with a girl, no more than sixteen or so. Kept her hidden in one of the houses by the main square. They betrayed us."

"But you don't know who *they* were?"

The archer shook his head. "What's your name?"

"Nathanial Garrett," I said. "Yours?"

"Thomas Carpenter. Everyone else is dead, aren't they?"

I nodded. "The French did this?"

"At first, yes. The women were forced to watch as their children and husbands were slaughtered and then...they had their way with them. They even raped and murdered nuns. Why would they do that? We fought as best we could, but we were captured and taken to the main square."

I fought the urge to go kill something. "What happened?"

"We were shackled and each of us forced to place our hands on an anvil. They used a knife and hammer to do...this." He raised his hand and stared at it intently. Bloody cloth sat where middle and forth fingers once did. They'd been taken to the knuckle. He'd never pull a bow again. It was a punishment that the French liked to give out after they'd captured English bowmen. Thomas watched his hand for a few moments, as if finally registering what had been done to him. And tears began to fall.

I took his hand and examined the wound. Or I would have if, under the blood and grime, the skin hadn't already healed. Before he could notice what had happened, I grabbed some cloth from the floor and wrapped it around his hand. I didn't need him to be any more afraid than he already was. "Why didn't the French kill you?" I asked once I'd finished.

Thomas swallowed hard and closed his eyes. "That bastard who betrayed us...told them to leave us for some friends of his." Thomas winced. "The French left and we thought we'd gotten away lightly. But that night eight men came. They let us loose and told us to run. They chased us, ate whoever they found. What manner of devil were they?"

"Werewolves," I said.

Thomas' face turned green. I dodged just in time for him to vomit the water he'd drunk onto the floor. "Werewolves," he said to himself. "This is a nightmare."

"You'll get used to it." I left out the part where if he didn't, he'd be dead before long. "How do you feel?"

Thomas sucked in air. "One of them brought down Christopher. He was my friend and I watched one of them eat his face. I can still hear his screams in my head."

"It'll get better," I said and then realized that lying to him helped no one. "Actually, it won't. But you'll be able to cope with it. It'll take a long time though."

Thomas sat back and breathed deeply for a few seconds. "Who are you?"

"I was on my way back to England; I'd heard about what happened here and wanted to find out if it was true. I found you on a pile of bodies, along with a large and angry werewolf."

"How did you get me away?"

"I killed it."

Thomas studied me, his eyes said he was curious, even mesmerized with what I'd told him. But there was fear there too—fear of the world he'd just been brought into, and fear of me. "What are you, and what do you want from me?"

"I'd hoped that you would be able to tell me why werewolves were here, and maybe who they were. As for what I am, that's complicated."

"A devil?" he asked, inching away from me.

I smiled. "No, definitely not a devil."

"Will you help me get out of this accursed city? I have to get home, to let my family know I'm safe."

"I need to find where that girl was kept."

Thomas looked away. He was obviously afraid, and I couldn't say I blamed him. He wanted to run as far away from this place as possible. But he also knew that I'd killed one of the things that had massacred his friends. That gave him a measure of confidence.

And he was a war bow archer who had been crippled. Vengeance is a good motivator.

"If I come with you, I want to find the people who did *this* to me, to my friends, and to those women and children. I want them dead. I want your word that we will bring down the wrath of God on whoever was responsible for what happened here."

Thomas seemed more lucid than I'd expected for someone infected in the way he'd been. Maybe he was one of the lucky ones, to survive a werewolf attack and not go crazy. And maybe that meant I wouldn't have to kill him. I picked up a bundle of clothes from the floor and tossed them onto the bed. "Get changed, we need to move soon."

Thomas found some trousers and a tunic that were a bit too large for him and got changed. When finished, he looked down at his bandaged hand. "Do we have a deal?"

I put out my hand, which he immediately shook. "By the time I'm done," I said. "They'll *wish* God's wrath was raining down upon them."

CHAPTER 5

I dropped onto the rain-sodden mud from the top of one of the stone houses. I'd used the high vantage to scout around, but still couldn't see anything living above the size of a large rat.

"You still haven't told me how we're going to find those werewolves," Thomas said as we continued through the city.

"I'm not trying to find them," I pointed out. "I want to find where that girl was kept prisoner."

"They kept her near the main square. I only saw her once." He looked up at the thatched roof that I'd been on. "Did you see anything?"

"The square is deserted."

"Why don't you sound happy about that?" Thomas pulled the cloak I'd found for him tightly around his chest, trying in vain to stop the rain's continued assault.

"Because that means either no one is waiting for us or, more likely, they know we'll come this way and want to surprise us." I unhooked my *jian* and passed it to Thomas. "You'll need this more than me. Do you know how to use it?"

"My father taught me when I was younger." Thomas unsheathed the sword, testing the weight in his good hand. "It's a lot lighter than I was expecting."

"You don't need heavy swings to kill, as you would with a great sword. The edge is razor sharp. Even the slightest contact will cut them to ribbons."

Thomas nodded and re-sheathed the blade, following me as we set off once more.

The closer we got to the town square, the nicer the living accommodations became. There was also an increase in dead bodies. People had run this way to escape the incoming French, creating an effective killing area for the invading army. A large pile of men, each wearing the English flag on their clothes, had been dumped next to an ornate fountain. Rats ran freely among the corpses and I tried to ignore the overpowering stench.

"Which house was it?" I asked as we walked past three women, their clothes ripped hurriedly from their bodies. They had been brutalized and then stabbed to death, left to rot on the sodden ground. The heat of anger rose inside me.

Thomas forcibly held his gaze away from them, pointing toward the building at the far end. "The Betrayer stayed there. He would come out and talk to the children as they played. But he wouldn't talk to anyone else."

We reached the front door, a huge piece of oak, which probably took three men to place, and I pushed it open. The weight of the door made it move slowly with ominous presence as it showed us the darkness beyond. "Stay here," I said. "If anyone comes, yell and get inside."

Thomas nodded. I stepped inside the building, closing my eyes and willing my magic to life. When I opened them a moment later, there were dim orange glyphs over my hands and arms and I could see perfectly despite the darkness. Unfortunately, everything had a slight orange and red tint to it, as if observed through a flickering flame.

I took a moment to search around the large room. Several wooden chairs sat around a long table that ran the length of the room. Dozens of leather bound books were piled high on it, and some had fallen onto the rug-covered floor.

A lap of the downstairs rooms produced only a kitchen and dining area, both untouched by the ravages that I would have expected. Paintings hung on the walls and ornaments were still prominently displayed. The Betrayer's home was untouched, and that meant the werewolves and French had been told that this property was off limits from ransacking.

I finished with the ground-floor search and made my way up the wooden stairs to the top of the house. It contained a few bedrooms and a latrine, but that was it. Something didn't feel right. There had to be something I was missing.

I took another circuit of the entire ground floor and this time noticed that the dining area looked much bigger from the outside than inside. I placed my hand against the stone wall inside the room. White glyphs immediately mixed with the orange. I used magic to create a fog, which traced the stone work as it left my palm, searching for an opening.

It wasn't long before the fog vanished behind the wall on one side. I tested the stones and found one loose, pushing it until a click sounded. The wall slowly moved back.

The stairs beyond led down, deeper into the darkness.

I stepped over the lower portion of the wall and descended the poorly made stone steps. An iron gate at the bottom, the empty keyhole taunting me, prevented further exploration. Or at least that was the idea. Once I'd placed my hand against the rough metal, the orange glyphs glowed brilliant and the lock began to melt. The door swung open a few seconds later.

The room inside was large, easily the length of the house. Despite the size, it contained only some tables, chairs, and more pieces of paper. Dirt covered the floor—presumably it was easier to leave it than keep it tidy. In the middle of the room surrounded by a dozen chairs was a large cell, probably the size of one of the bedrooms upstairs. A small bed sat inside it, the only clue that someone had been held prisoner.

The bars gleamed, even in the darkness. The closer I drew, the more I made out the runes carved into both the base and the top of the cell.

The solid silver bars made a dull thud as I tapped them with the tip of my finger. I pushed the cell door open. *What in God's name was kept in here?*

I stepped inside and was immediately blinded as my glyphs vanished. I darted out of the cell, my heart pounding in my chest. Panic and the need to defend myself fought for space inside me. I took a deep breath and reapplied my vision. The sight of orange glyphs reappearing on my arms calmed me.

There was no one else in the cellar, no imminent threat. I turned back to the cell. The runes carved into it had removed my magic. Runes are commonplace and can be created by anyone with access to magical energy. The more energy applied, the more complex and powerful the runes' end result. Most sorcerers learn them early in their teachings, although few ever use them in any meaningful way as they can take a long time to prepare.

I made a few more circuits around the cell, intently studying the runes. I touched one of the markings, it shimmered black. I immediately knew what magic had been used to create the runes.

I stepped back, stumbling over a metal bar that had been driven into the floor and concealed by the dirt. I took hold of the bar and pulled, revealing a hidden wooden trapdoor as it moved. More runes were carved into the wood, probably to mask the stench of what lay inside.

Blood magic had been used to make the cell's runes. To use that much energy would have required sacrifices. A *lot* of sacrifices. I looked down at the mass of bodies, men and women, even children. Throats slit, blood used to fuel magic and then bodies discarded.

Laughter and shouts rang in my ears well before I'd removed the magic sight so as not to damage my eyes when I stepped outside of the house.

Seven werewolves stood by the fountain in the center of the square, their backs toward me. They pointed and laughed at Thomas, who stood on the fountain, sword swinging from one wolf to the next. One of them had a deep gash on its shoulder, fresh blood running down its yellow-furred arm. I removed my *guan dao* and stabbed the spiked end into the saturated ground, causing a loud crunch when it hit rock. That drew the werewolves' attention.

"Another survivor," one of them proclaimed in French, its voice a deep rumbling laugh. "But, not for long." The remaining wolves joined in with the laughter, now oblivious to Thomas, who used my distraction and jumped off the fountain. One of the wolves darted into his way, forcing Thomas to swipe with the sword. The wolf easily avoided the attack, but his stepping back allowed Thomas to dive over a nearby wall. The wolf watched him with amusement before rejoining the rest of his pack. They were in no hurry to finish their fun.

I grasped the *guan dao*, lifting it out of the ground and lowering the curved, bladed end toward the pack. "Who's in charge here?" I asked, speaking French.

The largest of the wolves stepped forward. He was covered in black fur. His yellow eyes the only splash of color. "I am the alpha." His tone suggested he was humoring me. That was his first mistake. "Your pig-sticker does not frighten me. Run, little man, before I decide you've become a nuisance to me. Your friend will stay with us."

"I will not abandon him to your *hospitality*."

The alpha howled, his subordinates following his lead. "Your friend is one of us, one of ours. If you do as I say, you may live to see the next sunrise."

I placed the tip of the blade on the ground and adjusted my grip on the pole as three of the werewolves closed in on me from the sides. "If you want him, you'll have to fight for him."

The pack sprung into action. The first bolted toward me, claws extended, ready to kill me. I snapped the *guan dao* up, catching him under the jaw. I heard the wolf fall, but didn't see it as I stepped aside and continued the momentum of the pole, whipping it around to catch the second werewolf across the throat as he sprinted toward me.

The wolf's neck exploded in a sea of red, and he died before hitting the ground. The blade made a sickening crunch as I buried it in the top of the third wolf's head. The momentum and power behind the blow brought the *guan dao* to a rest just below the wolf's eyes, splitting the top of his head in two.

A quick pull would not free the weapon, so I released the *guan dao*, pushing the dead werewolf away. The first werewolf who had attacked me, clearly not as dead as I'd expected, took the opportunity to barrel into me from behind, slamming me into, and through, the front wall of the nearest house.

I managed to twist in the wolf's grip as we crashed onto the floor. Stone dust covered everything, making visibility minimal. The wolf's massive frame pinned me to the floor, with one of his arms stuck beneath me. If he wanted it free, he had to let me move, and that wasn't on his list of options.

I covered my chest in an armor of dense air in time to deflect a swipe at my heart with his free claw. Even so, he still managed to shred my tunic, exposing the dark, shimmering marks on my skin. He took another swipe—this time the blow held so much power that it drove the air from my lungs. I needed to get free, but I couldn't do that so long as I had the equivalent weight of a large horse on my chest.

I reached up into the dust cloud and grabbed the wolf's throat. It was slippery and warm as blood continued to spill from its face where the *guan dao* had cut it. My plan meant losing my shield, so for a few seconds I'd be completely helpless.

White glyphs erupted across my skin. A pulse of thick, heavy air shot from my palms into the wolf's neck, immediately decapitating it.

I rolled aside, pushing the werewolf's body off me, dodging his detached head, which struck the wooden floor, followed immediately by arterial spray. I watched through the hole in the wall as Thomas was dragged over to the alpha. The sword I'd given him was nowhere to be seen, but he was struggling with every step. The remaining pack members laughed and howled, occasionally throwing weak strikes in Thomas' direction to see how much they could scare him.

I picked up the werewolf's head from the floor and threw it out of the house. It rolled steadily along the ground, the werewolves oblivious to it, until it came to a rest by one of their feet.

One by one, each of the wolves looked down at the severed head of their comrade in arms and then slowly turned to watch the house. As they saw me step over the rubble of the house, their expressions changed from humor to horror. A whip of flame trailed down from each of my arms. The red and orange crackled as I moved, the whips scorching the ground they touched.

The fear-laden silence was only broken by the alpha's roar. "Sorcerer!"

He knocked Thomas into the fountain with a splash. His wolves advanced, spurred on by my killing of three of their pack. I spun and brought one of the whips around me, catching the closest wolf under the arm. The molten-hot magic sliced through the fur, skin, and muscle as if it weren't there. It left only the smell of burning flesh and the wolf's screams as the whip exited under the opposite arm pit, cleaving him in two.

I darted aside and brought the second whip across, catching another wolf in the throat, detaching his head from his shoulders.

The third wolf ignored his dead companions and charged at me, hoping to catch me off guard. I brought one whip up, catching the wolf under the jaw. The second whip hit him in the thighs. The wolf's leg and face were removed from the rest of the body and he fell to the ground, a gory mess.

I walked toward the squirming wolf, changing one of the whips into a much shorter pole of volcanic heat. His throat full of blood, choking him, stopped any screams from reaching his lips. He looked up at me, and then closed his eyes. I punched the pole through his head, ending his torment.

The alpha dove toward me, but I couldn't swing my arms around fast enough to catch him as he hit my ribs, knocking me off my feet.

I extinguished the fire magic before I hit the mud, blasting a jet of wind from my hands, which spun me in the air and back onto my feet.

"Impressive," the alpha said. He stepped over one of his dead pack, trying hard not to look down. "But magic won't save you from *me.*"

I pushed my hands forward. A jet of air slammed into the alpha's legs, dragging them out from under him and planting him face-first on the dirt. He struggled back to his feet, but another gust of wind swirled around him, pushing down on his legs and forcing him to kneel before me. I increased the speed and ferocity of the wind as it slowly climbed up the alpha's body. Before long, it would have the strength to rip trees from the ground. The effect on the alpha was no less impressive as the wind cut through his thick fur, slicing his skin. His cries of pain were lost to the roar of the wind.

The glyphs on my hands dulled as I moved them slightly, decreasing the power of the storm encircling the alpha. I waited until the noise had died down. "Who betrayed this city?" I demanded. "I want his name."

"Go to Hell, sorcerer. You'll get nothing from me." Blood oozed from cuts on his face, one eye almost swollen shut.

I nodded and started the storm again, this time increasing the intensity. The vortex spun faster and faster, ripping huge lumps of flesh from the werewolf's body. I allowed it to continue marginally longer than I had the first time, then stopped it just as suddenly.

"I don't know his name," the alpha said breathlessly as the winds died down. "But he *will* kill you for this." The werewolf sprung up in a feeble attempt to surprise me. But he was too far away, and too weak, to make it effective.

I stepped back and coated one of his legs in a thick gale. "You're an idiot," I said with a sigh and increased the pressure until the bones in the alpha's lower leg crushed like a walnut shell.

He screamed with pain and rage as he dropped back to the ground, managing to stay on his good knee. "I don't know his name," he repeated. "I swear."

"Why was he here?"

"He used the English to get inside the city. It was just meant to be a short stay, but the English were suspicious of him and refused to allow him to leave, so he arranged for the French to attack the city." The werewolf coughed, spitting blood onto the ground. "To kill all the English and leave no one alive."

"Why was his house left untouched?"

"He couldn't risk any of the French soldiers taking something important as a keepsake, so his house was to be left alone until we burned the city to the ground. But when we got here, the French still had English prisoners, so we thought we'd have some fun first. By the time we'd finished, we decided to wait for the inevitable English response to what had happened. We assumed they would send more men for us to kill, to make a name for ourselves."

"You're not like any sort of alpha I've ever encountered."

"The pack we're from is much larger than just the seven of us. I was the most senior member of this group. But I'm not the alpha."

Thomas walked toward us, the retrieved *jian* in hand. He positioned himself next to the werewolf and placed the edge of the blade against its throat.

"Wait," I said. "I have one last question. Where's the girl?"

"If I answer, will you let me go?"

I shook my head. "You will die here, today. The only question is how. Thomas there is a good man. Your death will be quick and painless." The werewolf looked up at the rage-filled Englishman. I motioned for Thomas to walk off as I made my way to the crippled werewolf. "I am not a good man," I whispered into his ear when we were alone. "I will strip the flesh from your bones and scatter your ashes to the wind. I will ensure that for the next thousand years, the merest mention of what I did to you in this city will evoke fear into anyone foolish enough to think they can cross a sorcerer."

Droplets of blood falling from the werewolf onto the wet ground broke the silence. "South," he said eventually. "They went south. Her name is Ivy, that's what they called her. She's sixteen, olive skin, dark hair. And I have no idea what they want with her."

"Neck or heart," I said to Thomas as I walked past the wolf.

"One last thing," the wolf called out to me.

Thomas placed the sword blade against the wolf's throat once more. I turned to see what he wanted. "These English weren't sent here by their king. Avalon sent them. Avalon sent humans to die for their sins." His deep laughter made me wish I'd had more time to question him. Thomas sliced the *jian* through the werewolf's neck, soaking himself in the contents of the beast's jugular.

Thomas washed the sword in the fountain and dried it before passing it, resheathed, to me. "What do we do now?" he asked.

"We find those who kept the girl prisoner. And then we wipe them from the face of the Earth."

CHAPTER 6

London, England. Now.

My past was catching up to me. That was fairly apparent as Holly and I walked the short distance to her building in relative silence. Until a few hours earlier, I'd never even contemplated injuring another person, let alone killing one. The fact that I remained so calm about it should have set great big alarm bells ringing. But then Lee was a colossal asshole, so maybe my lack of concern was linked to the fact that he thoroughly deserved to have the shit kicked out of him.

The only thing that worried me was what might happen if the wall between my present and past collapsed and I found out I was something I really didn't want to be. Like a cop. That would put a huge problem in my life. I found it hard to believe that many cops would have had no problems with killing, certainly not any that I'd ever met, but I couldn't rule it out. It wasn't like I had any new memories to go on that may give me a hint to who I was. The only thing I knew for sure was that whatever I used to do, or be, I had no issues with seriously hurting or killing someone. That gave me a few less-than-pleasant options for a previous profession.

I pushed the thoughts aside as we reached Holly's address. Long ago, her building used to be a massive house, but it was divided into two, both owned by her father. He left the downstairs one unoccupied, allowing Holly to use it for storage of all of her accumulated junk, leaving her flat nice and tidy.

Once inside her flat, I threw my jacket and rucksack onto her sofa. The main room of her home consisted of an all-in-one kitchen and living room. It was spacious enough to accommodate two sofas, a pale wooden coffee table between them, and a large-screen TV, along with a long dining table. Not once had I ever seen anyone sit at the almost gothic piece of furniture. The dark wood and curved ends were in stark contrast to Holly's personality.

"Where did you learn to fight like that?" Holly asked as she walked off to the kitchen.

"I don't know," I said, honestly. The feeling of having Lee's life in my hands, to decide whether he lived or died, was something I'd have expected my conscience to have battled with. But it didn't. It barely registered as something I needed to concern myself with.

Holly returned and handed me a cold glass of juice, and two packs of ice, one for the welt on my forehead and one for her face, before sitting on the sofa.

"You okay?" I asked.

She placed the ice pack against her cheek and winced. "It's sore, but I'll heal. You did a lot worse to Lee. You could have killed him."

I raised an eyebrow at the tone of her voice. She sounded almost pleased about how much Lee had been hurt.

At my reaction Holly immediately said, "I don't want him dead. Just…gone." She shook her head, a sad expression on her face. "Did I ever tell you why I hate him so much?"

"Not really, no."

Holly placed the can of Coke she'd been drinking on a coaster next to her. "He enjoys hurting people. Did you know he gets involved in extra fights? Ones Dad knows nothing about. Lee seriously hurt a few people because he won't accept leaving your opponent standing as a win."

"That does make him nuts. But why do you hate him?"

"He used to be such a good kid," Holly spoke with genuine affection, which seemed to make her hatred for Lee all the more difficult for her. "When we were little, we used to play together. We were really close. Then, when Lee was nine, he got sick. Really, really sick. The doctors thought he was going to die." Holly paused for a moment, her eyes moist. "He got better, but something was wrong. He was different. Mean and nasty to people.

"When I was fifteen and Lee was almost fourteen, I had a boyfriend. A nice guy by the name of John. He was a few years older than I was, and Mum and Dad didn't approve. They wanted me to end it, and I refused. John and I saw each other in secret for a few weeks.

"Somehow, Lee discovered what we were doing. He didn't like the idea of someone getting one over on any member of 'his family,' so he went after John and beat the shit out of him with a metal bar. Utterly destroyed his face. When Dad found out he went mental on Lee, told him there was no need to have done that. Dad had to buy John off and make the police investigation go away. But after all of it, Lee just shrugged and said maybe I'd think twice about who I dated."

"He did this because you refused to break up with John?"

Holly shook her head. "He did it because in his twisted head, we should have asked for his permission to start dating. Lee mentioned it several times as I was dating John. What Lee did was his way of showing me what happens when I don't follow *his* rules. That was the moment I knew my little brother was gone for good, replaced with the utter psychopath you know today."

"You're worried a little power will go to his head?"

Holly nodded. "I'm worried he'll start taking things into his own hands. And if he does that, a lot of people are going to get hurt."

"Do you think Lee will seek revenge for what I did?" I asked.

"Even if it means waiting for years, he'll want to. I'd watch your back. He won't forget what you did to him, and he'll take the humiliation of losing as a personal insult. But he won't tell anyone what happened. He wouldn't allow his pride to take that dent."

I sat in silence for a moment, mulling over what it would mean if Lee really did start to have more power within his family's business. And no matter what scenario I thought of, it never ended well for a lot of people, me included. Although after what had happened a few hours earlier, I doubted he was in any hurry to fight me. Which meant any reprisal would come when I wasn't looking.

I forced the negative thoughts away and suddenly remembered the money in my backpack. I took out five thousand pounds and placed it on the coffee table. "This is yours."

Holly's sour expression lightened as a smile forced its way through. "Thank you, this is my favorite part of the job. A bit of shopping should put my family out of mind for a while."

"You need to relax a bit more, Holly," I said with a smile.

She laughed and walked off down the only corridor in the flat toward her bedroom. I gave her a few minutes and finished my drink before following her. The bedroom door was open and Holly stood inside wearing just a black thong and bra. She unhooked her bra and allowed it to fall to the floor, exposing her large, firm breasts. She smiled seductively and climbed onto the queen-sized bed, lying back on the many pillows that were in front of the wooden headboard. "So, you fancy relaxing, Mr. Garrett?"

I removed my t-shirt and dropped it in the doorway, stepping into the bedroom with a smile on my face.

It was a few hours later when Holly and I finally fell asleep, exhausted and satisfied. You could never describe Holly as tender in bed—she's wild and energetic. By the time I woke, the sun had signed off for the day. Holly slept as I moved off the bed, stirring slightly when I grabbed my clothes from the floor. She soon returned to a deep sleep as I slipped out of the room.

I got dressed in the lounge as quickly and quietly as possible, but bumped into the coffee table, knocking over an empty glass. Air shot from my hands, cushioning the fall before it hit the ground. As I retrieved it from the floor, the six dark marks on my bare torso came to life. Each one swirled slowly in place.

Three of the marks sat high on my chest in a straight line, with two on my stomach, just below my ribcage. The last one was in the middle of my sternum, and each mark was the size of my closed fist. They only flare to life when I've used magic, so

Holly had never seen them. I'd never told her what I was, but six black, constantly changing marks on my chest would have given her a clue that all wasn't normal. So I made sure not to use my magic when I was around her.

The body art was another clue to whoever I used to be. I hadn't mentioned them to Francis either, although I couldn't say why. Something told me it was information I needed to keep to myself. Besides, they didn't seem to have any adverse effects on me.

I pulled on my t-shirt and went to open the door. As my hand touched the door handle, Holly asked, "So am I ever going to wake up and find you next to me?"

I released my grip, made sure that the marks on my chest weren't visible through my t-shirt, and turned to face my good friend. "This isn't a conversation we should have when you're still naked," I said.

"You'll just have to keep your eyes off my tits for five minutes."

"You do realize I'm a man, right? And that you have *nice* tits? Staring at nice tits is sort of a heterosexual male's hobby."

Holly sighed, darted back off and returned a second later wearing a large Wile E. Coyote t-shirt. It was baggy and old, and stretched down to her thighs, but she still looked stunning.

"Do you really want to talk about us?" I asked.

"I've never asked you for anything, other than that we have fun every now and again. When you're not around, do you think I sit and pine for you? I live my life, and enjoy myself. I don't expect anything more from you. So, why do you feel the need to leave at the first opportunity?"

"It's easier," I said.

"Easier for whom? For me? Because as I've just said, I know full well what our relationship is. So it must be for you."

"I don't want what we have to become complicated. If I ever remember anything and it's bad, I don't want to take you down with me."

"So it's altruistic? That's bullshit. You just like people to think you don't need anyone else."

I shook my head. "That's not it."

"You going to tell me what it is, then?" she asked.

I shook my head again. *How could I tell her that I wasn't even human? That I can control the elements? That somehow I know my past will catch up to me? And when that happens, I fear it's going to have repercussions for us all.* "No. I'm sorry. I'll see you soon." And I left the apartment.

CHAPTER 7

Four weeks passed since Holly and I had our little chat. Our relationship had continued as if nothing had ever happened. I spent the time back in my flat in Winchester, researching into anything that might jog my latent memory. I read up on special forces, assassins, various police and security agency training—hell, even different forms of combat—to try and pinpoint what I'd used, but nothing jogged a single memory loose, and by the end of week three, I was beginning to question if I'd gone mad. Maybe it wasn't my past abilities coming through, maybe it was just in the heat of the moment I lost my temper. I wasn't buying it, but I also didn't have a lot of good leads, so for week four, I tried, in vain, to push the thoughts aside and relax.

Winchester sits in the south of England. Hundreds of years ago it was the capital of the country. It was famous for, amongst other things, having a replica of King Arthur's round table in Winchester castle. Henry VIII had it made over four hundred and fifty years ago. Although it wasn't King Arthur's actual table—if such a thing ever existed—it's still a very popular tourist attraction.

My penthouse flat is close to the city center and overlooks a park and small river. I bought it a few years ago and keep it secret from just about everyone except Holly and Francis. I considered it my solitude away from the world, and my attempt at creating something that doesn't involve criminal activities.

I'd been out for most of the morning, enjoying the crisp February weather—you have to take the dry days when you can; there aren't many of them early in the year. I walked through the park to get to my building, crossing over a small red-bricked bridge.

I swiped my building pass over the electronic lock at the front entrance and pulled the door open. The foyer was decorated with various green potted plants, all of which were placed on the blue-and-white tiled floor. Paintings adorn the blue walls, mostly watercolor landscapes. The only other things on the ground floor were the stairs, a door that led to the basement, and a lift, the latter of which I avoided as much as possible. Running up five floors of stairs was a good way to get in a bit of exercise.

The journey up each flight proved to be utterly devoid of people until I reached the sixth floor, where a sixteen-year-old girl sat with her feet dangling between the wooden slats of the banister.

"You know that's dangerous," I said.

The girl shrugged.

I looked over the rail to the floor. It was a long way down. Fifty feet, easily. The wooden posts that the girl sat in front of stretched to the ceiling, and it would be impossible for her to get in between them further than she was. But if any of those wooden posts came loose, she'd have one hell of a fright.

"You look angry, Dani," I said as I sat next to her.

"*He's* back," she said and continued looking through the posts.

He was her mum's boyfriend, Phil, who from all accounts was a nasty piece of shit. And when a thief calls you a nasty piece of shit, you just know you're not a good person. "You've changed your hair again," I said, noticing the red coloring streaked through her normally dark hair. She had it tied back in two pigtails, one on either side of her head, behind each ear, and a ponytail at the back of her head.

She looked back at me with a mischievous smile on her face. "I fancied a change, and it made my mum go mad."

"How long you been out here?"

She shrugged again. "I need to get my homework done, but it's impossible when they're arguing."

"You want me to go get it? You can do it at my place." When I'd moved in, Dani and her mum had been living in the building for a few years. Her mum had won a few million on the lottery and bought one of the two penthouses in the building. For as long as I'd known the family, she'd argued with her ex-boyfriend once a month, *every month*. She'd left him long before I'd ever moved in, but he still came around regular as clockwork for money. Although my home was on the opposite side of the long hallway that separates the two penthouses, it didn't make me immune to the fighting, which often spilled out into the hallway.

Dani was good kid, smart, too. When she was thirteen, I'd found her crouched alone in the hallway, in a flood of tears. I'd sat with her and taught her how to play poker. She'd managed to win me out of three pounds worth of two's and five pence pieces by the time Phil had slinked past us and down the stairs.

"You sure you don't mind?" Dani asked.

"I wouldn't have asked if I minded." I walked to Dani's front door. "Any idea what they're arguing about?"

"The usual," she said sadly. "Money."

I knocked on their door, putting enough force into it to ensure that whoever was inside would hear no matter the decibel level they'd managed to create. There were raised voices, and a man cursed the interruption before the door finally opened. Dani's mum appeared, looking tired. She pulled down her sweater sleeves, covering a red mark on her arm. "You got Dani's homework?" I asked. "If it's okay, she can finish it at my place."

Dani's mum nodded, her blonde hair falling down across her face. "That's fine." She reached behind the door and brought out a green rucksack, decorated with so many drawings that the bag looked like a graffiti wall. I passed it over to Dani, who didn't make eye contact with her mum. "Thanks, Nate," Dani's mum said.

"Don't thank me," I whispered. "Sort out your shit so this doesn't happen again." I didn't wait for a response, just turned and escorted Dani to my door and into my flat.

We walked down the main hallway, passing the study and dining room, until we came to the large, open-planned living room and kitchen. Dani walked over to the windows, which ran the length of the flat, and opened the balcony doors. "We don't get to use the balcony in our place," she said. "Mum thinks we'll fall off or something."

"Homework," I said, as I walked into the kitchen. "Do you want a drink or something to eat?"

Dani stuck her tongue out in mock disobedience, but sat at the kitchen table all the same. She emptied the contents of her school bag onto the wooden surface with a loud bang. "A drink would be nice."

I removed a cold can of Coke from the fridge and took it over to Dani as she flipped open a schoolbook. "Anything interesting?"

"Fractions," she said with a sigh. "I hate fractions."

"Everyone hates fractions. That's why they make you do them. It's character building."

Dani smiled. "Did you do fractions at school?"

"Yeah." I had no idea if that was true, but I figured *everyone* did fractions. "I don't remember enjoying them."

I left her to work, grabbed a book that Holly had lent me, and tried to get past the second chapter. It was about vampires and werewolves and the love of a good woman. Apparently it had a lot of fans. I wasn't amongst them. About thirty pages in and I'd already come to the conclusion that it was shit, but I figured it could only get better.

I'd managed another twenty or so pages, with a solidifying belief that I'd been right all along, when Dani spoke. "You know, Phil seems to think he can act like my dad. Always bossing me about, telling me I'm useless."

It took a Herculean effort not to fling the book into the nearest bin as I looked up. "No, I didn't know that. So why does he come around all the time?"

"Money. My mum's a mug for giving it to him, but they always argue over how much and how often he comes around." Venom and anger colored her voice.

"Does he hit you?"

"Phil wouldn't dare." She looked out the window to the park. "He's hit mum, one time so bad it broke her jaw. That's when she kicked him out. But since she won the lottery all she seems to date are assholes that leech cash off her."

I had no idea what to say, but I got the feeling Dani knew that and just wanted to vent. I was about to ask if she wanted something to eat when there was a knock on the front door. A second later it happened again. And a third time before I'd even gotten to my feet. Each time, it sounded like someone was trying to use a wrecking ball against my door.

I opened it to face an angry-looking Phil. He had the type of largeness you find in a man who used to be solid muscle but has since degraded to flab. Skull tattoos adorned each arm, and someone had written love and hate on his knuckles so badly that it looked as if it had been done by an illiterate blind man.

"Can I help you?" I asked.

"You got my daughter in there?" he spat as he spoke.

"I'm not your daughter, you fucking bully!"

Phil's expression darkened. "Your mum wants you home, and I plan on taking you. Even if I have to drag you over there. Now get your fucking stuff, you little bitch, and don't give me shit." He yelled every word past me, as if I wasn't even there.

Dani nodded and put her stuff back in her bag. She walked over and hugged me, putting me between her and the brute at the door. "Thanks for helping today. I'm so sorry for all this. I didn't want to cause you any trouble."

"Don't worry," I said, trying very hard not to show Phil the error of speaking to Dani in that manner.

"Get your fucking ass back in the flat," Phil shouted.

Dani walked passed me and into the hallway. She glanced up at the larger man and looked away. The man smiled and nodded, satisfied that he still held sway over the young girl.

I started to close the door, but caught a glimpse of Phil shoving her along and re-opened it. Something washed over me, similar to how I'd felt when confronting Lee. It was like barely controlled violence, bubbling just under my skin. "You got a minute?" I called out before I could stop myself.

The large man stopped and looked back at me. "You talkin' to me?"

Slam my palm into his throat. With enough pressure, I could rip his voice box out in one go. "I don't think we've properly met."

"I know you're a pedo."

Break his nose with one punch, his ribs and knee after that, before he'd even had time to react. "Say again?" I asked.

"Offering to keep a young girl in your home, so she can do her *homework*. More like you're trying to get in her pants."

Dani blanched at Phil's words. "No, it's—" she began.

"Shut the fuck up," Phil said. "I know what's happening. And it's *fucking* sick."

I crossed the hallway toward Dani and Phil. *Feint with a left and catch him in the ear with an open palm, rupturing his ear drum and leaving him open for a kick in the stomach, and knee to the face as he falls.* "I assure you it's nothing like that."

Phil shoved me, and I allowed myself to be pushed back a few steps. "Yeah, well even if it's not, I don't fucking like it."

He turned to push Dani through the now-opened front door. I grabbed his arm. Phil looked down at my hand; anger flared in his eyes. "One last thing," I said. "If I ever see marks on that girl like the ones I've seen on her mum, I will end your ability to walk." I released his arm and he threw a punch with his free hand. Something I knew and expected—and something a part of me was hoping for.

I stepped back as the heavy punch sailed by and hit the wall next to me. Phil grunted with pain. I jabbed the side of my hand into his throat with speed and force that caught him unaware as his windpipe suddenly closed. His hands shot to his neck and I drove my knee into his stomach, forcing him to his knees.

He tried to push me away, but I locked his elbow and spun him around, ramming him, headfirst, into the wooden bars at the top of the banister. The wood groaned from the crash. He pushed himself back to an upright position, blood flowing freely from both a nasty gash on his forehead and his newly broken nose. He threw another punch, wild and powerful. I moved aside, caught his wrist, and smashed my forearm into the elbow joint, breaking the limb. Phil dropped to the floor in agony, cradling his arm. One more punch to his jaw ensured there would be no more fight in him.

He slumped to the floor, his breathing labored from the blow to his throat and broken nose. I looked up to see Dani now accompanied by her mum. "He'll need an ambulance," I said and turned, leaving the two ladies to deal with the unconscious man so that I could wash the blood from my hands.

I don't remember going back into my flat, walking to the bathroom, or washing my hands, but then I glanced up at the mirror and noticed the specks of blood on my shirt, blood that didn't belong to me. I began to think that maybe I hadn't done enough research into violent professions, that maybe I need to spend a lot more effort finding out what I used to do, before I killed someone. Because twice, in quick succession, I'd held the power to end someone's life without even blinking.

What the fuck was happening to me?

The sound of rain beating a rhythm against my bedroom window woke me from my slumber. The memory of the fight in the hallway jumped to the front of my mind, I probably wasn't going to get back to sleep anytime soon. I decided to get up and jump in the shower.

Once fully awake, I picked out a pair of dark blue jeans and green t-shirt to wear for the day. I was just eating some toast when the phone rang. I picked it up whilst I had a mouthful and tried to say hello. It came out "Murhm."

"Nate, that you?" Holly asked.

I finished chewing and swallowed the toast before attempting again. "Yeah, sorry, I'm just eating breakfast."

"You bored back in the suburbs?"

I smiled. "No, it's peaceful here." I thought once again about the fight with Phil a week before, and immediately decided not to tell Holly about it.

"Well your peace is over. You've got a job. That is, if you choose to take it."

I switched the phone over to speaker and replaced the handset. "Why doesn't that sound like I'll want to say yes?" I took another bite of toast.

Holly paused. "You'll need to break into a house to get it."

"No," I said. "No more houses. Too many opportunities for it to fuck up." And, given recent events, I wasn't certain if I would be able to maintain my "no violence" rule if trouble started. It wasn't a risk I was willing to take.

"But—" Holly began.

"No, Holly. I said, no more—"

"The offer is seven hundred grand."

I was glad I didn't have toast in my mouth. I'd have choked on it. "As much as it may depress me to say this, still no. It's not worth any amount of money."

"I thought you'd say that, so I asked them for a secondary option. They said the only other place it could be done is his office."

Office jobs are fun, lots of places to hide and sneak about when everyone goes home for the night. "Why did they change from home to work without a fuss?"

"Well, apparently this guy used to work for our would-be employees. He joined another company and stole some information when he left. They want you to grab his laptop and bring it to them."

That explained why the job could be done at home or work. "Sounds simple. What's the catch?" There is always a catch, and for that much money it was going to be a good one.

"He'll be in the office. He always works late, most of the time until midnight. You'll have to get the laptop from under his nose."

Yep, that was one hell of a catch. "What's the time scale?

"Within a week. Apparently, they can use the information to make a fortune. Hence the high pay-tag."

"Tell them I'll do it. I'll call you the day I go."

"I'll e-mail you the details. The office is in London, easy access by tube. Should allow you to vanish afterwards with few problems."

"Okay, I'll see you next week when I've finished."

"Take care," Holly said and hung up.

I switched on my laptop, entered my password, and left it to load completely, when there was a knock at the door. I opened it to find Dani's mum standing in the hallway. She looked better than when I'd last seen her. Her eyes no longer held the glimmer of fear in them. "I was hoping we could talk," she said.

I pushed the door open enough for her to walk in and closed it once she started down the hallway. "I'm sorry," she said. I followed her and motioned for her to take a seat on the sofa. I sat on my armchair and nodded.

"You don't like me very much do you?"

I shrugged. "Not really, no. You're more interested in your relationship with a thuggish bully than you are with your own daughter."

She stared at me for a few seconds. The silence didn't bother me. In fact, I preferred it to actually having to talk to her.

"You don't understand," she said meekly.

"Really? Okay, you're a special case then, are you? Unlike all the others in abusive relationships, your man really does love you. He's a good man deep down. Tells you he'll change."

"He's an awful man. A thug and a bully. I agree with you wholeheartedly."

I opened my mouth to disagree with her before I realized I didn't need to. "Say that again?"

"He's a fuckwit and we both know it," she said.

I wasn't really sure how to respond, so I wandered into the kitchen and put the kettle on. "Do you want a cup of tea?"

"You got coffee?"

"No, the stuff is horrible. I wouldn't touch it."

"Tea's fine," she said with a smile. "Milk, one sugar. I can see why Dani likes you."

I made two cups of tea, a normal one for Dani's mum and a green tea for myself. "Look…" I paused, trying to remember the woman's name, and placed a cup in front of her on my coffee table. "Diane, why are you here?"

Dani's mum went slightly red before regaining her composure. "I just wanted to let you know that Phil won't be pressing charges."

I found myself smiling as I blew steam from my cup. "I never thought he would."

"You broke his nose, arm, and several ribs. He was in hospital for two days. Why are you so sure he wouldn't have shopped you to the police?"

"He's what, six-nine?"

She nodded.

"So a foot taller than me, and outweighs me by five stone at least. And he got his ass handed to him like he was an altar boy. He's a bully and proud that those he judges weaker than him are intimidated. He's not going to tell anyone anything. What was it? Did he say he fell down the stairs, or was set upon by half a dozen lads?"

"Half a dozen jumped him on the way home from the pub."

I knew I could have done worse. And the scariest thing was that it didn't scare me at all. "That's it? You came over to tell me about how I wasn't going to be arrested?"

She shook her head. For the first time I noticed the lack of similarities between Diane and her daughter. Diane was nearly six feet tall, and Dani barely reached five and a half. Diane had long, curly strawberry blonde hair, and her features were hard and angular. She was attractive, and certainly didn't appear old enough to have a sixteen-year-old daughter, but more than anything, she looked tired and worn out.

Diane took a drink of tea, and a morose air seemed to settle over her. "You care for my daughter, for Dani, yes?"

I wasn't entirely sure where she was going. I was beginning to think Diane was going to offer me her daughter's hand in marriage in exchange for a few chickens and a goat. Eventually I decided to go with honesty. "She's a good kid, even for a teenager. She's smart, and opinionated, and argumentative, and in a few years is going to be beating off men with a stick."

"She looks up to you. Thinks a lot of you. I think she may have a crush on you."

"She's sixteen, and I'm..." I didn't know how to finish that sentence. "Older. Too old for any girl that age. I don't think you have a lot to worry about."

Diane shook her head. "That's not why I mentioned it. I just wanted to see your reaction."

I drank the rest of my tea. "Why?"

"I have a favor to ask." She raised her hand to stop my objections. "I know we've barely ever spoken. And I know you hate that Phil comes over, but you do care for my daughter. And she's who matters."

I motioned for her to continue.

"If anything should happen, anything that leaves me unable to care for my daughter, I want you to look after her."

I sat, mouth agape, like an idiot for an indeterminable amount of time. "Is this to do with Phil?"

Diane shook her head. "Phil is a moron. Unfortunately, he's a moron I have to deal with on a monthly basis."

"Why are you paying him off? What does he have on you?"

"Let's both hope that you never have to find out, Mr. Garrett... Nate." Diane drained her tea and placed the cup back on the coffee table. "So, will you do it? Will you take care of Dani if anything happens to me?"

I still wasn't sure how to respond. How would I look after a sixteen-year-old girl? How would I maintain my life, a criminal life at that? And more importantly, how in the world would I be able to keep the fact that I'm not human from her? All of these questions rattled around my brain. Every piece of common sense told me to say no and then shove Diane out of my penthouse as fast as possible. As much as I liked Dani, I was pretty certain that my life didn't need the added complication of a teenager. "Yes," I said. "If you're unable to look after her, she will always find a place here until she is ready to go out on her own."

Diane stood and kissed me on the cheek. "Thank you."

"No need to thank me." As we walked to my front door, I felt slightly conflicted about whether I was still meant to despise her. "I'm sure nothing will happen to you. Just get rid of that asshole."

Diane smiled sadly. "If only it were that easy." And then she left.

CHAPTER 8

True to her word, Holly sent me all the information I needed to do the job. I spent the next few days pouring over building blueprints alongside the previous few months' timesheets for everyone who worked there, grateful to have something to take my mind off *other* problems.

Patterns formed pretty quickly. Every Thursday and Friday my target worked from midday to midnight. The majority of the staff left between five and six, with a few stragglers going up 'til nine or ten. But for those last few hours the entire population of the building consisted of half a dozen cleaners and Daniel Hayes.

The big problem would be acquiring the laptop without him knowing, or at least without him trying to stop me. With too many things that could change during the op, I decided it would be best to come up with a plan on the fly for getting the computer.

All I knew was that I wasn't going to take it by force, and no amount of violent past was going to change that. If you can't finish the job without hurting anyone, then you're not good enough to be doing it in the first place—though, yes, it does help that I can use magic to incapacitate without causing permanent damage.

Dani's mum's request still hung in my mind. I wondered if she'd told her daughter what we'd spoken about. Probably not,

Dani would have said something if she had. Or more accurately, yelled something at her mum and I'd have heard.

I'd seen Dani a few times in the hallway, and each time she'd nodded hello and kept walking. Maybe what I'd done to Phil had frightened her. If that was the case I would be sorry, but it had needed doing. I was disturbed by how I'd felt during the fighting. Or at least I felt like I should have been disturbed. My concern was that it didn't really bother me at all.

The day before the job was due to take place, I caught a train to Waterloo station in London. I called on the way to book a hotel room near Canary Wharf, where the target worked.

When I got out of the subway at Canary Wharf, a freezing-cold wind was blowing through the area, coming off the nearby river with a vengeance. It made me immediately glad I'd worn a thick hooded top, as well as my black jacket that covered down to my thighs. It wasn't exactly executive dress. But even amongst the throng of people all wearing expensive suits and coats, I didn't stand out too badly, mostly thanks to the nearby shopping center, Jubilee Place, which was always busy with families and people off work for the day.

I'd been to Canary Wharf a few times, usually on business. The mass of glass-and-metal skyscrapers, along with One Canada Square, the tallest building in the U.K., looming over them all as it touches the sky, never ceased to amaze, especially at night, when the lights from the buildings illuminate everything around them.

I walked into the lobby of the hotel I'd used to reserve my room for the night. After getting my room's cardkey, and making a point of stating that I would carry my own bag, I made my way up in the lift.

My room was everything I'd paid for and more. It was massive, with an enormous king-size bed, large bathroom, and lounge area with flat-screen TV. A balcony overlooked the nearby park, and the huge windows running down one side of the room turned a nice view into an unforgettable one.

My backpack contained my outfit for the job, so I hid it under the bed. I'd rather not have some random cleaner finding it and discovering dark clothes and a balaclava. When ready, I left the hotel, making my way into the heart of Canary Wharf toward the forty-two-story monstrosity containing my target.

Daniel Hayes was forty-nine and a success in everything he'd ever done. He'd graduated with a first in economics from Leeds University, his hometown, and immediately moved down to London. He'd never married, but had an eleven-year-old daughter, although I had no information on her mother. My employers for the current job were Lionshead Pharmaceuticals, a company I'd never worked for before. They'd employed Daniel six years ago, and he swiftly rose through the ranks. All of which made me wonder why he would leave. He'd made six figures plus a bonus at Lionshead—though, as I'd learned time and time again, people always want more. But it was also strange that Daniel left a pharmaceutical company to work for Mars Warfare, a military weapons designer.

After taking a seat on a bench outside the massive structure, I removed a book from my backpack and feigned reading as I watched through the windows surrounding the entire ground floor. I made mental notes of the number of guards inside. I was going to bring a note pad and pen, but that would have been far too obvious. The guards moved in twos. Four pairs in all, each guard carried a submachine gun and a holstered pistol.

Employees and visitors moved around them with little fuss or concern, apparently accustomed to their armed protectors.

Two women sat behind a large reception desk opposite the three massive turnstile doors and across an expansive lobby. They were probably mild-mannered receptionists, but they appeared more akin to someone you'd meet in the dead of night with a large knife.

Pictures of weapons—ranging from rifles and knives to tanks—adorned every cream-colored wall. And the company's logo, the planet Mars with a sword and shield in front of it, had been painted onto the white tile floor directly in front of the reception area.

After a few minutes of covertly scanning the building and its inhabitants, it became apparent that the bruiser-like receptionists had taken to watching me a little more intently than I'd have liked.

I glanced around, as if looking for someone I was waiting for, and spotted a beautiful, curly-haired redhead nearby. She wore a dark trouser suit and tiny-rimmed glasses on her button nose. I'd noticed her watching me with interest and wondered whether someone had sent her to keep an eye on me.

I put my book away, keeping one eye on the receptionists, who by now had called over one of the armed guards, and waved at the redhead. She looked confused for a moment, but tentatively waved back.

I walked over and offered her my hand. After a brief pause she shook it. "My name's Nate," I said with a smile.

"Jenny," she replied. "I was going to come over and say hi."

"I thought I'd beat you to it." I hoped our conversation would make it look like I'd been waiting for her and not trying to scope out the building. Besides, learning more about a stunning red-head is always more interesting than recon work.

Jenny's smile lit up her face. Her green eyes sparkled. "I was just finishing work for the day and wanted to ask if you'd like to join me for lunch. I was building up the nerve."

"I was just about to suggest the same thing," I said with a relaxed smile.

She laughed. "Okay, well, a date it is. In the past six months my dating experience has been limited to men who could barely read their own name. You were sitting there reading alone and looking…well, looking like someone I'd like to meet."

One of the guards began to walk toward us. I motioned for Jenny to lead the way. "Shall we, then?" I said. The guard lost interest in me and wandered back over to his colleagues.

I'd wanted to get inside and look around a little, but that was going to be impossible. Besides, I'd already figured out *exactly* how I was going to get inside.

I looked at Jenny as we walked together and wondered if I was being set up. And if so, why? No one knew about me, or my plan. So what was her game? Whatever it was, I was happy to play along.

Hell, this might be fun.

"I know this little Italian place," Jenny said as we walked together through the increasingly crowded financial mecca. "It's a bit out of the way, so it shouldn't be full of people talking about nothing but work."

"Lead the way," I said.

We reached the restaurant shortly after. Like Jenny had said, it was nowhere near as busy as the rest of Canary Wharf. I opened the door for her and we both entered the warm restaurant. The smell of tomatoes and spices wafted out of the kitchen, making me hungry. A young woman seated us in a booth, and Jenny removed her jacket, revealing the black blouse she was wearing. The waitress placed menus in front of us and, after taking our drink order, left us alone to look over what we wanted to eat.

"So, what do you do, Nate?" Jenny asked as she fidgeted with her napkin.

I'd been thinking about my answer to this since we'd left Mars Warfare. "I'm in-between contracts at the moment," I said.

"You're unemployed?" The slight *oh crap, another one* in her voice was easy to hear.

I shrugged. "Not exactly, no."

"So if you're not unemployed, what are you?"

It was time to spin my tale. "I was in the military; I left a year ago with enough money to allow me to spend some time doing things that I want to do. When I've had enough, I'll get a job. I've done some consultant work for Hollywood, and I've been told I have a job if I want it. But at the moment I'm happy just not having to get up every day at five a.m. for a ten-mile hike."

"That's a lot more interesting than 'I'm in-between contracts.'" She finished her Coke and ordered another. "So what films have you worked on?"

"A few. There was one a couple of years ago with giant robots. It made buckets of money."

"I remember that film." Jenny looked sheepish. "I thought it was a bit...."

"Shit? Yeah, it was a *dreadful* film, but I had fun making it."

Jenny laughed, putting her hand over her mouth. "I didn't want to offend you by saying what I thought of it."

"It's pretty hard to offend me. And, like I said, I enjoyed myself."

"When I was little I wanted to be an actress."

"What stopped you?"

"I was terrible at it, mostly," she said, causing us both to laugh. "So I went to uni and now I'm a secretary for an overpaid scientist. Not exactly glamorous."

"You make it look pretty glamorous."

"Thank you," she said with a slight grin. "You have to dress well around here, no matter how much your wages may groan under the idea."

"I'm certain you'd look amazing no matter what you wore."

We chatted about her days at university, where she studied history. We even got onto the topic of her family for a while. A brother and a sister, both older, both more successful, both assholes. I always managed to deflect questions she asked me back onto her. I wanted her to feel comfortable. We continued to talk as we ate; I had spaghetti and meatballs and Jenny an Italian ham pizza.

As time passed, my original concern that I was being set up had begun to evaporate. If Mars Warfare did know about me, I wouldn't have thought they'd have set me up on a date. What I would have expected was more guns, perhaps some torture. Besides, she gave far too much information about herself and her job. Even so, that left me with a startling opportunity to glean some information about Daniel Hayes. "What do they actually do in that place, anyway?"

"Research new tech for the most part. The top fifteen floors are totally off limits to anyone who isn't high on the corporate ladder. They even have their own lifts and stairwells, just in case us plebs get nosy."

"Wow, segregation in the work place, eh?"

"Tell me about it! There's also a basement lab, which is even more off limits."

"I know a guy who works there, Daniel Hayes." I appeared to ponder this for a moment. "At least I think he works there."

"Doctor Hayes, I know him. He's one of the nice ones. Always says hello. He's brought his daughter in a few times, Samantha's her name. Good kid. You should have mentioned earlier, I'd have called up to him."

"I only just remembered to be honest, when you mentioned scientists."

Jenny drained her Coke before speaking. "You should go and say hi. He's working really late tonight, won't be in 'til at least midday tomorrow."

I doubted that after I'd stolen his laptop he'd be in the mood for me to say anything to him.

We chatted a while longer, until the staff began making hints that we couldn't stay since offices were emptying for the day and it was starting to become busy. I paid for the meal and we left the restaurant, the sunset casting the sky in a brilliant orange and red. "You know it's only five," Jenny said.

"You fancy coming back to my hotel for a drink?"

"Just a drink, though, I am a good girl after all." She linked her arm through mine and we walked back to my hotel.

CHAPTER 9

We tumbled through my hotel door, lips pressed tightly against one another. Jenny pushed me up against the wall and began to undo my belt one-handed, sliding the other one down my trousers and grabbing me. I hardened at her touch. If she was setting me up for something, then it was the best setup I'd ever known.

She moved her hand slowly up and down. I groaned. I didn't want her to stop, but I needed more. I broke the kiss and undid her blouse, kissing her neck and chest as I moved down her body. She dropped the blouse off her shoulders to the floor as I kissed her stomach. I ran one hand up her back, unhooking her dark-red bra with two fingers and using my free hand to pull it away. I threw it behind me and ran my tongue back up her body. Her perfume only served to heighten my passion. I took one of her pierced nipples in my mouth, flicking the metal bar with my tongue. A gasp escaped Jenny's mouth and she moved both of her hands to the back of my head, holding me in place.

I dropped back to my knees and unfastened Jenny's trousers as I kissed her smooth stomach. I pulled her trousers down slightly, uncovering a dark and jagged scar on the top of her thigh. A knife wound. Jenny must have noticed my slight hesitation because she kicked off her heels and allowed her trousers to fall to the floor as she walked to the bed. She lay on the covers, wearing only a pair of French lace underwear.

I immediately forgot all about the scar and allowed my jeans to fall to the floor, along with my shirt soon after.

Jenny removed her underwear, revealing a thin strip of dark hair. A smile on her face remained as she threw the tiny panties at me. I tossed them to the floor along with my black shorts.

I climbed on the bed beside her, lowering my head to her thighs, where more perfume enticed me, and, after teasing a kiss between her legs, I kissed my way up her body.

"That was cruel," she said before our mouths touched once more.

I pulled away and ran my hand up the inside of her leg, pushing one finger up inside her. She arched her back for a moment and let out a low moan. "Still being cruel?" I asked and began to move my finger slowly.

"No, that's good." Jenny grabbed my head and lowered my mouth to her own. There was hunger and fire in her kiss. She reached down with her hand and began stroking me once again as I sped up my finger's movements.

"I want something else," Jenny said her voice throaty. She pushed me onto my back and climbed on me, lowering down onto my erection with another gasp. She rocked back and forth slowly. A moan escaped my own lips.

"Oh, Nate," she said and began rubbing herself as her movement quickened.

I grasped her hips, moving myself to keep in time with her thrusts. Jenny arched back, and sped up her movements as she screamed my name.

Jenny screamed my name twice more that night. The last time seemed to last forever and ended with us crashing onto the bed, spent and exhausted. I woke to find daylight streaming through the windows, bathing our naked bodies in soft light.

"Good morning," Jenny said as she swung her legs out of the bed and stood, treating me to the perfect view of a perfect ass.

"Yes, it is," I said with a smile.

She turned, giving me her profile and reminding me of the nasty scar on her thigh. "Got it a few years ago," she said after following my glance. "In a club up north—some psycho bitch did it with a broken bottle."

"What happened?" I asked as she walked into the bathroom.

"She accused me of fucking her boyfriend. I told her where to stick it. So she glassed me. I think she's probably still in jail. Hopefully she got attacked by some gang as she ate lunch."

Jenny had been in the shower for a few minutes when my phone rang. Holly's name appeared on the touch screen.

"Hi, Holly," I said. "I was going to call you later."

"Just thought I'd see how things are going. I'll be going out later to have lunch with my mum."

"Say hi for me." Holly's mum, Lyn, instilled fear in people just as easily as her husband. She was always hospitable and pleasant, but had no qualms about what her family did. I'd seen her stare down hardened killers without breaking a sweat. Her husband might have been the boss in the operation, but he had one hell of a second in command.

"Shower's all yours," Jenny said as she reappeared in the bathroom doorway wearing her clothes from the previous day. I placed my hand over the phone trying to stop Jenny's words from reaching Holly's ears.

"I'd love to stay, but I've gotta go," Jenny continued. She walked over to me and kissed me gently. "I had a great night but, be honest, if we exchanged numbers would you ever call? So let's just leave it at that. If we ever meet again, we'll see how it goes."

We kissed again, and then I watched her leave the hotel room.

"Nate, Nate?" Holly's questioning voice took me from the night's memories. "Is that a woman in the room with you?"

"Yeah, I had a sort of date last night."

"And you haven't left her in bed and made your escape? I'm impressed." Her tone said that she was trying to keep anger out of her voice, but I heard it all the same.

"This is my hotel room."

"Oh, so *she* gets to walk out on *you*? That should be novel for you."

"Holly, we met yesterday, had a date. Yes, she spent the night. That's all there was to it."

"You don't owe me any sort of explanation. Why should I care whom you fuck? Like I said before, when you're not around I don't sit at home and pine for you. I've had sex with someone since you, Mr. High and Mighty."

"I never assumed—"

"Anyway, I've got to go. I've got a date tonight. Looking forward to it."

"That's gre—"

"Good luck with the job." With that the phone went dead and I was left in silence. I'd been fooling myself for a long time that Holly and I were not getting serious. She went out on dates when I wasn't there, and I saw other people too. I assumed it was perfectly fine for both of us. From her reaction, I knew I'd been wrong. And I felt guilty for upsetting her. But there was another thought in my head—why had Jenny lied about how she got her scar?

CHAPTER 10

Job days always moved at light speed. After Holly's barely hidden anger, and my mulling over why I'd been lied to, the day was no different. I poured over the Mars Warfare building blueprints and cemented the strategy for my entrance. And more important, my exit.

One of the buildings next to Mars Warfare was twenty stories high and lacked the security of its big brother. There was a second building on the opposite side, which you could actually use to look into the office of my target, but it was also over six hundred feet away. I've been considered many things. Bat-shit crazy isn't one of them. Which is why, after I'd gotten dressed in dark fatigues, boots, and hoodie, I found myself on the smaller building's roof at just after ten p.m. I stood at the edge and looked down onto the streets below.

Five floors beneath me, thirty feet away and across a gaping twenty-stories-deep chasm, lay my entrance into the Mars Warfare building. It was a small balcony with a door. They'd been put in every ten floors, presumably as some sort of smoking area.

There's no way a human could jump it. Not without leaving a very big red stain on the concrete pathway far below. Even a sorcerer like me had just one chance at this. Get it wrong, and I'd be that big red stain.

Once my rucksack was secured properly, I backed up to the opposite side of the roof and positioned myself against a large air conditioning unit. I mentally prepared myself for what I was about to do and breathed out slowly as white glyphs covered my hands. I shoved myself off with everything I had, sprinting the fifty feet across the flat roof. Air magic can make my body lighter than it is, giving me amazing agility and speed.

I planted my foot just below the roof edge and pushed off. My heart raced like a jackhammer as I flew across the alley far below.

I hit the balcony with a resounding thud and rolled across the floor to lessen the impact as the smell of stale cigarette smoke hit my nose. I came to a stop against the cool glass door and stared up at the roof I'd just left. If I hadn't been capable of using air magic, I'd never have made the jump. Hell, I wouldn't have even attempted it.

My glyphs died down and I forced myself to calm. When I could no longer feel my heart trying to burst out of my chest, I set about letting myself into the building. There was no need to conceal that I'd been here—Daniel Hayes was going to realize that someone had stolen his laptop. Unless he was an idiot. But I doubted that would be the case. I ran my gloveless finger up the side of the glass door, melting the lock. A slight push later, and the entrance opened. I stepped inside, acutely aware of any sounds that might indicate someone nearby.

When I was certain the coast was clear, I continued through the building to the lifts. Getting into one of them was out of the question. There were enough cleaners and security staff inside the building to notice if one started to move when it wasn't meant to.

But that didn't mean the lifts were a totally no-go area.

The darkness inside the building was occasionally broken with wall lights, creating an eerie atmosphere. Shadows criss-crossed over one another, trying to claw back the darkness from the low-level lights.

The lift doors were surrounded by ornate bronze work. I took a few seconds to study the artwork. It really was quite beautiful. Dozens of figures carved into the bronze, most in full ancient armor, stood in front of their boats, waiting for whatever war the artist was depicting.

I placed my hand close to the steel of the lift doors and noticed something in the carvings. On the opposite side of the waiting warriors was a huge walled city. Men stood on the ramparts, staring down at those before them. Suddenly I realized that it was a depiction of the battle of Troy, or at least the beginning of it.

Air rushed out of my hand, forcing the heavy lift doors apart and keeping them there as I peered into the darkness beyond. I closed my eyes briefly, aware that orange glyphs would be mixing with their white counterparts as I drew on the fire aspect of my magic. When I opened them I could see in the dark. The lift shaft was a mesh of orange and reds, but I made out the lift itself a few floors below me, idly waiting for its next journey.

It's probably a common thing to hate lift shafts, but when you're a thief sometimes they're your only means of getting from one place to the next undetected. They're drafty, dirty, and full of things whose entire mission in life is to tear the skin from your body. It was why I spent a moment to take climbing gloves from my bag and put them on.

I pulled a balaclava down over my face. The blueprints showed no internal cameras, but I didn't want to accidentally walk into a cleaner and have my face plastered all over the news in the morning.

A quick jump later and I found myself holding onto the thick lift cable. Once I'd wrapped my feet around the cable and made sure my grip was iron tight, I began my twenty-two-floor climb.

There was no way of telling how long it took—I wasn't about to wait for a second and take a look at my watch—but it felt like years. By the time I'd reached the top of the lift shaft my arms and shoulders ached and my hands felt on fire, cramped from how tightly I'd needed to grip. There was also another problem—the lift doors were closed. Jumping over to them would have left me with about an inch to grab hold of. An inch between life and death wasn't big enough for me to take the risk.

I wrapped one arm around the cable and stretched out my free hand, palm facing the door. A jet of air exploded from it, ripping the glove to shreds before slamming into the door. I kept the gale focused on the crack between the doors, forcing them aside. Anyone outside them would easily hear the howl of the wind, but it was the quickest way.

Once the doors were apart, I moved around slightly so that my back faced the now open lift doors. I pulled my feet up, planted them on the cable, and launched myself back, twisting in mid-flight with a slight blast of air and landing beyond the lift doors as they began to close. I hit the thinly carpeted floor hard, but rolled, the backpack taking the brunt of the blow.

I remained motionless for a moment and listened for any signs of approaching life. It was soon apparent that I was alone. The information I'd received from my employer stated that the cleaners didn't normally get to the thirties until after midnight, and it was only quarter past eleven. But it was better to be safe than sorry.

The information had also told me that level thirty-two was as high as I could go. The next few flights would have to be done in the private lift or stairwell, both of which were armed with alarms and wouldn't open without a key card. So no more climbing up lift cables, which wasn't the worst news in the world.

The plan was to disable the stairwell lock and use the stairs to gain entry to the restricted floors.

Unfortunately, I hadn't counted on the stairwell being guarded as well.

I peered around a corner and watched one giant of a man sitting directly in front of the door some thirty feet away, a book in his hands and a stun gun at his waist. That was definitely not in the dossier from my employers.

For the life of me, I couldn't figure out how he hadn't heard me, and then I noticed that he was wearing headphones. He started tapping his foot to whatever beat he was listening to as he read his book. Listening to music probably wasn't one of his usual duties, but I was glad he had, otherwise that stun gun would probably have been pointed at me.

I ducked back around and wondered how in the world I was going to creep past him. There was a good chance he'd notice me from a few inches away, even if he was listening to music. Unless he was blind, and then he'd be sort of useless as a security guard.

I sat, cross-legged, on the floor and concentrated on my breathing. The space around me shifted and moved as I dragged all of the air away from the far end of the corridor. The guard's cough was the first indication that it was working, followed soon after by wheezing, as the air around him became thinner and thinner. He stood and cursed as he searched for something, and then a quick puff on an inhaler. All the while I kept concentrating, kept dragging all the air toward me, holding it in place just in front of me. I'd tried it out a few times, and it had gotten easier with every attempt. But it wasn't a quick bit of magic and required *a lot* of effort.

Footsteps sounded, as the now panicked guard walked toward me, each step accompanied with another wheeze. And then a second later, as he reached halfway down the corridor, the steps stopped just before an almightily bang signified the guard crashing to the floor.

The air rushed back down the corridor, passing over the guard as it refilled the void its movement had left behind. I walked to the prone man, rolling him into the recovery position and stole his card key from his belt. "Sorry, mate," I whispered.

After using the key card to unlock the door, I dropped it onto the floor. It would look like it had fallen out of the guard's pocket when he stood. Hopefully that meant he'd be in no hurry to raise an alarm.

The stairwell had an oak banister, behind which more carvings depicted warriors from different times—Greek warriors, Roman legionnaires, and even a few English war bowmen, sat on the wall. If I'd had time, I would have taken a few to sell to Francis. Unfortunately I was in a hurry, so I was forced to leave the bounty alone.

I tore my gaze away from the splendor surrounding me and jogged up the next few fights of marble stairs, stopping outside the entrance to the floor I needed.

The door pushed open without incident. No one was hiding behind it waiting to apprehend me in the act, so I stepped through and into a brightly lit corridor. Glass windows faced me, allowing me a peek into dark offices as I made my way along the floor to find my destination.

Daniel's office was the largest on the floor. Easily two or three times larger than any other. According to the blueprints, he had his own private bathroom, too. The higher up the pecking order, the less you have to mix with those beneath you.

I crept along until I reached the closed door. Daniel's name was painted onto the dark wood in a golden font. Instead of having glass windows that stretched from floor to ceiling down the length of the wall, Daniel's office windows stopped at about chest height, giving him a measure of privacy. At least his new employers thought highly of him. Not sure the same would be said tomorrow.

His blinds were closed, which made getting close to the office a lot easier than it would have been otherwise. I sat next to the door and was about to fish out a snake camera from my bag, when part of the door exploded above my head showering me in wooden shards and splinters. I dove aside, my ears ringing like bells, and glanced through the jagged hole now in the door. It was about a foot above where my head had been.

"You're not going to kill me," I heard when the marching band in my ears finally stopped playing.

"I wasn't *planning* on killing anyone," I shouted back as another round ripped more of the door apart, putting a hole at what would have been my stomach height.

"Don't lie! You're here to kill me and take my daughter. Well, you can't have her." He ejected a shotgun shell, instantly loading another.

I placed my open hands in front of the door, showing Daniel that I wasn't armed. "Wait! I have no idea what you're talking about."

Moving slightly had let me peer through the door and into the office, where Daniel Hayes stood, eyeing me suspiciously.

"Just put the gun down," I said. "We can talk about this." I wasn't about to inform him that if he didn't, I was going to take the shotgun and put it where the sun doesn't shine.

I pushed the shredded door a little. His response was immediate. "Stay there," he screamed and fired at the door once more. "Try that again and you'll look the like the doorframe with my next around."

The wood resembled Swiss cheese. I was surprised it was still upright.

I glanced through the closest hole, getting a good view of the obviously agitated Daniel in the process. The shotgun was still pointed at the door. His arms were beginning to wobble and sweat creased his forehead.

"You going to let me talk to you?" I asked.

His answer was to load another cartridge.

"Your choice." I threw a small fireball through the hole. It moved with speed, until it struck the barrel of the shotgun, where upon it exploded. Daniel dropped the weapon in panic, which gave me the opening I needed to dive through the remainder of the door and fling a blast of air in his direction. It caught him square in the chest, driving him into the far wall with enough force to hopefully knock the fight out of him.

I picked up the shotgun. "We done now?"

Daniel slowly made his way to an upright position. "You won't find her," he said defiantly.

"I'm here to steal a laptop, your laptop, to be precise. No idea what the hell *you're* talking about." I emptied the shotgun and tossed the cartridges into a waste paper bin next to a large wooden desk, dropping the empty shotgun onto the desk. "How'd you know I was outside your door?"

He pointed to the carpet outside the office. "Pressure plates, I activate them when everyone's gone home."

That was pretty damn smart. I was impressed. "As it looks like this job has gone to shit, give me the laptop, I'll run off, and you can go back to being crazy guy."

"What laptop?"

My alarm bells couldn't have begun ringing any quicker if they'd tried. "Your laptop—your old employers, Lionshead Pharmaceuticals, want it."

"Who the fuck are they?"

Now the alarm bells were going apeshit. "Your old employers. You worked there for ages. You left with some of their secrets."

"Never heard of them. I'm afraid you've been given wrong information."

Or been set up. "Who did you think was after you?" I asked.

"I'm not telling you shit. You're a thief. A thief who's currently still wearing a balaclava. How do you expect me to trust you?"

He had a point, and if I was set up, then it looked like Daniel had been too. He was definitely expecting trouble. I pulled off my balaclava and tossed it onto the desk. The expression that crossed Daniel's face wasn't good. "What?" I asked.

"Nate?"

"You know me?"

"Of course, I know you. Why are you here?"

I ignored his question. "How do you know me?" My heart raced. What was going on?

Daniel walked over to his desk and opened a drawer, removing a cigarette and lighting it up. He exhaled a moment later and I expected the sprinklers to go off. "I disabled them years ago," he said, anticipating my thoughts. "Occasionally I need a sly one."

"That's great, now how do you know me?"

"You're the one who got me into this fucking mess in the first place. I helped you get that damn psychopath Welkin, helped you get those people out. Then you vanished. What the fuck are you doing back here now?"

"I. Have. No. Idea," I said, as the "easy" job had a meltdown all around me. "I don't remember anything before ten years ago. Now can you start from the beginning, please?" I tried to remain as calm as possible—the man in front of me knew who I was; he had answers. Despite my ten years of trying to convince myself that I didn't want them, it was pretty damn obvious that I was lying to myself. I needed to know who I was, and Daniel could help with that. Whether he wanted to or not.

Daniel ignored my insistence. "Everyone thought you were dead. It would have been safer if you'd stayed that way. I guess they found you." Daniel turned to look out the window, when he turned back his face was ashen. "You know the real kicker? This whole fucking mess started over three thousand years ago. If it wasn't for that damn Priam, none of this would have happened."

Daniel raised his cigarette to his lips and his head exploded, covering me in gore. An eyeball flew past my head as he fell toward me. I caught him and blasted a gust of air under the desk, flipping it onto its side to use as cover. Wind sucked through the small bullet hole in the thick glass window. I looked down at Daniel. He'd known who I was, and yet all I got were even more questions. I needed answers. But more than that, I needed to leave.

Another gust of air left my hands and the desk shot upward, twisting behind me as I ran for the still open door. I made it out of Daniel's office and back to the ornate staircase when a female voice sounded from behind me. "Hi, Nate."

I stopped and turned; the voice was familiar. "Jenny?" I asked.

She nodded once, and then shot me.

CHAPTER 11

1414, France.

The English archer, Thomas, had remained deathly silent since we'd left Soissons a few hours earlier. I'd expected a barrage of questions, but since leaving the city and the death it contained behind, he'd become mute.

We'd walked at a steady pace, heading south and keeping away from major cities or towns. Two armed men covered in blood would invite attention. It was a complication I didn't need.

"We need to find somewhere to sleep," I said and walked toward the nearest stretch of woodland. It would offer as much shelter as possible outdoors, and much more safety than being out in the open.

It didn't take long to find a nice spot, an opening about twenty feet square. The thinning trees offered no help against any rain or wind, but the sky was cloudless, and once I'd placed ferns on the floor to keep the cold earth from seeping through my clothes, I was ready to go.

Thomas did the same as I removed my *jian* and *guan dao*, placing them next to me. Then I waited patiently. I knew what was coming.

"I'm a monster, aren't I?" His words were sad, but with something resembling acceptance tucked deep inside.

"That depends on you. If you're asking me if you're a werewolf, then yes, you are. If you're asking me if that is a prerequisite for being a monster, no it isn't. It's up to you to decide what you'll be."

"What's going to happen to me?"

"I don't know for certain. During their first change, most werewolves do it in front of others of their pack. They find strength in numbers and help one another. I *do* know that it will hurt, inhumanly. It lasts only a few seconds, but that will feel as if you've gone to hell and back. And after that you'll feel the presence of the beast inside you. During your first change, the beast will be more prominent. It will try to make it easier for you to accept the bloodlust, to allow the beast to do as it wishes. You'll want to fight that."

"And if I don't?"

I tapped the sword. "A beast-driven wolf is exactly what you saw back in Soissons. You will kill and hurt for fun. If you allow that part of you to take control tonight, you'll come after me or someone else. Neither of those options will let you see the sunrise."

Thomas nodded that he understood. "How long before I change?"

"Sunset is in about an hour—anytime after then. Werewolves can change when they like, day or night. But the first time must be on the second night after they're infected. It'll be tonight; I'm sure of that."

"When I was a boy there were stories about men who could change into wolves," Thomas said. "Turns out I should have paid more attention."

"The stories are rubbish—I know that much. Wolfsbane does nothing, and you don't have to change on a full moon. However, you must change at least once a week, otherwise you'll start going mad. And a mad werewolf is dangerous. Silver will kill you almost outright, depending on where the wound is, as will decapitation. Fire will cause serious problems, as it does almost everything else on the planet. And while you can heal most injuries, your limbs don't grow back, so be careful."

"Anything else?"

I searched my memory for anything I'd missed. "Right now you can turn into your beast form, basically one of those we saw back in the city. But over time you'll learn a third form to go alongside the beast and human. The wolf itself. It's the hardest to transform into, as it's the least human. But you're a long way off from that."

"Do I age?"

"You're not immortal, but you'll age slowly now. A hundred years will look like only a couple has passed to a human."

Thomas silently held his head in his hands. He understandably needed time alone.

I wandered off into the woods, leaving him to sit and ponder my words. When deep enough inside, I set a snare trap by an old tree. The tracks I wanted were easy to discover. It would just depend on whether they smelled Thomas before the trap was sprung.

I sat up the nearest tree for twenty minutes, perched on the end of a branch, as rabbits and deer walked under me. Each was nervous, tentatively looking around for unseen predators, and not quite sure why. Then my prey trotted past, oblivious to the danger. A quick gust of air from me and the trap sprang shut, hurling the boar five feet off the ground by its hind legs.

I dropped to the forest floor and approached the massive animal from the rear; I didn't want it to see me and go any more insane than it already was. The squealing alone would wake the dead. I removed the air from its muscular body, rendering it unconscious without a fight, which allowed me to examine it more easily. An older male, which was good. I didn't like killing females. Sometimes they're pregnant and sometimes they're too young. Adult males are fair game.

I removed a small dagger, the same one I'd used to kill the first werewolf in Soissons, and slit the boar's throat, avoiding the warmth that escaped. Then I cut it down with a loud crash and dragged it back to the clearing.

Thomas stared at the dead beast with hunger in his eyes. "What's that for?" he asked.

"Later," I told him and removed the ropes from the animal, leaving it to bleed out onto the freshly leafed earth.

"I have another question for you." Thomas' words were meant for me, but his vision was firmly on the boar. His change would be soon.

I sat back on my ferns, cleaning the blade with some nearby leaves. "Go ahead."

"What is Avalon? And why did hearing their name make you unhappy?"

Now that was the question I'd hoped to avoid. "I work for Avalon. In a sense anyway."

Thomas raised an eyebrow. "What do you mean?"

"I work for some people in Avalon, carrying out certain... *tasks.*" Assassination, murder, theft, infiltration, and spying, all things I've done in my life. And all things I'd have no problems doing again. "All the gods and goddesses of old, Zeus, Hades,

Odin, and the like, well, they're all real. Although, not actually gods. They're a mixture of sorcerers, elementals, the fae, and other magical beings. A long time ago, all of these deities were left to their own devices, and that created constant chaos. Many of them don't like one another, and when you throw in the various other species that exist in the world, like vampires and weres, what happens can be all-out war.

"So a few thousand years ago, there was a war amongst the various gods. In the aftermath, they all agreed to join Avalon. They're all left to do what they want, but they have laws and rules regulating them. For example, Ares can't just go and kill Apollo without reason. Unfortunately, those powers are abused. The highest-ranking member of each faction is nigh-on untouchable. It's created a darkness at the heart of Avalon, where these people fester away, doing whatever they desire."

"Is Avalon an actual place?"

I nodded. "It's an island off the west coast of England, although it's not on any maps or charts that I've ever seen. But apart from being a place, it's also an organization, consisting of several different entities all working together. It's a little bit like when the Lords of England bring their men over to fight for a common goal—in this war's case, King Henry's desire to take France."

"Was Avalon being in Soissons bad?"

"It meant all the English soldiers were sent there to die. Someone in Avalon probably contacted King Henry and used his men to do as they wish. Either to provoke all out war between countries or to guard a small girl with humans, because Henry's men are expendable in Avalon's eyes. It's conceivable that it could be both."

"They can get the King to do what they want?" Thomas asked, incredulous.

"Normally the heads of countries are surrounded by Avalon advisers. They ensure that Avalon's needs come first."

"So who wanted the English to be in Soissons?"

I shrugged. "No idea. There are so many gods and goddesses, so many Lords, Ladies, and Knights of Avalon, that it could be anyone in a few hundred."

"So, which god do you…"

A scream pierced Thomas' lips, doubling him over onto the ground. He reached out to me, his face contorted with pain. "Help…" he started.

Another scream cut through him, dragging him to a kneeling position before dumping him back onto the earth. Once his screams could no longer leave his constricting throat, the only sounds echoing through the night were that of snapping bones and muscles. His face changed first. His ears grew upward and the bones in his nose and jaw crunched. Tears fell from wolf-like eyes.

When his face was finished, now covered with thick black, only then did the rest of his body follow suit. Pain continued to show in Thomas' eyes as his arms and legs grew, increasing not only lengthwise, but in terms of mass as well. They formed huge muscular monstrosities. Long black talons were at the end of each finger once they'd dislocated and grown.

Grunts and groans of pain stopped, replaced with a low growl as Thomas' midsection changed—the last thing to do so. Ribs popped and healed almost instantly, each accompanied by a small grunt. The collarbone snapping brought a howl of pain and Thomas raked at the ground.

I sat and watched, hand around the hilt of my *jian*, as Thomas stood tall for the first time. He was over three heads taller than before, and likely weighed twice as much. An inhuman killing machine, designed to hunt and inflict damage. He looked up at the sky and howled again, showing the razor-sharp teeth within his mouth.

He moved toward me, each step tentative and uncertain, testing out his new body. "I wouldn't do that." I tapped the sword next to me.

Thomas stopped and followed my hand with his eyes, growling slightly.

"If you're hungry, I brought you some food." I motioned toward the wild boar.

Thomas dove onto the carcass, claws ripping at the large animal. He tore huge chunks out and fed them into his waiting maw. He sliced open the boar's belly, spilling its insides onto the ground, and pushed his face up inside. The sounds of ripping flesh and snapping bones echoed throughout the clearing.

By the time Thomas finished, the boar was almost picked clean, a few hundred pounds of animal devoured in no time at all. Still covered in blood, he fell asleep soon after. Even though he'd only been a wolf for an hour at most, exhaustion took him.

I waited until his body had transformed back into his human form, a process much less painful, before covering him with some ferns and letting him sleep.

I managed to get a few hours rest before waking up. Thomas slept soundly, still covered in ferns. He needed to change regularly for the coming months, until his body allowed it to happen within a few seconds instead of the dozens it took the first time.

By the time Thomas woke, I'd dragged the boar into the woods for whatever carrion decided it was hungry enough. When finished, I had a wash in the nearby stream. The cold water certainly helped wake me up.

"My body hurts," Thomas said as I entered the clearing again. He staggered to his feet, ferns and leaves clinging to him.

"It will do that when you first change form. There's a stream about a hundred yards that way." I pointed into the woods. "I put some clothes on a tree stump. Go wash the boar off and get dressed. I can't have a naked Englishman covered in gore walking around with me. People might get suspicious."

Thomas nodded and walked briskly into the woods, leaving me alone to eat some bread and fruit.

"Where'd you get the food?" Thomas asked on his return.

"There's a village not too far from here. I stole it from a house down there as everyone was sleeping."

"That's wrong; you shouldn't steal."

"I think they'll get by with the loss of half a dozen apples and some bread."

"And the clothes?"

"Those are stolen too. They seem to fit OK."

Thomas looked down at the peasant outfit I'd found. It was mixture of browns and grays. When dressed, he looked as inconspicuous as I've ever seen a person. He might not have been happy about my thievery, but he'd get over it. Or go naked the next time he ripped his clothes apart mid-change.

"So where are we going?" Thomas asked as we set off.

"There's a larger village about two hours walk away. I'm hoping they'll have a few answers for us."

Thomas returned to the previous day's mute as we started out. But as we passed the village whose wares I'd stolen the night before, he piped up. "You mentioned knights. Are they like the knights of Arthur?"

I stopped walking and turned to face him. "They *are* the knights of Arthur. The legend is real. Neither Arthur nor most of the knights are human. And many of them are still involved in Avalon's running and continued wealth. Arthur…he is a separate matter. He's no longer involved in day-to-day matters."

Thomas' jaw dropped open. He stood silent for a moment as the information sunk in. Greek gods are one thing, but the Arthurian legend was something every Englishman knows. To discover it was real must have been quite a shock. "Why isn't he involved?"

"He got hurt long ago." It was true, although not the full answer. Arthur was betrayed and seriously injured. Only magic keeps him alive. I turned and started walking as thoughts of Arthur filled my head. Arthur's betrayal had taken many forms over the years: Mordred, Guinevere, Morgan, and Lancelot. All more than any one man should suffer. But it had been my betrayal that had led to my King—my friend—fighting for his life.

CHAPTER 12

The walk took a little longer than I'd anticipated, mostly because Thomas was sore. He grimaced and winced with every other step on the hilly terrain. Normally, werewolves rest for a few days after their first change, but Thomas didn't have that luxury.

We walked past several men and women. Some rode on carts or lone horses, but most were on foot. None of them gave Thomas a second glance, but they avoided me. "That *guan dao* is scaring people," Thomas said after the fifth person purposely left me with enough room to swing a horse.

"Oh good, for a moment I thought that my rugged handsomeness was scaring folk off."

Thomas' laughter filled the air but was cut abruptly short when I stopped walking. "What's wrong?"

"Soldiers," I said. The road we were on moved with the land. The sides rose steeply the farther it went, leading down to an open field below us. The forest, which had been on either side of us for much of our journey, ended a few hundred yards before the road split in two. One side of the road followed the steep decline to the lower ground, and the second curved sharply, leading toward a small village. A soldier stood guard at the village limits.

"Do you speak French?" I asked.

Thomas shook his head. "Only a few words."

"Then as of right now, you're a mute. You just nod and keep your eyes on the ground. If this all turns to shit—and let's be honest, the chances are high—you don't get involved."

Thomas opened his mouth to protest, but I cut him off. "You're not ready to fight. You'll have to change once a night for the next few weeks, or even months, before the pain from changing goes away. Until then you're in no condition to fight unless you have to. And right now, you don't have to."

Thomas didn't argue and we made our way toward the village. Despite the many people we'd passed on our journey, this close to our destination there was no one else on the road.

The soldier spotted us, and ran closer. "Keep your hands in your pockets," I whispered before the soldier reached us. "Your lost fingers will give you away."

"Who are you?" the soldier asked once in earshot. One hand rested on the hilt of his sword.

"I'm just a traveler, on my way to the silk road," I said in French.

"What's with the weapons?"

"There are many unsavory types on the road, and it is a long journey. Being prepared is common sense."

The soldier nodded an understanding before glaring at Thomas. "Who is he?"

"He is my servant. And a mute."

"Lucky you," the soldier said with a laugh. "Although he doesn't look French."

"He's Prussian, and an awful servant in truth. But I can't very well carry everything myself. And he makes for a second target when bandits appear."

The soldier regarded Thomas for a moment longer. "You can't stay here," he said eventually.

"I've no desire to stay. A drink and some hot food before we move on would be nice."

"There's an inn just down this road. They should give you something to eat, but we've taken all the rooms." He glanced at the *guan dao* again. "Don't start trouble or I'll cut your balls off."

"No trouble," I said and raised my hands, palms out, to show I meant no harm. "Why are there soldiers in the area? Is trouble expected?"

The soldier laughed again. It was low and menacing. I didn't like the man one bit. "We're here to protect the villages from... *undesirables.*"

"I heard that Soissons was attacked. Do you think those responsible could be coming here?"

Laughter rang out again. "We're already here, you idiot. We attacked the city. It was full of English bastards and those who supported them. They all deserved what they got. Cut off a few English archers' fingers too." He laughed again.

Thomas bristled behind me, and for a second I thought that he was going to lunge at the man, but he kept his temper in check. I looked past the French soldier and saw none of his brothers close by. "So you know where the girl is? Is she in the inn?"

The soldier's face changed from smiles and laughter to concern in an instant. He reached for his sword, but I plunged a dagger of air magic up into this throat, turning it slightly and removing it, the dagger immediately vanishing.

His tunic, once white and blue, rapidly turned crimson. I used a little air magic to push him backward and he lost his footing, falling down the hill beside to us. Once at the bottom, he was out of sight from anyone in the village. The curved road made sure of that.

"We could have gotten answers from him," Thomas said.

"The girl's in the village. Probably at the inn itself, which, as it happens, is our next destination."

The start of the village was only a few hundred yards away. The inhabitants peered out of their homes, watching as we made our way toward the inn. They all vanished when three soldiers walked up to us.

"Who are you?" the largest of them asked. A poleax and dagger hung from his belt. He scratched his raggedy beard. Possibly mites.

"A traveler," I repeated from earlier. "We spoke to one of your friends out on the road."

The three men exchanged a glance. One of them, a man with a pox-marked face and a scar that ran from ear to nose, walked away and looked up the road.

"I don't see him," he said on his return.

The large man took a step toward me. We were in the middle of the village, a large open space with houses circling us. Violence here would rapidly escalate to involve innocent people. "He walked into the woods," I told them. "Said he needed to piss."

The large man chuckled and looked at Pox-face. "He's been on the ale all day. He'll be back soon enough." He then turned his attention to me. "Are you walking through?"

I understood the threat. Get out of the village, *now*. But I'd never responded well to bullies. "My servant and I just want a drink to sate our thirst. Then we'll be on our way."

The larger man nodded, but Pox-face and the third companion, a thin weasel-like man with a vicious-looking curved dagger in his belt, didn't look so convinced, and once I was a few steps away all three walked off in the direction of their dead friend.

"This is going to shit pretty fast," Thomas whispered when we reached the inn's front door.

"We'd better hurry up then, hadn't we?"

The wooden door felt rough under my hand. It rubbed against the floor as I pushed it open and stepped inside, Thomas close behind me. Three pairs of soldier's eyes turned toward us from a table of the corner in the small, dark room. A man and woman stood behind a counter next to what was probably the kitchen, their arms laden with bowls of what appeared to be stew of some type. They glanced our way and immediately looked elsewhere, not wanting to get involved.

"Who's in charge here?" I asked.

One of the three men stood. The meager light in the room bounced off his bald head. "I am."

He wore an expensive ring on his index finger, and the sword hanging from his belt looked worth more than all of his companions' weapons combined. He wasn't lying. I nodded and shot a blast of air at the two other men, flipping them out of their chairs and slamming them violently against the far wall. From the cracks that sounded, I doubted either man was getting up again anytime soon. If ever.

The soldier in charge had little time to react before a bolt of fire struck him in the chest, lighting his tunic. He dropped to the ground, beating his chest as I walked over to him and kicked him onto his back. I planted my foot firmly on his sternum.

"The fire," he cried.

I clicked the fingers on one hand and the fire vanished. "Better? Good. Where's the girl?"

"I will not…"

"Yes, you will," I told him pointedly. "You will tell me, or die."

"Then I shall die." He spat at me and retained a smug look on his face. I clicked my fingers again and set his right arm on fire.

The screams started immediately and continued until I removed the fire once the smell of burning linen and flesh filled the air. I waited for the whimpering to die down. "Feel like answering now?"

He nodded furiously and moaned as the skin on his forearm blistered. "Up…upstairs, third…door."

"Thank you," I said as I punched him in the face, snapping his head back.

"Do you two have a cellar?" I asked the man who appeared to be the owner of the inn.

"Yes, sir."

"Take your family there. Do it now."

He nodded once and vanished into a back room.

"You're not killing him?" Thomas asked. He'd removed the soldier's sword and pressed the tip against his neck, drawing a thin line of blood.

"We might need him. But if you want to, be my guest."

Thomas looked down at the man with fire in his eyes. He was still angry about what had happened to him and his friends, but he was not a murderer. Thomas sheathed the blade and hung the sword from his waist.

"Good choice," I told him as I started up the stairs.

"Would you have done it?" he asked once we reached the landing. "If our roles were reversed?"

We walked down to the third door. Runes, similar to those I found back in Soissons, were carved into the wood.

"Yes," I said and opened the door.

A girl sat on a small bed. Her long, light-brown hair cascaded over a deep-blue dress. "I knew you'd come," she said without looking at me.

I entered. "Glad I could help."

The room was large and had probably served as the owner's main bedroom. Several bottles of what I assumed were perfume sat on top of a chest of drawers. Lace-lined dresses in various shades of greens and blues hung over the back of a cushioned chair. A full-length mirror, the edges lined with gold leaf, sat in one corner of the room, reflecting the back of the girl who sat regally posed on the bed's mattress. The contents of the room cost more than anything an innkeeper's wife could afford.

The girl turned to look at me for the first time, and I noticed she was leaning more toward woman than girl. Probably seventeen years old, although her eyes said she had lived more than most her age.

"Are you the girl from Soissons?" I asked.

She nodded once and turned her gaze to Thomas. "Thank you for coming, Thomas."

For a second I thought he was going to sprint out of the room. "How...?"

"I'm psychic." She said it in the same way a person might say they were English. It wasn't what she could do; it was what she was.

I remembered what the werewolf in Soissons had told me about the girl from the cage. "Ivy?"

She nodded again. "They're scared of me. Scared that I'll see their deaths."

"Can you?"

She shrugged. "Sometimes."

Her utter calm in the face of what she said was unnerving. I checked the room for runes that might cause problems with her leaving and found nothing suspicious. "We need to leave."

"I can't," she said calmly. "They won't let me."

I was about to ask who, when Thomas said, "I think we have a problem." He stared out the window, which looked down on the village square.

I joined him just as a howl cut through the air. Several werewolves stood motionless in the square, all looking up at the window. Another howl filled the air. This one filled with rage. Someone had gone through a lot of effort just to keep one psychic prisoner.

"Who are you?" I asked Ivy.

"My grandmother was Cassandra of Troy, daughter of Priam, and the spoil of war for Agamemnon, King of Mycenae."

Goddamn it. "Now we have two problems," I said.

CHAPTER 13

London, England. Now.

My first thought upon waking was that heaven looked surprisingly like my hotel room. Or maybe it was hell. It was hard to differentiate. The loud buzzing of a mobile phone, as it vibrated against the wooden table it sat on, was definitely from hell.

My body hurt, and my mouth was dry. I reached over and picked up the small, black phone. The second thought of the day ruptured in my mind. It wasn't my mobile. It was probably never good to wake up after being shot and find someone else's phone is ringing next to you. At least that's what I'd gleaned from my limited experience.

The number on the screen was withheld. I pressed the button to answer the call. "Yes," I said tentatively, still feeling woozy.

"You have ten minutes to get up and out of that room." It was at that moment that I realized the person on the phone was female and that I was wearing only my shorts. "Some very bad people are about to burst through the door."

That woke me up. I sat bolt upright, and immediately wished I hadn't. "What's wrong with me?" I said, holding my head.

"You were tranquilized about six hours ago. It was enough to put out a rhino for a day. You're probably feeling a little sluggish."

Jenny had shot me. "Where's Jenny?" I noticed the bit of growl in my voice.

"She's not here," the woman on the end of the phone said firmly. "You now have seven and a half minutes. I'd get dressed."

"Not until you tell me what's going on. I'm not in the habit of trusting mysterious female voices over the phone."

"Look, I'm sorry about the dart. But my lord wants you taken in so he can pull your brain apart. I can't allow that to happen. Our orders were to drug you and leave you in your hotel room. He wanted to wait until he'd sorted everything out at Mars Warfare before dragging you away. There was a murder there last night. And rules have to be followed, even if he was behind it. But Jenny gave you less tranquilizer than she was meant to. You're waking up five or six hours early."

"Why not leave me where I fell?"

"Because then you'd be implicated in Daniel Hayes' murder and Avalon might get involved. He didn't want that."

"You killed Daniel," I said as my body continued to remove the effects of the tranquilizers, clearing my head slightly.

She paused for a heartbeat. "I had no choice." Her voice was soft, almost regretful. "And you now have four minutes. If you don't hurry, what Jenny and I planned will be for nothing. And people will die."

"If you're fucking with me…"

"I assure you, Mr. Garrett. No one is *fucking* with you. *Now* get dressed."

I thought of a witty remark about how Jenny had certainly fucked with me, but decided it probably wasn't the time. I turned on the phone's loudspeaker, dropped it onto the bed, and hastily pulled on a pair of jeans and red t-shirt. "Where's my bag?"

"In a car downstairs. I will explain soon. You have two minutes. I arranged to have the room below you paid for the night. You will need to jump off your balcony and catch the railing below."

I slipped my shoes on and hurried to the balcony. "Which one?"

"There's a red chair on it."

I found the red chair on the balcony one story down and to the right of mine. "Call me back," I said and disconnected the phone, placing it in my jeans pocket before I climbed the railing.

It was windy out, and sitting precariously on top of a railing a hundred feet in the air does not make for a good thing to do. Even worse when you've been shot and drugged the night before.

There was shouting from the hallway. After a bang on my room's door, I immediately launched myself off my balcony, using air magic to steady my fall, but I used too much and almost flew over my target, knocking the red chair flying as I slammed into it and rolled back to my feet. I really hoped that was because I was still woozy and not because whatever was happening to me was affecting my magic. I opened the unlocked balcony doors and darted into the room. Although I didn't trust the anonymous voice, it wasn't like I had a lot of choices.

The phone rang again as I made my way through the room. "I assume you made it," the mysterious woman said.

"No, this is my ghost." I looked around the almost identical room to my own. "Why didn't you just put me in here?"

"We had others with us. They would not have allowed a deviation from the plan."

"So how do I get out of here?"

"Take the lift to the ground floor. The desk has a set of car keys for you. A Nissan GTR, black. It's completely clean. And don't worry about speed cameras or the congestion charge. It's registered to a dummy corporation."

I opened the room door and looked into the empty hallway, ready for any nasty surprises. With none forthcoming, I started toward the lift. "Where do you want me to go?"

"The address is already placed into the car's sat nav. A young girl's life hangs in the balance. You have just over two hours to get there."

The lift doors opened, the mirrored sides and lack of inhabitants made it appear much larger than it was. I stepped inside and pressed the chrome button for the ground floor. "And what do you want me to do when I find her?"

"Take her somewhere safe. You can't involve anyone; it will only lead to more problems."

"Do you at least have a picture?"

"No. She should be the only girl at that address."

After a brief conversation with the desk clerk, I left the hotel with a set of car keys in my possession. "Why are you doing this?"

"None of your concern. In the boot of the car is a bag with a hundred and fifty thousand pounds. That is your fee for carrying out this job."

I clicked the alarm on the keys. The beautiful Nissan beeped softly. I opened the boot to check if she was still being honest and found my bag exactly where she said it would be along with a small bag containing crisp fifty-pound notes. A silver briefcase was next to it. "What's with the extra baggage?" I asked as I removed my own phone from my bag and put it into my pocket.

"The code is one-four-seven-one."

CRIMES AGAINST MAGIC **123**

I tapped in the code on the numeric keypad and opened the case, immediately slamming it shut again. "A rifle? Are you fucking kidding me?"

"It's a sniper rifle—an Accuracy International Arctic Warfare Covert, to be precise. It's fitted with a suppressor. There's also a Heckler and Koch USP with .45 ACP silver-tipped ammunition."

"Why in God's name would I want those? What about Holly? She booked the job. Is she safe? Why do these people want me?"

"Who's Holly? If I don't know, no one else does. And you might need those guns. A decade ago you crossed my lord…" She paused for a moment. "There isn't time to explain further. You need to go. *Now.*" She hung up before I could say anything else. So I got into the car and started the engine that roared to life.

I had no idea what was going on, but she could have left me to whatever doom awaited my waking in my hotel room. And she knew my past. As much as I didn't want to think about it, it still burned a hole in my stomach to wonder what my old life was like.

I clicked the power button for the sat nav and watched the screen flick to life, the route already shown on the screen as a red line. I tapped one of the buttons to reveal my destination and felt all the air rush out of me. It belonged to the penthouse flat directly opposite mine. It was Dani's home.

CHAPTER 14

I sped home, breaking more than my fair share of traffic laws in the process. My journey was marked by the flash of speed cameras, but I didn't see any police. No one followed me or tried to pull me over, for which I was thankful. The last thing I wanted was to have to outrun the police.

Not that I didn't think the Nissan GTR could do it—it was like driving a rocket. Whenever I put my foot down the acceleration pushed me back into my seat. And braking was the same. Never have I been more thankful for a seatbelt.

On the way, I called Holly on my own mobile, getting her machine and voicemail. I left a message on both asking her to call me. My gut told me she wasn't in any danger, but I still needed to make sure.

I pulled into my building's garage, switched off the engine, and got out as quickly as possible. I had a half hour left. Before I made my way upstairs, I removed the Heckler and Koch USP from the boot of the car and loaded it with .45 bullets. I put on the back holster that had also been left for me. I'd not used a gun in the past decade, not even for practice, but I felt at home as I flicked the safety off and placed the gun in its holster. Once comfortable, I replaced my zip-up hooded top to conceal the weapon.

The only way to get from the garage to the main building was to walk around the outside of it, which left me exposed to anyone watching the building. Whoever built the place didn't even bother to make sure you could access your car when it was raining without having to get drenched, so it was no wonder that security features didn't make it into the design. Once outside I instinctively eyed places where someone might lurk in ambush. I was soon confident that no one was around. Whoever was coming either wasn't here yet or was keeping a low profile. There was a third option—I was late and they were already gone—but I pushed that out of my head and entered the building I'd been calling home for nearly a decade.

I jogged up the stairs. The thoughts of what might already have happened popped back to my mind and refused to be banished. Once I reached the stairs one floor below my penthouse, it was obvious that I was utterly alone. I was early. I still had time.

I unzipped my hoodie and placed my hand on the grip of the gun before knocking on Dani's door. After a few seconds, I tried again. No answer. I counted to ten and tried a third time. I was about to kick the door in, when someone walked up the stairs behind me. I turned, ready to draw my gun, and found Dani making her way toward me. She wore a strappy red top and dark blue jeans and carried a pair of high heels in one hand.

"You okay?" she asked.

I removed my hand from the gun. "I've been trying to get hold of you. No one's answering."

"I was out all night. Mum and I had a fight; she told me I had to stay in so I snuck out and went to a friend's party."

"How do you sneak out of a penthouse?"

Dani smiled. "I waited until she got drunk and fell asleep."

That would do it.

"You look freaked out. Everything OK?" She walked toward me, key in hand, ready to open the door.

"I heard a big bang in your place. Was a little worried something had happened."

"Mum probably broke something." Dani unlocked the door and pushed it open to reveal her mum, Phil, and a third man I'd never seen before all standing by a large brown couch further into the flat.

Something was wrong with the picture before me. Dani's mum and Phil looked nervous. And the new man's smile held more menace than I'd ever seen one manage. "She's here now, so give me my fucking money," Phil shouted.

"I was told…" Dani's mum started before the stranger raised a gun and shot her through the eye. The bullet entered her skull, and the back of her head vanished in a cloud of red.

"Mum!" Dani screamed as she lurched forward. Phil's eyes were wide, his mouth agape, as he stared at the dead body of Dani's mum.

I grabbed Dani by the waist and darted back to the hallway. The murderer, still smiling, aimed the gun at Phil's head and pulled the trigger.

"Let me go," Dani screamed as I dragged her from the flat. Phil's body toppled onto the cream carpet.

"They're dead, and you're next if we don't leave *now*." I all but carried her down the hall and into my apartment, locking the door behind me. Once inside, I pointed toward the living room. "Down the hall, *go*." I said. But Dani just stood in shock, unable to take in what she'd just seen.

I picked her up, threw her over my shoulder, and sprinted down my hallway. I dropped her onto my couch before using air magic to fling my heavy wooden table toward the front door. It cracked and bounced down the hallway, tearing huge chunks out of the ceiling and walls with deafening roars, until it hit the front door with an almighty crash. It didn't matter how much of my home I'd just wrecked. I wasn't planning on coming back.

"I need your help, Dani," I said, grabbing my laptop and stuffing it into my rucksack. "Dani!"

She looked up, tears in her eyes. "What's happening?"

I knelt beside her and held one hand in mine. "I don't know. But we will find out, and we will have justice for your mum. But right now, if we don't leave, we're both dead. And I promised someone I would get you to safety."

"Who?"

I didn't see the point in mentioning her mysterious savior. "Your mum asked me to keep you safe. I intend on following through with that. So let's go now, grieve later."

She nodded once. "What can I do?"

"Pack. I need the USB sticks on the desk over there, in this bag."

Dani ran off, tears streaming down her face.

A loud bang sounded against the front door. Then a second and third. The bastards were shooting through my door. Hopefully the table was going to prove a bigger problem than the front door locks.

"Knock, knock," shouted a male voice through the remains of my front door.

I ignored him and ran into my bedroom, grabbing the ready-prepared blue travel bag I kept beside the door. It contained clean clothes, ID, money, and a few other odds and ends that I figured might be useful in an emergency. I removed the hoodie I was wearing and stuffed it into the bag. Being able to get to the gun would be more useful than concealing it. I slung the strap over my head and positioned the bag until the weight felt comfortable. My plan to escape wouldn't pay off very well if I had to worry about how heavy a weight I was carrying on my back.

"Done," Dani said showing me the bag.

"Put it on, and go to the balcony."

I waited until the sliding door was opened and Dani was outside before I went to the kitchen. I hoped the rest of the inhabitants of this building would forgive me.

I ran into the living room and removed two white phosphorus grenades from a lock box under the sofa, placing one in the microwave and setting the timer for twenty seconds. The front door exploded inward, the makeshift barrier turned into thousands of deadly shards of wood, imbedding in anything they touched.

I pulled the pin on the second grenade and tossed it toward the surge of men who spilled over the debris to enter the flat. The sounds of their clambering were soon replaced with the yells of those desperate to get out of the way as the grenade went off, filling the hall with a brilliant white flash, followed by thick white smoke.

I didn't wait for the intruders' response. I pressed start on the microwave and sprinted toward Dani. The microwave and anything in its immediate surroundings exploded just as I reached her, scattering pieces of metal and wood at high speed throughout the kitchen and living room. Windows shattered around us. I held Dani tightly, launching us both up and over the railing. Dani's screams accompanied us as we freefell toward the rapidly approaching pavement.

The sounds of my home's destruction filled my ears, but I had no time to be sad. I placed one hand in front of me and glaring white glyphs exploded to life. A column of massively compressed air shot from my palm, far more powerful than I'd ever created before. It not only slowed us down enough that when we hit the ground only a short roll to lose the momentum was needed, but it tore huge chunks from the earth below.

"We landed," I told Dani, who still had her eyes closed as she lay next me, pieces of dirt raining back down around us. "And we're not done yet."

She opened her eyes and looked around her, the disbelief that she was in one piece written all over her face. "How did you...?"

"Explanation later. Running now."

I pulled her to her feet and felt reassured that the H&K was still where it should be. Together we ran to the parking garage and reached the Nissan only to be met with the loud sound of a fired gun. Dani and I froze and turned toward the noise as the man who had murdered Dani's mum and Phil stepped from around the Bentley Continental owned by Dani's mum.

"Hello, Dani," he said with an evil grin. "This has been a lot more fun than I'd imagined."

"Who are you?" I asked. He looked about eighteen, with long, dirty-blonde hair tied back in a ponytail. But his dark eyes definitely didn't belong to anyone as young as he appeared.

"Not really important, is it? Dani, you'll come with me. And you." He pointed the gun at my chest. "Who knew all this time *you* were living next to her? If I'd known, I would have killed you long ago."

I remembered what the woman on the phone had said about her 'lord' wanting to get into my brain, and took a chance. "Your lord wants me alive doesn't he?"

"That doesn't mean I do," he said.

"You killed my mum, you fuck!"

"That alcoholic bitch? She's not your mum, just some woman our lord put you with. Although that prick Phil wasn't part of the deal. *And* she told him the truth. Fucking idiots had to die." He shook his head in exasperation. His hair moved loosely over his broad shoulders.

"He's not my lord, you psychopath," Dani spat.

"Not yet, but he will be." He reached into the trouser pocket of his dark suit and threw a pair of handcuffs at Dani's feet. "Put these on."

"Go to hell," she spat, kicking the cuffs under the nearest car.

I pushed Dani behind me and slipped my car keys into her hand. She darted off to my side. A second later the GT-R beeped, unlocking the car before the door opened and closed.

"That's not going to stop me," the man said.

"This might," I replied and hit him in the chest with a blast of air, which lifted him off his feet. He slammed into the car behind him, causing an alarm to go off. He didn't pause, just reached inside his jacket. I whipped the gun out from my holster, shooting him between the eyes. It was instinctive; I knew he was going for a weapon and I knew he would kill me given the chance. I'd used a gun very few times in the last decade, and never on a person, but as I watched him crumple to the ground, I wondered just how many times I'd done this very thing over the years.

After what felt like hours, but was probably only a few seconds, I ran to the car and got into the driver's seat. I floored the accelerator as we sped out of the garage and into the night, not slowing down until we'd reached the motorway a few miles away. Dani stared out the window the whole time, tears steadily falling.

When my heart rate finally lowered, I expected my actions to overwhelm me. I'd killed someone. But I didn't feel sad or sick. Just like my recent fights, there was no panic or concern in me. Only acceptance for what needed to be done. I didn't even know how I'd made the shot. But I did know that whoever had sent the men to take Dani wouldn't stop.

I left the motorway as soon as possible, taking the quieter back roads in case anyone was watching the main roads. At one point I parked the car down a dark lane when I heard police sirens nearby. Once they'd revealed themselves to be ambulances instead, I knew I needed to wait before I set off again. I was too wired on adrenaline, and that doesn't bode well for driving safely or making good decisions.

I sat in the car and stared at my hands. Before the fight with Lee and the craziness that had followed since then, I'd genuinely thought that the strangest thing to happen to me would have been the woman bumping into me and then vanishing. Show's what I knew. Everything had gone to shit, and I needed help.

By the time I reached London and stopped the car, it was midnight. I left Dani asleep in the car and ran the short distance to ring the bell for Holly's flat. "Who is it?" she asked a moment later, playfulness in her voice, accompanied by a second voice somewhere behind her.

I'd forgotten about her date. That could cause an interesting situation. "Holly, it's Nate. I'm in deep shit."

CHAPTER 15

Holly stood in her open door, motionless, mouth agape, for what felt like hours. "Can we come in, then?" I asked.

She looked behind me. "We?"

I raised my index finger to get her to wait a moment and dashed back to the car. Dani had woken up and was sobbing into her hands in great big breaths. I opened the car door and crouched beside her.

"I'm sorry," I whispered. Asking her if she was okay would have been beyond stupid.

"She wasn't even my mum. Do you think he was being honest about that?" she asked through the tears.

What could I say to that? There was no answer I could give that would make what had happened into something better. But I decided the truth was the way forward. "I don't think he had any reason to lie."

She nodded once, as if understanding my words, but I doubted it was going to sink in that easily. "I always wished I'd been adopted and my real family would come find me. But now...I..." She trailed off as fresh tears fell from her eyes.

"I know. Come on, let's get you somewhere warm." Dani took my hand, falling onto me once out of the car. We walked together, toward Holly, with my arm around her. "I'll explain when we get upstairs," I told Holly.

She moved aside and led the way up two flights of stairs to her flat. "What happened?" Holly whispered as I lowered Dani onto her couch and passed her some cushions and a throw that had been draped over the back. Within seconds, Dani was asleep.

I was about to explain what my day had consisted off when a man walked out of Holly's bedroom. He wore only a pair of dark blue jeans and a smile, which faded when he saw me. I had to fight whatever instinct inside me reached for the gun.

"Who are you?" he asked me.

"Slight change of plans, hon," Holly said. "This is my friend, Nate. Something's come up. I don't think it's going to work tonight."

"Fucking what?" he asked her with more than a little anger in his voice. "You're the one who asked me to come over to see you. These guys can wait out here for half an hour."

Holly laughed. "More like ten minutes, isn't it really? Anyway, you can get your stuff and go."

He stormed off into the bedroom, reemerging a few minutes later wearing boots and a shirt, which was still open down the front. "You're a fucking cock tease," he said pointing at Holly.

His eyes went wide when he noticed the gun barrel against his nose.

"I'm so very much not in the mood for this shit." My voice was utterly calm. "Say sorry and leave."

"You're...fucking insane," he stammered, looking down the barrel at me. He glanced at Holly. "Sorry." He almost ran from the building.

"I could have dealt with him myself." Holly's eyes were set on the gun.

"Of that I have no doubt. But time's sort of a factor here. Besides, I'm not in the mood for assholes."

"When did you start using one of those, anyway?"

"Tonight. It was a gift from whoever decided to hire me to save Dani."

Holly stared at the gun for a moment longer and I replaced it in its holster. "What happened?"

"It'll be easier to explain once I've got my bags." One quick journey to the Nissan later and everything in the car's boot was on Holly's bed.

"Whose car is that?" Holly asked.

"Mine, I guess. It was left for me by my mysterious employer."

"Explain everything. Slowly."

I started the story from the job at Mars Warfare and finished when I arrived at her home. "Holy shit," she whispered. "So Mars Warfare is involved. Is it safe here? Do we need to leave, because that is some seriously fucked up shit."

"Really? That's the impression you got?" I sighed. "Sorry to snap. But, yes, they're as bent as a nine bob note. And I can't see any reason why you wouldn't be safe, but do you have anywhere you can go?"

"A safe house," she said. "It's not too far from here. I can stay there for a few days until all this shit is over. You're not planning on going to Mars Warfare, are you?"

"Unfortunately, I think going back there would have stark similarities to the end of 'The Charge of the Light Brigade.'"

Holly raised an eyebrow in question.

"Seriously? The 'Charge of the Light Brigade,' you've never heard of it? It's one of the most famous poems ever." Her quizzical look made me sigh. "How about Custer's last stand? Or Butch Cassidy and the Sundance Kid? Would they be better references for you?"

"Ah, right, gotcha. Everyone dies." Holly got up and left the room.

"Do you trust the woman who got you out of that hotel?" Holly asked when she returned with a bottle of vodka fresh from the freezer and two glass tumblers. She poured herself a measure and passed me the bottle. I half-filled the tumbler, steam coming off the near-frozen liquid, and drank a large portion. The cold in my mouth turned to warmth as it passed down my throat and chest into my stomach. I closed my eyes as the alcohol did its job and made me relax.

"She murdered a man directly in front of me. Something she didn't seem too fussed about. But she wants Dani safe. I believe that just from her tone. She's not setting me up. It would be a ridiculously long-winded approach to kill or capture me."

"But her...*lord* wants you?"

"Apparently, although I have no idea why. It's not good that they're playing with a full deck and I've only got one suit. Can you tell me more about who gave you the job?"

"All done electronically. I checked them out, Nate. I used some of my dad's contacts. Same people as always, paid them for a full background check. MI5 don't go as deep as they did. It was solid; every single detail checked out. I can go back to them, see if they know anything."

I shook my head. "If your dad thinks someone gave you bad info on purpose, what'll he do?"

"Crack heads until he gets what he wants."

"So either that gives away that we're checking into someone and they run, or it puts your parents in danger."

"My dad can be subtle." She paused. "Okay, my mum can. I'll talk to her, try and see if she's heard anything about a set up."

"What if your brother's involved?"

Holly thought about it. "It's a little high-brow for his usual revenge, but that's a fair point. I'll do some checks on my own; I have people too."

"Could he be trying to branch out on his own, or working with someone else?"

"If either of those things are true, my dad will quite literally cut his bollocks off. In the meantime, you could go to Francis."

I raised an eyebrow.

"Yeah, he's a money-grabbing dick, but you seem to trust him, and he's got his fingers in enough pies that he may know something I don't. As much as it pains me to admit it."

"Thanks. Is Dani okay staying with you?"

Holly nodded. "She's going to be a mess. Her mum, who isn't really her mum, murdered in front of her. The safe house is well stocked. We'll be okay there."

I opened the briefcase, staring at the sniper rifle it contained. It was in several pieces and I wondered if my subconscious would be able to put it together without help. I closed the case and opened the duffle bag, pouring out the hundred and fifty grand onto Holly's bed.

Her eyes went wide. "That's a lot of money."

"Take what you need and hide the rest. Anything I need is in my bag by the door."

"So what's your plan?"

"I'm going to take your suggestion and see Francis tomorrow. He might know a few things. Or at least point me in the right direction. I don't want to sit around and wait for them to find me. Especially when I have no idea what I'm up against." I rolled my neck, which cracked. It had been a long day. "You mind if I take a shower?"

She gestured toward her en-suite bathroom. A second later I was letting the hot water wash away the day's events. I wondered how long it was going to be before I'd need to shower again, to get blood off me. Something inside me said things were going to get much worse.

I'd been in there for a few minutes when the bathroom door opened and Holly walked in. She pulled the shower curtain aside and my eyes took in the beauty of her naked body. "Care for a back rub?"

I smiled. "My muscles ache."

She stepped inside the shower and began to stroke me until I was hard. "Let's see if I can't do something about that," she said as she dropped to her knees.

CHAPTER 16

My sleep was restless. More than once I woke, grabbing the gun from the bedside table next to me in preparation for an unseen assault. When I finally decided to get up, the sun had started to creep through Holly's wooden blinds.

The red numbers on the digital clock next to me said it was just after eight in the morning. "You didn't sleep well," Holly said as she appeared in the doorway. She stretched, raising the t-shirt she wore to give a small glimpse of her toned stomach. She caught me looking and smiled. "You've got no chance this morning, Nate. I don't think my other guest would be too thrilled at hearing that sort of thing."

I pulled my best "damn it all" face and walked off to have a shower. This time I remained alone for its entire duration.

When I was dried, I found Holly had left a pair of blue jeans and a black t-shirt on the bed. "I told you one day you might need those," she said as she went to have a shower of her own.

"Yeah, yeah." I thought back to how awkward I'd felt keeping clothes at Holly's place. I had some of my own in my suitcase, but that was still in the car, and I was just grateful to wear something that didn't smell like I'd run through a burning building. *My home,* fucking hell that hurt more than I'd expected it to. I didn't have a huge amount of stuff, but it had still been mine.

"Your friend's been up a while," Holly said.

"She okay?"

Holly shrugged. "Not really, no. She's barely holding it together."

Holly left for the bathroom, a huge orange towel in hand. I finished getting dressed and went in search of Dani.

I found her sitting cross-legged on the couch, the blanket I'd placed on her before going to bed myself draped over the couch's back.

"What the fuck are you?"

"Excuse me?" I asked and sat on the chair next to her.

"Yesterday I watched a woman who I thought was my mum murdered by a man I've never met. And then I was caught up in an explosion and *thrown over a balcony*. You stopped us from hitting the ground. So *what* are you?"

"It's complicated."

"People only say that when they make it complicated. My whole life is a lie. I just want some truth I can hold onto."

She had a good point. Everything in her life had just crumbled down around her. Having one truth in all that mess might make the difference between despair and hanging on with her fingertips. After checking that Holly wasn't around, I told her. I didn't go into everything. But enough about who—and what— I was to set her mind at ease, making sure to keep an ear out for Holly finishing in the shower as I spoke.

When I'd finished, Dani sat very quietly for a few seconds, hands in her lap as she stared at me. "So, you're not human," she said eventually, her voice barely above a whisper.

I nodded as Holly's shower fell silent.

"Why do they want you too?"

I shrugged. "I plan on finding out. Don't mention what I told you to Holly, about my magic. She doesn't know about it, and I'd like it to stay that way." After everything that had happened, I'd considered telling Holly about my magic, but something had stopped me. A fragment of doubt, as if it was the sort of information that shouldn't be shared. Francis had told me that the majority of the wider world knew nothing of the different species that inhabited it. He made it sound like it was very much meant to stay that way.

Dani nodded as Holly entered the room.

"That woman who called you, any idea who she was?" Holly asked as she walked to the kitchen, returning a moment later with two cups of coffee and a cup of green tea for me. She passed one cup to Dani and sat next to her.

"No idea," I told them. "She said she would contact me soon. Hopefully today."

"Will you find the people responsible for what happened?" Dani asked me.

I nodded.

"Will you kill them all?"

I paused for a second, a little concerned at the ease with which Dani had asked me that question. "I'll do what I need to." I caught Holly's eye; she seemed to have the same concerns as me.

Dani shook her head. "They've taken away my life. I can't ever go home. Hell, I don't even *have* a home. I want them to feel what I feel." Dani stood and looked down at me as tears fell in steady streaks down her cheeks. I stood and held her against me as great sobs burst from her, coating my shirt and chest in tears. Holly looked away, with tears in her own eyes, which she wiped away.

"Why am I crying?" Dani asked. "My mum…" the word seemed to cause her pain. "That woman and I…we fought all the time. She hated me. She couldn't even be done with that twat, Phil."

"She came to see me," I said, remembering Diane's visit.

Dani looked up from my tear-stained top. "What? Why?"

"Just after the fight with Phil. She told me that she hated him, but that he had to be there."

"Why didn't she stop him coming over?"

"I got the feeling that she didn't have a choice in the matter. She was paying him off for something. If the attacker was being honest, then he probably knew something he shouldn't, and she was keeping him quiet."

"Was that all she said?"

"She asked me to take care of you if anything should happen to her. I don't know what she was preparing for, but she wanted to make sure you were safe. You were all that mattered."

Fresh tears rained down from Dani's puffy eyes.

"I think she loved you, Dani. Really loved you. And I'm sorry that you lost that."

Dani took a deep breath, and I could tell that she was trying with everything she had not to keep crying. She turned away and rubbed her eyes before taking one last deep breath.

"I'm sorry for that," she whispered.

"You never need to be," I told her. "Holly's going to take care of you today."

"You're going away?" Dani asked, her bravado evaporating and replaced with fear. "You're not staying here?"

"You'll be very safe here. But I need to find out who those people were. And that means going out."

"Can't I come with you?"

"It's too dangerous. And besides, you have no shoes."

"I'm going to take you shopping," Holly said. "You need some clothes and things if you're going to be staying here."

I picked up the remote and switched on Holly's widescreen TV, turning to the news channels. A portly man with a shit-eating grin and possible toupee sat behind a desk going through the main stories of the day. It didn't take long to get to what I was interested in and I watched with shock as every word out of his mouth was a lie. Even if he was unaware of it.

"What the hell?" I said and sat back on the chair.

"I assume that's not what happened," Holly said.

That was putting it mildly. The news stated that a man murdered his lover after an argument. Then, in an attempt to hide the body, tried to burn the place down, killing himself in the process. Their daughter was missing and if anyone saw her they needed to phone the number that flashed up on the bottom of the screen next to a photo of Dani.

I'd hoped that what had happened might have slowed them down. Instead, they hadn't even missed a step. "So they can doctor the news. Which basically means, they can do whatever they feel like."

"That's all it says anywhere," Dani said. "Even the net is quiet about it. I checked the statuses of a few people I know in our building. No one else was hurt. Although, I've got a lot of messages asking where I am."

Dani's photo appeared on screen once more. "You didn't respond, did you?"

"Of course not," she said. "And I switched my phone off."

"Well, we won't be going anywhere with your picture all over the news," Holly said. "Not with you looking like that." She took Dani's hair in her hand and bunched it up at the back. "I've got hair dye, and used to cut hair when I was younger. By the time I'm done you'll look like a whole new person."

"You could always stay in," I said.

"Dani needs clothes, and we all need food. She's about my size. She can borrow some of my clothes until we get her some of her own. Besides, like you said, she needs shoes. Those high heels won't be much good if we need to move fast."

"Just be careful. Right now we have the advantage of being invisible. I'd like to keep it that way until we know what's going on."

"Are you a cop or something?" Dani asked.

Holly's riotous laughter pretty much put stop to that idea. "He's a thief," she said once she'd calmed down.

"You're a criminal?" Dani asked, shocked.

"I'm a thief." I tried not to smile at the notion that Dani was more shocked that I was a criminal than she was that I wasn't human. "Is that going to be a problem?"

Dani shook her head. "No, I just wanted to know."

I passed Dani my mobile. "This is untraceable. As I seem to have acquired another, it'll be a good idea if you have this."

She nodded thanks and started playing with her new electronic toy.

Holly gave me a hug. "Take care."

I grabbed my jacket and walked to the front door. I picked up the gun and placed it in my holster, fastening my jacket up afterward. I caught a glimpse of Holly's worried expression.

"Just in case," I said. "I won't use it unless I have to." Somewhere inside me a voice whispered—*but if I have to use it, I'll make sure I'll be the one walking away.*

The phone in my pocket began to vibrate before I'd even made it down the stairs to the front door of Holly's building. The number said "withheld." I answered it and a familiar female voice filled my ear. "Is she safe?"

"I'm good, thanks. Blew up my flat, got shot at. Oh, killed a man in cold blood. Been quite an eventful day. Least it's not raining though, eh?"

"Are you quite finished?"

I had more, but I thought it better to save them for a more willing audience. "Dani's fine."

"Dani." Her tone was hard to pinpoint. She sounded angry, but sad too. "Where is she?"

"At a friend's."

"I told you not to involve anyone else."

I pushed the front door to Holly's building open with more force than strictly necessary. It slammed against the fence behind it. "Yeah, well I was running out of options. Did I mention the being shot at and blowing-up incident?"

"Involving others will lead to complications."

I stopped walking. "Look, I did the best I could." Anger rose inside me, and I had to force myself from snapping at her any further.

"Yes, I'm sure you did." She sounded a little sorry, but maybe it was just the sleep deprivation on my part. "Where are you?"

"London, why?"

"You need to get to Tower Hill within the next hour. Is that possible?"

It would take me about twenty minutes from where I was. "No problem. Who am I looking for, you?"

"No, not me. That would be foolish. Once out of the tube, go to a nearby pub, The Friar. It's five minutes walk from the station. My advice would be to get a cab in case you're followed. You'll know your contact. Just keep…Dani safe. I'll contact you when possible."

"Whom do you work for? And what do they actually want from me?"

"See your contact. Good luck, Mister Garrett."

"Wait," I snapped. "Just tell me, why is Dani so important?"

"My lord is interested in having control over fate itself. With Dani's help he will ensure that happens." And she hung up.

"More cryptic shit!" I shouted at the now disconnected phone. A young woman walked past with a small, yappy dog trailing after her on a bright pink lead that matched the color of the woman's tiny skirt. She turned and gave me a stare of disgust. "Lovely day we're having," I said tipping an imaginary hat. The woman glanced away and increased her pace, her heels clicking against the pavement.

Great, now I'm scaring members of the public, I thought and made my way to the tube station at Bank, which as usual was full of people all vying for that little bit of extra space. Luckily, it was a short ride to Liverpool Street and then an only slightly longer one from there to Tower Hill.

Tower Hill is the closest tube station to the Tower of London. The huge and impressive building looms above everything else around it. The fact that it used to be a prison, and that more than a few people died in it, seemed to be all the reason it needed to become a massive tourist attraction. People from all over the world have long congregated outside the Tower's imposing gates, which is probably why every shop in the area charged three times more than anywhere else.

I walked past a group consisting of a mother, father, and their two children, a boy and girl, both I guessed to be younger than ten. The dad was telling the girl off in rapidly spoken Italian, which I immediately translated in my head without thinking. Apparently, Italian was one of the languages I could understand, something I hadn't been aware of beforehand. The girl didn't want to wear the Beefeater-style hat she had on, and the dad wasn't happy with his daughter's tantrum. To be fair, it was an ugly hat, and making his child wear one probably went against the Geneva Convention.

I left them to it and passed a few dozen middle-aged American tourists eating ice cream cones that they'd probably had to remortgage their houses to afford. A few of them wore those ridiculous Union Jack hats that stores sell Americans so everyone else can tell them apart.

I got into the first black cab I reached and asked the male driver to take me to The Friar. Despite the close proximity of the pub to where I was standing, I wasn't exactly shocked to discover that he was happy to oblige.

The journey took all of two minutes and cost more than the tube ticket I'd used to travel twenty times the distance. *I'm in the wrong bloody job.*

The pub had been built inside a beautiful old building, possibly Georgian—it was hard to tell after all the work that had been done to the exterior. Several gray-stone gargoyles hung from the rooftop, peering down on those beneath them with a set indifference.

I entered the pub and it took a second for my eyes to adjust. A large stained-glass window down one side only allowed a small amount of light in. Low-hanging lights had been placed throughout the interior, but they could only help so much. I walked to the bar and ordered a scotch from a tall, skinny man who looked like he needed to get a bit of sun and eat a good meal. He returned with a glass containing a shot of scotch, neat. He hadn't even asked if I wanted ice in it. I liked the place already.

I drank a measure of the golden liquid, feeling the warmth as it cascaded down my throat. The door to the pub opened and I looked up just as a familiar voice said, "Hello, Nate."

I turned to see Jenny. And downed the rest of the scotch.

CHAPTER 17

"I'm not here to fight, Nate," Jenny said.

That was strange, because my first impulse was to throw a giant ball of flame at her. "You shot me," I said holding back my sudden anger.

"With a tranquilizer dart."

"Oh, that's *okay* then. Wanna shoot me a few more times?"

Jenny smiled; she had a nice smile. She'd changed her hair color to a deep purple, left loose over her shoulders. She wore a pair of blue combats, a tiny black vest with a picture of AC/DC on it, and some white Nike trainers. A black rucksack hung over one slender shoulder and she had a small jacket in one hand. My mind crept back to the last time I'd seen her naked, moving on top of me. And then it went to the moment she shot me. The memory of being shot by a woman pretty much kills *any* sexual urge you have toward her. And if it doesn't, you have issues.

"I was sent to help you," Jenny said as she walked past me and took a seat in a booth at the rear of the pub. I ordered two Cokes—alcohol was not going to be a good idea—and took them over to our table.

"How very gentlemanly," she said.

"I just didn't want you to get me one and lace it with sedatives."

Jenny laughed and my groin did a little happy dance. OK *apparently I have issues.*

"So, you fancy explaining why you shot me?"

"It was my job. Shoot you, take you to your hotel, and leave you there for pick up. But I used a lot less tranquilizer than I was meant to. It took a little explaining about how you'd managed to wake up and escape by the time my lord's men arrived." She smiled at the memory. "Apparently, I'm very persuasive."

"So sleeping with me was part of the plan?"

Jenny's smile intensified. "Oh no, that was definitely all for *me*."

It took a Herculean effort not to drag her somewhere secluded and have my way with her. I pushed the thought aside before it took hold. "Who do you work for?"

"My lord is the only name I have. He's not exactly personable with his staff. Sorry." Jenny rummaged through her rucksack, where I caught the glint of gun metal. She passed a red file across the table to me.

I opened it to find my name written on the first page. "What is this?"

"It's a copy of the file we have on you. And a few things my lord managed to acquire from *other sources.*"

I flicked through a few more pages, but Jenny's voice drew my attention back to her. "Read that later; right now there are more pressing matters." She reached back into her rucksack and removed a brown envelope, which she passed to me. I opened it, spilling the contents onto the table.

"Photos?" I asked, trying to make sense of what I was seeing. I stared at myself, caught in black and white. "What's happening here?"

"I've been ordered to do a few things at this meeting. One of them is to explain why my lord and his vast resources are currently after you. These photos help do that."

"Who ordered you? Who is the woman on the phone?"

"Nate, please look at the photos." Jenny's sharp change of tone from playful to all business was a little jarring, but I did as she asked.

There were a dozen photos in total, all of me. I wore a dark jacket and combats, although the shading suggested they weren't the same color. The photos could have been used as a flip book, showing the seconds pass as I entered a building and attacked its inhabitants. After the third photo, two bodies were on the floor and a gun had appeared in my hand.

"Nate?" Jenny said and placed her hand against mine. And my brain went nuts as I collapsed against the wall and passed out.

Ten years ago.

I entered the building, an old abandoned office block near the London docks, aware of what I would find inside. Six humans and my target. He had to be kept alive; everyone else was expendable. They were mercenaries, no one I needed to feel sorry for. They'd been paid to work for a monster like Dr. Welkin. They'd witnessed the atrocities carried out at his hand. They deserved their fate.

I opened the door and faced the first of the humans. Shock crossed his face before I slammed my fist into his throat, crushing his windpipe. I spun around to face a second man, who had been standing behind the door when I'd opened it. A quick elbow to his jaw snapped his head to the side before he could reach for the gun in his hip holster. I took advantage and stepped behind him, breaking his neck and dropping him to the floor.

I grabbed the gun from his holster and placed a round through the temple of the suffocating man—they deserved to die, but I was not in the mood to watch people suffer needlessly.

The gunshot brought a third merc out from a nearby room, pistol at the ready. He was dead before he had the chance to fire off a single shot. The contents of his head decorated the beige wall behind him.

The mercs wore body armor, Kevlar, over normal street clothes, but nothing to protect their heads. It was an oversight they wouldn't live to regret. With three down, that left only three to remove from this world before tracking down Dr. Welkin, a man I was sure would be cowering somewhere. Men like him always do. They torture and rip people apart behind the safety of bulletproof offices and drugged victims.

I ejected the magazine from the dead guard's Ruger and checked the contents—ten bullets left, although the fact that they weren't silver meant these men were only expecting human problems. I reloaded the gun and continued through the nondescript building, checking all of the offices along the lengthy corridor and finding nothing but rats and spiders.

After a few minutes of walking around the maze-like structure, I stopped outside a large gray door. I'd heard a slight noise from inside. It had been quick and soft, but it was something that needed checking. I placed a palm against the door and concentrated. The glyphs on my hand glowed white and air seeped through the cracks in the frame, pouring into the room and flowing unseen through it. Every time it touched something with a heartbeat I received a sonar-like ping. In my head I could map out where everyone was. It wasn't a hundred percent accurate, and had taken a lot of time to perfect, but it had saved my life more than once. The noise from the gunshots ensured that the three remaining mercs would now be prepared for me. That didn't mean they stood a chance, but it didn't mean I had to be stupid either.

The glyphs subsided and I walked a few feet to my left, unleashing a torrent of air at the thin wall. Brick and plaster dust exploded around me. I stepped through the hole and fired twice, once at each of the two men inside the room. Both fell to the floor, their fates the same as their friends.

The room was about twenty foot square and consisted of nothing but two dead men and a group of sockets that had been pulled from the wall. Wires spilled naked from the holes the damage had created. There was another gray door opposite me. I walked over ready to try the sonar trick again, but the door was ripped apart in a hale of gunfire. I dove aside, landing on one of the dead mercs as the bullets came once more, this time just above my head, perforating the thin wall. A submachine gun, probably an Uzi from the sound. I kept low and made my way to the wall. Some of the bullets had punctured through, giving me a good view of the room beyond.

The last merc stood about five feet inside the room, the gun trained on the door, ready for me to make my move. I placed a finger inside one of the holes and shot a stream of fire through it.

More bullets hit the exact part of the wall where I'd been sitting, but I was already on the move, kicking the door open and firing twice before he realized what was happening.

The Uzi clattered to the floor, followed soon after by its user. I moved around them into what amounted to a large storage room. Several small windows sat on one side, none of them big enough for a grown man to get through. That didn't stop the doctor from trying.

He'd shattered one of the windows, cutting himself on his thigh when he tried to climb through, blood dripped slowly onto the dusty, bare wooden floor. I walked over, grabbed him by his leather belt, and dragged him back into the room, dropping him on the floor with a loud thud.

I looked at the window, about two foot square, and then glanced at Dr. Welkin, who could never be described as two foot anything. He was six feet tall and weighed in excess of twenty-two stone. There were sumo wrestlers with more flattering physiques.

"I won't tell you anything," Dr. Welkin said, his voice shrill and nasal. He reached behind him for the discarded Uzi, which I kicked out of his reach, through the open door and into the room beyond.

"You can torture me," Welkin yelled. "I won't tell you anything."

I crouched beside him, placing the end of the Ruger's barrel against his knee. "Wanna bet?" I said and pulled the trigger.

"Nate, Nate," Jenny was saying over and over, as she held my hand. "You okay?"

I blinked several times before forcing myself back to a seated position. "I had a flashback. I was killing the men in those photos. I was after a doctor."

"Are you sure?" Jenny looked temporary taken aback, but any confusion soon vanished, replaced by her usual calm demeanor. "The magic that was used to make you forget was very powerful. Could you be mistaken?"

That got my attention. "No, it was real. Did you say magic was used to make me forget?"

"Blood magic. Powerful Blood magic too. They were meant to rip the memories from your mind before killing you. You escaped before whoever was tasked with the job could finish."

"Who was it?" My voice was filled with anger. I'd never realized how much I wanted my old memories back until everyone else suddenly wanted them too.

Jenny shook her head. "I'm sorry, but I don't know. All I know is that my lord wanted you hurt, badly. I remember how angry he was with you. How much he...hated you, although I don't know why."

The need to read through the file was immense, but it had to wait. Jenny was my chance to get answers, and I wasn't about to waste it. "Who's Doctor Welkin?"

Jenny briefly scowled, and then stared at me for a long heartbeat. "It would be easier if I just explained from the beginning."

I drank some of my Coke and motioned for her to continue.

"About twenty years ago, my lord hired a man by the name of Doctor Philip Welkin, a human geneticist, to oversee his newest round of soldiers."

"Soldiers?"

"My lord is in the arms business. He supplies his weapons to anyone who can afford them. And very few people can."

"These weapons, they're living beings, yes?"

Jenny nodded. "Have you ever heard of the Harbingers?"

I shook my head.

"They're the elite warriors of Avalon. They undergo a series of mental and physical trials to ensure that they operate at peak performance. It involves increasing their abilities, both magical and otherwise, through the use of psychics and rune work. The point of the trials is twofold. Firstly, they give the participants access to power that would otherwise take them a hundred years to learn and develop. And secondly, it creates a loyalty and bond between each other, which is almost unbreakable."

Francis had told me about Avalon, about it's power and how if you have any sense you stay under their radar and as far away from them as possible. I was pretty certain I wanted to keep it that way. "Your lord wants his own version of these soldiers?"

"For centuries my lord has taken those who crossed him and changed them, making them into vessels of destruction—gargoyles and nightmares—for anyone with enough coin. But my lord has always wanted to have his own Harbingers. His own elite soldiers."

"Why not just stick with what he was doing?"

"The creation of nightmares and gargoyles is long and complex. It more often than not leads to the subject's death. Avalon calls them crimes against magic, and it's a death sentence to be one. Making a Harbinger-like soldier should be much easier and produce a more pliable subject, but Avalon has always kept their creation a closely guarded secret. Or it was until my lord found someone within Avalon who thought as he did. Over time he was able to discover the secrets of the Harbinger's creation. After that he hired Welkin, a man notorious for both his brilliance and his lack of ethics."

"What aren't you telling me?"

"The process of creating a Harbinger is not without its dangers. It takes anywhere from one to five years of intensive treatment, and that's on people who are already hundreds of years old. Normally, the survival rate of a Harbinger creation is ninety-six percent."

A cold feeling started in my stomach. "Normally?"

"Welkin theorized that it would be better to use children, those from thirteen to eighteen, to create Harbingers. He surmised that they would be more loyal and capable than their adult counterparts. Welkin also suggested that they could be used as a surprise offensive. And he said it could all be done within eighteen months.

"He used children of nonhuman parentage whose abilities hadn't yet surfaced. Having nonhuman parents is no indication that the child will gain any abilities, but despite this, Welkin never checked to find out if the children were human or not. Of the forty-one children he used in his experiment fifteen years ago, six survived the process."

I felt sick. Welkin murdered over thirty children for an experiment. An experiment conducted all in the name of making more money. "Where are those children now?"

Jenny looked down at the table. "I don't know. They were sold and I'm not privy to the buyers list."

"When did I get involved?"

"You raided the warehouse where the next group of kids were being held—sixty-four children, the majority of whom were waiting to go through the Harbinger process. Welkin claimed to have refined it, that seventy percent would survive it."

"You said the majority."

Jenny's expression hardened. Her eyes became cold and narrow, but I saw sadness in them alongside the anger. "To prove his point, Welkin took ten of the children and forced the experiment on them. He said it would be done within a year. And he was right, it was. Seven of those ten survived."

Ten years ago would put Jenny at about fifteen. "You were one of those kids."

She shook her head. "My sister was. She died in the initial wave of experiments. I was deemed too valuable to use in such an experiment."

"Why?"

"It's complicated," she said and wiped her eyes with the back of her hand. "Anyway, before Welkin could run the experiment, he began to get paranoid, saying he was being stalked and that his life was in danger. He wanted to postpone it, but my lord refused. Welkin vanished soon after. At first we thought my lord had removed him, but when those kids were freed it became apparent that someone else had gotten to Welkin. The doctor's body was found a few weeks later. The details of what you did to him are in the folder."

I didn't want to wait that long to find out. "What did I do, Jenny?"

"You tortured him, kept him alive long enough for him to give you what you needed. Welkin died hard—broken bones, lacerations; part of him had been turned to charcoal." A small smile spread across her lips and hatred shone in her eyes.

"Welkin was a *fucking monster*." Her words dripped bile. "He experimented on *children* and made Josef Mengele look like a nice rational human being. He deserved a lot worse."

"Why do you work for him? Your lord, I mean."

Jenny looked away for a brief moment and then continued as if I'd never spoken, "You were ambushed when removing the kids from the labs."

"What about Dani? What does she have to do with all this?"

Jenny shook her head. "Welkin's replacement wanted to try some sort of nature versus nurture crap. Two girls. One was placed with Daniel Hayes, a scientist who was meant to be cold and scientific about the whole thing. And another with the woman who died yesterday, Dani's fake mum. The scientists wanted her to shower Dani with presents and trinkets. They paid her millions to take the job. The plan was then for both girls to be taken back at the same time in order to find out how their lives had affected their abilities."

The scientists hadn't counted on both Dani's mum and Daniel actually loving the children placed with them. "Dani's not human?"

Jenny shook her head. "I hope for her sake she is, but the truthful answer is I don't know. We're working off the basis that she will retain the abilities of at least one parent."

"And they were?"

"Her mother is psychic. I've no idea about the father."

How was I going to tell Dani that she might not be human? I decided to get my other questions answered as I tried to figure out that particular puzzle. "Why did your friend murder Daniel Hayes?"

"My lord willed his death. We might be going against him now, but if we'd refused to kill Daniel, or to set you up, we'd never have gotten Dani out. All the planning would've been for nothing. Daniel had to die. It was a sacrifice we were willing to make."

The detached tone in her voice chilled me slightly, and I knew that if she'd been the one behind the rifle, she would have killed Daniel just as easily as her mysterious friend. "Do you know where Daniel's daughter is?"

"She's safe right now. I have her hidden."

That was one weight off my mind. "Why are you helping me?"

Jenny took a long drink of her Coke. "Because you tried to help those kids. This operation has been a long time in coming, and I want to see everyone involved in it burn. Besides, despite trying not to, I actually like you."

I couldn't help but smile, which was returned in kind with one of Jenny's own.

"It's quite the coincidence that I ended up in the same building as Dani and her fake family."

"I've been thinking about that. I didn't have any ideas until you had your little episode just now, but I think your memories are a little closer to the surface than your attacker intended them to be. I'm no Blood magic expert, but maybe subconsciously you knew where she was and sought her out."

It was as good an explanation as any I'd managed to think of. I finished my Coke and was about to ask Jenny about Daniel's last words involving King Priam when I noticed her eyes narrowing as she watched something behind me. Her hand went into her bag, and I reached for the H&K in its holster.

"Jenny, you traitorous bitch, how did I know I'd find you here?" A man's voice sounded from the front of the pub. His footsteps tapped on the wooden floor as he moved toward us.

"Remember me?" he said as he stood between me and Jenny, resting his hands on the table.

I looked up with shock at the unblemished face of the man who had murdered Dani's mum. His dirty blonde hair fell over his shoulders, a large smile spread across his lips.

"That's right, not dead. Bullets can't kill me," he said to me before turning to Jenny. "And what should I do with you? Our lord knew you'd betray him. You fucked up back at Mars Warfare. You'd never make the mistake of not using enough tranquilizer."

"So, Achilles, you're here to kill me?" Jenny said.

"Achilles?" I said with a laugh. "Wow, you must have had the piss taken out of you at school. Did your parents hate you or something? Or had all the other Ancient Greek names been used in your household? I pity the kid named Ajax the Lesser."

A flicker of hatred started in Achilles' eyes as he looked down at me with distain. "I'll come to you, asshole," he said angrily. "First, I'm going to take you both in. I've got six men outside, ready to come in here and take you by force if necessary. So you can do this the easy way or the hard way."

"Eat shit and die," Jenny said and shot Achilles three times in the stomach. Each loud shot caused every other occupant in the room to dive to the floor or hide under the nearest table. Achilles smiled briefly, then crumpled to the floor as Jenny darted from her seat. "Come on, we haven't got long," she said to me and started to run to the back of the pub.

I grabbed the file and followed her, bursting through a fire exit into the alleyway behind the pub, and almost running directly into Jenny who was looking up and down the alley.

"My lord's men will have stormed the pub by now, probably left a few out front in case we were stupid enough to use that exit. This way." She sprinted toward one end of the alley.

I followed her in silence for the next few minutes. We kept to the back alleys, not wanting to risk running out onto the busy streets. The thickening crowds would make it difficult to tell innocent from combatant, and I doubted our pursuers cared too much who they hurt in their need to get to us.

We stopped running outside a large building, which probably contained a few dozen flats. "We need to get to shelter. They can track us from above."

I hadn't heard any helicopters above us. "How?"

"Let's hope you don't find out," Jenny said and pressed the entire set of buzz-in buttons for the flats. At least one of them unlocked the front door without ever checking to see who it was. I would have expected people in London to be a little more security cautious.

Jenny opened the door and we hurried into a dark foyer, one flickering halogen bulb all that was left to illuminate the way. "Most of these old buildings have fire escapes close to one another. We'll check the sky when we reach the top and if it's all clear, we should be able to jump between buildings and lose them."

We started to run up the stairs. "That doesn't sound like the best idea."

Jenny stopped just shy of the top stair on the first set. "This is our only choice. If we keep running around the streets they will catch us." She paused and took a deep breath. "If this goes to shit you've got to get that file away from here and read it. They want Welkin's research. You took it when you killed him, and no one else has been able to duplicate the results. You're the only one who knows where it is."

"Except that I have no idea."

"You have to try to remember. They won't stop coming after you and Dani until they've got you. Your only way of defending against them is attacking them. To do that, you'll need what's in those notes. They're terrified it'll get into the wrong hands and ruin them. Swear you'll try. But no matter what happens, you must keep Dani and yourself safe."

I nodded. "I swear."

She took a step toward me and kissed me tenderly on the lips. "Just in case." For the briefest of moments, she looked incredibly sad. "Let's go."

She bounded up the remaining stairs and along the third floor corridor with me close behind. On the stairs to the fourth, Jenny slowed her stride as if more cautious about what was above.

About halfway down the fourth floor corridor, Jenny stopped. "Remember," she said. "You must keep Dani and yourself safe. And find those notes."

"I will," I assured her. "Now let's go." I managed another step before the wall beside me exploded, accompanied by a roar that couldn't possibly belong to anything human.

Several bricks slammed into me as I dove to the ground. Pain shot through my arm as I rolled aside to get distance between me and whatever had destroyed the wall.

Dust and screams filled the air. I forced a small breeze to clear my view, and immediately wished I'd brought a bigger gun. Or an Apache helicopter.

Jenny's feet dangled a meter off the floor, her head slightly imbedded in a plaster wall opposite the now-demolished flat. The *thing* held her by her neck. I'd never seen a living being that looked like it. Six and a half feet tall with gray, stone-like plates interlocked over each other, creating a sort of armor. Huge wings, easily the length of the main body, flicked gently with the breeze. The edges dripped blood onto the green-carpeted hallway floor.

The monster turned to look at me, its face familiar despite the gray armor and foot-long horns growing from each temple. Somewhere inside me a name reverberated, I knew what this thing was. Gargoyle.

"Guess who?" Its voice was raw and deep.

"Achilles," I responded. Two dead bodies were inside the flat he'd torn through, both of them sitting in chairs watching the TV, their backs to me, heads missing from their shoulders.

"Collateral Damage," Achilles said, a long red tongue—the only part of him that wasn't a shade of gray—licking Jenny's face.

Jenny opened her eyes and emptied her revolver into Achilles' face, but the plates stopped the bullets from doing harm as they ricocheted off, striking the ceiling and walls around him.

"You fucking whore," he screamed smashing her against the wall once more.

I couldn't use magic, I couldn't risk the fluctuation in power I'd been experiencing. It could increase the damage I did to not only Achilles, but Jenny. She was too close to him for me to reliably get a good shot. But, as I'd recently learnt, I could fight up close.

I darted forward, any reservations about using violence had long since been done away with, as I hoped to use the distraction to get Jenny free. Achilles was too fast and one wing slashed across my face, knocking me back to the ground. The wind was knocked out of me. Blood dripped from a cut above one of my eyes. I touched it instinctively, my finger easily finding the sides of the wound. It needed stitches. A few millimeters lower and I'd have lost my eye.

"You're lucky our lord wants you alive," Achilles yelled at Jenny. Her gaze fixed firmly on me. "Him? You're worried about him?" The monster dragged Jenny over toward me, showing me to her and then launching into a kick that broke my ribs as it connected.

"Run," Jenny whispered. "You promi—"

"You shut up," Achilles said and threw Jenny into the nearby wall. I used the change of attention to wrap tightly compressed air around my fist and caught him on the jaw with everything I had. He rocked back, blinking twice before kicking me in the chest so hard I thought he'd broken every bone from my waist up to my neck.

I flew along the corridor, impacting the wall thirty feet away with a crack as I broke plasterboard and a few more ribs. I fell to the floor unable to breathe, barely able to see what was happening. One eye had a veil of blood, and the other kept seeing dark spots.

If I couldn't use magic, Jenny would be taken to who-knows-where. And I'd be killed. I picked up the file I'd dropped, forced myself back to my feet, and planted myself as best possible, using the nearest wall for support. "Hey, dipshit," I shouted.

Achilles turned to face me. He appeared amused, or consti-pated, it was hard to tell with a face made of solid rock.

"You are becoming an irritant," he said and raised his hands to stop his newly arriving comrades from using their guns to turn me into a colander.

White glyphs blared along my arms as I willed a tornado-like ferocity to throw at Achilles and his friends. I stepped forward, hands out, and watched as the nongargoyle members of the party dove for cover.

Then, there was a sharp pain in my arm, and the sound of a gunshot. I spun wildly to the floor followed with an explosion of agony. The magic I'd released had torn through the wall of a the flat I was next to. Luckily, no one appeared to have been home. I got back to my knees and saw one of Achilles' friends pointing his rifle at me. Achilles pushed him aside and began to run at me; after a few steps he took off, moving at a speed I would have thought impossible for something his size. He flexed his fingers, razor-sharp claws glinting as he passed bright hallway lights.

If the claws touched me they'd slice me to ribbons, but I moved too late. And instead of avoiding Achilles altogether, I only avoided his claws. The rest of him barreled into me, launching me through the window and into the outer brick wall of the building twenty feet opposite.

I fell about ten feet, crashed stomach first into a steel fire escape, which spun me in the air and sent me toward the concrete earth several stories below at an accelerated speed. My glyphs sprung to life and slowed my descent, but I still hit the ground hard, losing whatever air was in my lungs as the fire of pain made breathing an unbearable struggle.

I had to move. Achilles and friends would be after me, and I had promised Jenny that I'd make sure that Dani was safe. *Holly*...shit, if they went after Holly. I looked around for the file but couldn't find it. Then I remembered. When Achilles had hit me, the impact had knocked it out of my hand. Any chance of finding out what was going on went up in smoke.

Gunshots sounded from the window high above me, the bullets hitting the ground all around me. Apparently, "alive" and "in one piece" were not the same thing to Achilles' boss.

I got to my feet and moved as fast as possible down the alley, trying to keep myself out of the public eye as I used a small amount of wind magic to put pressure on the bleeding. The gunshot had hit my shoulder, and my arm had gone numb. I really hoped it wasn't as serious as it felt, but even breathing caused me pain.

I had no idea how long it took me to reach my destination, but by the time I did, the dark spots in my left eye had turned into a permanent fixture along with dizziness and nausea.

I walked along the final alley where Jerry stood at the end. His eyes narrowed, first in suspicion and then shock as he recognized me. I fell to my knees, my body refusing to move any further. "Little help," I said and then darkness consumed me.

CHAPTER 18

1414, France.

"Exactly how is she a problem?" Thomas asked pointing at Ivy, who remained sitting on the edge of the bed. "Compared to the large number of angry werewolves outside, I mean?"

"We'll discuss that later," I told him and looked out the second-floor bedroom window. The placement of the inn gave a great view of the surrounding village, the center of which now contained fourteen werewolves, and their alpha. He stalked back and forth behind the others, his yellow eyes never leaving the inn.

"Can't you just go down there and fight them?" Thomas asked.

I shook my head. "A dozen wolves and an alpha? I think that's a little beyond my scope for keeping both myself and you two alive." I glanced out the window again. Thomas was in no condition to fight alongside me; he'd only had his first change the previous night. He'd be more of a liability than a help.

Could I have taken them all by myself if I didn't have to worry about Thomas and Ivy? I couldn't have said with certainly that I'd have made it out in once piece. Fifteen wolves in total, not a large pack by any standards, even if you added those I'd already killed in Soissons. I could get through maybe seven or eight before they swarmed me. I'd been lucky in the city. The wolves had been young and stupid, unprepared for a sorcerer. I would not have that surprise on my side again.

Besides, even if I survived, using that much magic again so soon after Soisson could cause my magic to start making me think I could use it to solve all of my problems, and then…it wasn't worth thinking about.

"They won't kill me," Ivy said as I tore myself away from watching the beasts below. "They brought me those bottles of perfume and some dresses. They wanted to make me happy and comfortable. Besides, their master won't let me die. They'd be severely punished."

I filed the information away for future reference and continued to search the room for something that might help. I grabbed several of the rainbow-colored bottles, each filled with scented contents.

"I don't like the perfumes," Ivy said, mostly to herself. I passed the bottles to Thomas, who gave me a quizzical expression as he held them in his arms.

"Trust me," I told him with a smile. His expression didn't change. "Is there anything you want to take with you?" I asked Ivy, who shook her head.

"Then we should probably take our leave." Thomas and Ivy followed me down the stairs. The perfume bottles clinked as they jostled against one another, trying to escape the confines of Thomas' folded arms.

I stepped into the inn's main hall and caught the flash of the blade and its wielder's movement as it tore toward me. I dodged in time to avoid both, but the soldier's momentum was unstoppable and he collided with the wall, still slashing wildly at me, his eyes blazing with rage. Thomas and Ivy stopped and took a few steps back, out of reach of the crazed soldier.

"Put the knife down," I said as the soldier moved steadily toward me. One arm hung uselessly at his side, the skin red and blistered where I'd set it on fire.

"You did this to me, you bastard."

I pushed a table aside with a loud crash and weighed my options. Removing the knife would be simple, a blast of air and he'd bounce off the wall. "Cut me then," I challenged.

The solider roared in defiance and ran at me, the knife held like a tiny lance in his hand. I waited until the last second and stepped slightly aside and then immediately toward him, grabbing his arm and snapping it back over his shoulder, all in one fluid move. The solider was lifted off his feet and landed head first, his knife clattering to the floor beside him.

I kicked the small blade aside, but held onto the soldier's arm, locking it at the elbow. "I let you live because you might be useful. If not, I can always rectify that."

"I'll not help you," the Frenchman said. "You are monsters. People who would do our country harm. That girl will make France the greatest nation on earth."

"Says the child murderer. You were at Soissons, yes?"

Fear dotted his eyes as he nodded slightly. "The English deserve...."

I raised my hand to silence him. "You will answer one question or I will pass you to my *English* friend over there." The Frenchman's eyes darted to Thomas. "He's not happy with what you did to his countrymen. He'll take pieces of you before you die, and I don't feel like stopping him. Apart from the wolves, what's out there?"

"Nothing," he said. "They are beasts sent to us by God himself, to make our country great."

"I'm sure they are," I said and knocked him out with one punch.

"So, do you have a plan?" Thomas asked.

"The perfume should mask our escape. I just need to figure out the escape bit."

Thomas jumped slightly as the door to the inn opened and a man stepped inside. The door slammed shut behind him. He wore long, dark-red robes, which covered him entirely, leaving only the dark boots on his feet and his bare hands visible. Under the hood, his face was shrouded in darkness. But something about him was familiar, and dangerous.

"I thought I would come and see those who cause us so much trouble." The man spoke in English, although I didn't recognize the accent. "What a surprise to find it's *you*, Nathanial." He placed more hatred and bile in my name than few I could remember.

My mind raced as I tried to figure out who he was. "Have we met?"

The man chuckled. It was much more disturbing than I'd ever thought a chuckle could be. "Maybe a demonstration is in order." He raised one hand toward the unconscious French soldier, who began to spasm as he was lifted off the ground and forced into an upright position.

Thomas' eyes never left the soldier, a look of horror on his face. Ivy was also terrified, but there was something else there too—anger. She hated this man with a fury. I studied the hooded figure, aware of what he was doing, and felt some anger of my own.

A dark spiral, almost black in color, appeared on his outstretched palm. The tail followed along the artery in his wrist and down his forearm, where it vanished from view under the sleeves of his robe. A crunching sound gained my focus as the soldier writhed in midair. Suddenly, there was an almighty crack, and blood exploded from the sides of the still-living soldier, drenching the surrounding furniture and floor.

Another crunch followed immediately after and the soldier's eyes vanished in a mist of red as his skull was crushed.

Finished with his sickening display, the sorcerer casually dropped the Frenchman's body to the floor. "Understand now?" The sorcerer asked in an amused tone.

"Who are you?" I demanded as my glyphs glowed against my skin.

"Still don't recognize me? I suppose it has been a very long time." He opened the door. The wind outside had picked up, blowing leaves through the strangers legs and into the inn. "How about now? he demanded as he pulled his hood back in one flourish.

"Mordred," I seethed with anger as my glyphs burned brightly.

He gave us a wicked smiled. He'd grown a long, dark beard since I'd last seen him, plaiting the ends into several individual strands. He'd also shaved his head bald. His red eyes were a product of the type of magic he used exclusively. "Nathanial," he whispered. My name sounded wrong on his lips, and that infuriated me all the more. "This is where I take my leave."

I unleashed a torrent of flame at Mordred, but he darted from the door, vanishing into the village.

"What in God's name was that?" Thomas asked.

"Not now," I said between clenched teeth, anger burning brightly inside me. The fire I'd cast had taken hold of the inn and was quickly spreading across the wooden floor. "Throw the bottles into the fire."

Thomas did as I asked, the exploding bottles spreading their scent and flammable liquid all over the entrance to the inn.

"In the cellar," Ivy said, followed by a creak as the trapdoor was pulled up.

We descended down a long, well-made ladder into a large cellar as the mixed smells of the perfume followed us. The inn was about three yards above us. The fire would have a hard time reaching this far underground. Candlelight illuminated the entire cellar, casting eerie shadows along the stone walls.

"So, do we just hide down here?" Thomas asked.

"The monster who kept me locked up didn't trust the soldiers or wolves. So the man who owned the inn was ordered to bring me my meals," Ivy said as she wandered through the cellar. "I read him once. He wanted to know if his family would be safe. He'd been leading them through tunnels down here and into the hills above us."

"And this wasn't information you were going to give us?" Thomas asked.

"I would have, yes. But I wanted to know what Nathanial's plan was. I knew that he would rescue me; I didn't want to jeopardize that by giving him the answers. The things I see aren't set." Ivy stopped, placed her hands against a stone at the far end of the room, and pushed. A hidden door silently released. A cool breeze swam through the resulting crack.

I gripped the smooth edges of the stone and pulled the door fully open. The tunnel inside was small, fit only for single-file movement. It had probably been designed for smugglers. There were plenty of such tunnels dotted over both France and England, and there was no telling how safe or long it might be. But it was a way out that didn't involve fighting my way through a wolf pack.

I removed my *guan dao* and held it horizontally by my side. The three of us moved through the narrow passage as fast as we dared, closing the door behind us to conceal our exit. It looked well made, but one wrong step and the tons of earth above us could very quickly become our tomb. I took up the front, with Ivy a few steps behind me to avoid the spike on the end of my *guan dao*, and Thomas behind her. The only sounds inside were the pounding of our footwear on the soft earth and the occasional crunch as a bug came too close.

The further we went, the staler the air seemed to become. Even so, I was grateful it wasn't the smell of burning flesh. Nor that of those perfumes, which had not formed a pleasant odor once mixed together. *Although, they had burned well.*

The tunnel seemed to go on forever. The complete absence of light combined with the size of the tunnel created a growing sense of claustrophobia. I considered using magic to make me see in the dark, but the inferno I'd caused back in the inn meant I needed time without its use. Despite how small an amount it takes to allow me to see in the dark, it just wasn't worth the risk to let my magic take more control of my thoughts.

Eventually, I started to see tiny pinpricks of light and I hurried forward, hoping to spring any traps that may await us.

At the end of the tunnel I discovered that the tiny lines of light were making their way through a huge amount of ferns and leaves piled up at the exit, which was a large hole in the side of a mound of earth. I pushed the flora aside and stepped into a forest. Probably part of the same one Thomas and I had stayed in the night before. After the darkness of the tunnel, even the insignificant amount of sunlight was enough to make me blink and rub my eyes. I took a moment to get used to my new surroundings.

The village behind us was easy to spot by simply following the black, billowing smoke. It was probably a mile away, certainly far enough that we were safe from any immediate hunting on the part of the werewolves.

"So what do we do now?" Thomas asked, emerging from the tunnel.

"We find my sister," Ivy said as she sat on the grass. "That man in the hood has her."

"Mordred?" I asked. "He's the one who kept you imprisoned in Soissons?"

Ivy nodded.

"I recognized him from Soissons, too," Thomas said. "What he did to that man...I...what in God's name is he?"

I stabbed at the entrance to the tunnel with the spike on the end of my *guan dao*, partially collapsing the earth to ensure no one could easily follow us through it. "Evil," I said when I'd finished. "A crime against magic."

CHAPTER 19

Thomas and Ivy had a lot of questions about what had happened. I ignored them and walked deeper into the woods without looking back. The only way I knew Ivy and Thomas were following me was the constant cracking of twigs and rustling of the many dead leaves on the ground.

They both left me alone when we reached a clearing near a small lake, a waterfall providing a beautiful backdrop to my melancholy thoughts. I washed in the lake, scrubbing dried blood from my arms and hands whilst the sunlight began its descent into darkness.

I found Thomas and Ivy sitting on the edge of the tree line. Thomas was busy preparing a fire, but the wood was damp and refused to do anything beyond smoke. "Can't you do your magic again?" he asked.

I shook my head and sat against a large oak tree, the old bark felt nice between my shoulder blades.

The click of flint on flint sounded once again, as did the mumbled curse that followed. "Why not?"

"Because he could kill us all," Ivy said.

I turned to look at her and found that she was staring at me. "Magic is alive," I said to Thomas. "It's inside me, inside all sorcerers. It needs to be used. The more you use it, the more powerful you become. But that power comes with a price." I rubbed the back of my neck. It had been a long few days. "Magic heals us, makes us stronger and faster. Hell, it makes us almost immortal. We still age, but much slower than regular humans. The more magic you use, the better you become at it, the faster you learn, and the more likely you are to turn into a monster.

"If a sorcerer stops using magic, just one day decides he's never going to use it again, the magic will start to feed on him. It'll take months, but eventually the magic's feeding will start to age the user at a human level. Those who stop using always die quickly.

"It doesn't want to be dormant. It wants to be used, to do amazing things. And if you won't do it, it will escape the confines of your body and go back to the world around us to be used again by someone else.

"I've used a lot of powerful magic in the past few days, and I'm starting to think that magic can resolve everything. That it would make my life so much easier if I just embraced the use, allowed it to wash over me. But doing that will eventually turn me into a crime against magic."

Thomas cursed the fire's inability to start and flung the flint into the deep forest. "That's what you called Mordred," he said.

I nodded. "There are over a dozen crimes against magic. Most of them are creatures that can be created by using magic either on yourself or others. If a sorcerer uses too much magic his body begins to change. And his mind cracks. Eventually, depending on the magic used and the speed at which you allowed it to consume you, it will turn you into a one of several things."

"Such as?" Thomas continued.

"There's too many to go into right now, but there are two that stand out. The first is a gargoyle. Near impervious to any weapon and covered in thick stone armor. Killing one is hard work. Strong magic is pretty much your only chance. And that's if you manage to avoid the gargoyle's speed and strength, or the venom they have in their claws and bite. They don't have any magic of their own, though; they give that up once their armor encases them.

"The second, and much more common, is a nightmare. And it's exactly what the name suggests. Magic is all but useless against them. They're fast, strong, and will kill anyone in their way. Unlike gargoyles, nightmares possess very little independent thought. They're used as weapons. You point them at someone and they go kill him."

"Can they use magic?" Thomas asked.

"They can absorb magical energy used against them and direct it back at their attacker. But they can't use their innate magic, no. The energy they use is different to my magic; it's raw, almost primal."

Thomas glanced around the forest before speaking again. "Is that why you carry those weapons?"

"Not everything is susceptible to magic. And not everything to silver. But most things can be hurt by one or the other. It certainly reduces the odds of getting caught without something to defend myself with."

"So, what is Mordred?" Thomas asked.

Ivy's expression matched my own feelings. What had that evil bastard done to her?

"I've known Mordred for centuries. He's evil, cruel, and capable of horrific acts, but as for what he is. Well, that's...

complicated is probably the word," I said. "There are three sets of magic. Elemental and Omega are the big two. But the third is Blood magic. It's not a crime to learn how to use it. In fact, most sorcerers who are powerful enough learn some of the more useful aspects—how to increase spell power, healing abilities, tracking people, that sort of thing. But some use it to do terrible things—curses, controlling another's actions, demonic possession.

"All magic demands to be used, but Blood magic is addictive. The power's a massive rush, and some use it to the exclusion of all other types when they become obsessed with it and their power grows. They're called blood leeches. They sacrifice people and drink their blood in an attempt to become ever more powerful. Mordred is one of those."

Thomas looked slightly nauseated. I'd had a similar reaction when I'd heard about what a blood leech did. "So why hasn't anyone killed him?" Thomas asked.

I tensed slightly. It was a sore subject. "We've tried, again and again. Every time, he kills those sent against him or escapes and we don't hear from him for fifty years. But this time, I intend to find him and ensure he doesn't walk away again."

"So you'll help me?" Ivy asked.

I nodded. "We'll find your—" A scream escaped Thomas' lips and he doubled over, clawing at his clothes to remove them before the change ripped them apart. He'd managed to drag off his tunic when he screamed for a second time, this one mixed with the howl of a wolf.

The change lasted a few seconds less than his first time, although it appeared to be no less painful. Ivy was unable to tear her gaze away from what she saw, but there was no fear or horror in her expression.

When Thomas finished, he lay on the soft grass panting heavily, his thick fur matted with sweat. He looked up at Ivy and darted toward the lake, diving in with an enormous splash.

Ivy followed him and stood by the water's edge, utterly unafraid of what Thomas could do to her.

My hand slid toward my sword and I pushed myself to my feet.

"Wait," Ivy said to me.

Thomas had exited the cold water a few yards from Ivy and shaken himself dry, sitting hunched on all fours. She took a step toward him and I instinctively followed suit, but Thomas didn't move. He showed no signs of aggression or unhappiness at having Ivy near him. I expected him to be more feral than he was. It was still early in his life as a werewolf, and his control over the wolf portion of him should still be weak.

Ivy took a couple more steps and raised one hand toward Thomas' face. He lowered his muzzle to the ground, sniffing loudly as the young girl continued unabated. When she was in touching distance, Thomas moved forward and pushed her away with his gigantic front paw. There was no anger or threat in the gesture. He merely didn't want her too close.

Ivy ignored the push and placed her hands on Thomas' head, one on either side of his face. He shook his head slightly, but she held on and said something I couldn't hear. Then she started shaking, her entire body convulsing as she released Thomas and fell to the ground.

Thomas' wolf eyes looked at me with easy-to-read concern, and I sprinted the distance between us and scooped Ivy up from the ground. "She's having a vision," I told Thomas, who had started pacing back and forth. I hoped my words would calm him, but he looked up at the moon and howled.

"It's not your fault," I shouted at Thomas. He ignored me, only calming when he saw Ivy's body relax. She grabbed my forearms, holding on for all she was worth. I tried to push her away, but it was too late and she started to convulse once more, this time even more violently.

"Shit," I said as she let go of me and crashed back to the ground, her dress riding up her legs to reveal a dark swirling mark on one thigh, about the size of her fist.

Almost as fast as the convulsions started, they stopped and Ivy opened her eyes. "A thousand years of your life in an instant," she said. "I had no idea you were that old."

"Don't move. I'll get you some water."

Ivy shook her head. "I know what you are. You're the thing the monsters fear...." She coughed. I tried to get her some water for a second time, but she grabbed my arm and pulled herself toward me. When she spoke her voice was barely a whisper, but she might as well have shouted from the top of a mountain, "Merlin's Assassin."

CHAPTER 20

London, England. Now.

I wanted to submit my application for being shot in the shoulder as the most gut wrenchingly painful experience someone could have.

The pain takes your breath away. The red-hot, burning evilness running through your body, stopping any thought that doesn't involve the fact that you've been shot. And I had the joy of broken ribs and a general shit-kicking to add on top. It hadn't been a good day.

I vaguely remembered Jerry carrying me down into Francis' place of business. And then nothing until I heard Francis' voice above me, "Are you awake, Nathanial?"

I didn't even have the strength to tell him to fuck off for getting my name wrong. "My body hurts," I managed, as I opened one eye and tried to look around me. I was on a comfortable bed with metal bars on either side of me. It had probably once belonged to a hospital. The pillow covers were cold against my neck, and I found myself wanting to go back to sleep.

I forced my eyes to stay open and took in the rest of the room. The walls were familiar brick from the rest of the abandoned tube station, and like those, at one time it had been white. Some time ago it had been transformed into a strange mixture of old white paint and red brick dust.

My head felt like it was stuffed with cotton balls. "What's wrong with me?"

"Apart from the gunshot?" Francis asked, placing something on a tray next to me with a clank that made me wince. "We had to give you something for the damage you sustained."

"What did you give me, Francis?" I asked concerned. I sat up and leaned back against the headboard. I felt woozy, like everything would start spinning the moment I tried to stand. I'd never been in the room I found myself in. A long wooden shelving unit sat along one side of me. It held boxes of what looked like surgical equipment. Each box had a large label on the front; some said needles while others contained gloves

An expensive looking freezer was on the opposite side, like the type they use in hospitals to keep vials of medicine. Another metal tray sat on a table next to me with two vials on it; both labels were pointed away from me, but I could see that they were empty with two hypodermic needles beside them. Bloodied gloves and some gauze were next to the needles. I absentmind-edly touched my bare chest and found the lack of a hole there to be worrying.

"Why has the bullet hole closed?" I asked.

"Are you complaining?" Francis commented. "You should be grateful." He watched my expression for a few moments and sighed. "Firstly, you need to understand. You had several broken ribs, a punctured lung, and bullet hole just below your clavicle, the latter of which resulted in some silver poisoning but managed to miss anything important. Your magic would have sorted them all out within the next few days, but I assumed you wouldn't want to rest for the time that would take. So, I hastened things along a little."

"What did you do, Francis?"

Francis' mute bodyguard entered the room and sat next to the arch. Francis turned to look at him. "You're avoiding the question," I said with an edge to my voice.

"As I said earlier," he started. "You were seriously injured. The biggest problem wasn't any of the injuries I listed, but this." He removed some gauze from my stomach, showing me three small claw marks, oozing a clear liquid. "The gargoyle must have hit you."

"Bastard was faster than I thought," I said with a forced smile.

"That *bastard*, as you so eloquently phrased it, nearly killed you. Gargoyle-s are pretty much immune to all but the most powerful magic, certainly enough to have killed that girl he was holding. On top of that, their claws and teeth excrete a highly efficient toxin. They use it to incapacitate victims so they don't fight back while they're being eaten, like a snake or a spider. To combat this, I had to inject you with antivenom." Francis tossed me a small empty vial, the word *gargoyle* inscribed on the front in bold letters. "A few years back I acquired the venom gland of a gargoyle. I've had people synthesizing an antitoxin since then."

I should have been going nuts, at the very least I should have been questioning what was happening, but it just felt...right. As if I should already know this information anyway.

"That vial you're holding is worth ten thousand pounds."

I looked down at the small glass object, which I'd started to crush without thinking, in my hand. "Are you serious?"

"Don't worry," Francis said with a wave of his hand. "We'll work out some sort of repayment scheme."

"Repay…" I began, but stopped.

"Of course repay. How do you think my mute friend came into my service? A gargoyle ripped off his tongue, and I saved his life. He's indebted to me, although he does seem to enjoy his work."

"Is that how you know so much about them?"

Francis nodded. "I've never come across one myself. Something I'm very much grateful for."

The bodyguard smiled, thankfully without opening his lips to show the remains of his tongue.

I told Francis about what Jenny had informed me.

"So, whoever's behind this is trying to make their own army. That's not good news. Neither is going up against Avalon."

"Can we just go to Avalon and tell them what's happening?"

"We have no proof. And what if they're involved? Avalon isn't exactly whiter than white about everything. They could just kill us all and decide it's better left forgotten about."

"Well, that's just great. I guess I'm on my own then. So, what's numbing the pain, and why did I heal so fast? I assume that's not the antivenom at work."

"This is the part you will be unhappy about. I had to inject you with something else. Something to heal you quickly. I have a number of things that would work, but under the circumstances…"

"Francis."

"Vampire blood," Francis said. "My own to be exact."

Words actually failed me. I felt as dumb as my tongue-less friend in the corner. "You injected me with vampire blood?" My words were said slowly, ensuring I didn't get one wrong or accidentally call Francis a fucking asshat. "You're a vampire?"

Francis' expression managed to convey how stupid he thought that question was. "I live underground, and you've never seen me outside. I'm pale in complexion and obviously hundreds of years old. What did you think I was? Agoraphobic?"

I shrugged. "It just never occurred to me, that's all. Although, with all the crazy shit I've seen in the last few days, I probably should have figured it out for myself. Would have been nice for you to have shared what you are—you know what I am."

"How would you have knowing I'm a vampire have helped you in any way?"

I shrugged again and swung my legs off the bed, grateful that Francis had left my jeans on along with my shoes and socks so that I didn't feel the coldness of the tiles as my feet touched them. I winced slightly at the movement, but felt happy that I wasn't utterly numb. "That's why I don't feel anything but a little dizziness," I said. "Because your blood is acting like an anesthetic."

"Vampire blood, from someone of my power, has incredible healing qualities."

"Your power?"

"I'm several hundred years old and have sired a dozen vampires, although I'm no where near master status. They mostly live in the tunnels around us. I assumed you would be angry with me, so I wanted to do it before you woke up."

"What other great effects might this have?"

"Well, it could lessen your inhibitions, or cause hallucinations. But any of that will only be for the next few hours. Which is why you've got to stay here."

"Hallucinations? You've injected me with nonhuman PC-fucking-P," my voice rose about a hundred decibels at the last word.

Anger flashed on Francis' otherwise calm face. "I saved your life, *Nathanial*. The side effects are temporary and a tiny concern compared with the fact that you're capable of breathing. That is something you should be grateful for."

I sighed. Francis was right, I should be grateful I wasn't dead. A few hours of trippy weirdness wasn't a lot to bear, considering the alternative. "Can I get something to wear?" I asked and sat back on the bed.

Francis' bodyguard left the room and returned a moment later with a stunning brunette woman who wouldn't have looked out of place on a catwalk. She wore dark jeans and a red t-shirt that had a picture of a comic book character that I vaguely recognized as Blade. The phrase "real vampires kick ass" was written underneath it. She passed me a plain black t-shirt. "My name's Laurel; I'll be watching over you tonight," she said. "Apparently you shouldn't be left alone." Her voice made a shiver go up my spine, something I really didn't need with a body full of something designed to lessen my inhibitions.

"Tomorrow we'll discuss how you managed to get in the state you were in," Francis said. "It's eleven p.m., you've been unconscious all day, and I need to feed. I will see you in the morning." He turned to Laurel. "If he gives you any shit, knock him out."

She nodded and then smiled at me.

We'd been at the cabin for hours on end, talking about our future in between bouts of love making. We'd explored each other's bodies several times over, learning every inch by taste and touch alone.

When we were finally spent, we lay naked in each other's arms. I caressed her pale shoulder. Her long auburn hair cascaded across my chest.

"This is going to be it, isn't it?" she asked, never looking up at me. "Tomorrow there will be war. I am your friend's enemy, and you shouldn't be here."

I pushed the thought aside, but the shadow of it lingered, reminding me what I would lose if my love for the woman were to be publicly acknowledged. "Yet I am anyway. He is my friend...my king, but he doesn't control my feelings." I sat up in bed, pushing the thick covers away.

"You do terrible things for him, for Merlin too. I've heard what they call you. The rumors cast a darkness over you."

I sighed. I'd heard the rumors, too. And they didn't go anywhere near far enough to describe the things I'd done in the name of Avalon. "Horrible things need to be done to maintain a peace in this kingdom. Arthur is a good man...a great man. But he's not capable of such things. He would find the very idea of murders and assassinations to be abhorrent. I do whatever is needed."

"Would you kill me? If Merlin ordered you to?"

"Merlin is—was—your teacher. He has a great affection for you and would never ask me to do such a thing. And if he did..." I let my answer trail off, afraid of what that thought would lead to. "Let's not discuss such matters." I crawled across the bed and took Morgan in my arms once more, kissing her hard on the mouth. She reciprocated and began to trace her tongue down my neck and chest.

"You're going to tire me out," Morgan said slyly as she began kissing my stomach.

"Then I'll know I've done my job right," I said and laughed, stopping immediately as she took me in her mouth. The next few minutes were

awash with joy and ecstasy as Morgan did things with her tongue that no woman had ever done to me before. Morgan stopped abruptly just before the point of no return, moving back up toward me. "That's cruel, leaving me like that." My voice was ragged and full of need.

She kissed me hard and the door exploded open. I immediately raised a shield of dense air alongside us, deflecting the tiny shards of wood as we rolled off the bed and onto the floor.

I stood ready to kill the intruder, daggers of pure white air formed in my hands. Morgan was no slouch with magic, either. Her body became covered in thick rock, both protecting her and giving her a dangerous weapon.

"Who dares..." I began.

"I dare," replied a familiar voice, and a man stepped inside the room, the darkness from the forest beyond no longer casting thick shadows over his handsome face, and huge frame. Torches flared to life inside the cabin, orange glyphs blazing along his hands and forearms.

"Arthur," I whispered. The stone armor encasing Morgan vanished, along with my own daggers.

He took another step inside. "Get some goddamn clothes on."

My eyes shot open and I bolted upright, taking in huge breaths as I fought to calm myself. Laurel was at my side in an instant, her hand on my chest, lowering me back to the bed. "Are you okay?" she asked.

I nodded. "I...I'm not sure. I don't know what I just saw, but it was so real."

She smiled slightly as if recalling an old memory. "Probably a hallucination; they can be real mindfucks sometimes."

I stared at Laurel's hair. It was almost the exact same shade as the woman in my dream. Maybe it was exactly what Laurel said it was, but something inside me remained unconvinced. "Probably. How long was I out?"

"About three hours. I managed to finish my book." She pointed over to a comfortable leather armchair and a table, neither of which had been here when I'd fallen asleep.

"Any good?" I asked. "And any chance of some food?"

"It was about vampires, and they got most of it wrong. But it was enjoyable. The vampire died though, which wasn't the best ending ever." She walked over to her chair and removed a blue cooler from behind it, placing it next to me on the bed.

I opened it to find sandwiches, crisps, and an assortment of chocolates and soft drinks. I grabbed a large BLT roll and set about filling my stomach, which growled in response. "So you're a vampire, I take it."

Laurel nodded.

I opened a can of Coke with a loud hiss and savored the cold as I took a long drink. "Shouldn't you be feeding too?"

"Already did; that's why I was late in coming. I didn't fancy rat hunting first thing in the morning, because I couldn't eat during the night."

"So do you all use humans?"

"Some of us do. But Francis owns several clubs that cater to our needs, as well as a few slaughterhouses. As nice as human blood is, it's good to have a change once in a while."

I raised an eyebrow and started in on a second sandwich and a chocolate bar. "Really? I thought human blood was the best you could get."

Laurel smiled, showing a tiny amount of fang. "You like steak, yes? Would you like steak every day for the rest of your life? Of course not, that would be stupid and you'd soon get bored. So we mix up the human with cow, chicken, or any other animal we feel like. A few years ago one of us started biting the animals at London Zoo; apparently lion blood is delicious."

For some reason I couldn't help but find that ridiculous and laughed. It was the kind of laugh that makes your ribs ache, which, as I'd had mine broken not long ago, made me wheeze and cough in pain. "Don't do that," I said with a smile.

"You're an odd man for a sorcerer," Laurel said, removing the cooler so I could lie back down.

"Why do you say that?"

"Most of your kind are suspicious of vampires. They think we're only one step away from one of your fabled crimes against magic. You don't appear to have that problem."

"Maybe the old me did, I just don't remember. You know, I hadn't even thought about my past in a long time, until all of this kicked off. I knew I wasn't the only sorcerer—Francis told me as much years ago—but gargoyles and vampires and who knows what else? It's a lot to take in, but not a single bit of it is causing me to freak out. That's probably a good thing, right?"

She shook her head. "Maybe, but ever since I was turned against my will fifteen years ago, you're the first sorcerer I've met who has looked at me with honesty in his eyes. Not fear, suspicion, or the need to use me for his own agenda."

"Who turned you?"

"A bitch. Francis saved me from her, and he has looked after me ever since. He likes you, and that's rare."

"He charged me money for saving my life," I pointed out.

"But he saved your life. With his own blood. Anyone else he would have just had Jerry toss the body into the Thames."

What a pleasant thought.

CHAPTER 21

"**N**athanial, we need to have a conversation."

I didn't bother to open my eyes. "What time is it, Francis?"

He paused briefly, probably looking at his pocket watch. "A little after seven."

"Wake me up at ten," I said and smiled as Francis exhaled in annoyance.

"Nathanial..." he started.

I opened my eyes and sat up, immediately wincing with the sudden movement. "Nathan or Nate. For crying out loud, Francis, it's not that bloody hard. How would you like it if I called you Frank?"

Francis' eyes narrowed. "That would be...*unwise.*"

"Then don't piss me off." I swung my legs off the bed and stood, causing more muscles to protest. I felt like I'd been hit with a car, and then backed over to make sure I got the point.

"Feeling sore?" Francis asked and motioned for me to remove my t-shirt. He examined the bullet hole and ribs, ignoring the six dark swirling marks on my chest and ribs. "They're healed, almost to the point you'd never know you were shot. The deep gash above your eye has vanished. The ache you're feeling is the gargoyle venom and remains of the silver poisoning. They're leaving your system, but you'll feel stiff and achy for a few days."

Apparently the vampire blood wasn't a total miracle worker. Still, I couldn't help but be impressed. "You should bottle your blood and sell it; you'd make millions."

"And kill millions more," he said without missing a beat as he removed the gauze from my stomach. "Drinking any more than a miniscule amount of vampire blood by someone who is not gravely injured will kill them. Painfully and slowly—and that's if the madness doesn't drive them to suicide first. Your magic stops most of the blood's adverse effects. It's lucky you were as hurt as you managed to get yourself, otherwise you'd still be nursing a bullet wound. Besides, it's a one-shot deal to humans; they can take it once and if it saves their life that's it. No second try."

"Why?"

"Anymore than one dose in a human will heal the wounds, but drive them insane." He started washing his hands in the nearby sink. "Basically, all the bad shit that could happen to a person who takes it *will* definitely happen if it's your second time."

"How do you know all this doctor stuff?"

"Laurel taught me." He motioned for me to replace my t-shirt. "She used to be a nurse and likes to keep up to date with modern medicine. She's probably better than most doctors."

"Where is Laurel? I wanted to thank her."

"Gone to sleep for the day—she had a long night." Francis walked over to a blue teapot placed on the table next to the arm-chair and poured two cups of white tea. He stirred some honey into both and passed one to me. I took the hot china teacup in hand and hoped my days of passing out were firmly behind me. I didn't need the cost of a tea set added to my bill. Knowing Francis, it was probably worth thousands and had belonged to Queen Victoria.

I took in the aroma of the white tea and honey before taking a sip. "What do you want to talk about?"

"Why you got shot, and generally how much shit you've brought down on me by coming here."

I took another drink of my tea and started to tell Francis about the past few days, the job at Mars Warfare, the murder of Daniel, and rescuing Dani. It took a while, but Francis never interrupted, not even a cough. He got up once to refill his cup, but that was the extent of his reaction to what he was being told.

When I got to the meeting with Jenny and my slight brain spasm, he leaned closer, as if that was the really interesting part, and then moved back when I recounted my escape.

"So you and this Jenny girl are lovers, I assume," Francis said. As an opening gambit, it had style.

I had to smile at his lack of tact. "Yes, we did the dance of forbidden love. Why?"

"Did you have any visions or, as you put it, brain spasms, as you were mating?"

I shook my head and tried not to think about Francis' use of the word *mating*. "Only the one at the pub, although I had a strange dream last night. You think Jenny's a psychic?"

"There are several types of psychics. Some have convulsions when they see a vision. Some enter a trance-like state. Some even cause both themselves and the person they're viewing to go into that trance-like state. The one common denominator is that they need body contact; the more powerful the psychic, the less contact they need. Did she have contact with you?"

I raised an eyebrow.

"Other than the sex," Francis said impatiently.

"She touched my hand with her finger."

Francis chuckled at whatever it was he found amusing—I wasn't about to ask what it was. I was already sure I didn't care. "Psychics live a shortened life, even shorter than a human *normally* does. I've known many, and only a few live into their fifties, let alone beyond. And even those have to be the most powerful. I once met a psychic who could cause visions just by caressing your skin. She was sixty-three years old. How old is this Jenny girl?"

"Mid-twenties."

"In that case, unless she is the single most powerful psychic in a millennium, I would say it's a coincidence. Maybe she slipped you something in your drink."

"I got the drinks."

"The photos could have jarred something loose. But no matter, I'm more interested in this Blood magic talk. When we spoke about possible causes for your memory loss I hadn't considered it. Mostly because I know little to nothing about it. Sorcerers keep the secrets of Blood magic close to their hearts."

"What do those marks on my chest mean? Could they be part of the spell on me?"

Francis looked confused for a brief moment. "What marks?"

I lifted my t-shirt again and the six marks came into view once more. "These, what else am I talking about? You just examined me and they were there; you going blind in your old age?"

Francis walked over and lowered my hands gently. "Nathan, I don't see any marks."

The news hit me like a freight train. I blinked in shock, my mouth refusing to work. When I could finally speak again, I said, "I have six dark marks on me. They're always changing, each about the size of my fist. How can you have never seen them?"

CRIMES AGAINST MAGIC **199**

"Has anyone, in the ten years you remember, ever asked you about them? Even once?"

"They're not always there," I said weakly. "They only come when I'm using magic, or if I think about them."

"No one has, have they?"

I shook my head. "What are they?"

"I don't know, Nathan. But I'll find out for you."

I laughed. "And how much will *this* favor cost me?"

"We'll make a deal. You don't pay a penny, not for my help or for the vial of blood. But in exchange you'll do certain jobs for me at a much-reduced cost. You do that, and I'll help you with this in any way I can."

"And why would you do that?"

"If I involve myself in whatever crap you're in, that will use my time and resources. Favors might need to be called, and as information is power in my business, that could cost me in the long run. So instead of making you pay a cost, you'll help me in return.

"And to answer your question, I'm going to help you because, despite myself, I like you and you need my help. But nothing's for free in this world, Nathan. This is about as good a deal as you'll ever get from me."

Having Francis' full help would certainly make my life easier. But the idea of working for him on a more official basis concerned me. In the long run, it wasn't like I had a whole lot of options. The mystery woman on the phone wasn't exactly in any hurry to tell me what was going on, and with no memory of whom any of the people trying to kill me were, I couldn't go straight to the source and end it all.

In the end I had one choice. "Three," I said to Francis' obvious confusion. "I'll do three jobs, no pay, in exchange for your help and support. And I pick them. I'm not going to spend six months trying to infiltrate the mafia so I can steal a fifteenth-century oil lamp."

Francis' smile reminded me of an Orca that's just found its next meal. "Deal. As of right now, I work for you. What do you need?"

Well, that stopped me in my tracks. What did I need? A missile launcher? Some sort of guide on how to kill a gargoyle? "Information," I said after a minute's silence. "I stole the *Iliad* for you. I want to see the people who wanted it."

"Out of the question."

"Francis, since I stole that book I've met a psychotic murderer called Achilles and been told that this whole mess started with King Priam. I've been shot at, thrown out of a window, injected with venom, and had everything I've worked the past ten years for blow up in my face. It's not that far fetched to add being lied to on that list, and I don't think that job was a coincidence. The *Iliad* was written about the Trojan War, so either whoever hired you to get me to steal the book either knows what's going on, or that is one of the largest coincidences of all time. Either way, I need to see them. Preferably before the well-funded bastards who set me up get their wish."

Francis removed a pad of paper and a pen from his pocket and began to jot things down. "If I do this, you can never mention it to anyone. I can't have people know that I betrayed my clients."

"My lips are sealed."

He looked to be fighting something internally before finally nodding. "I'll see what I can do."

"One last thing. Blood magic. I need to know how to get rid of whatever crap someone cast on me."

"Not even I have pockets that deep. I checked for you once before, when you first came to me. I figured knowing what it was could aid me in the future. The only way someone will tell you is if you find a sorcerer. And I don't happen to know any who I trust enough to not go running off to whoever pays the highest and tell them I asked about it," he said.

"Thanks for checking anyway," I said, slightly surprised that he'd bothered.

"Like I said, I thought the information would come in handy. Come with me." He led the way as we left the room and walked down a dark corridor, the tiny amount of lighting coming from fading bulbs in the ceiling. Eventually, we came to his main office. The mute bodyguard was once again in his seat by the front entrance. He nodded a greeting at me as I entered.

Francis ducked behind the counter and there was the click of a safe being opened. I didn't know why he would need a safe. The fact that somewhere in the darkness of the tunnels there was a pack of vampires was a pretty good security system.

He stood and placed a small red bag on the table. I picked it up and Francis vanished into the back of his office, returning a moment later with a sword cane, placing it on the counter. It was black with red slashes that gave the appearance of claw marks. The bottom half of the cane was covered in a single piece of steel. The handle was made of ivory, a deep-red dragon set on the tip. I opened the bag and removed the contents—a black Heckler and Koch USP.

"I never noticed before," Francis said. "But don't you find it odd that someone gave you the exact same type of gun you were using the night someone fucked with your head?" He opened a green box behind him and retrieved my wallet, mobile, and the gun I'd been given a few days previously.

I picked up both guns; they looked identical. "She was there," I said, mostly to myself. "She had to have been if she knew the type of gun I used."

"So maybe she's not telling you everything you need to know." He thumbed the catch on the sword cane and removed the rapier-like blade from its home, passing it to me.

It felt a lot heavier than I'd have expected it to be. Francis had told me long ago that the blade had a high silver content. Despite the fact that it was one of the few things I had with me when I woke up a decade ago, I always felt strange holding it. "That dragon still reminds me of King Arthur," I said.

"No one in King Arthur's court has ever carried such a weapon. And I doubt they'd want to. Rapiers are a stabbing sword. You could do some damage with it, but it's not a good weapon to fight with in the long term."

I replaced the sword in its scabbard. "Could be ceremonial."

"Maybe, but everything I know about it says that Arthur didn't use ceremonial swords such as these. He would have used *proper* swords."

"I'd better go see Holly and Dani, make sure they're okay and try to figure out our next move." I put on the holster and the newest USP, replacing my wallet and phone in my jean pockets.

Francis passed me an old army coat to wear and cover the gun. It was made of wool and weighed a ton, but it was better than being arrested. "There's a cab upstairs for you. Jerry called it." Francis turned to place the sword back where he'd retrieved it and a shout broke through the subway.

I darted out onto the platform in time to see Dani, wearing a set of red pajamas and some white trainers, fly down the stairs, Jerry right behind her. She crashed into me, knocking me back, as giant sobs escaped her. "What happened?" I asked Jerry.

He shrugged. "No idea. She said she needed to see you. She was in this state. I figured as she was human, and carried no weapons, that she was of little threat."

"They came," Dani whispered. "Holly told me to come here."

"I don't understand. Who came?" I asked as a cold feeling settled inside me.

"The man who killed my mum. Holly got me out of the building, but he took her. Holly told me to run to this address and ask for Francis."

The cold feeling began to change into the warmth of anger. "You'll stay here," I said to Dani and turned to Francis "Keep her safe."

"Where are you going?" Dani asked, fear easy to hear.

"I'm going to go teach this asshole the error of going after the people I care about."

CHAPTER 22

I'd made it as far as the top of the subway staircase when my mobile rang. I'd retrieved it from Dani, just in case I needed it. The number on the screen showed as unknown. For a moment I thought about not answering. But something inside me said it was important, so I slid my finger across the phone's touchscreen, answering the call.

"Nathan Garrett, I assume," a man's voice said.

I stopped dead on the staircase. The hairs on the back of my neck stood on end. "And you would be?"

"You don't recognize my voice? That leaves me sad. It's Achilles. You sound a lot healthier than I'd expected. Remember me kicking the shit out of you now?"

"I was about to come find you." Anger resonated in my voice. "I think we need to have a chat."

"Oh, indeed we do. I have a lovely friend of yours. Say hi, my dear."

"Fuck you," Holly snapped followed by the sound of flesh meeting flesh in violent impact.

"She's got quite the mouth on her," Achilles said.

"If you hurt her—"

"You'll do nothing. You're not even aware of who you used to be, are you? The old you, I may have been concerned about. But you? You're not going to do a damn thing to stop me."

I had never wanted to kill someone more than at that moment. "What do you want?"

"I'm going to be taking your friend to a nice, secluded place. I'll text you a London address in one hour. Be there ninety minutes later. If you're late, she dies. Are we clear?"

I closed my eyes and took a deep breath. "Yeah, we're clear."

"If you fuck with me, she dies. You come alone, with no tricks or weapons. Your friend is a beautiful woman, but if you screw with me on this, I will replace that beauty with something ugly and horrific. And I will film myself doing it and send you a copy. And after all that, I will still track you and the little bitch down and take you both in." And then the call ended.

Rage poured out of me and I spun on the steps, punching the wall next to me with raw power. Dense air had enveloped my hand, stopping me from breaking any bones but producing a deafening sound as the wall broke apart. Pieces of tile and brick flew into the air all around me. I allowed the glyphs, which had blared to life only a moment before the punch had struck home, to dissipate as I tried to calm down.

Jerry ran to the foot of the stairwell and stared up at me as I slowly made my way toward him. He was soon joined by Dani and Francis. "They have Holly," I whispered. "And there's fuck all I can do about it."

Twenty minutes later, a message tone sounded from my mobile. I took the phone from my pocket and opened the text message. All it gave was an address and a warning—*Alone. Ninety minutes.*

"You know the place?" Francis asked.

I nodded, dumbstruck and fearful of where I knew Achilles had taken Holly. "It's an industrial estate consisting of half a dozen warehouses on the waterfront. It's a half hour from here."

"So why are you worried?" Francis asked.

"One of the warehouses is used by Holly's parents to front an underground fighting operation."

"Why would he take Holly to her parents?" Dani asked as she returned to the room.

"Two reasons. Either to get more hostages, or more worryingly, because someone there is allowing him to use the place as he sees fit." Neither of those options appealed to me. "I need to know everything that happened tonight," I said to Dani, who had been quiet since arriving

"We were watching TV," she said, her voice almost detached. "There was a knock at the door, and Holly asked who it was, but there was no answer. She told me if anything happened that I should come here." Dani paused, allowing a sob to escape her lips. "The door...it just...vanished. And this...this *thing* flew into the room.

"Holly screamed at me to go into the bedroom. I glanced back to see...it had Holly by the throat." Tears began to fall down her cheeks again in slow, steady lines. "I just ran. I didn't know what else to do."

"If you'd stayed, they would have taken you too," I said. "You did the right thing."

I watched Dani with new eyes. She looked much more grown up, even if she was wearing a blue Cookie Monster t-shirt and a pair of jeans, a gift from Francis, she still carried herself differently. She was afraid, terrified really, but refused to let that rule her. If she had, she'd still be hiding in Holly's flat. Instead, she ran a few miles, through nighttime London, to get to me. That took some guts.

"This is going to get worse, isn't it?" Francis said.

I nodded. "I'm going alone and find out what he wants."

"That's not the best idea, Nate," Francis said. "He doesn't sound all that sane in the first place."

"If I don't go, people will die—Holly, her family, anyone unlucky enough to be working there. Until I know what's going on, Achilles has me by the balls."

"You'll be okay," Dani said. "I know you'll get through this."

"You have a lot more faith than me," I said.

"You'll be fine," she said again and kissed me on the cheek lightly.

My smile vanished as Dani fell toward me, shaking uncontrollably, her eyes rolled back in her head. "Help!"

Francis didn't wait a heartbeat; he moved toward us so fast that it was almost a blur. "Don't hold her," he said. "Let the fit happen—if you hold her it could seriously hurt her."

I let go of Dani, laying her on an old couch and waited until the shaking died down. Francis left us alone, returning with a fresh glass of water. The previous one had shattered on the floor when Dani had started her fit.

"She'll be fine," Francis said. "She's just having a seizure. If what you told me about her is right, she could be psychic. Either way, touching her will make it worse."

Laurel entered the room and made her way over to a still-unconscious Dani. "She'll be weak and need to be looked after. She's going to have to stay here for a while. I hope you weren't planning on going anywhere with her."

I shook my head. "I want her as far away from everything as possible. She escaped with her life this evening. I won't put her back into a situation where she's in jeopardy again." I looked up at Francis. "If anything happens to me tonight..."

"Nothing will happen to you, my friend," he said with startling assurance. "You're too good to let a thug like this take you down. Discover what he wants and then get out."

"And leave Holly and her family to his devices?"

Dani began to come around before we could finish our conversation. She opened her eyes and sobbed. Not the cry of the confused, but a deep uncontrollable sobbing. She looked between Laurel and me and then dove toward me, pinning herself around my neck. "You were being hurt, Nate," she said between cries. "Strapped to a table, with people all around you."

"It's okay," Laurel said. "Nate's fine."

Dani shook her head. "It didn't feel like a dream. It was so real," she said. "You screamed in pain. You cried and begged someone to stop. Nate, they're going to kill you."

CHAPTER

Dani's description of what she'd seen sat with me long after I'd left her in Francis and Laurel's able care. I couldn't be late to the meeting with Achilles; there's no way he would let that pass without incident. I tried to show everyone that I was fine, that I thought Dani's vision was just the creation of her fears, but I knew that it wasn't. And that scared me.

So, I left with an uneasy feeling in the pit of my stomach. And for the entire cab journey, that feeling spread inside me. By the time I'd reached my destination, I was beginning to wonder if I was actually going to make it out in once piece. I had to figure out an escape plan, one that resulted in innocent people not dying. If it came to it, secrets be damned, I'd use enough magic to take Achilles out. So long as I was capable of using that much. I suddenly regretted not practicing with my magic more.

I left the cab and watched it drive off into the night as rain began to fall in a steady stream. A guard stood at the entrance to the industrial estate, next to a small hut where he could operate the barrier. He wore dark combat fatigues, black boots, and a dark blue camo jacket, under which a holster was visible. He aimed an M4 carbine at me. "I'd walk away," he said.

"I'm here to see Achilles. He's expecting me."

"Hands on the hut." He waved the gun's barrel slightly and I complied, placing my hands on the cold glass. He patted me down without comment, a professional just doing a job.

"Let's go," he said when satisfied I wasn't hiding anything.

I turned to walk off in the direction of the warehouse and spotted someone's legs stretched across the floor inside the hut. The body had been shoved under the desk, but it was done carelessly. The light in the hut fell over the side of his face, showing his neck at an impossible angle. I knew him, or at least I'd met him a few times. I couldn't remember his name, but he was only a kid, nineteen at most. He'd worked at the fights as a favor to his dad, someone Holly's own father was friends with. "You didn't have to kill him," I said.

The guard pointed behind me at a fast-approaching black Saab 9-3 convertible. The Saab belonged to Holly's mum, Lyn. She was not a woman who was easily forced into giving up anything. To get her car, they must have really piled on the pressure.

"You're going with them," the guard said and shoved me forward.

The car pulled up beside me, where one man got out and the driver pointed another M4 at me. Both wore the exact same uniform as the guard at the front gate. "Get in," the passenger said.

"Do you know who killed the kid in the hut?" I asked as the passenger got into the rear of the car and motioned for me to get into the front passenger seat.

Once seated, I was cracked in the skull with the butt of an M4 from the man behind me. "Keep your mouth shut."

I rubbed my head as black spots appeared in my vision, but did as I was told.

We drove around to the rear of the farthest building, following yellow arrows on the ground, and parked up next to a black BMW M3. The rain had eased off, giving everything a fresh feel and smell. I exited the car and looked around at the array of expensive rides all around us. Only the wealthy turn up to Mark's fights; they're the only ones who can afford the bets.

The whole operation was very slick. No one got close without someone noticing. I knew from past experience that when the fights were on, two men would be positioned on the roof with night vision. One extra piece of security. I also knew that when the police did come, everyone would dash off to one of the other warehouses, parking there until the coast was clear. And Holly's dad, Mark, was jeopardizing all of that by giving it to his psychotic younger son. The man had lost his damn mind. But first, everyone had to survive whatever Achilles had planned.

"This way," the man who'd hit me said, shoving me in the back.

The three of us walked to the large double doors, which signified the entrance. I noticed the Nissan GTR I'd been driving, parked farther down the row of cars. I would need to find another ride, as I doubted I'd be getting it back. Two more men in the same uniforms stood outside, both bald and overly muscular, with tattoos on their hands and necks. They could have been interchangeable. One nodded to the man behind me and knocked on the door twice. It opened and we all stepped inside.

The smell was the first thing that hit anyone arriving. It was akin to your nasal passages being assaulted. Blood, sweat, alcohol, and sex all featured in the smorgasbord of scents. There was an underlying smell of lemon bleach too, but it wasn't strong enough to overwhelm the force of everything else in the room.

"The boss is waiting for you upstairs," the man said. "Don't fucking try anything."

I was marched through the ground floor, past the caged fighting area known affectionately as *The Pit*, where fresh blood was easy to spot on the padded canvas floor, and toward a set of double doors. The man escorting me entered a PIN number into the pad before pulling one of the doors open.

"You never told me why you killed that kid," I said.

He ignored me as we walked down a long corridor where signed pictures of various sporting legends adorned the walls.

We continued up two flights of stairs in silence and stopped outside yet another set of double doors. The man knocked twice and pushed one open, shoving me inside. "I brought him for you, sir," he said.

Mark and Lyn O'Hara, Holly's parents, were bound and gagged on the floor of the family's main office. Lee's hands were also bound, but he'd been propped up against the wall. A cut above his eye had dripped blood down one side of his face and onto his blue shirt.

Holly was lying on top of a full-size snooker table, in an identical state as her family. Another man lay underneath it, blood pooled under him, his face a crimson mask. He'd been one of Marks' bodyguards, a highly trained ex-soldier. Half of a snooker cue protruded from his throat.

A noise to my left made me turn away from the carnage. Achilles rose from the comfortable leather sofa.

"I like it here," he said tossing the TV remote onto the sofa. "I like the snooker table, the old arcade games. Look here," he said with enthusiasm as he pointed out an old Gauntlet arcade machine. "And I need to get me one of these." He picked up a second remote and pressed a button. The red curtains along one side of the room opened, showing a window that stretched almost the length of the room. "They can watch the fights without ever getting involved with the little people."

"You didn't want me here so you can show me cool stuff."

"Thank you, soldier, you can leave," Achilles said to the man who'd brought me in.

The soldier nodded and walked around to face me. "I killed that kid because he was a snot-nosed little bitch who dared to challenge me. But most of all, I killed him because I could." A smug satisfaction spread across his face.

"I have one a question for you, before you leave," I said.

He moved slightly to my side so that he could glance back at Achilles, who nodded his permission for him to answer.

"What wears blue and screams like a bitch?" I asked.

The soldier shrugged.

I kicked at the side of his knee, snapping it with a loud crack. The soldier dropped to the floor like a sack of flour, screaming in pain.

Achilles never moved. "Apparently, there's still a little of the old you left," he said with a smile.

The reminder that he knew who I used to be was like a punch to the gut. I couldn't just try to kill Achilles. Not only was I not even sure it was possible, but he had information I needed. "He might need a doctor," I said in what I hoped was a detached tone. I didn't want to give anything away to the monster in front of me.

Achilles picked up a radio and asked for assistance. Two more men, dressed in the same uniform as all the others, dashed into the room moments later. They glared at me as they helped their injured comrade, dragging him gingerly from the room and drawing a look of displeasure from Achilles.

"I do so hate dealing with stupid people. But I can't kill him either. He's a good soldier. Or he was before you broke him." He walked around the couch until he was within striking distance. "You want to kill me, don't you? Give it your best shot. I'm curious to see if you're all that the stories I've heard about you suggest."

I had to will myself not to launch at him. Even if I got past Achilles, there was still Holly and her family to get out safely. I wasn't sure if I'd be able to do that.

"Does it anger you that I know who you are?" he taunted. "That must drive you insane."

"Why did you want me here?" I asked, trying to keep my temper in check. "I assume it's not to show off the people you've killed."

Achilles smiled and glanced at the dead bodyguard. "I left him there as a reminder to everyone what happens when you cross me. I think it's sort of effective." He turned back to Holly, who flinched as he touched her leg. "It helped to eventually subdue this one's personality enough that she's now acceptable to have around."

"Why am I here?" I demanded.

Achilles removed his hand from Holly's leg and stared at me. "You stole something from my lord. And you will retrieve it."

I opened my mouth to speak, but Achilles stopped me. "If you speak before I've finished, I will rip the legs off one of Holly's family members. Clear?"

I nodded.

"Good. A decade ago you murdered Doctor Welkin, and then proceeded to ruin his experiments by helping dozens escape my lord's hospitality. That is neither here nor there. We can find more *patients*. However, you also stole Welkin's research. All of it. We'd like it back."

I stood silent, waiting for Achilles to finish.

"Oh, you can speak now," he said.

"I don't remember any of that. I don't remember stealing it, or killing Welkin."

"Ah, now that's not true. Jenny informs us that because of her, you had a little vision back in that shithole of a pub I found you in."

"I don't know what the vision was," I said. I didn't let on that he'd given me information I was unaware of. "Where's Jenny?"

"You care do you? Did she fuck you?" A measure of anger slipped into his voice as he asked the second question. "Did you see that scar on her leg? That's so she'll remember what happens to those who refuse me. Besides, you have bigger problems than Jenny's whereabouts.

"You have twenty-four hours to bring me Welkin's research and the girl you stole. You will then submit yourself to us, so that we can discover exactly who you told about what you knew. Failure to do those things will result in your friend and her family dying horribly. There's also another thirty people in the fighters' changing rooms downstairs. I've almost got *too many* people to kill."

"I told you, I don't know where I put the research," I said with a sigh. "For all I know I might even have destroyed it."

"Find it," Achilles snapped. "You would have needed it for evidence, so we know it's around somewhere." He looked down at Holly. "Do you know what happens when a gargoyle in rock form fucks a human woman? It's not pretty. Not for the woman anyway. They tend to die of blood loss. And they scream. *A lot.* This is exactly what I'll do to your friend here." He ran his hand over Holly's legs one more time. "Shussh," he said as she screamed against the gag. "I'll be gentle."

"Enough," I said. "I'll find the research. I'll bring it to you."

"And the girl?" he asked.

What was I supposed to do about Dani? I couldn't just hand her over to Achilles and his psychotic employer. And if I did, we'd all be dead within moments anyway. There was no way that Achilles was going to let anyone else live, even if I'd brought him everything he wanted. I needed time to think of a way out of this, to figure out how to get everyone away in one piece. So I did the only thing I could. I nodded.

"Excellent," Achilles said. "You have until midnight to-morrow to bring me what I want." He looked at the clock on the wall beside him. "In fact, that gives you an extra two hours. Plenty of time to get back to whatever hole you crawled out of and try to figure out where you stashed everything."

I glanced over at Holly, who stared back at me with absolute terror in her eyes, and swallowed a lump in my throat. Holly's parents looked defiant and strong, but behind that mask lay more fear. Only Lee wasn't afraid—he looked at me with hatred. Some people can't let go.

"Twenty-six hours," I confirmed. "And if you've hurt them, you get nothing." I waited for Achilles to nod an agreement. "And then I'll end you," I finished, knowing full well that even with my magic I couldn't beat him.

Achilles darted forward with incredible speed and struck me on the cheek. It was enough to send me sprawling to the floor, tasting blood. I looked back up at the gargoyle who smiled with amusement. "You wouldn't stand a chance, little man."

CHAPTER 24

Once Achilles had made his point, I was marched from the industrial estate by gunmen. If any of them made any unpleasant comments, I didn't notice. I was too busy trying to figure out how I was going to unlock memories that had remained buried for a decade. And even if I did manage that, I still had to figure out how I was going to get Holly, her family, Dani, and myself out of this without the loss of life or limb. Unfortunately, nothing came to mind. But I had twenty-six hours, plenty of time to come up with a plan that didn't end with the untimely death of people I cared about.

I walked through London for a few miles, enough to ensure I wasn't being followed by unseen foes working for Achilles and his people. When I was certain I was safe, I flagged down the next taxi that passed me and got the driver to take me back to a location a few streets away from Francis', where I continued the rest of the journey at a brisk jog.

Since it was still the middle of the night, Jerry was no longer needed on guard duty. But that meant the door to Francis' place was locked from within. I pounded on the door for a few minutes, hoping that someone downstairs would have hearing as good as what I'd been led to believe about vampires.

Sure enough, after banging on the door long enough to make my fist ache, it finally opened. Laurel stood in the doorway, hands on perfect hips. "You'll wake the dead," she said with a smile.

"That was terrible," I pointed out as she stepped aside to let me pass.

"I've waited for years to say that to someone," she said walking alongside me when we descended the stairs. "You can't say all that time was wasted."

I forced a smile.

Laurel placed her hand on my shoulder once we'd reached the subway platform. "Is your friend okay?"

I nodded. "For the moment. Although I don't know how long that might last."

"Nate," Francis said. "I assume it didn't go well."

Dani appeared from behind Francis. "Is Holly okay?" she asked, a tremble in her voice.

"She could be worse," I told her, thinking of the dead teenager and Mark O'Hara's bodyguard. "We have a few very large problems, though."

"Such as?" Francis asked.

I told him what Achilles had demanded of me.

"So you either sacrifice Holly and let Dani go, or you give up Dani and you all die. That about right?" Francis asked when I'd finished.

"There's always a third way. We just need to find it."

The four of us walked in silence through to Francis' office, where he brought us all cups of freshly brewed green tea.

"So, what's your plan?" Francis asked, sipping his hot drink.

"I don't know," I said. "I don't remember getting the documents, much less where I actually hid them. And unless you happen to know how to remove whatever magic was cast on me, I don't know how I can bring the memories back."

"I could help," Dani said. She seemed to visibly shrink when everyone else in the room turned to stare at her. "Well, I could," she said defensively. "I may have only found out I was psychic a few hours ago, which is still weird by the way, but Laurel was telling me about how psychics work."

"I doubt you would be able to give Nate full recall. Whatever was done to him was far too powerful for you to turn back, my dear," Francis said. "No offence."

"Okay, so I can't bring Nate's memories back," Dani said with a shrug. "But I want to help."

"Actually, I have an idea," Francis said. "Nate had a vision of his attack on Doctor Welkin. So where did that attack take place?"

"An office somewhere," I said. "I didn't recognize it."

"Maybe Dani can help with that. She could try and pick apart that memory, and from there figure out where it was you last saw Welkin. At least it gives you a starting point."

Francis' plan certainly had merit. If I could figure out what I'd done with Welkin, maybe I could find his research. I didn't want to give it over to Achilles or his employer, but I figured it might jog something loose in my own brain. And, worse-case scenario, it could be used as collateral in some sort of exchange for Holly and everyone in the warehouse. "Works for me," I said.

"Except, I have no idea how to do that," Dani pointed out.

"This is our best shot right now," I said. "But if you agree to do this, it'll be a learning curve for both of us."

"Could I hurt you, or me?" Dani asked.

Francis shook his head. "It's unlikely. You'll have to find the memory and work within it. But so long as Nate thinks about it, it should be quite near the surface. Worst-case scenario—you trap your subconscious inside Nate's brain."

"I'm sorry," Dani said. "I do *what*?"

"I've heard it's happened in the past. Although it's very rare, and more than likely won't happen this time." Francis stood and motioned to Laurel. "We should leave, let them get ready."

"I'll be just outside," Laurel said to Dani before leaving with her boss.

Dani and I sat in silence for a while, neither one of us seemingly sure of how to start. "So, what do I do?" Dani asked eventually.

"I have no idea—you're only the second psychic I've any knowledge of ever meeting."

"Did you know? About me being psychic, I mean?"

"Jenny told me when I met her in the pub. I didn't know before then, and after I got shot. And with Holly being taken, I didn't have time to tell you. I'm sorry about that."

"That's okay," she said. Dani was young and scared, and she had just found out that she was capable of reading people's minds and memories, pasts, and futures. It was a lot to take in. "Did Jenny mention anything else about me?"

"She said your mum was psychic, that's it."

Dani smiled a little, her eyes moist. "My mum." Her voice was croaky, the words hard for her to say. She wiped at her eyes with the back of her hand. "When this is over, when we're all safe, can you find out who my real parents were?"

"I'll try," I told her.

"Thank you," Dani said and placed her hands on either side of my head. "Now, let's get this over with."

I suddenly felt dizzy as the memory of finding Welkin took hold. I ran through what had happened, trying to get as far back to the start of the memory as possible.

Dani's eyes rolled back into her head. Her body twitched slightly, the movements increasing in strength until she flew back from me, her whole body shaking. I sat with her, making sure not to touch any exposed skin; I wasn't sure if that would make things worse.

After a few minutes she opened one eye and stared at me. "I think I got it," she said. "And you're about to get a phone call." Then she passed out. A second later my phone rang.

"I was wondering when you were going to call," I said and sat opposite Dani, watching her as she rested.

"I haven't exactly been able to get away," the mystery woman said. "It's been a bit crazy here since...well, since they brought in Jenny."

I forced myself to remain calm. "How is she? Achilles mentioned that she told them about my vision."

"She would not have done that if given a choice," she said tersely.

"I wasn't being shitty," I pointed out. "Just wanted to know how she was."

"Surviving. At the moment, they need her. But if they find Dani, all bets are off."

"Did you know Dani is psychic?"

There was a brief pause. "I assume you mention that because she's revealed her abilities."

"Answer the fucking question," I said. "Did you know?"

"We weren't certain, although it was highly possible."

"Yeah, well you can be certain now. She had her first vision and it was of someone being tortured to death." I decided to leave out that it was me, and that she'd just delved around inside my head to get information. "A little heads up would have been nice."

"There was no time," she said.

"Make fucking time," I almost shouted into the phone. "You tell me everything I need to know. Right now. No more bullshit, no more clandestine meetings. Achilles has my friend and her family held hostage. I have twenty-four hours to find Doctor Welkin's research or he'll kill them. Research I don't fucking remember in the first place. And he wants me to give over Dani too, so if you can help me not do either of those things, then now is a good time to start." I sagged into the comfy chair. "I need help here, or people are going to die."

"We have a file on you," she said. "It's the one Jenny gave to you. Achilles brought it back with him. Your real name is Nathanial Garrett, so you got that bit right. There's no date of birth, but we know that you worked with Avalon before your memory loss. It's probably how you managed to get a man into my lord's operation so easily. Daniel Hayes."

"What else did that file say?"

"We know very little about what you've done in your life. And I don't mean you've led a quiet life. I mean your entire existence is hidden so well that you're a ghost. That alone means you worked for some powerful people, high enough inside Avalon to ensure everything you did was hidden. It's why Achilles wants to kill you. I think you scare him."

"He has a funny way of showing fear." I absentmindedly touched the side of my face where I'd been hit. "Why not kill Daniel back then? When I broke people out?"

"My lord didn't look into it too closely until Daniel tried to hide his daughter."

"Do you still have her safe?"

"Jenny gave up her whereabouts. It was the only thing she could do to stop them from...They hurt her."

I closed my eyes and sucked down my anger. There would be time for that later. "Achilles thinks that Jenny unlocked memories hidden in my head. He said that she's a psychic, is that true?"

There was a brief pause. "Yes, Jenny is psychic," the mystery woman said. "Although I doubt she's powerful enough to unlock memories hidden by Blood magic."

"She didn't unlock my memory," I said, certain that I was right. "I saw the look of confusion and shock on her face after I came around. There's no way she was expecting to do that. So, she's either incredibly powerful and doesn't know it, or...."

"Or something else happened."

"Exactly. I've no idea what though." Although the vision in the pub was my first memory, the first time I'd felt strange was when I'd fought Holly's brother a few weeks earlier. "Could she trigger memory without knowing it?"

"Jenny's not powerful enough to do that without help. Someone else would have had to plant the suggestion on you."

"And that person would be?"

"Not person, *people*. You took three important women from him ten years ago. They are why you must keep that research and Dani from my lord. If he gets his hands on it, he can start from the beginning—he can make them again."

"What are you talking about? What women? Make who again? If you can help me, please do."

I waited a few seconds and, when no reply came, asked the same thing again. Once more all I got was silence, and then the sounds of someone moving the phone around. "Mr. Garrett, I presume," said a man's voice.

"And you would be?" I asked.

"If you don't remember me, there's no point in reminding you. It seems that you've had some help from within my organization. I assumed we'd caught it all when Jenny was apprehended, to find yet another greatly disappoints me. And if you did remember me, you'd know how much I hate to be disappointed. I believe you now have less than twenty-four hours to get me what Achilles asked. If I were you, I'd hurry before my patience becomes lax." And he hung up.

CHAPTER 25

1414, France.

Ivy fell into a deep sleep after having visions of both Thomas and me in such a short space of time. Thomas lay down next to her, once he'd changed back from werewolf, and was asleep soon after.

I dozed off for an hour or two, but it was fitful. Visions of Mordred, and of all the pain and suffering he'd been responsible for, swirled around my head.

Eventually, sunlight streamed through the treetops, bathing the lake next to us in a brilliant sheen, a sight that was far too tempting not to take full advantage of. By the time Thomas woke up, I was just getting back onto dry land.

"Ivy still asleep?" I asked.

Thomas nodded. "I think we need to talk, don't you?"

I shrugged and allowed the orange glyphs to burn brightly, raising my body temperature and drying me in the process before I put my clothes back on.

"You're not too worried about using your magic now?" Thomas asked.

I tapped the side of my skull. "I don't think I can solve the world's problems with a flick of my hands anymore, so I think it's safe."

Thomas sat on the lake's edge, his back up against a nearby tree. "I can't go home, can I?"

I sat on the ground one tree over. "This is what you wanted to talk to me about?"

"I have a wife and son. His name is Edward. He'll be four now. It's been so long since I've seen him. And I'll never see him again, will I?"

"Before I answer that, let me ask you a question. Last night, when you changed, how did you manage to control the beast so easily?"

Thomas shrugged and threw a stone into the lake, watching the ripples it made across the otherwise still water. "I don't know. It wanted me to rip Ivy apart when she touched me. But I wouldn't let it. I forced myself to control it. "

"About one in fifty can control the beast like you did last night. Even fewer would have stayed as calm. The only werewolves I've ever met who could claim that were alphas. The most powerful of your kind."

"What does that have to do with my family?"

"Even if you weren't an alpha, if you go back home eventually you'll change. You'll have to. It's one of the laws of being a werewolf. Your wife will see you, and if not her then someone else. The alarm will be raised. People will try to kill you."

"What if I stop changing altogether? Force myself to stay human?"

I threw a stone into the lake. "If you somehow manage to force yourself not to change for the first few weeks, maybe even for a month or two, eventually your body will break and with it your mind. It was the most common reason why people like me were called to kill a new werewolf. They go mad and start killing people. Usually beginning with those they love.

"And if someone like me doesn't get to you, the local werewolf pack might. And they have very different ways to punish those who turn themselves into a mindless beast. It usually involves torture and a slow death as a warning to others."

"So I can't see my family, that's what you're telling me?"

"Even if you could go home, and your family could accept you for what you are, others will challenge you for power. Eventually, someone will use your family to get to you. Right now your wife and son think you're dead. If you go home, you'll destroy not only your life, but theirs too. Is that what you want?"

Thomas wiped his eyes, not wanting to show the tears falling from them. I turned away to give him a moment of privacy. "I want them to never need anything," he said. "I need them to be taken care of."

"If we get out of this in one piece, I'll talk to some people. They'll make sure that your family live a comfortable life. You have my word."

We sat in silence as a strong breeze lifted the fallen leaves from the ground and threw them into the air. "Merlin's Assassin," Thomas said after a short time. "Who are you, really?"

"I figured you'd heard," I said. I'd tried to decide how much to say if either Thomas or Ivy brought it up. I'd killed people in the past for knowing who I am, or rather, what I am. But something about Thomas told me that he could do great things, and more important, I liked and trusted him. And that was a rarity in both my business and personal life. "Whatever is said between us goes no further. If you repeat anything of what I am about to say, I will kill you. No questions, no excuses. Clear?"

Thomas kept eye contact for a moment before nodding once.

"I am a thousand years old, give or take. I was found outside Camelot as a child of about eight or nine. Merlin took me in and we discovered that I had an aptitude for magic and fighting, so he taught me magic whilst the many knights in the city taught me the other.

"Being trained to fight in Camelot was where I met Arthur, Gawain, Galahad, and the other knights. Arthur and I soon became friends, more like brothers really. He was destined to be king, to be a great ruler, and the knights who pledged their allegiance to him and Camelot were always similarly great men. They believed in doing what was right, most of the time, and like Arthur, saw things in shades of black and white. I see things in terms of gray.

"Merlin noticed this in me from a young age, during a training session. Arthur and some of the other boys were being schooled on chivalry. The man-at-arms in charge of one lesson told us that we were never to kill an unarmed opponent, that it was tantamount to murder. I suggested that an unarmed opponent was actually the best person to kill, as it was safer than fighting someone armed to the teeth. It didn't go down well." I recalled the day with a smile, the mouth of the man-at-arms dropping open in shock. And Arthur laughed so hard he fell off the bench he sat on, causing everyone else to laugh. I didn't find out until much later that Merlin had been watching and listening to our lessons.

"So Merlin recruited you?" Thomas asked.

I nodded. "He suggested that some people needed to be removed from the world before they could endanger others. And that there would always be some who got away with their crimes simply because they were too powerful. I agreed with him, and he set about training me in other talents. It wasn't about how to fight, but how to kill, incapacitate my opponents, and leave as if I were never there. He took me away to China. He'd visited the country a thousand years before I was even born and learned a lot.

"I was thirteen at the time. It took a year to get there by foot and horse. Merlin stayed for the first year, and I for ten more. By the time I got home I was nearly twenty-four and had killed more men than I had fingers and toes.

"Arthur was king when I returned, yet he greeted me as his equal. He asked me if my training was done and introduced me to his wife, Guinevere. I always regretted not telling him what I was, but he wouldn't have understood."

"So you started killing for Merlin?"

"Some things out there need special *attention*; sending Arthur and his knights to kill every evil bastard would have gotten more innocent people hurt. Removing that evil just became a way of life. And I didn't just kill people. I found information on some, infiltrated their homes and friends, searching for clues about their motives and guilt."

"Does Merlin still tell you where to go?"

"These days I tend to do my own thing. Merlin will give me information or a request every few months, but I'm left to do what I need to."

"How does he contact you?"

"Merlin's one of the top three or four sorcerers on the planet. He can project himself into someone's dreams. At first, it's a bit disorientating."

Thomas stood and stretched, glancing over at a still-sleeping Ivy. "You skipped a lot of your life in that telling."

"Most of it, in fact." Thomas didn't need to know my entire life story. I wasn't sure any one person did.

"Were you honestly at Soissons by accident?" Thomas asked. "It seems very coincidental."

"I think maybe Merlin knew what direction to send me in. He likes to do that—not tell me exactly where to be, just point me roughly in the direction he has in mind and leave me to sort it out."

"I have one more question," he said. "Why is Ivy a problem?"

"From what I know about the Trojan War and its aftermath, Cassandra died at the hands of Agamemnon's wife. And she died childless."

"So how does Ivy exist?"

I glanced over at the girl, still sleeping soundly. "I don't know. But I'm planning on finding out at some point."

He smiled and walked off a few paces before turning around. "Thank you for being honest with me."

I couldn't help but smile as Thomas went to check on Ivy. I got the feeling that smiling would be something I wouldn't do much of before this was over.

I sat around and waited for Ivy to get up and wash in the lake. She was unsteady on her feet to begin with, as if just shaking off the remnants of being drunk on the visions she'd had.

Thomas had found an apple tree not too far away and picked a few of the ripe green fruits, throwing me one as he went to make sure Ivy was alright. I watched him behave like a parent around her, even though he was at most seven or eight years older. The idea of never seeing his family again must have torn him up inside.

I felt guilty for not asking about his family, for only thinking of finding Ivy and stopping those who attacked Soissons. Sometimes I got so used to not answering questions about my life, or forming lies about it, that I forget about asking others.

Ivy and Thomas sat beside one another and spoke for a while. I was too far away to hear normally, although I could have used a gust of wind to bring the words to me. Instead, I dozed on the soft grass. I always tried to get sleep where possible, and being half asleep was better than none at all.

Ivy and Thomas' approaching footsteps woke me. I opened my eyes as the young girl sat beside me and took my hand in hers.

"There was so much pain in your past."

"Keep it there," I said coolly, unwilling to get into a conversation regarding whatever she'd gleamed from her vision.

"She betrayed you," she continued unabated. "The woman you loved betrayed you for her ideals. And Mordred was there."

I sat bolt upright, jerking my hand from Ivy's. "Drop it."

"But I know now why you hate him."

I shook my head. "You have no idea why I hate him. What did you see? Me semi-conscious on the floor, Mordred standing over me? Maybe Morgan was with him…"

"You and the woman, Morgan, were in a room; your friend burst in. Arthur. He demanded an explanation. You fought—you were angry, resentful of how he spoke to the woman. It spilled outside, and he was ambushed. Mordred stabbed him with a sword of some type. When you went to stop him, the woman hit you from behind with powerful magic."

I rubbed my eyes. I really didn't want to relive this. "Why are you telling me this? I was there."

"I wanted you to know that I understand why you hate him. But I hate him too."

I stood with the intent of walking off. I managed a few paces when I turned back to Ivy. "He has that effect on people."

"I was born in a cage, inside what can only be described as a prison, just outside Orleans," she said.

I froze mid-step, my intention of leaving suddenly evaporated.

"It's where I lived until I was twelve. Then Mordred took me to see the King of France, and then onto England. Both times, my job was to do readings of people's future. Of not only the king but of anyone Mordred deemed worthy of trying to impress, or needed to blackmail and threaten. The things some of these *men* did made me sick, but I was to show no feeling. Or I was punished.

"Mordred's method of punishing me depended on how creative he felt. Sometimes he would urinate in my food in front of me and make me eat it. Sometimes he would beat me with a birch switch, or his sword cane. Once he made me walk across broken glass to get to my bed. As I said, he was creative." Ivy's hatred seeped out of her like the beginnings of a burst dam.

"Why the rune-inscribed, silver cage in Soissons?" I asked. "You're not a sorcerer; the runes would have little effect on you."

"He was paranoid that someone would try and take me, so that's where I slept. In an impenetrable prison that would nullify the abilities of anyone who managed to break in."

I leaned against the nearest tree. "That explains why you hate Mordred. But not why he left you alone in that nice room back in the village."

"When we left England, King Henry required an escort for us. Mordred didn't want one, but Henry insisted. It was why the English archers died. It was the only way Mordred's could get out the city without a trace.

"Every morning while we travelled, Mordred had me read for him. He wanted to know what would happen each and every day. Two days after we arrived in that village I told him that if he stayed another night, he would be killed in the morning. So he ordered his men to stay in the village and guard me, and then he left. He was meant to come back in a few days. He told me that he had other things to do."

I couldn't help but smile. "He was scared. He would never have left without a fight if he thought you were wrong."

"But he came back," Ivy pointed out.

"Could he have thought you were lying?" Thomas asked as he rejoined us.

"Psychics can't lie about a vision," I said as Ivy shook her head. "They can't fake one either. Whatever they see, they're compelled to tell the truth. They have no control over it. Mordred knows this."

The question bounced around my head for a short period of time until I came up with an answer that best suited Mordred. "He was worried about leaving you alone for any length of time. What were his plans for you? Do you know?"

"No," she lied.

I turned to Thomas. "Can you give us a moment?"

He stuck an apple in his mouth and took a large bite. "Be over there," he said between chews.

"I like him," Ivy said. "He's a noble man. I've met very few."

"You have five seconds to tell me the truth or I leave you here to sort yourself out."

"We both know that's not going to happen," she replied with a sly smile.

"Fine, you're right, but you're going to tell me anyway."

"Thomas cannot be made aware of what I'm about to tell you. Promise me."

"Tell me what it is and we'll go from there."

"Promise me," she repeated, her eyes cold and hard. She was not going to be dissuaded from her course of action.

"Tell me why first."

"If Thomas finds out, he'll attack Mordred at first chance. We both know how that will end up."

Badly. Thomas would be dead in seconds.

"You've got a deal. What's going on?"

"You were right, Mordred needs me. He's using people, making them into weapons. Training them, selling them to those with the highest bids."

"And you're to be sold?"

"No, I'm his. Or at least I'm to be used only by him. He has two other women, the three of us together are going be something he's worked for a thousand years to put together."

That was nearly as long as I'd known Mordred; he would have been working on it soon after betraying Arthur...after nearly killing me. "What does he want you for?"

"I can't tell you. And no threats will make me. If you know these things...." She wiped away a tear as it ran down her cheek before rolling up her sleeve to show a dark swirling mark on the top of her arm. She grabbed my hands in hers— they shook slightly; she was scared. But something told me that she wasn't just scared for herself. "He cursed me, and I cannot speak of his plans unless he allows. Or until those plans are completed."

"I hate Blood magic shit," I said with a hard-fought smile.

"If it makes you feel better, I feel the same way."

I decided it best to change the subject. "I've seen the other mark on your thigh," I said without breaking eye contact.

"I thought you might have," she said. "I'd hoped to keep it secret. Just like you didn't want to mention the six you have on your chest."

"Who did that to you? Mordred?"

She nodded. "I have two, one on each thigh. Like the one on my shoulder, he wanted to put them somewhere that they wouldn't easily show to others who have been cursed with Blood magic. They stop me from aging."

I couldn't believe what I'd heard. "How did he do that?"

"He used a sacrifice. In fact, about two-dozen people were killed. These marks will ensure that I don't age, although I am just as vulnerable to the elements and other human conditions. I can die."

"So he murdered two dozen people to make sure you don't age?"

"I was seventeen. He sat me in a gigantic bath and poured the blood of twenty-four men and women over me. He forced me to drink some of it. And then he conducted his spell, using their souls, their essence, as a basis for it. It apparently took him years to prepare it all. He was very proud."

"How old are you?"

Ivy glanced over at Thomas, who was busy skimming rocks over the lake. "One hundred and thirty-one."

My mouth dropped open. "And you've been with Mordred all that time?"

Ivy nodded.

"Why did he do it? I mean, why did he want a one-hundred-plus-year-old psychic?"

Ivy didn't reply for a heartbeat. "Why do you not get your blood curse removed?" When she said it, her tone was soft, almost a whisper, as if afraid of the question. Or afraid of my answer.

I thought about lying, saying that I didn't care about the marks, but that would have been doing Ivy a disservice. "Because I know what it takes, the sacrifice that would need to be made. And so long as I have a say in it, I won't have anyone do that for me. Not now, not ever."

Ivy nodded, satisfied with my answer. "It's part of his plan. I'm not the only one he marked in this way. The others, the ones he's going to sell as weapons, are at his castle near Orleans."

Ivy and I sat in silence for some time. My mind raced at the possibilities of why anyone would want to create an ageless psychic.

My thoughts were broken by Thomas, who had decided to rejoin us. "What's the plan?" he asked.

I explained about Orleans, which Thomas absorbed with quiet thought. "Do you have a plan for getting into this fortress?"

"I'm thinking on it. We've got to assume that Mordred is already there," I said. "He'll be fortifying their defenses. You both sure you want to come?"

"I won't let him hurt anyone else," Ivy said with conviction. "And I want to be free of him."

I looked over at Thomas.

"You know I'm coming," he said. "I've got some vengeance of my own that needs to be inflicted on those bastards."

"How long until we reach this...prison?" I asked Ivy.

"By foot? Two, maybe three days."

"Well, we'd better get moving then. You'd both better get some water to drink and something to eat, because we've got a hell of a march ahead of us."

Both Thomas and Ivy brimmed with the expectation of getting revenge on the man who had destroyed their lives. But I knew that Mordred would rather see everyone he held captive die than allow anyone to take him alive. Innocent people were going to die, I was sure of that.

CHAPTER **26**

The large city of Orleans sat on the river Loire and was one of the richest cities in France, with one of the few bridges passing over the river leading right into her heart. The only problem for us was getting past Paris. As Orleans was directly south of our current position, going around Paris would have taken precious time, so we walked through it. A calculated risk, but Thomas played the mute servant well, and Ivy took the role as my niece, whilst I continued to play the part of a man on a pilgrimage. None of us were bothered by the guard or citizens, but we didn't stay, no matter how nice the idea of a fresh bed might have been.

We did, however, buy plenty of food, mostly bread and cheese, enough to last several days.

After Paris, we kept moving for two days and nights, rarely stopping for longer than a few minutes during the day, and finding somewhere safe and off the roads for short periods at night to get some sleep.

At some point our luck at remaining undisturbed was going to run out, and the closer we got to Orleans, the more likely we were to be attacked by Mordred's forces. I wanted to avoid a confrontation for as long as possible.

"We're close now," Ivy said as we passed a derelict old hut, scorch marks evident on the wooden beams used as the frame.

She pointed down a small dirt road. "The prison is down there, about a mile. One of the prisoners, a boy named Simon, managed to escape and get through the woods." She turned to Thomas. "He found this place, and an old man and woman lived here. They gave him shelter. Mordred found them and killed the old couple before dragging Simon back. I can sometimes still hear his screams at night."

She hugged herself tightly, until Thomas placed a strong hand on her shoulder. "He won't hurt anyone again." I had to give Thomas credit; he certainly believed his words—though I doubted it was going to be an easy thing to achieve.

"Get some rest, we leave at nightfall." I turned and walked off toward the prison.

"Where are you going?" Thomas called after me.

"Research." I stepped through the tree line and into the dark forest.

I ran, avoiding any bushes or patches of mud by virtue of using the tiny amount of light on offer. The *guan do* occasionally caught a branch, slicing it in two, the sound of it crashing to the ground echoing behind me, but I had little interest in removing the weapon, or repositioning it. If anyone was out there and came to investigate…well, it wouldn't end happily for them.

After a few minutes, the trees began to thin out, sunlight crept back in through the densely packed leaves above me, and I slowed down. By the time I'd reached the edge of the forest I was walking slowly, careful not to give my position away to anyone watching.

The good news was that the prison wasn't surrounded by a moat. Unfortunately, that was where the good news ended. I sat at the top of a steep hill. The only thing between me and the ten-yard-high stone walls of the outer ring of the prison was a huge expanse of open space.

I could see inside the prison grounds from my vantage point. After the sheer walls, there was a large courtyard, with three buildings feeding off from it. Two of them were quite small. Armed soldiers, none of them with any marking to tell country or allegiance, came and went from one of them, suggesting it was the barracks. It was about the right size to house twenty men. Maybe fewer if they had a lot of equipment.

Smoke rose from the chimney of the second, smaller building. It was probably the kitchen.

The last building was the most interesting. It was also the most imposing, as it resembled an actual castle. At least five floors high, and maybe ten times the size of the other two buildings combined, it would be like a maze in there. And that was if it didn't have any below-ground levels, which didn't seem likely even as I thought it.

The sun decided to expose my hiding spot and I moved farther to one side, partially concealing myself behind a large tree. The outer ring of the prison had a walkway with crossbow-wielding archers moving along it. There were also several armed guards at the front gate.

Across an open stretch of ground, up ten yards of rock wall, past several archers all watching for an attack, across a court-yard, and past the barracks. And after all that we had to gain entry to the main building, find those we were here to rescue, and kill Mordred. Maybe I should have gone back to England first and collected an entire army before attempting to carry out this mission.

I tried to find somewhere that we could get inside without being filled full of arrows before we were even halfway there, but found very few options. Then something occurred to me. If there wasn't an entrance, make your own.

"Tell us this plan again?" Thomas said.

I'd explained it three times, but neither Thomas nor Ivy seemed to like it any more than the first time. "We get in, Ivy shows us where everyone is kept, and we get out."

"It's more the *getting in* portion of the plan I'm not too fond of," Thomas said.

"What about killing Mordred?" Ivy asked.

"You get everyone out. *I'll* find Mordred. You just wait for me to distract the guards, and then you get inside."

Thomas sighed. "If this place is as you described, we've got no chance. Those walls will be thicker than my arm is long."

"It'll be fine." I looked up at the setting sun. "We need to leave soon. Get yourselves ready."

Thomas walked off to the woods so we didn't have to watch him change. "What am I going to use as a weapon?" Ivy asked.

I hadn't thought about that. Thomas was pretty much sorted for killing equipment, as was I, but Ivy's entire offensive abilities came from harsh language and shouting loudly. I drew out a silver dagger, and passed it to her. "Only if necessary. I'd rather you not go all barbarian horde on me and run screaming at a bunch of crossbow-wielding Frenchmen."

Ivy took the dagger and unsheathed it, weighing it thoughtfully in her hand before replacing it. She kept hold of the sheathed dagger and stared at it for a moment longer. "I've never killed before."

"Don't start now then," I said. "Unfortunately, killing gets easier the more you do it, so don't begin that tally unless you have no choice. Otherwise, run like hell and hide."

"I won't fail you, or my sister," Ivy said.

"I know," I said with honesty as Thomas appeared and sat at the edge of the forest. "You ready?"

He nodded once and growled slightly. He still had trouble speaking in werewolf form. It would come with time, but that wasn't soon enough for him. Besides, being able to bite a person's head off was a lot more useful than conversation. He was still sore from the changes every night. He hid it well, but the pain was easy to read on his face when he changed back into human form. I hoped he wasn't pushing himself too hard.

The night had fully taken its place around us, and only a glimmer of moonlight made it through the thick clouds. Although I could see at night with a little help from magic, and Thomas' night vision was as good as a wolf's, Ivy couldn't see more than a foot in front of her. Thomas had offered to carry her, but she refused. If we met with any immediate trouble, Thomas would be unable to involve himself until Ivy was safe. So she opted to walk beside the giant wolf, holding onto his fur. Thomas moved around anything that could cause her to fall or make a lot of noise.

I moved off in front, ensuring there were no ambushes waiting for us when we reached the forest's edge. I crouched close to where I'd been earlier in the day and searched for the guards walking along the high walls. Concern crept through me as I waited for my companions.

"What's wrong?" Ivy asked as she moved next to me.

"Watch the prison. The walls, what do you see?"

She stared straight ahead for several heartbeats. "Nothing."

"That's it, there's nothing there. No one is walking the walls or guarding the entrance." I looked over at Thomas. "Can you smell anyone?"

He raised his head into the air and took several deep breaths before letting out a low growl. "D…eath," he managed in a low rumble.

"What does that mean?" Ivy asked.

I set off in the direction of the front gate, moving quickly. I kept low, just in case my concern proved baseless and I needed to drop to the ground. I made it to the iron portcullis without incident. Two thick ropes held it up—whatever had happened took place with enough speed that the guards hadn't used the fort's defenses. I waved Thomas and Ivy over, knowing that Thomas would be able to see me, before stepping through the entrance and into the courtyard beyond.

The torches attached around the large courtyard were still burning away. The light they created made it easy to see why Thomas had smelt death. I passed three dead bodies before I'd even made it a few steps. "How did they die?" Ivy asked as she entered the courtyard with Thomas.

I knelt by one of the soldiers. He was slumped at the bottom of the stone wall I'd seen archers walking along earlier. His chin touched his chest. I moved his head slightly and saw the jagged circular wound, which had ripped through the center of his throat. He'd died where he fell, his sword still in its scabbard.

Thomas prodded one of the dead bodies with his massive paw. The soldier was missing his arm. It lay a distance from the body, the sword still held in a useless grip. Thomas glanced around and pushed open the door to the closest building, the one I'd assumed was the kitchen. He walked inside, and the smells of fresh cooking carried through the air. He returned a moment later with a shake of his head.

"What could have done this?" Ivy's words dripped with fear.

I opened the barracks door and found eighteen beds, nine along each wall. Five dead bodies occupied the beds closest to the door. Their blood saturated the walls and floor as the smell of death began to overwhelm me.

The men hadn't stood a chance. Most were missing limbs— a few decapitated by their attacker before they'd even had time to react. More bodies were easy to spot at the far end of the room, weapons in hand. I walked through the mass of death and destruction and found that these men had died just as suddenly as their friends. One had tried to hide under the bed; he'd made it part of the way before something sliced him in half, just above his hips, spilling intestine and organs over the already slick floor.

I'd seen some horrific sights in my time, but the level of violence exhibited inside the barracks certainly ranked pretty high. Mordred had outdone himself in terms of brutality. I quickly left the building, ensuring the door was closed behind me.

"Mordred's cleaning up," I told Ivy and Thomas, who were crouched by the entrance to the larger building. "He probably wanted everyone who was aware of what was happening here to vanish. He's planning to move his work."

Ivy's hand shot to her open mouth. "Mordred did this?"

"Thank you for thinking so highly of me," Mordred said.

I spun to find him standing atop the wall above the kitchen area.

"There was no need for this," I said. "You could have just vanished. We'd never have found you. But you stayed to kill, and that will be your mistake."

"I've killed no one," Mordred said with glee. "Didn't want to get my clothes dirty with French blood. It's a bastard to remove."

There was movement from above, and I threw myself side-ways as someone crashed into the ground, throwing up loose dirt. The shockwave knocked me farther than I'd anticipated, causing me to slam into a nearby stone wall. I got back to my feet in front of the kitchen as my would-be assailant slowly stood.

Thick, black, leathery skin stretched over every inch of its human-like body. The muscles in its arms and legs were massive, easily capable of causing devastation with the broadsword it held in one hand. It regarded me with cold, dispassionate eyes the color of ice.

"I believe you've met a nightmare before," Mordred almost sang.

The creature known as a nightmare stepped toward me. Its movement was fluid, quick, and deliberate, the broadsword held loosely by its side, as if it weighed nothing more than a child's toy.

I moved away from the building. My hand gripped the *guan dao* and I removed it from the holster on my back, holding it in a position that was ready to attack. There were maybe ten yards between us, but I knew from experience that the nightmare could close that distance within the blink of an eye.

Mordred raised one hand high into the air and the nightmare stopped moving, his gaze never wavering from me. "You wanted to know what I'm trying to achieve here, Nathanial. Well, here it is." He motioned toward the evil creature. "The ultimate weapon for use against the English, or the French. Or, to be honest, anyone who gets in my way."

"That used to be a person," I said. "He was a sorcerer. You've committed a *crime against magic* in turning him into this."

"Really? And will Avalon send someone to kill me? You're a fool if you believe they didn't know what was happening here."

"Merlin doesn't."

Mordred spat at his feet. "Merlin is too set in his ways to be useful. You'd best remember that." He smiled brightly. "For the next few minutes anyway, then you'll be too dead to bother me any longer. Enjoy yourself, Nathanial. I'll be sure to send pieces of your corpse back to Merlin." Mordred dropped down behind the building, vanishing from view. The nightmare charged, his sword swinging forward with an ease that should have been impossible.

I rolled aside as the blade smashed into the wall, rendering the brick to dust. I came back to my feet a short distance away, ready for the next assault. The nightmare turned toward me, dropped the sword, and darted forward, hands out to strike. Thomas slammed into it, driving it into the nearest wall with an explosion of sound. Thomas' movements were a blur as he tore huge chunks out of the nightmare, goring its face and chest in an attempt to kill it.

"Thomas…" I started to shout, but it was too late. Blasts of magical energy it must have stored from a previous encounter with a sorcerer hit him square in the chest, throwing him back across the courtyard and into the wall beside Ivy.

I didn't dare turn my back on the nightmare, or I'd be dead in seconds.

It moved toward me, its face and chest, which had been a mass of raw flesh only moments previously, already knitting itself back together. It darted to one side, scooped up the broadsword, and swung it at me, all in one smooth motion. I deflected the attack with the *guan dao*, forcing his blade upward. I stepped toward the creature, slashing at its face, but catching nothing but air as it dodged away.

"Thomas will be okay," Ivy called. "He's not going to be any help though."

I didn't bother replying, my concentration was needed elsewhere. The nightmare tried another swing, this one aimed at my hips to try and cleave me in two, but I blocked it with the *guan dao's* blade. The power of the impact took me off my feet and dumped me on the ground a few yards away. The nightmare didn't pause; it came at me with another swing of the broadsword, striking nothing but earth when I rolled aside just in time. The dust and air struck the side of my face, reminding me how close I'd come to losing my head.

I kept rolling and struck at the nightmare's chest with the sharp spike on the end of the *guan dao*, but once again it dodged aside. I needed to get some space between us, to try and figure out how I was going to kill him. Or at least stop him from killing me.

I sprung up and dashed forward, slashing the *guan dao's* blade up at the nightmare's face. He deflected it, leaving him open for the jet of flame I smashed into him, driving him back into the wall of the barracks. Magic might not be able to kill a nightmare, but it was still good to use as a distance maker.

"Get Thomas inside the prison," I called to Ivy. "And don't come out."

The nightmare got back to its feet and lifted the broadsword, pointing the tip of the blade toward me. It looked angry. Or as angry as something can possibly manage with no emotions. Its black lips opened and it spat a lump of dark, thick blood onto the ground.

The nightmare took a step forward, then charged. I dodged a sweep of the blade, but the nightmare blasted me in the chest with the magical energy it had stored from my fire attack. It threw me back against the nearest wall, the impact of which forced the air from my lungs and caused my head to spin.

I fell roughly to the ground and just avoided another powerful swing of the blade, but he caught me with a punch to the jaw that hit with enough force to knock me from my feet. I landed awkwardly in the dirt, losing my grip on my *guan dao*, which clattered beside me, allowing the nightmare to kick it aside as I rolled back to my feet and created a sword of fire in my hand.

"You can't use magic back if I don't throw any at you," I said.

He paused for the briefest of moments before covering the distance between us in a heartbeat. I sliced up with the sword and used my free hand to throw a gale of air into its face, picking up all the dust and muck that littered the ground.

The nightmare tried to guard its face, but some of the matter must have struck him in the eyes, because he shook his head and tried to create some distance between us. With his attention diverted for a split second, I threw a second gale of air into its legs, hardening the air at the last second. It would have been like getting hit by something from a cannon. Its knee snapped with a loud crack. The nightmare opened its mouth and a sound escaped that would have left no one in doubt that there was nothing but a monster left inside the creature. It staggered away and grasped its leg, snapping the knee back into place with another cry of pain.

Then, it turned its attention back to me. I was already on my feet when it charged with a guttural roar. There was no way I could beat a nightmare in a one-on-one fistfight. They can kill werewolves with their bare hands. But I still had options.

I slammed a powerful tornado of air into the monster's legs, tripping it before it got too close. But it didn't work, the nightmare recovered at the last second and barreled into me, lifting me from the ground and running with me into the barracks wall. Wood and stone broke around us. The nightmare refused to let go, crushing my ribs until they popped, before finally throwing me farther into the barracks.

I landed on one of the dead soldiers and skidded off onto the sticky, wet floor, eventually slamming into the adjacent wall. It was difficult to breathe, difficult to think, but I had to get back to my feet or I was dead. The nightmare was beside me in an instant, lifting me from the ground by my tunic and throwing me back across the room and into the remains of the far wall. Any breath I'd caught left me once again, and dark spots began to form on the edges of my vision. The only way to kill a nightmare was with silver, but they're too fast and strong to get close to easily.

As the nightmare stalked closer, I threw myself through the hole in the wall, causing my ribs to protest once more as I hit the ground in a roll. I moved into the middle of the courtyard and removed my *jian* from its scabbard. Every breath was agony, my ribs screaming in pain as I tried to suck in more air and waited for the nightmare to reappear.

The barracks' door exploded outward, pieces of it raining down onto the ground. Another blast of magic from it tore into the building behind me, destroying the entire wall with ease and forcing me to create a shield of dense air to stop the larger of the rocks from doing me damage.

The nightmare stepped through the ruined barracks entrance and moved toward me with silent purpose. It raised its hand and...nothing. It was out of magical energy to throw at me. The creature quickly noticed the sword in my hand, and for the briefest of moments I thought a smile crossed its lips before it attacked.

I threw the sword into the soft ground and flung a vicious gust of wind at the nightmare, tearing up the ground beneath its feet. I hardened the air, making advancing all but impossible for the nightmare, but I couldn't keep up the power use for long.

Molten eyes flared, the only part of the nightmare I could see as the winds increased in power getting closer and closer. When it was exactly the right distance from me, I stopped the gale and threw the *jian* like a javelin into the remnants of the storm. The monster didn't even see the sword coming as it plunged into its chest, driving it back. The nightmare dropped to one knee, its hand gripped around the guard of the sword, desperately trying to pull it out. But the creature's blood was pumping out fast enough that a thick and dark essence covered the sword within seconds, ensuring it was too slippery to gain purchase.

I dashed toward the dying nightmare and pushed the sword in still farther, until the hilt was touching its bare chest. The creature opened its mouth, but only blood escaped. I cast air magic to afford me a better grip on the sword, and twisted. The wound opened further and more blood gushed onto the ground as I dragged the *jian* from the nightmare's kneeling body and kicked the monster over. A soft gurgling noise left its lips.

The door behind me flew open and Ivy rushed toward us, sprinting past me and kneeling by the dying nightmare. "Don't," I said. "It can still kill you."

Ivy ignored me and placed her hands on either side of its head. The nightmare tried to get back up, shuddered, and dropped to the ground as the leathery darkness that covered it began to leave its face.

"What did you do?" I asked Ivy as Thomas padded over toward us, limping slightly on his right front leg.

"I reminded him of his old memories. Of who he used to be."

I stared in shock as the pale face of a young man peered at me through patches of the dark skin. "Thank you," he said and coughed more blood onto the ground.

"Simon," Ivy said with obvious affection as she took his hand.

"Little one," Simon said. "They caught me, turned me into this. They forced me to keep using my magic. Didn't quite work...you brought me back for a moment." He looked at me. "You have to stop them. They want an army of these. More...kept in the basement...behind you." He pointed at the main prison structure.

"We'll stop them," I said. "I'm sorry it had to come to this." I meant it, too. Someone was going to pay dearly for this.

He nodded and looked back at Ivy. "I'm sorry, I have to leave." Simon coughed up more blood and cried out as the pain from the wound did its work. "You need to go. Stop Mordred."

"I'm sorry I couldn't stop them from hurting you," Ivy said. Tears fell onto her dying friend.

"You helped me more than you could ever know. You kept me sane all these years. It was as honor to call you my friend."

"The honor was mine," Ivy said.

"Now go, find your sister and the others and free them."

Ivy nodded and then kissed Simon once on the forehead. "I'll always remember you," she said as she released his hand and stood.

"Take her in there," I told Thomas, who nodded and motioned Ivy back inside the building they'd just left.

"Take care of her," Simon said to me when we were alone. "They need Ivy, and her sister." He had to stop talking as a fit of coughing and pain wracked his body. "Don't leave me like this. Please."

I knelt beside Simon and removed a silver dagger from my belt, the twin of the one I'd given Ivy. "Ready?" I asked. He took a deep breath, nodded, and I plunged the long blade up through his neck and into his brain, killing him instantly.

I allowed the rage I felt to build inside of me and got up, intent on killing Mordred once and for all.

CHAPTER 27

London, England. Now.

"**D**ani's awake," Laurel said to Francis and me.

We stood in unison and followed her from the old bench on the subway's platform through to Francis' office. After Dani had passed out, and I'd received my unpleasant phone call, I'd asked Laurel to look after her. Although based on how fast Laurel had motioned for us to leave, I wasn't sure how much of my decision that actually was.

"How you feeling?" I asked Dani, who was sitting up on the couch, a cup of hot tea in hand.

"Okay, I guess," she said. "Sorry I fell asleep. How long was I out?"

"About an hour," Laurel said. "It was a lot for you to take on at once."

Dani drank some of her tea. "I know where the office is. Or I will once we drive around the area."

"We?" I asked.

"I'll have to go with you. There's no way I can tell exactly where it is without seeing it."

I didn't want Dani to come with me. For a start, I didn't want her in any more danger. But I also didn't want to have to look out for her if it all went to shit. I'd rather she was somewhere I knew was safe. "You just give me the location and I'll do the rest."

"Doesn't work like that." She swung her legs off the couch and placed her cup on a coffee table beside her. "I know the area, it's by the docks, but unless you want to go building to building in search for it, I *have* to go with you."

"It's my memory, I think I'll know what building it is," I pointed out.

"Did you see the outside of it? Or what the buildings next to it look like? Because I did."

I opened my mouth to speak and then realized that I actually couldn't have picked the building out if I was standing right in front of it. I'd have to check out every single one of them in the area, and that would take hours, if not days, to finish. "Okay, you can come. But you do what I say."

Dani mock saluted. "Will do, boss."

I shook my head. "You've got twenty minutes to get ready," I called out as she walked off.

I turned to Francis. "How's it going getting the information on your client who wanted the *Iliad* stolen?"

Francis walked off toward the main area of his business. He walked with purpose, and a little anger. Something was bothering him.

I followed and watched as he made his way behind the counter, pulling up a large box from the floor and placing it in front of him.

"What's wrong?" I asked.

He waved his hand at me in a dismissive gesture.

"Let's try again," I said and walked toward him. "Why are you angry?"

Francis opened the box and began removing small pieces of jewelry from it and placing them on the glass counter. By the time he'd finished the glass was no longer visible—it was covered by dozens of broaches and rings, necklaces and cameos. Hundreds if not thousands of pounds worth of jewels gleamed before me. "I can't seem to contact my last client," he said eventually.

"And that makes you reorganize jewelry?"

Francis sighed. "I will not be used to further the ambitions of others. I was used for a long time, and that period in my life is very much over. If these people have set me up, I have to consider my response." He looked up at me and for the first time I noticed the predator lurking behind his eyes. It was hidden, but definitely there. He blinked once and it was gone.

I thought about asking more, but Francis' tone made it perfectly clear that he would not be taking questions. "I will keep trying though," he said.

Dani's footsteps sounded throughout the subway. "All ready," she said. She'd changed into black combats and a dark blue hoodie, much more suitable attire for traipsing around the docks in the still-dark early morning.

"You'll need this," Francis said, throwing me a set of car keys. "It's parked around the corner in a resident's parking space."

I glanced at the badge on the keys. "You drive a Jag?" I asked.

A smile crept onto Francis' face. "I like to drive in style."

I couldn't help but laugh.

As it turned out, Francis didn't just like to just drive in style, he liked to drive in style at very high speeds. The Jag was a black

XK 4.2, a car that, as I discovered, went like a rocket the second I put my foot down. The V8 engine, given the freedom to work without having to stop due to congested traffic, roared to life as I drove through the early morning streets of London.

Dani dozed on and off through the journey. It was only just coming up to three in the morning, and she was probably still tired from having to use her newfound abilities. Even so, by the time we reached the docks, she was wide awake and keen to start searching.

I drove slowly around the twisty streets, giving Dani an opportunity to look at all of the large warehouses and assorted office buildings that littered the area. It took all of five minutes before she spotted something. "Up there," she said, pointing toward the end of the road we were on. "That looks familiar."

I followed her directions and turned off the road to drive through an unmanned security gate. The barrier had long since broken, leaving only the jagged remains of splintered wood protruding from the mechanism that would have raised and lowered it.

The entire complex beyond was deserted, and vegetation had started to encroach on the structures, giving the whole place an *end of the world* vibe. More than once I had to dodge potholes at the last moment.

I continued to follow Dani's directions, which took us to an office building several stories high. I parked behind it and stepped out into the bitter coldness of the early morning. The smell of the river Thames hit me in one gigantic wave. The sounds of seagulls, and the occasional boat moving along the river's dark surface, sang through the air. I'd always liked the river. There was something soothing about its scent and sound, as the waves lapped against the banks and concrete walls that surrounded it.

"That's really freaky," Dani said after I'd applied my night vision. "You're like a walking torch."

I glanced down at the orange glyphs as they vanished from my arms, and smiled. "That's probably not how I'd put it, but thanks none the less." Graffiti covered whatever could be reached on the exterior walls without a crane or climbing gear, including one particular piece that could only been achieved by hanging from the roof. At first glance it appeared that all of the windows had been broken, but as I got closer I noticed that one window on the third floor remained whole. "How did you find this place from my memory?"

She flicked on a small, but powerful, flashlight that she'd retrieved from her pocket. "Have you ever seen those crime TV shows, where they see an image and then turn that image around and measure the distance from it to a landmark or some such?"

I nodded.

"I sort of did that. When I came into your memory, you were standing by the door. I just sort of flipped the image and looked around for something to recognize." Dani pointed off past the buildings and back to the main road. "There's a sculpture back down that road, next to a sign that tells you the road name. You can see it during the daytime, but we passed it on the way here. I just knew to look for it and go from there."

"How come I didn't see it?" I asked. "I don't remember it."

"You weren't looking for it," she said. "You can't freeze frame your own memory and have a look around. Even if your subconscious spotted something, your conscious memory wouldn't remember."

I raised an eyebrow in surprise at her knowledge of memories.

"Laurel told me," she said with a sly grin.

"How'd you know it still existed?" I asked.

Dani smiled and held up her mobile phone. "Google Street View said it did."

"So you could have just told me the address and let me do this alone?"

Dani nodded. "Could have, but I want to help. And besides, wouldn't you rather have the company?"

I probably should have been angry. After all, Dani had just placed herself in more danger. But part of me was actually quite impressed with her ingenuity. "Just tell me next time," I said and poked my head through the entrance, seeing nothing but more graffiti and the occasional rat. "You don't mind big rats do you?" I asked Dani, who was a few feet away. She shrugged in response. *Well, we'll soon find out.*

I stepped inside and the rodents stared at me before scurrying off to wherever they lived, the sound of tiny claws tapping against the tiled floor sent a slight shiver up my spine. "Safe to come in?" Dani asked from outside.

"Yeah, you'll be fine," I said and looked around the hallway. It was definitely the one from my memory.

Dani shrieked a little and I whipped around. "Really big rat, fucking thing ran past me."

"I thought you didn't mind rats," I pointed out and began to walk through the corridors to where my memory had taken me.

"I don't," Dani said right behind me. "At least not until they get to the size of a Great-fucking-Dane." She mumbled a curse under her breath. "So you know where we're going?"

"I hope so." I followed the corridor until I found one of the walls that had been partially destroyed. "Now I know so."

We stepped into the room. It had been cleaned out long ago, and any remnants of those who had died here long removed. The same could be said of the adjoining room, where I'd dragged Welkin from the window and shot him in his knee.

"There's nothing here," I said and kicked a tin can against the far wall. "It's a dead end."

"I'm sorry, Nate." Dani placed a hand on my shoulder.

I squeezed it gently and left the room, my hopes evaporating along with the time I still had to find the research. I stood in the corridor and stared at the mess of graffiti on the wall in front of me. Most of it looked old, certainly more than a few years. It reminded me of the graffiti outside, in amongst the broken windows. "We need to go to the third floor," I said.

Dani appeared beside me wiping dust from her top. "Why, what's up there?"

I was already walking down the corridor and she had to run to catch up to me. "You going to answer the question, or what?" she asked.

"Outside, the windows were all broken. Except for one on the third floor."

"Maybe stoned people have a shit throwing arm."

"So how'd they manage to get the others?" I asked. "The law of averages suggests that if they can break the rest, then enough stones thrown should break all of them."

We reached a stairwell, where more graffiti adorned the walls, and headed up to the third floor. "I don't think it's glass." I opened the door and went through first. If there was anyone about to attack us, I'd rather Dani wasn't in the front line.

"So what is it?" she whispered as we walked down a corridor identical to the one on the ground floor, the only difference was lot less graffiti.

We opened every door we came to, checking for either the research, or potential threats, until we reached the door at the far end. "This is the room with the intact window," I said.

"I think there's going to be a problem," Dani said with a tap on my shoulder. I turned and followed her flashlight. Blood splatter covered the far wall.

"That's not good." The blood was old and had soaked into the exposed plasterboard. "It's about chest height." I touched the board. It was peppered with tiny holes. "A shotgun did this."

"You sure?"

I shrugged. "Somehow I know it was a shotgun." I turned back to the door and a thought occurred to me. I gathered up some compressed air in the palm of my hand and threw it at the wall next to the door. Plaster dust ripped from the wall, causing Dani to sneeze.

"Little warning next time," she said with a cough.

"Sorry," I said and examined the hole I'd made in the wall. Shiny metal stared back at me. "This whole wall is reinforced. Someone wanted to keep what's inside this room hidden."

"So bust it down," Dani said with another cough.

"Can't, I think there are shotguns behind the door." I pointed to the lock on the door. "And the deadbolt from the lock actually goes into the wall. To get inside I'd need to rip off the door, which is probably also strengthened, opening myself to a rather nasty blast of shot."

Dani moved aside, no longer standing in the path of any shot. "So how do we get inside?"

I placed a hand against the lock and concentrated. The white glyphs on my arms mixed with orange and grew in brightness until it was almost unbearable to watch. "I'd move back," I said, and the lock began to melt. I used my spare hand to slam air magic into the lock; a second later the door vanished in an explosion that shot out and destroyed part of the wall opposite where I'd been standing.

Fortunately, I'd dove to the ground after grabbing Dani and covered us both in a thick shield of air. Little pieces of red-hot metal bounced off the shield and pinged around the corridor.

"Well, that was new," I said, as I removed the shield. "You okay?" I asked Dani once the ringing in my ears had subsided.

She nodded. "What did I say about warning me?"

"You'd have argued with me," I pointed out, getting back to my feet and helping her up.

She stared at me for a heartbeat. "I hate you."

I laughed and went to examine the damage. "Well, that definitely wasn't a shotgun behind the door." I knelt down and picked up part of a claymore mine. "The door was rigged with mines."

"And it stinks," Dani said.

"Burning wood, plastic, paper, metal. Not the most pleasant of combinations." I stepped through the still-smoking shell of the doorframe and into a small room with one metal door in front of me. "No lock," I said and turned the handle, pushing it open carefully with a lot of effort—it was thick enough to be used in a bank vault.

Dani gasped as she saw the dozens of filing cabinets, each one with three drawers, all lined up in rows. In the middle of everything was a single desk. A PC sat atop it. A white envelope had been taped to the silver tower. Dani walked over and pulled the note off and reading the front before passing it to me. "I think we've found the research."

I turned the envelope over in my hands to read the front. It had two words written on it. *For Nate.*

CHAPTER 28

I had no idea why someone would leave me an envelope with my name on it. It wasn't in my handwriting, and the contents had turned out to be a solitary USB stick. It felt weighty as it burned a hole in my pocket, willing me to find out what it contained.

"What is this place?" Dani asked, tentatively moving through the room after I'd given it a clean sweep to check for any more explosive surprises.

I opened one of the filing cabinets and removed a file at random, flicking through its contents. "I'm going to guess that it's where I hid all of Welkin's research." I removed a photo from the file and passed it to Dani. "That man in the picture is Welkin."

He'd posed for the photo in front of a table full of scientific paraphernalia—test tubes, microscopes, and equipment to separate liquids. A beaming smile sat frozen across his face. "He's creepy," Dani said, passing me the photo back. "Should I recognize him or something?"

I shook my head. If what Jenny had said was true, she'd have been far too young to remember Welkin. It was something to be thankful for.

I placed the file back in the drawer and closed it. "So, are you going to see what's on that thing?" Dani asked and switched on the computer, which generated a low humming noise as it booted up.

"I was checking the rest of the room first," I said and joined her at the desk.

"Liar, you're just worried about what you might find."

Dani's words may have been spoken in jest, but there was a sliver of truth to them.

I waited until the computer had finished loading before placing the USB stick into the port and opening Windows Explorer. The stick contained one file, and it was large in size.

"It's a video," Dani said, allowing me to take a seat on the only available chair.

The file name said *Nate*, and according to its properties, it had been created just under a month ago. I double clicked on it and another window popped up, an image of Daniel Hayes speaking in silence. Dani found the on switch for the speakers and Daniel's voice filled the room. I adjusted the volume to no-longer-ear-bleeding level, and restarted the video.

"Nate," Daniel said looking directly at the camera in front of him. It appeared that he'd filmed it in the same building where Dani and I stood. Daniel drank a dark liquid from a glass he'd placed on a table next to him and took a deep breath. The date on the bottom of the screen read four weeks previous.

"I'd written down some things I wanted to say, but I don't really know where to start." He smiled, although it was filled with sadness. "At the beginning always works well, I guess."

"He's really nervous," Dani said.

"He probably knew his employers were after him."

Daniel took another drink, this one much longer. "So, Nate, I've heard rumors that you're actually alive," Daniel started, his voice more confident. He sighed. "I don't even know why I'm doing this, or if you really have lost your memory. But in the hope that you see this before they kill me, or you, and that somehow it might help you finish what we started a decade ago, I have to try."

There was a noise behind Daniel, and he looked around for the culprit. Finding nothing, he returned his attention to the camera. "Fucking rats. You could have picked a better bloody spot."

Daniel sighed again. "Okay, from the beginning. I work for Avalon. I'm not high up or anything, just a human scientist who mostly works at universities. Genetics are my field, and I've always thought myself pretty good at my job. I fed Avalon information on human breakthroughs, or, indeed, nonhuman ones. Anything that Avalon would find useful or interesting. It was hardly the most exciting life, but I loved doing it. Still do. But I wanted to do more, to help more.

"You contacted me long ago, maybe fifteen years now, and asked for my help. You said there were few scientists in Avalon who had any interest in genetics, and even fewer you could trust. You wanted me to infiltrate Mars Warfare and discover what they and, more specifically, Doctor Welkin, were involved in.

"I was happy to do it, so don't think for one second that I'm complaining. It was a chance to help a lot of people. And, if I'm honest, it was exciting. I knew Welkin by reputation. He'd been seen as a genius in the field of genetics, but his ethical line was somewhere just below that of a psychopath." Daniel took another drink. "Quite far below as it turned out. You arranged for me to get a job there—I never asked how, I don't think it was something I wanted to know—and for years I was simultaneously excited, and terrified, in awe and sickened, by the practices that went on in that place."

"He sounds like he enjoyed it there," Dani said with a touch of anger.

"That sounds awful," Daniel said as if on cue. "It makes it sound like I enjoyed working for those who killed people. But they gave me everything I could ever want to do my job. It was a good feeling to finally have unlimited funds to explore the ideas I'd always wanted. And for a while that was it. Create, hypothesize, and test them in carefully controlled experiments, all the time feeding you information about what was happening. And whilst Welkin was odd, I had no idea of the kind of man he'd become.

"It took three years before I learned about the things Welkin had done—murder, torture, and experimenting on people just to see how they work. All in the name of some twisted science." Daniel paused, thoughtful for a moment. "No, not science. In the name of profit. He did anything if it could advance his standing within the company, or make him richer.

"Welkin forced sorcerers to use magic until they'd changed into gargoyles and nightmares. My entire life I'd fought against those who created crimes against magic, and here I was sitting back and allowing it to happen."

I realized that Achilles used to be a sorcerer and wondered if he was broken before he transformed, or if that was a result of it. I had a horrible thought: How much magic use was too much? How much would I need to use before turning into one of those…*things*. I pushed the thought back down inside me and continued watching.

"Creating gargoyles takes a long time, days and weeks of forcing someone to use magic. And nightmares take an unpredictable amount of time, too. They both need to be manipulated and molded. So, Welkin decided they weren't worth the effort and focused on other species. He stopped werewolves from transforming, just so he could record how mad it drove them. The things he did...they were awful. And I had to participate the whole time. Oh, I fed you the data, dates and times of experiments, photos, and case notes, but it was like every day I saw and heard those things, a little piece of my soul died. You stopped what you could, intercepting convoys with prisoners and aiding the occasional escape, but there were always more. And you couldn't shut Mars Warfare down without a lot of evidence— Welkin's research. But his experiment a decade ago changed the time frame we'd set in place to acquire that evidence.

"Welkin decided to push forward with a second set of Harbinger trials. These were meant to be safer. The first set had taken place before my time, and Welkin was secretive about who knew what he was planning for the second trials. I was definitely not included in his inner circle, but eventually he informed everyone that a batch of ten children had been put through the process and most had survived."

Daniel cupped his hands to his face, rubbing his eyes. When he next looked up at the camera they were slightly red. "*Most*. How do you quantify that you'd allowed 'most' of the children to live. And he was proud of this. I couldn't stand by and let these kids die. And neither could you.

"Within a few days Welkin had vanished. At first it was put down to the pressures of work. But it didn't take long for panic to set in around the building. I was interviewed three times about my knowledge of Welkin. I don't think I've ever been more scared in my life. You helped all of the kids from Welkin's experiments escape, along with thirty other inmates. But even as you helped them escape, you were captured, and that was the last any of us heard about you.

"I was meant to be hidden soon after the breakout, but without you there, and with the crackdown in security, if I'd left they'd have killed me. And then they gave me Samantha to look after. I was meant to be scientific, cold, and clinical about the whole thing. But she brought out fatherly instincts I'd never known existed. And once I had her, there was no way I could leave. They would have hunted both of us."

Daniel finished the rest of the drink. He looked sad and tired. He'd been living a lie for a good portion of his life. It must have been hard on him. "The building you're in was where you found Welkin, and where you killed him after getting the access codes and information about the facility.

"You forced Welkin to tell you where his research was, and then you brought it all back here, to this crap-hole of a building, before the break-out. After you vanished, I bought the building to protect the information it contains. You probably found the claymore. It used to be a shotgun, but some drug dealer decided to break in and I had to rethink things after he decorated the far wall. I assumed you'd be the only one capable of getting inside without blowing yourself up."

"Yeah, didn't that work well," Dani observed sarcastically.

"You weren't blown up," I pointed out.

"I wish I could tell you more about who was in charge at Mars Warfare, but he doesn't tell anyone his real name, just 'my lord.' He scares the shit out of me, though. Him and his psychotic gargoyle bodyguard. If you get the chance, kill him. You'll be doing the world another favor."

Daniel grabbed some paper from beside him, the list of things he'd wanted to mention, and started reading. "Oh yeah, someone contacted the organization behind Mars Warfare with a lot of info about you. It's how they found you. Not sure who, though. We scientists aren't exactly privy to a lot of sensitive information these days.

"One more thing. They need this research. They haven't been able to figure out how Welkin got the Harbinger project to work with increased efficiency. You wanted to keep all of it. You said you needed it all for leverage. I just wanted to burn it all." Daniel flicked through the paper once more. When he found what he was looking for, he took a deep breath before speaking. "Samantha, the girl I think of as my daughter, wasn't the only girl placed. And the second girl wasn't just any girl. She's Samantha's older sister."

I looked at Dani. Her mouth had dropped open, and tears had begun to run down her face. "That's me, isn't it?" she asked. "He's talking about me?"

I nodded, barely believing what I'd heard. "You have a sister."

"Nate," Daniel said as he got back to his feet. "If you're seeing this, then I'm probably dead. So I have to ask you, please keep Samantha safe. If they've got her, you must get her free. They use psychics. I'm not privy to the details, but they change them somehow. This is how you can repay me for the years I worked for you. Get my daughter to safety." Daniel was crying now. "And thank you. Thank you for helping me, for allowing me to do something meaningful, for trusting me to work with you. If I am dead, I want you to know; it was an honor to know you. You are singularly the best and most terrifying person I've ever met."

Daniel's stare hardened. "And if they've hurt Sam, if they've harmed one hair on her innocent, beautiful head, bury them for me. Turn that whole fucking place into rubble."

Dani walked off the second the video finished, saying that she wanted to be alone for a while. I could hardly blame her. She'd only just discovered that she had a sister. I gave her a few minutes before following her; I didn't want to give more bad news, but Dani needed to know the truth.

I found her huddled next to a filing cabinet, staring off out of the unbreakable window. "I have a sister," she said. "Welkin's lord has her, doesn't he?"

"Yeah," I said and sat beside her. "When they took Jenny, the girl I was with when I got shot, they forced her to give over information about Samantha's whereabouts."

"We have to get her out." She refused to turn back and look at me.

"We will," I said. "They need Samantha to do something. Until they get you, they can't do it."

Sobs rocked her body. When she turned back to face me, her eyes were puffy and red. "I want to go through these files," she said. "I want to know why they're doing all this."

I agreed and we spent the next few hours trawling through file after file. Most of them contained information on experiments that had been conducted, or ideas that Welkin had about future experiments.

"I need to stop," Dani said after what felt like years of reading true horror stories.

"Yeah, me too," I said and threw the file at the nearest cabinet, spilling paper and photos over the floor. "This guy's work does not make for pleasant reading."

"He got them to fight, to find out what they could do," Dani said. "Did you really kill him?"

I nodded.

She thought about it for a moment. "Good. He deserved it."

There was so much anger and venom in her voice, born of frustration, sadness, and fear. Even if she'd been the happiest person in the world when she'd said it, I still wouldn't have felt anything wrong in her words. Welkin had needed to die. I'd done the world a service by fulfilling that need.

"The Harbinger stuff is just as bad," I said and held up a file. "This is what they want, and there's no way we can let them have it."

"But if you turn up empty handed, they'll kill you and Holly. And then her family."

I walked to the nearest cabinet and emptied the contents onto the floor, about forty files in all. "There's no way I'm giving them the knowledge to run those experiments on anyone else." I looked over at the ruined front door. "But we can't leave it all here. Someone will eventually find it." I took the USB stick out of the computer and put it in my pocket. "Empty all the filing cabinets."

Within a few minutes we had several huge piles of paper dotted around the room. "So, now what?" Dani asked.

"Grab those files there, the ones about the Harbinger project. They're coming with us." We shared the files between us and made our way to the scorched exit. The claymore had made a massive mess, and anyone standing in the way of its blast would have been killed instantly.

Dani and I stepped back into the hallway and I put the files on the floor. "Those involved with Mars Warfare, who helped do all this, are never going to see the inside of a court room, let alone a jail cell. I must have known that."

"So what leverage did you want?"

"I think I was going to use them to get information on Welkin's boss. I think the removal of my memories was him hiding his own involvement." I raised my hands, orange glyphs adorning them, and threw one steady stream of fire into the room. It soon caught hold of the stacks of paper, turning the interior into an inferno within seconds.

"So what's the plan?"

I picked up the pile of files and took one last look in the room. The fire had engulfed everything, including the computer. There would be nothing left of anything by the time it had finished.

"I don't know yet," I said honestly and looked at my watch. "But I have six hours to figure one out."

CHAPTER 29

"That's a terrible plan," Francis said with more than a hint of anger, after Dani and I returned to the subway station, files in hand.

"Francis has a point," Laurel said. "You're planning on engaging a gargoyle and his men in combat. It does seem...unnecessarily reckless."

"It's bloody insane," Dani chimed in.

I raised my hands in surrender. "It'll work. I'm pretty certain of it. Achilles likes to think of himself as the greatest warrior ever, a man who can't be bested in combat. He'll see no threat going somewhere alone with me. He knows in a straight fight he could kill me without breaking a sweat."

"You're sort of proving our point," Dani said.

"But the only way I'm getting everyone out of that place alive is if Achilles is no longer an issue," I pointed out. "He has to be removed, or he'll just start killing everyone."

Francis glared at me.

"If anyone has a better idea, I'm open for suggestions." When no one else came up with anything, I decided it best to go sit by myself on the station bench.

I'd closed my eyes and rested the back of my head against the cold tiles when Laurel spoke. "What do you need us to do?" I hadn't even heard her walk up.

"The files I brought with me need to be scattered inside the boot of Francis' car, so that one glance will show exactly what they are." I opened my eyes and found that Jerry was standing beside her. "If there's not enough paper, get more. I want the boot almost full to the brim. Any paper will do, just make it look full."

Laurel walked off up the stairs and I glanced down at my watch. There wasn't long before I had to be back at the warehouse.

"You got a minute?" Jerry asked.

I nodded, and he took a seat next to me. "You really think this will work?"

I nodded again.

"You've got the boss' feathers ruffled. He's not happy that you haven't told him everything."

"That's okay, he'll be even less happy when he hears it."

Jerry laughed. "If anything happens to you." He raised his hands. "Not saying it will mind, but if it does, Dani will be safe here. I think Laurel has taken a liking to her. And they won't turn her either. Not unless she asks to be. Francis doesn't like turning people without needing to."

"So, what are you, Jerry? Because you're not a vampire."

"Human," he said and noticed my surprise. "I was a Marine, left just before the whole shit with Iraq."

"So how did you come to work for Francis?"

"Just sort of fell into it. I needed a job, and he supplied one."

"It's not exactly the sort of place you can bring a date though," I said.

Laurel returned, carrying some bundles of paper and smiled at Jerry, who winked.

Jerry looked down at his feet and smiled. "I don't think that's ever going to be much of a problem."

"You and Laurel, are…?"

Jerry nodded.

"Good job."

He smiled and stood. "I wanted you to know that the girl will be safe."

"Thank you."

"Just don't get yourself killed," he said and shook my hand. "Francis would complain for years that you never paid him back for that gargoyle cure."

I laughed. The tension in my shoulders relaxed a little. "I'll do my best."

"We're done," she said to me. "Now for the rest of the plan."

We made our way back to Francis, who was showing Dani how to operate a semi-automatic gun. "Is that necessary?" I asked.

"Yes," Francis said without looking up. "She's not going with you. Don't argue, girl," he said before Dani could even open her mouth. "But, she needs to know how to defend herself, just in case."

"You want to know the rest of the plan, then?" I asked.

Francis placed the gun on the counter and looked toward me, followed by Dani and Laurel.

"Okay," I agreed. "But first things first. I'm going to need a couple of claymore mines."

Francis' response to the rest of my plan had not been one of joy. In fact, out of Dani, Laurel, and him, he'd been the most upset with my idea. It probably didn't help that I was using his car to drive to the warehouse.

I was going to be early, but I didn't see the point in waiting around for an hour, getting more and more agitated and nervous. I stopped Francis' Jag at the guard post where I'd been searched on my first visit. The same man, in the same blue uniform, left the hut and motioned for me to get out of the car.

As before, I placed my hands on the side of the hut and the guard searched me without a word. When he'd finished, he walked around to the back of the car. "Open it," he demanded.

"No, this is for Achilles. And Achilles only," I said. "My friends' lives are at stake here. So if you don't want to let me through, then go get your boss."

The guard stared at me, and for a moment I thought he was going to call my bluff. Instead, he relented and allowed me through.

I took the car around to the back of the warehouse Achilles and his cronies occupied, parking it opposite the Nissan. The two guards from my last visit radioed Achilles before allowing me inside.

"Come on, fight," someone bellowed from inside the warehouse. In the center of the pit were two men, both naked from the waist up, and both bloodied and bruised. They were standing opposite a shirtless, entirely human-looking Achilles, who was beckoning them to fight him.

The closer I got, the easier it was to see blood on Achilles' hands and arms. Blood that I was certain wasn't his.

"I said, come on," Achilles shouted.

One of the men sprang forward, hoping to catch Achilles off balance. I recognized him as one of the regular fighters, a capable and intelligent combatant. But against Achilles, he was hopelessly outmatched.

Achilles easily dodged his attack and landed a huge right hand to the jaw of the regular, who hit the floor and didn't move. With Achilles' attention diverted, the second man decided to pounce, but Achilles was already moving to intercept, and by the time the man had closed the distance it was too late. Achilles stepped around him, grabbed him by his hair, and yanked his head back, driving his elbow into the man's exposed throat. I knew he was dead before he hit the mat.

Achilles, appearing satisfied with his kill, turned back to the regular, who was getting back to his feet, and kicked him square in the ribs. They audibly broke, along with his arm when Achilles followed up with a vicious kick to his elbow.

"Enough," I shouted as Achilles was about to stomp down on the back of the man's neck.

Achilles paused and looked down at me.

"You said that no one would be hurt," I said.

"I offered them an out. Beat me and everyone goes free. I did warn them what would happen if they lost." Achilles stepped between the ropes and dropped to the floor. He picked up a bottle of water and took a long drink, using the liquid to wash the blood from his hands and arms. "Did you bring everything?"

"Dani is somewhere safe."

Achilles craned his head slightly, a look of pity on his face. "Did I not tell you to bring her? I didn't dream that, did I? I said, you bring her and the research or people die."

"You didn't expect me to bring her. That would make everyone here redundant. You'd take me and her and then kill everyone else."

"True, but an order is an order." He nodded to one of his guards who, before I could stop him, removed a silenced pistol from his holster and shot the regular fighter in the back of his head.

The man slumped to the mats beneath him. "Now, shall we go see this research?" Achilles asked cheerfully.

I tore my gaze away from the dead man, using every ounce of willpower to keep my temper in check. "Holly and her family, where are they?"

"They're upstairs, where they were last time. And they're not dead. So unless you want that to change, I suggest you get on with it."

I set off toward the exit with Achilles alone, right behind me. "I'll be back soon; get rid of this filth in my ring," he told the guard who'd killed the fighter before we both stepped outside.

"Nice Jag," he said, running his hand along the back of the car. "Not really you though."

"It's on loan," I told him. "The stuff is in the boot."

Achilles held up one hand. "Keys."

I tossed them to him. He caught them easily and opened the boot. A smile appeared when he saw the mass of paper inside. "I'm impressed." He picked up the first piece of paper he came to and started reading. "This is the stuff."

"So you don't need to go messing in my head for that information anymore."

Achilles grinned. It reminded me of a shark. "We need your head for something else."

My mind raced as I tried to figure out what else they could need me for, but my thoughts were broken by Achilles as he grabbed a handful of the paper. "You could have at least tried to keep it all organized. It'll take hours to sort all this out."

"It had to be done like that," I said.

Achilles placed his hands deeper into the pile of paper and pulled out a bunch of shredded newspaper. "What the fuck is this?" he yelled.

"Kindling."

Orange glyphs roared to life along my arms and fire erupted from the boot of the car, igniting the claymores I'd hidden beneath the paper. Francis hadn't owned many claymores, so I'd packed the boot with C4 too. The effect was spectacular. The back of the car exploded, engulfing Achilles in flame as he changed into his gargoyle form, driving him back at enormous speed and right into the Nissan, which crumpled from the gargoyle's impact.

I'd been spared the majority of the force from the explosion by creating a shield of dense air all around me, similar to the one I'd used back at the abandoned office building to cover Dani and me. Even so, I felt the blast pushing at my hands, trying to force me off my feet.

The energy soon dissipated and I lowered the shield and looked over at the smoking ruin that used to be the Nissan GTR, with Achilles somewhere in the middle of the wreckage. It was too much to ask that he'd be dead, but hopefully he'd be otherwise occupied long enough for me to finish getting everyone out.

I made it to the warehouse door just as an armed guard darted through, almost barreling into me. I used his momentum to take him off his feet, twisting my body and dumping him on his head behind me, knocking him out cold. There was no more feeling different, or wondering where it had come from, as I performed acts of violence; it was just natural instinct.

A second guard ran through the door like he was on fire, slamming into me before I could move aside. Before we hit the floor, I hooked my arms around him, locking his arms in place, and moved my body to the side. It had the desired effect. The guard lost his footing and fell face first onto the cold, hard concrete with a crunch as his nose and jaw broke.

I pushed him away and got back to my feet, but he turned his head toward me. His face was ruined, but he still reached out one hand to a knife in his belt. He didn't get to it in time to stop me driving my boot into his face.

That was two guards down in less than ten seconds, but when I turned back to the door I came face to face with the guard who had coldly killed the fighter only minutes earlier. A gun was aimed at my head and a smile was on his face. I pointed to the building beside me, but his gaze didn't waver. For about two seconds.

There was a small noise, almost lost in the wind around us, and an unseen force struck the guard in the temple, snapping his head around and driving him to the ground. I removed an earpiece from my pocket and put it into my ear. "Took your time," I said and glanced down at the growing pool of blood beneath the guard's head. There was an entry hole the size of a penny. But the bullet didn't leave the guard's head; it wasn't designed to. It was made to shatter on impact and bounce around inside the target, creating massive internal damage.

"Sorry, had to get rid of the guard from the hut," Jerry said from on top of the empty warehouse beside me. "Looks like your plan worked."

"So far," I said. Discovering that Jerry had been a Marine changed the plan. In hindsight, that was probably for the better. "There's more inside."

"Two," he said. "I've got them on my scope. Those big windows down the side of the building make for good visibility. You want them gone?"

"If you don't mind."

The sound of breaking glass assured me that Jerry had finished what he'd started. "Both down," he said. "I'll stay here and keep an eye out for our stone friend. But from what I've heard, I don't know how well I'll be able to keep him down. I didn't bring a bazooka."

"Do what you can," I said and opened the door, peering inside. Two dead guards lay by the pit. It appeared that both had been making their way outside to see if their colleagues had managed to resolve whatever was happening. "Be back soon."

I darted inside and sprinted across the main floor, taking in every detail as I moved toward to the exit, something else to add to the ever-growing list of new experiences. I hit the door at high speed with a shield of air already up in front of me just in case.

As it turned out, I needn't have bothered. The entire way up to the O'Hara suite was utterly absent of anyone, friend or foe. One kick to the door and the lock gave way. Mark and Lyn O'Hara sat where I'd last seen them, although more disheveled and tired in appearance. Holly and her brother were both missing and fear pinged inside me. I used air magic to create a hardened blade across my fingers, cutting through the plastic ties used to hold Mark and Lyn's hands behind their backs. "Holly?" I asked Mark as he rubbed his shoulders and winced.

"They took her upstairs," he said.

"I'll go get her," I said. "Can you check everyone else?"

Lyn hugged her husband once and then reached under the pool table, pulling out two shotguns that had been attached to the underside. Mark had grabbed a box of shells and began loading them.

"How many more guards are left?" Mark asked.

"Not sure, but probably one or two," I said. I wasn't concerned about leaving Mark and Lyn to deal with any stragglers. I was pretty certain they'd be human and no match for a very angry married couple with experience in killing people.

I left them to their preparations and darted out of the room, sprinting up the stairs two at a time and pausing at the top, just below the next floor. I peered down the corridor and quickly moved back before the single armed guard saw me. There were only two rooms on the corridor. One was used to store medical supplies, and the other was a soundproofed chamber so that those who crossed the family could have...discussions.

I started to make my way back down the stairs, wondering if there was another route, but the next thing I knew, the guard was standing at the top of the stairs, his eyes widened in shock as his hand went for his holstered pistol. I moved quickly, covering the distance between us and slamming my open palm into the side of his knee, dislocating the joint. He tried to stop himself from falling forward, but I grabbed his jacket and pulled him toward me, twisting my hips as I moved and launching him head first down the stairs. He hit the first stair at an awkward angle, the loud crack and sudden limpness of his body signaling that he wouldn't be getting up again.

"Nate, you there?" Jerry's voice said. I'd forgotten I was even wearing an earbud.

"Yeah, how's things at your end?" I asked as I walked toward the room where Holly was being kept.

"I'm fine. There are police cars and ambulances turning up—someone must have heard that explosion—so I'm about to run too."

"Thanks for your help," I said.

"No problem, but your gargoyle friend ran when the sirens started. He didn't look too happy about the fact that you'd set him on fire. He's going to want payment for that."

"He can take a ticket," I said.

Jerry wished me good luck and my earpiece fell silent. I removed the little bud and slipped it into my pocket.

I opened the door to Holly's makeshift prison and what I found caused a lump of worry to grow in my throat.

The place resembled something you might see after a tornado hits town. Everything was broken, the remains thrown around the room, creating as much devastation as possible. A wooden chair protruded from a small TV; the chair cushion's stuffing hung out of the smashed glass like a mortal wound.

My gaze fell downward to a naked leg lying on the floor behind a sofa bed that had been tipped over. I rushed over and pulled the bed free, revealing Holly beneath it.

Blood saturated her clothes and the floor beneath her. Tightness filled my chest, and a lump stuck in my throat as I realized how badly she was hurt. There was so much blood that it was hard to know how much one person could have left. It pooled behind her, drenching her hair and turning it a deep red as it stuck together.

I wiped her neck with the palm of my hand and searched for a pulse, but found nothing. I grabbed a nearby t-shirt and cleaned her neck more thoroughly, before trying again. "Come on

Holly, can you hear me?" I pleaded as I struggled to find signs of life, eventually discovering a faint pulse.

It looked like she'd been cut repeatedly, all over her body. Each slice into her skin had bled her a little more, and they seemed to get deeper the further down her body they went. I searched to see if there was one wound that might have caused the massive blood loss and found two gouge-like wounds in her abdomen. The holes were large and had ripped the skin on both ends. The weapon had been pushed inside and then twisted.

"Holly, please?" I said again as I pushed the t-shirt over the deep wounds, trying to stop the bleeding.

"I need you, you can't die," I demanded, my voice full of desperation. "Come on, fight. I can't do this alone."

A wail sounded from the door and I spun around to find Lyn standing in the doorway. "Get an ambulance, now! And a first aid kit," I shouted.

She nodded and fished a mobile from her jeans pocket, immediately dialing as I kept trying to stem the flow of blood. When Lyn finished she rushed off, returning a few seconds later with a large first aid box. She ripped into the bandages, passing them over to me so that I could use them to apply pressure to the worst of the wounds.

We worked like that until two paramedics arrived and pushed us aside, assuring us that they'd do the best they could. I couldn't get up from the floor as they placed her on a gurney and wheeled her out of the warehouse. My legs didn't seem capable of movement. I just sat on the floor, numb with shock, as Mark arrived and held his wife, crying together as they left to follow their daughter.

CHAPTER 30

I couldn't say how long it took me to walk down to the ground floor of the warehouse, where more paramedics had rushed into the building, accompanied by several human police. The paramedics checked me over, but once they'd cleaned the blood off my face and hands and discovered that none of it belonged to me, they left me alone. Instead, they began looking at everyone who'd been taken captive, requesting that many of them be taken to the hospital.

The O'Hara's were already gone by the time I'd gotten outside, the ambulance too. They hadn't wasted any time in getting Holly to the hospital.

I passed several police who were hunched over the dead bodies outside. From what I'd overheard, the detective in charge of the investigation wasn't too happy to have had all his witnesses leave at once, but there was no force on earth that would have stopped either Lyn or Mark from being with their daughter.

After answering a few questions and being told that I'd need to make a statement, the detective offered to give me a ride to the hospital, which I accepted.

I knew what he was trying to do, hoping that I'd divulge information that he wanted, but by the time we'd arrived, I was pretty certain I'd told him absolutely nothing of value.

The O'Hara family was easy to find inside the hospital, as the shock of what had happened finally began to dull. We were taken down dingy corridors that wouldn't have looked out of place when Florence Nightingale was running around. I was told to wait in a small room with half a dozen chairs, none of which were occupied. A few seconds later, Mark and Lyn joined me, holding each other's hands in comfort.

"How did this happen?" Mark asked.

I remained silent, unable to face him.

"I asked you a question," he repeated, and this time menace crept into his voice.

"They were after me," I said without looking up, as a lump caught in my throat. It was my fault Holly was hurt, I should have just been honest with her about who I was from the start. I should have done more to keep her safe. "They wanted me to do things for them. But I don't know how they found out about Holly and you."

"This is your fault," Mark roared and dove toward me, dragging me from my chair and slamming my back into the wall. "You got my daughter killed." Mark's forearm pressed into my throat, his face a mass of red rage.

"Let go," I managed as Mark pushed harder against my throat.

"Mark," Lyn said from behind her husband. "This isn't Nate's fault. He saved us."

Mark blinked once and the tension against my neck eased. "I want to know who did this. And why," he said. "And you will tell me."

I'd never seen Mark angry before. Sure, I'd heard the stories of what he was capable of, but seeing the rage in his eyes as he was inches from my face put a whole new slant on it. And I understood how Mark had managed to gain the reputation he had. I was grateful that Lyn had been in the room. If Mark hadn't let go, I would have had to make him. It was hardly the time to be fighting.

"I can't," I said. "I'm not really sure why any of this is happening. All I know is that they want me and Dani."

"The girl Holly mentioned." Lyn said. "She told us that she was taking care of someone—apparently Dani was in some trouble."

"They murdered my mum," Dani said from the doorway.

I turned to Dani, about to ask how she'd gotten to the hospital, but she continued talking before I could say anything.

"Nate saved my life, but destroyed his in the process. They're after me because I'm important to them. It's my fault that Holly got hurt." Dani began to cry and Lyn rushed to her, holding the young girl against her.

"You're safe here," Lyn said and looked back at Mark with daggers. "And you, Mark O'Hara, will threaten no one. Our daughter is fighting for her life, and you're in here threatening the man who tried to save her."

"Where's your son?" I asked.

"Lee was taken down to the fighters' locker rooms," Mark said. "We saw him outside talking to the police when we left the warehouse. He said he'd escaped and managed to get outside just as the police turned up. He's dealing with them back at the warehouse, now."

"Why don't you make yourself useful and go call him, see if he's finished," Lyn said.

Any remnants of Mark's anger evaporated instantly and he left the room to do as he was told.

"You've got to give his mind something to occupy itself," Lyn said when the three of us were alone. "Otherwise, he'll go mad. You okay, Nate?"

I rubbed my throat. "I'll be fine." I looked over at Dani. "How'd you get here?"

"After Jerry got back and told Francis what had happened, Francis called a police friend of his to ask for an update," she said. "I begged Jerry to bring me here. I wanted to make sure you and Holly were okay. Jerry said to give him a call if we need anything."

Lyn was about to ask something else when a doctor entered the room. She was a brunette, probably no older than thirty, and appeared to have had a very long night.

"Your daughter is in surgery," she said to Lyn, without looking at the clipboard in her hands. "Someone will let you know her progress. But it's going to take awhile; you might want to go home and get some rest."

"Would you go home and rest if it were your child?" Lyn asked her.

The doctor's answer was immediate. "No. I'll get you some pillows and blankets."

Half a dozen pillows and three large pink blankets arrived a few minutes later, just as Lyn was leaving to find her husband. Dani settled in one of the chairs and switched on the TV. I took one of the pillows and tried to get comfortable in a chair that had never been designed for anything resembling comfort. The clock on the wall said it was just after three a.m., although with a constant tick every second, it soon became clear in my mind that the clock might not make it to four a.m. before being thrown through a window.

Evidently, I fell asleep before then, because the next thing I knew Dani was poking me in the shoulder. "You were asleep for a few hours," she said.

"You should have woken me," I told her.

"You needed your sleep," Lyn said from the doorway. Mark stood behind her, holding his wife around the waist. "The doctor has news about Holly. We wanted you to be there to hear it."

I pushed the thick blanket off and stood as the doctor from earlier arrived in the room. "Holly is out of surgery," she said.

"What are her chances?" Mark asked.

"There were a large amount of lacerations. Most of these are shallow, but a few were quite deep, especially those on the lower extremities. Whoever did this made a point of cutting muscle and tendons. If she recovers, Holly will need months of physical therapy and, no doubt, psychological counseling. She also has two further puncture wounds on her abdomen. One of these nicked a kidney and the other touched her spleen. The damage to the organs themselves is fortunately mild.

"We've controlled the bleeding for now and closed the wounds. We're replacing the blood she lost and have started her on a round of antibiotics. There's also what appears to be a claw mark on her spine, just at the base. It's quite deep and could have easily severed her spine, but on the face of it, it caused very little damage. But, we have another, greater concern."

"What is it?" Lyn asked as she sat on one of the chairs, looking up at the doctor with an expression of hope and expectance that science and medicine could save her daughter.

"Unfortunately, Holly appears to have been suffered a head injury and it's given her some swelling on the brain. We're going to keep her in an induced coma for the next few days. We need to find out what the damage is, and whether waking her up will cause more problems. We should have a much clearer picture soon, but until then we're taking it cautiously."

The doctor told us where Holly was and said that if there were any further developments, she'd let us know. She then asked to have a moment alone with Lyn and Mark.

Dani had followed the O'Hara's after they'd finished talking to the doctor, and I caught up with them as they walked through the hospital toward Holly's room. The tension inside me ratcheted up with every step. My heart pounded in my ears and the lump in my throat grew until I thought I'd be unable to breathe.

We walked for what felt like an eternity, up flights of stairs, following brightly painted green lines on the floor. Different colors, red, blue, yellow, all led to other parts of the hospital, but I barely paid attention to the route we took. I just watched the never-ending green line as we passed through double doors after double doors, along identical hospital corridors.

Finally, the green line vanished, and I looked up to see the intensive care ward. Lyn and Mark had been told that Holly would have her own room and went to talk to one of the nurses, coming back soon after. "We can only go in one at a time," Mark said.

"We'll wait here," I told him.

"We want you to go in first," Mark said.

"Are you sure?" I asked, taken aback by the gesture.

Mark nodded. "You need to get going, to find the men responsible. Go see her before you leave."

"Go," Lyn said pointing to the room opposite a nurses' station, which was a sedate place, even as nurses and doctors alike tried to save the lives that had been brought to them. Not all of those patients would make it. It was a thought I forced aside as I took the short walk to Holly's room.

I stopped breathing as I opened the door—I didn't want to see this, didn't want it to be real. The blinds looking out into the corridor were half closed, as were the thick blue curtains. The only sound was the beep of the heart-monitoring equipment.

I took a chair from the end of the bed and placed it next to Holly, but didn't sit down. I watched her for a moment, taking in the bandages wrapped around her head, the left eye swollen shut and split lip. Her right arm was in a plaster cast and she's been intubated to help her breathe.

I sat beside Holly and took her good hand in mine. "You're strong, Holly. You need to be. You need to get better." A tear fell down my cheek. "You made it easier to not know who I was. It didn't matter who I used to be because I had people like you in my life." The tears began to flow freely. "I can't lose that, can't lose you. You need to fight, and when you wake up you'll see that I've brought down everyone responsible for what happened today."

The door behind me opened and I turned to see Lee, silhouetted in the doorframe. "This wasn't supposed to happen," he whispered and sprinted away.

CHAPTER 31

Within a fraction of a second I'd launched myself up from my chair and sprinted after Lee. We raced through the hospital corridors, drawing glares from nurses and patients alike, as glyphs blared along my arms. I had to shut them off before the temptation to use magic became too great and I did serious damage to the hospital or an innocent bystander. Neither of which Lee cared about. He shoved his way past people, knocking some to the ground.

He reached an open lift, marked *employees only*, and darted inside just as I got to it. I slammed my fist on the metal and watched the green floor numbers above the lift as it made its way down. There was no point chasing Lee if I didn't know what floor he was getting off at.

Dani yelled something from down the corridor as she made her way toward me, with Lyn close behind. But I didn't respond. I just kept watching the green numbers get lower and lower until it finally stopped on *GF*, Ground Floor.

I didn't waste another second. I burst through the door into the stairwell and raced down the stairs, taking them three at a time. I flung open a set of double doors at the bottom of the stairwell and found a long corridor with shops and fast food outlets dotted all around, making this one of busiest parts of the hospital, where visitors bought their loved ones some comforts. I followed the corridor to the front exit of the hospital and spotted Lee outside, running toward the car park. I set off in pursuit, ignoring the passing cars and pedestrians as I hurried toward him.

Lee kept running, past the car park and toward an empty, secluded road nearby. He'd opened the rear passenger door to a large black four-wheel drive car when I grabbed him, slammed his head into the roof of the car, and shoved him to the ground. The driver side door opened before I could continue the assault and a large bald man got out, ready to protect his paycheck.

I kicked the open rear door into the bodyguard, forcing him to move aside, and then hit him in the jaw with my fist wrapped in compressed air. It was the same trick I'd used against Achilles when he'd attacked me and Jenny, and it had rocked the gargoyle. It lifted the human bodyguard off his feet, spinning him in the air and dumping him back on the ground, unconscious and no longer an issue.

I spun back on Lee who had watched the exchange. There was real fear in his eyes now, and it took a moment for me to realize that he was staring at the white glyphs on my arm. "What are you?" he managed.

I grabbed him by his jacket collar, lifted him off the ground, and threw him at the car. He landed on the bonnet and almost skidded off, but I grabbed his leg and pulled him back toward me, punching him in the solar plexus as he got closer. Lee dropped to his knees on the concrete, sucking in a large amount of air. I grabbed his head in both hands and forced him to look at me. "What did you do?"

"It wasn't meant to be like that," he said.

I pulled him upright and punched him in the solar plexus again, allowing him to fall back to the ground. "What did you do?" I repeated.

Without warning a knife appeared in Lee's hand. He tried to stab at the top of my thighs, aiming for an artery. I kicked his arm away, grabbing it before he could swipe once more, locking the joint at the elbow. I was about to ask him again, but a rage, cold and calculating, swept through me. Instead, I smashed my forearm into his elbow.

I let Lee fall to the ground, screaming in pain, clutching his useless limb. I was about to rain down kicks on him when Lyn stepped in front of me.

"Don't do this," she pleaded.

"He's involved with what happened to Holly," I told her. "He will tell me what he did. Or I'll cripple him."

Lyn nodded and knelt next to her youngest son. "What did you do, Lee?"

"What I had to," he spat. "He humiliated me." Lee pushed his mum away and forced himself back to his feet, his movements jerky. "After you beat me in that fight, I wanted to hurt you. I got my guys to show your picture around, see if there were any takers. And one person bit. Offered me half a mil for information on you. So I gave it.

"Then a few days ago he called again, asked where you might take someone you wanted to hide. So I gave them Holly's address. She needed to be taught a lesson not to go against her family. They said that they wouldn't hurt her, just scare her a little."

A red haze fell over me, but before I could get to Lee, Lyn had punched him in the jaw, snapping his head around. It was the punch of a professional boxer, and if she'd followed up with another, they probably would have given her a TKO, but she backed off and let Lee get to his feet once more. "How dare you," Lyn snapped, her face red with fury. "You endangered your own sister, for what? Petty vengeance?"

"He humiliated me. Beat me like a fucking dog. I couldn't let that slide. When that fucking monster, Achilles, arrived at the warehouse, he made it look good. Gave me a bit of a kicking, and then took me down to the lockers to wait until he left. The deal was that he'd not hurt Holly, but she fought them."

Lyn shook her head sadly. "Where are the men who did this?"

Lee shrugged, the tiny movement of his arm causing him to cry out in pain once again. "Don't know. I didn't know she was going to get all fucking heroic."

Lyn looked back at me, her eyes red and saddened. "My son is a thug and a bully. I look into his eyes and see nothing but violence and hate there. I'd hoped over time he would change. But he won't."

I tried to interrupt, but she raised a hand to silence me before continuing. "He knows where those people are." She looked back at Lee who was dabbing the split lip his mum had given him. "I beg you not to kill him. But get that information."

She stepped aside, giving me a clear path at Lee, whose eyes widened in terror as I stalked toward him.

"No, Mum, I didn't mean for her to get hurt," he pleaded.

"It's too late, Lee," Lyn said and she walked away.

When we were alone, I whispered in Lee's ear, "I'm going to make you tell me what I want to know. And it's going to hurt." I grabbed his broken arm and twisted, increasing my grip on it, causing him to scream out. "I know Mars Warfare is behind all of this," I whispered to him. "But I'm going to hurt you like they hurt Holly."

I squeezed on his broken arm a little harder, drawing a concerned look from a young woman as she got out of her car nearby
and hurried off to the hospital. Orange glyphs came to life and I
soon smelled burning flesh as I began to cook Lee's arm.

Lee screamed, raw and guttural.

I considered hurting him further, but I glanced over and
found that Dani had joined Lyn, so I pushed him back against the
car and left him there, whimpering. "I know where the people
who did this are," I told Lyn as Dani glared at Lee.

"Are you doing this alone?" Lyn asked.

I nodded. "I have to. This needs to be finished." I turned
back to Lee. "If I ever see you again, I'll kill you."

Lyn moved to kneel beside her son and kissed him tenderly
on the cheek. "You betrayed your sister."

"No," Lee shouted. "No, she wasn't meant to get hurt. Why
won't you listen?"

Lyn ignored him. "You have twenty-four hours to leave the
country. That's as long as I can give you before I tell your father
about your involvement. After that you're a dead man." Lyn
walked off and Dani launched her foot between Lee's legs, as if
trying to kick him into space.

Lee screamed and crumpled to the ground, holding himself
as best he could, and Dani followed up with a second kick. A
third would have followed if I hadn't grabbed her, dragging her
away. "You bastard," she screamed at Lee, trying to get away from
me and finish her assault.

"Come on, Dani, we've got a lot to do," I said as we followed
Lyn back to the hospital, Lee's cries following behind us, lost on
a sudden gale of wind.

CHAPTER 32

My mobile rang before I'd even made it back to the hospital.

"I got you a meeting with the people who hired me to steal the *Iliad* for them," Francis said.

I rubbed my eyes. "I don't need them now—I know who did all of this. I'm going to go to Mars Warfare."

"Nate, going anywhere near their building will get you shot or taken, probably both. As much as I know you want revenge, doing anything without the facts and without some serious planning will lead to your death. And then what was the point of Holly getting hurt, and it you being dead won't help Dani stay safe."

I sighed; he was right. It wasn't just about me and my need for vengeance. "Okay, but if this is a trap..."

"It doesn't feel like one. But if these people can help increase your chances, you'd be insane to ignore it."

"Yeah, you're right. One last thing, they said they were there ten years ago."

A dozen bodies littered the tiled floor; I'd been responsible for most of them. Blood saturated my clothes as alarms sounded all around me. It was all going to hell, but at least people had gotten out.

I dove aside as semiautomatic fire ripped through the air. I turned to tell people to run, to leave me to fight, as more soldiers appeared before me. A sheet of hardened air protected them from the soldiers' weapons, but it wouldn't last forever.

As the bullets finally ceased and the last person escaped from view, I stood and walked out into the center of the hallway. Six men aimed their MP5s at me, but no one pulled the trigger.

"If you want me, you'd best come get me," I said, a sword of fire appearing in one hand.

"What an excellent idea," a man replied as his armed guard parted, allowing me to the view the man I'd been wanting to kill for centuries.

"Nate," Francis asked, clearly concerned. "You okay?"

I nodded slightly, then realized he couldn't see me. If I hadn't wanted to see the book buyer before then, that little piece of info and the memory that followed made it a necessity. "Yeah, I'm good. Tell Jerry I'll meet him out front in twenty."

"Are you going to say bye to Holly?" Dani asked once I'd ended the call and put my phone back in my pocket.

I nodded and explained what was happening.

"I want to come with you," she said.

"You're going to stay with Francis. I just need to talk to some people. Who, based on the past few days, will probably want me dead."

"Don't joke about that," Dani said.

I folded my arms around Dani, holding her against me. "I'll be fine. It's you I need to keep safe. And there's not much safer than Francis'."

Dani nodded, her head striking my chest. "Can I come with you? To see Holly, I mean."

We walked toward the lift without a word. I had no intention of running up the stairs again, so we waited in silence as the lift slowly made its way down to us.

"By the way, nice kick," I said once we were inside the steel box and moving upward at a snail's pace.

Dani's smile was easy to see in the reflection of the polished metal. "I was hoping they'd come out his mouth."

"At least he won't be able to sit down for a few weeks. And he won't forget you in a hurry."

"If I see him again, I've got a whole other foot just waiting for a shot."

"He'll run abroad," I said. "You'll never see him again. And if you do, take a run up next time and twist with your hips as you catch him."

Dani's smile broke into a giggle, which died down the second the lift doors opened. It was as if someone had hit the stop button on a song; one second there was sound, and the next— nothing.

I walked to the nearest public bathroom to wash Lee's blood off my hands before we made our way to the intensive care ward. We caught Mark just leaving Holly's room. Lyn had arrived back well before us, thanks to Francis' call, and I could see her sitting at her daughter's bedside, stroking her hand. "You got a minute?" Mark asked.

I got the impression that he wasn't asking, since he didn't even wait for an answer, but just walked off toward one of two waiting rooms on the floor. I decided it best to follow him without comment.

He waited until we were both inside, and then he closed the door, turning the small catch to lock it. For the briefest of moments, I wasn't sure if Mark was going to try and finish what he'd wanted to do earlier in the day. I really hoped not, because there was no way in hell he was going to pin me up against the wall by my throat again.

Mark placed his head against the door and took a deep breath. I readied myself for a fight. "How long did my wife give Lee to run before I go after him?" he asked

The question took me by surprise, something he must have noticed. "I know my wife," he said. "Lee and you run off down the corridor, and then Lyn brushes off my questions. She wouldn't have done that unless she hadn't thought of a good lie."

As much as I liked Lyn, I held no allegiance to her son. "Twenty-four hours."

Mark nodded as if that was what he'd expected. "So he really was behind it all."

"Not all of it. But he did get the people who hurt Holly involved. It was some sort of revenge for what I did to him."

That got Mark's attention. "What did you do to him?"

I explained what had happened in the alley all those weeks ago. It felt like I was talking about something that had happened in another lifetime. When I finished Mark remained silent, staring at his hands.

"I'd hoped giving him responsibility would help," he said eventually. "Twenty-four hours. If that's what he was told I'll honor it."

I couldn't help myself. "And then what?"

"Lee will be in Ireland within the next few hours. He'll spend just enough time there to get a new ID, probably using my name to get it faster. We have family and friends there.

"When he's done, he'll fly to the States, probably Boston, and make a good show of meeting everyone over there who knows the family. Then he'll use his secret ID, the clean one he's had for years, and vanish. He'll continue moving across America until he arrives in California."

I was astonished that Mark had already considered the possibility of Lee running away. "How do you know he'll do any of that?"

"I always knew Lee would fuck up at some point. I'd hoped this move would be done with my blessing, to escape the law, or a rival gang, but I trained him to have a clean ID and always be ready to leave in a hurry.

"California will be his destination, because it's big enough that he can get lost in it, and very few people there know him. It's a fresh start. Besides, it's the opposite end of the country from where he thinks I'll expect him to go. My son is many things, but his unpredictability is, unfortunately, utterly predictable."

"So what will you do?"

"I'll leave it twenty-four hours and then start to put feelers out. Let everyone know that anyone who meets Lee and doesn't let me know will have to deal with me. None of the big families in the States, the Italians or Irish, will want to work with him. They need London for importing and exporting—they wouldn't be too happy if I started interrupting their cash flow. If Lee wants work, he'll have to go it alone, or join one of the less stable members of the criminal community."

"What if you find him?"

Mark glared at me, his eyes hard and cold. "He's responsible for my daughter being tortured within an inch of her life. Because of him, I lost six good men. If I find Lee, I'll kill him."

"Good," I said and noticed Mark tense a little. "Sorry, Mark. But after what he's done…"

"I know," he interrupted. "But if he dies, it'll be by *my* hand." The implied threat was obvious.

A knock on the door caused Mark to slowly turn away from me, as if unsure he was safe in doing so. He unlocked and opened the door, revealing Lyn. "Everything okay?" she asked and looked past Mark to me.

"Just chatting," Mark said and then left without another word.

To Lyn's credit, she didn't ask any more questions. But she did thank me for my help with everything that had happened and allowed me to go say my goodbyes to Holly by myself. I was grateful for it. I wasn't sure if either one of us would live long enough to see each other again.

After Jerry picked us up, the drive took mere minutes, even in the rapidly increasing London traffic. He pulled over in front of a small bookstore, Le Tre Donne. "The three women," I said to myself.

"Be careful," Dani told me as I got out of the large four-wheel-drive Volvo.

"I'll see you soon," I said and closed the door, wasting no time in making my way to the bookshop's front door. A small bell above the door chimed as it opened. I stepped inside, but didn't see anyone in the immediate vicinity. After closing the door behind me, and noticing that Jerry had already left, I took a look around the shelves of books.

They were stacked from floor to ceiling, which was a good few feet above my head. A small metal stool sat beside one of the shelves, next to a moveable ladder, which allowed a person to get to the books out of reach.

Most of the books appeared old. Certainly the shop didn't cater to the usual reader who wanted the latest popular piece of fluff. There was philosophy, poetry, and some copies of Charles Dickens and Sir Arthur Conan Doyle that looked original. I removed a copy of *The Memoirs of Sherlock Holmes* and was about to look through it when a throat cleared behind me.

"You could just say hello," I said without turning around.

"My apologies, Nathan," a woman said.

I gently replaced the book and turned around to find a woman sitting on the stool I'd seen earlier. Her olive skin appeared flawless, presumably a testament to whatever anti-aging creams she used. Her dark hair was tied back into a ponytail, and she wore a green dress, which stopped just above the knee. But it was more than mere looks; there was a radiance about her that was captivating. I couldn't put my finger on it, but although she only appeared to be in her thirties, something told me that she was wasn't human, and that she was *a lot* older than she looked.

I offered my hand, which she took and shook gently. "And you are?" I asked.

"Oh, now where's the fun in just telling you." She smiled and glanced behind me at the book I'd been looking at. "That contains 'The Final Problem,' the one where Sherlock was meant to die fighting his nemesis, Moriarty. Sherlock's death didn't last long though. He was too popular."

"Is this to be a lesson in classical literature, then?"

She smiled and ignored my question. "Let's go into the back room, we can talk freely without concern for interruption." She stood and walked off to the rear of the deceptively long shop, where she opened a light-blue door leading to a lengthy corridor.

Beneath a window at the far end, two more women sat playing cards. Both had light-brown hair with olive skin, and they could have passed for mother and daughter. The younger of the two looked about the same age as Dani. In fact, she looked a lot like Dani in almost every respect. She glanced up at me and appeared incredibly sad, her eyes hiding a lifetime of pain. A forced smile broke her lips. The second woman placed a loving hand on her shoulder and whispered something. The younger girl nodded and went back to her card game. The woman with me ignored them both, opened a second door, and stepped inside. I joined her a second later and was utterly astounded by what I saw.

Compared to the drab hallway outside, the room beyond was a haven of tranquil beauty. Indoor water fountains sat around the room, all in various guises. Some were small mountains, where the water trickled through carved rock. Another depicted several large stone carp, water moving across them in a display that probably took the designer years to perfect.

"They're beautiful aren't they?" the woman said as she stood by a third fountain—a miniature representation of a Japanese garden. The water moved under a small bridge and passed several cherry blossom trees.

She motioned for me to take a seat on one of chairs dotted around the room. Each one was made of black leather and looked about as comfortable as you could make a chair. I sat down, and they felt as good as they looked.

The woman sat on the chair next to mine, barely a finger's width between us, and stared at me intently. "Why are you here?" she asked.

"You had Francis steal a copy of the *Iliad*. I need to know why."

She moved back in the chair. "Let's be honest here. Because without honesty you'll discover nothing. Francis didn't steal anything, you did."

I'd assumed that Francis had already told her about my involvement. "Yes, I stole the book. I want to know why you wanted it in the first place. I want to know what ties the *Iliad*, King Priam, and Mars Warfare together, because I know they're linked, I just can't quite put my finger on how."

"I could tell you I'm a collector, or that it had been stolen from me, but as I want you to be honest, I guess I should be too. I wanted that book, because I want to destroy it."

"You spent two hundred and fifty grand to get a book, just so you could destroy it?" I couldn't believe my ears. "I thought you were being honest."

"Oh, I am, Nathan, very honest. After receiving the book and verifying that it was the one I wanted, I incinerated it. I smiled the whole time too; it was very cathartic."

That wasn't the answer I'd hoped for. I'd wanted to examine the book to get answers, to figure out why it was worth so much. And why people were willing to kill for it. Instead, it felt like the bottom had fallen out of my hopes.

Before I could gather my thoughts, she asked. "Do you have a nemesis? Like Holmes?"

I stood; I'd hoped this woman could have answered my questions, could have given me the information I needed to stop Mars Warfare. Instead, she'd told me nothing of value. "I don't have time for this."

The woman moved like a snake, grabbing my hand. "Sit, you might learn something."

I stood for another few seconds and thought about how much effort it had taken to get this meeting in the first place. If the crazy lady beside me could answer my questions, my journey would be worth it. So I did as she asked.

The woman nodded and removed her hand, before standing and wandering around the room. "The *Iliad*," she said. "The story of Troy." She smiled again when she saw the surprise on my face. "That's why you're here, yes? To learn why everything that's been happening is linked to a book that's about a five-thousand-year-old war?"

"Did Francis tell you that?" I asked.

She tapped the side of her nose and continued as if I'd never spoken. It was a trait in her that I was beginning to find annoying. "The version that almost everyone knows is based on Homer's *Iliad* and *Odyssey*, but everyone is wrong." She opened the drawer of a side table and pulled out a book, one identical to the volume I'd stolen. "This is now the only remaining copy of the original *Iliad*. We keep this one, because one day people should know what really happened all those years ago, and why so many people had to die for one man's insane vision."

"You've lost me."

The woman put the book back on the table and re-took her seat next to me. "The story of Troy, as you and pretty much everyone else knows it, is that Paris and Helen eloped, drawing the anger of Agamemnon and his brother, who, with a massive Greek army, raced to Troy to get revenge. Thus starting a decade-long war. A war that only ended with the use of a giant wooden horse containing hidden Greek soldiers, who at night massacred the sleeping inhabitants of the city. Sound about right?"

I nodded. "You've missed a fair bit, but that's the backbone, yeah."

"Hundreds of years after the war, Homer wrote the *Iliad* and the *Odyssey*, two epic poems, retelling the story of the Trojan War and its immediate aftermath. What you may not know is that there are in fact eight books telling the events of the Trojan War. However, the other six were written by different authors."

"So why not destroy them too?" I asked.

"Because they don't exist anymore," she said with a smile. "The six other books are lost to the annals of time. But the Homer epics were too popular, and removing them from circulation would have been impossible. But they contained something more dangerous than mere tales. Information.

"You see, Homer wrote the stories with help. He thought he was writing fantastical tales based on fact, but whoever helped him—and we don't know who it was—told him the exact details of why the war took place and what really happened.

"Over the centuries, Avalon realized what the books contained and went about getting them removed from circulation. Peisistratus, a Greek tyrant during the sixth century B.C., was charged with this task. He changed the stories, outwardly saying that he wished for them to be more consistently in line with one another, but in reality he was changing the story to omit anything that Avalon wanted to be censored. That is why copies such as the one you stole are so rare. They were mostly destroyed thousands of years ago."

"So these books, poems, contain the entirety of what happened at Troy. And you, along with Avalon, don't want that information getting out?" Her mention of Avalon had linked her to Jenny, and thus linked her to Mars Warfare. It finally felt like I was getting somewhere.

"Avalon stopped caring a millennia ago, when they believed every original copy was either in safe hands or destroyed."

"So what really happened in Troy? And how does that relate to what's happening now?"

The woman got up and rang a small brass bell that sat on a nearby table. A young girl came through the doors seconds later. She was one of the two I'd seen at the end of the corridor outside. "Can you fetch us some tea, please."

The young girl glanced over at me, and her eyes held a sadness that made my heart ache. Then she vanished. "Do you recognize her?" the woman asked.

I shook my head. "Should I?"

The woman ignored me yet again and waited for the girl to come back with the tea. When she returned, she carried a large tray containing a red teapot decorated with pink lotus flowers and two small bowls that matched the pot. The woman helped the girl set everything on the table. Then the girl turned back, giving me a final sorrowful glance, before leaving the room.

"She knows me," I said to the woman. "Is she your daughter?"

The woman poured some tea into each of the bowls and passed me one. The fragrance was intoxicating. "Troy first, questions later."

I motioned for her to continue as I blew on the steaming-hot liquid.

The woman nodded and sipped her tea before beginning. "In the years building up to the war, King Priam was one of the most powerful men in the known world. Troy was rich and bountiful, and Priam enjoyed showing that wealth off at every occasion.

"Another thing he enjoyed showing off was his daughter, Cassandra. In the story as you know it, she's cursed by the god Apollo with visions of the future that no one believes. But in reality, King Priam believed every word. He would get her to tell him every morning what he should expect of the day. And then at parties, he would drag her out to give the guests something to talk about." The woman looked suddenly weary and there was real emotion in her voice as she spoke.

"So she wasn't cursed then?" I asked and took a sip of tea..

She shook her head. "Not that I'm aware of. Cassandra's mother was from a very special bloodline and passed the gift of foretelling on to her daughter." She drank her own tea and poured herself and me some more. "Priam continued to show off the power wielded by his own flesh and blood, for years. Cassandra was paraded about, telling fortunes until she could barely stand from the visions. And then one day Agamemnon was present, and King Priam decided to give the Mycanae king his own private reading, away from the ears of his other guests.

"Cassandra was fourteen at the time, still a child in today's eyes. But back then, old enough for many to have asked Priam for his daughter's hand. Something he had always refused. Agamemnon was not so easily dissuaded, and after the vision, Cassandra was all he wanted."

"What did she see?" I asked.

"Death, fire. The destruction of Troy at Agamemnon's hands, King Priam dead on the steps of the city. Psychics cannot lie, and Priam was furious with what he'd heard. He removed Cassandra back to her room at once, ending the party in a violent temper. And, all the while, Agamemnon had already begun to plan and plot. He wanted the girl for his own, but he couldn't just invade, or attack. It would be suicide. So he thought of a way to get what he wanted, something that took time. It also allowed him to establish why Cassandra was so powerful."

"And the answer was?"

"She was one in a million. Her abilities far exceeded those of a normal psychic. One of her power comes along rarely, but it does happen. Agamemnon discovered this, and so he went to war.

"He arranged for Helen to seduce Paris. He knew full well that Helen was hard to resist, and that Paris was never one to turn away a beautiful lady, no matter who she was married to. And it worked even better than he'd hoped, when Paris and Helen actually fell in love. The young idiots gave Agamemnon the perfect excuse to go to war."

"Why didn't Priam know what was going on?" I asked. "I mean, his daughter was a powerful psychic."

"After Agamemnon, he never asked for another vision and barred anyone else from hearing them under pain of death. Cassandra saw everything that was about to happen; the horse, the death of her brother Hector, but no one was allowed to hear it. Troy was destroyed because of King Priam's foolish pride."

"So Troy *was* still destroyed?"

The woman nodded. "Burned to the ground, its people raped and murdered and its contents pillaged until there was nothing left to give. Even Cassandra didn't escape the Greeks' fury. She was found by Agamemnon as Ajax the Lesser raped her on the steps of Athena's temple." An expression of utter loathing washed over her face. "The story suggests that Ajax the Lesser was eventually killed by Athena and Poseidon for this act. That isn't what happened. Agamemnon, in a rage, had him skinned alive. He conjured the tale of the gods' vengeance as a way of keeping his men in line."

"So, Agamemnon got what he wanted, a powerful psychic. That doesn't explain how it links to what's happening now."

"That's because I haven't gotten there yet," she snapped. "The voyage back to Mycenae was long and difficult. Agamemnon's own daughter died on the trip—she'd stowed away when they'd first set sail and had served as a nurse during the war. But when they finally reached home, Agamemnon's wife, Clytemnestra, hated that not only had her daughter died during her husband's war, but that he'd brought home a young, beautiful woman to be by his side always.

"Clytemnestra had already begun an affair with her husband's cousin and was trying to figure out how to remove Agamemnon from power. The idea of having a psychic around didn't go over well. Although Agamemnon was human, Clytemnestra was a sorcerer. Not a particularly good one—in fact, if anything she'd have been utterly average—but she was determined and eventually figured out a way to turn Cassandra to her advantage. So she arranged her husband's murder and set her plan into motion."

"And that plan was?" I asked.

The woman smiled slightly, obviously enjoying my need for information. "She realized there were Blood magic spells that, when used on a psychic, had interesting results. So she sacrificed some of her people and placed a Blood magic curse on Cassandra. With enough death, even an average user of magic can perform incredible spells, and she had more than enough.

"Unfortunately, her remaining children, both sorcerers themselves, hated their mother for what she'd done to their father and murdered Clytemnestra and her lover. But Electra found the dozens of scrolls left behind and deduced what her mother had been trying to do. Clytemnestra was breaking one of the rules of magic—she was trying to re-create the Fates."

It was possible that my jaw dropped open—it's hard to remember, as my brain had been turned to a kind of mush by the news. "As in, the three Fates of Greek mythology?"

The woman nodded. "Clytemnestra would have needed to wait years for Cassandra to have a child, and then a grandchild. But she was a sorcerer, so it wasn't as if she didn't have the time. Or would have, if not for her murder. But the plan was already set in motion. Except it didn't take a few years; it took a few thousand before three of the same bloodline were found who were not only psychic but capable of surviving the Blood magic ritual."

"If you know about Blood magic, can you tell me how I'm meant to rid myself of whatever was done to me." My mind raced and I barely noticed the door opening, as both the girl and woman from outside walked into the room and stopped. I looked up and immediately recognized one of them. Age-wise, she sat comfortably between the other two, maybe in her late twenties or early thirties. "You were at the tube station in Whitechapel," I said. "You brushed past me."

She nodded. "I needed to touch your hand, just enough to start the ball rolling. My name's Grace."

"*You're* the Fates," I said.

"My name is Cassandra of Troy," the woman who had been telling me the story said. "And you..."

Cassandra walked toward me and placed one slender hand on my cheek. "You need to remember who you are."

CHAPTER **33**

Ten Years Ago.

"**Y**ou should just kill him and be done with it," a man said. His voice held the hint of fear in it. I was curious who was speaking, but I didn't want to open my eyes and give away that I wasn't unconscious anymore.

"That's not your decision though, is it?" a second man commanded. His tone made it clear that he wasn't used to people refusing his order.

"He's dangerous," the first man exclaimed. "You're being personal."

There was a noise of flesh striking flesh and a grunt of pain. "Do not argue with me," the second man said. "He's tied to a table, with runes inscribed into it. Nathan Garrett is at my mercy. And I need to know what he discovered. After that, I intend to rend the flesh from his bones. Now leave."

There were footsteps on the tiled floor, and a gust of air when a door was open, and then silence.

Unfortunately, it didn't last. "You can open your eyes; I know you're awake," the second man said.

I did as was asked and stared at the man who stood by my feet. He hadn't changed a day since I'd last seen him; in fact, no matter how many times I'd seen him, he never changed. "Hello, Mordred," I said. "You should really listen to your friend."

"*Employee,*" *he corrected with a sigh.* "*He might want to think of himself as a powerful and dangerous man, but he's nothing but a bloody fool. He wants to call himself Achilles, can you believe that? Achilles? Proud, arrogant asshole. But he's a good bullet sponge, and does as he's told, for the most part. Gargoyles are rare, so if it doesn't work out I can always sell him for parts.*"

"*You want to know where the Fates are, I assume.*"

"*I'm going to rip the information out of your head. And then find out who you told about them. Achilles is scared that some friends of yours will come rushing through the front door to try and find you. But you didn't tell anyone, did you? You don't trust too many people these days, that's what I heard.*"

I turned my head to look at the thick rope holding me against the table. "*The rope's a little old school, isn't it?*"

"*I didn't exactly have time to do anything else, and besides the runes will stop you from trying to kill me.*" *He picked up a large bowl and placed his hand inside, drawing it out a second later and flicking the liquid it contained at me.*

A deep, white, rage built inside me. "*A sacrifice,*" *I said as Mordred flicked more warm blood at me.*

"*A secretary from upstairs—made the mistake of saying hello to me in the lift. Well, she won't be doing that again, although I understand some people upstairs are pissed off. She was a good secretary.*" *He upended the bowl over me, drenching me in sticky redness.*

"*I will kill you,*" *I said.*

"*I'm going to lobotomize you, and then I'm going to torture you to death. It'll be good. For me anyway, not so much for you.*"

I glanced over to the large window behind my captor. "*How high up are we?*"

ABOUT THE AUTHOR

 Steve McHugh was born in Mexbrough, South Yorkshire, but grew up in Southampton, Hampshire, where he now lives with his wife and three young daughters. While at school, Steve discovered a love for history and mythology, along with the beginnings of a passion for writing, which despite of—or maybe because of—numerous sucky jobs, never went away. When he's not writing or spending time with his kids, Steve enjoys watching movies, reading books and comics, and playing video games. *Crimes Against Magic* is his first novel, and the first book in the Hellequin Chronicles.

Mordred looked at the window and back, a smile plastered to his face. "That's your escape plan? Jump through a window?"

I shook my head. "You're going to let me go."

Mordred laughed so hard, he had to put one hand on the nearest wall to steady himself. "And why would I do that?"

"Because killing me like this nets you nothing. You've wanted me dead for over a thousand years. I know you. I know how your twisted little mind works. You want to beat me, to look me directly in the eyes and know you're my better."

Mordred stopped laughing. "I'll live with just knowing you're dead, and I'm not." He raised his hands above me and began to chant as black glyphs appeared on his palms and arms.

Pain racked my body, and I screamed, desperate to break free, to stop the barrage of torture that was inflicted. Then suddenly, the agony stopped.

Mordred stared down at me. "I've done enough that in about ten minutes you'll forget your own name. I want to see that fear of not knowing what's happening before I crack your mind like a walnut. Then, when I'm finished, I'll untie you and gut you like a fish."

"Mordred," I whispered. "I'll always be better than you."

His rage exploded and he dove for me, his hands around my throat, choking the life from me as he screamed obscenities in my face. Part of my mind panicked, but the part that knew what I was doing smiled. And I kept that smile on my face as Mordred's turned bright red with hatred.

"I fucking hate you," he screamed.

"And I know you." I positioned the blade of the sword cane I'd removed from Mordred's belt to cut through the rope. I'd almost succumbed to the darkness, when the rope gave way and a surge of magic rocked through me.

His shock that one of my hands was free lasted about two seconds before a sledgehammer of air wrapped around my fist slammed into his temple. He rocked back and I kicked him off me, using the brief moment to cut the other rope and roll off the table.

"I've always been better than you," I said and forced every ounce of strength into a blast of air that would have flipped a truck. It hit Mordred in the chest and drove him back and through the window, accompanied by an explosion of noise as the thick glass shattered.

I wasn't going to have long before my memories faded. I grabbed the sheath for Mordred's sword cane, which had clattered to the ground when he'd left the building, and replaced the sword inside. It wasn't much of a weapon, but it might still come in handy. I took my gun from a nearby table and looked out the window. The river Thames was just below me, maybe two hundred feet. A survivable distance, so long as my fading memories didn't take my magic with them.

The decision was made for me when armed guards burst into the room. I jumped out into the abyss, falling rapidly until my air magic slowed my descent and I hit the water as if I'd jumped from only a few feet above it.

I part swam, part drifted in the strong current, allowing it to take me as far as I dared. The whole time everything became increasingly difficult to remember. When I was far enough from danger, I forced myself to swim to one side of the river, using an old metal ladder to climb up and into an abandoned parking lot for a derelict warehouse.

I took one last look at the deep, dark water. I needed shelter; Mordred was not easily killed, and fighting him in the state I was in would not end well for me. I found an old black biro pen on the ground and some paper. The pen was broken and the paper torn and damp, but it allowed me to write my name before I put the paper into my *pocket and dashed into the building. A few seconds later darkness took my mind.*

I opened my eyes to find myself in the same room I'd been in before my brain had gone nuts, a feeling I was becoming depressingly familiar with. I looked around and noticed Cassandra sitting alone by one of the many water features. "What just happened to me?"

"My daughter, granddaughter, and I are Fates. Each of us holds a mastery over the past, present, or future. As the oldest of us, mine is the past. I unlocked one of your memories, or at least allowed it to become clearer."

"I fought Mordred. I escaped from him and that asshole Achilles." I shook my head in a futile attempt to clear it. "What do you want from me? And what did your daughter mean when she said she touched me to get things rolling?" I searched the room for the two other Fates. "Where are they anyway?"

"Gone outside. It's easier if I explain everything." She picked up a bottle of water from the table and offered it to me. "You should drink. Visions can have some tiring effects on people."

I took a long drink of the cool water. "Now, please explain."

"The Fates are not merely powerful psychics. As I said, we have mastery over a person's past, present, and future. Between the three of us, we can see far into the past or future of someone we touch. My daughter sees the present, but doesn't need contact with a person to have a vision. She has flashes of what is happening now, usually within a few months before or after the current date. We'd wondered what had happened to you since you rescued us and had tried to find you, but with little success. A few months ago my daughter had a vision of you in Whitechapel and realized that your memories had been blocked.

"A plan was put into motion to help you. We knew where you'd be and what day, so it was easy for my daughter to bump into you and touch your hand. That small contact started bleeding your blocked experiences into you."

"So the reason I started knowing how to kill people was because of that touch?"

Cassandra nodded. "Grace used a lot of power to do that. She passed out in the car and didn't wake for three days."

"What else did you do?"

"Nothing," she said. "We knew that your friend's brother would betray you and involve our old captors. That you, in turn, would meet Jenny, and that she would spark your memories to come through."

"How did she do that?"

"My daughter, Grace, was responsible for that, as well. Allowing your experiences to trickle through into your conscious meant that any further contact with a psychic would widen the hole. Jenny is very powerful. Her touch was all that was needed to accelerate the flow of memories."

"So eventually I'll remember everything?"

"Sort of," Cassandra said and raised her hands to subdue my next comment. "They will continue to come out, but you will have no frame of reference for them. You won't be able to put them in chronological order, or even distinguish actual memories from dreams or fantasies you may have had. The only way to totally recover your memories is to have the Blood magic curse removed."

"And how do I do that?"

Cassandra looked nervous, almost as if she didn't want to answer my question. "There are two ways. The first is the most difficult—find the sorcerer who originally placed the curse, and have him remove it."

There was more chance of me landing on the moon than getting Mordred to remove the curse. "I think we can skip that one," I said.

"The other way is to have another Blood magic user remove it. This isn't always easy. If the user isn't powerful enough, it could jumble your existing memories up with the blocked ones and turn you into mindless husk."

"What aren't you telling me?"

Cassandra sighed and closed her eyes. "The first requires only the original caster of the curse. The second will require blood. Not necessarily human blood, I might add, but something must die for the curse to be removed."

"So to remove the curse, whoever does it may have to kill someone?" That wasn't even close to being an option.

"Not necessarily," Cassandra argued. "If you can convince the person to use animals, then the spell to remove the curse may not be as powerful, but it should get the job done."

"So, to get my memories back, I need to find a blood mage. Which Mars Warfare probably has in spades."

Cassandra nodded.

"And then what? Why did you do this for me? What do you want out of it?"

She didn't speak for some time, and when she did her words were spoken softly, a hint of pleading behind them. "For a decade we have run from place to place, hiding who we are in an effort to stay one step ahead of the world we left behind. We are tired of running, we like living here, we like our lives, and we like ridding the world of the knowledge of how to create more Fates. We need your help. We need you to stop those people from finding us. But to do that, you need to be whole again."

"You *want* me to get grabbed by Achilles and his psychotic friends?"

Cassandra hesitated and then nodded once. "We can't think of another way. And I know that what we ask is a lot, but Grace's visions say that you must give yourself over to these people."

A horrible thought occurred to me. "Did you know that Holly was going to get hurt?"

"You have to understand," she said. "The timeline is flexible—there are many versions of events that could unfold, and we don't always see what happens."

"Did. You. See?"

"Yes."

Anger bubbled to the surface. "You mean, telling me would have changed your precious path."

Cassandra met my gaze and never wavered. "Yes, it would have. Telling you what was going to happen would have gotten you and Holly killed. Those were the only alternatives—let her become injured or let you both die. Do you have any idea what it's like to know that if you try and stop something horrible, some unmentionable evil from happening, that it might make things worse?"

The fury that Cassandra put in her words took me aback. I couldn't imagine living with the knowledge that allowing a horror to take place was the better of two evils. "You should have told me," was all I could manage, my anger having vanished.

Cassandra's face softened. "No. We couldn't."

"So why tell me now? Why explain what I need to do."

"Because if you don't, we'll be dead within the week." Cassandra looked away and held a hand to her eyes, unwilling to let me see tears fall. "Achilles will find us, and he will rape and murder my daughter and granddaughter. He will do this in front of me, saving me till last. My daughter saw this, and at nearly three thousand years old, she still wept at what she knew would happen."

"But don't they need you alive? They want me to tell them where you are so they can take you back and go on controlling their own destiny."

"They do want us back, that's true. But for some reason the visions have changed; either we go free or we die. I don't know why that is."

"I can't just walk in there," I said. "They'll kill me and then Dani. And I won't let them take Dani."

Cassandra opened her mouth to speak, but a knock on the door changed her mind and she closed it. "You should go. My daughter says that your friends will need you."

"How…?" I started.

"The three of us are linked—what one sees, we all see if necessary. And you're needed back at Francis'."

I started to ask another question when my mobile rang. I hastily answered it. "Francis…"

"Nate," Laurel said, breathless and pained. "They came for her, Nate. They took Dani."

CHAPTER 34

The door to Francis' subway home was destroyed. Pieces of it hung uselessly from its hinges. It could no more stop a man than a light breeze. I ran past it and down the steep staircase, dread and fear building up inside me, threatening to stop my legs from moving lest I see something I wished to forget.

"Francis," I called out as I reached the bloodstained platform. Smears of red adorned the walls and floor, some ending at the side of the platform. I stood still and took in everything around me: at least two bodies lay on the disused train tracks, both of them in the same uniforms as those who worked with Achilles— one had lost an arm, the other two bullet holes in his head. Two more lay farther up the track, just inside the darkness that signified the vampires' home. Probably vampires. Damn it.

"Francis," I shouted once more, this time with an edge to my voice, after stepping into his work area, which now resembled a bomb blast. Anything that hadn't been nailed down covered the floor, most of it broken, none of it replaceable.

"Nate," a female voice called out from Francis' office.

I found Laurel kneeling on the floor, covered in blood; Jerry lay next to her, his head in her lap, his eyes looking up at the ceiling as fear wracked his face. One arm, from just below the elbow, was missing, leaving jagged lumps of bare flesh. A belt had been wrapped around his bicep, stopping the loss of more blood, but he needed a hospital. And soon.

"Laurel," I said, and she looked up at me, her blood-soaked face unable to hide the anguish it showed. "He needs a hospital." She shook her head. "He won't make it," she said. "I've given him something for the pain, but he won't let me make him into a vampire."

"I can't live forever," Jerry said weakly. "Not even for the woman I love."

"I cannot let you die," Laurel yelled at Jerry, who raised his good hand and placed it in her's, squeezing gently. "Please, let me…"

Jerry shook his head, the movement small and barely noticeable, before looking up at me. "They took Dani," he said in between coughs. "We had no chance. I brought her into the office to hide, but that damn stone fucker ripped my arm off."

"You should let Laurel turn you, Jerry," I said. "It's got to be better than dying like this."

"What if the power drives me mad? What if I kill innocent people?" He looked back at the Laurel. "You say this won't happen, that you'll help me, but we both know there's no way of predicting how I'll react."

"I'll make sure it doesn't happen," she pleaded before looking up at me. "Make him agree." Her words came out angry, hurt, but as much as she wanted Jerry to be with her, she would not go against his wishes. But that didn't stop her fighting him until he changed his mind.

"Why don't you inject him with vampire blood?" I suggested.

Laurel shook her head. "He's already had it once, a few years ago. Doing it again would heal his wounds, but drive him insane."

I tried to think of a way I could possibly help. There had to be something I could do. "If you do this, if you become a vampire," I started. "I'll make sure you never hurt an innocent."

"How?" he asked.

"Because if you do, I'll kill you," I said. The words came easily and there was no doubt in my mind that I'd follow through if I had to. "Let her save your life."

Jerry stared at me for a heartbeat. "I'll hold you to that."

I stood. "Now let Laurel save your damn life." Laurel's relief was almost palpable.

"Where's Francis?" I asked her.

"Hospital room," she said and I left before she could start turning him, closing the office door behind me and running toward Francis.

I found him sitting beside the obviously dead Robert. The mute man was missing part of his chest. "I'm sorry," I said.

"He fought the gargoyle. But apparently even werewolves can't survive having their heart punched out of their chest."

So, if werewolves and vampires couldn't stop these guys, what hope did I think I actually had? As the question settled inside me another formed. What choice did I have? "They took Dani." The answer to my own question was easy. None.

Francis nodded. "We were out matched. They came during the morning when the vampires were sleeping. Hell, *I* was sleeping until it was too late. How's Jerry?"

"Laurel's turning him now," I said and covered Robert's body with a sheet from the floor. "Where are your vampires?"

Francis didn't bother to hide his shock. "He agreed? And the vampires are resting; it is still daylight out after all. I don't need any more angry and tired vampires wanting revenge."

I told Francis what I'd said to Jerry.

Francis raised an eyebrow. "Did you mean it?"

I nodded. "Of course."

"My vampires are dealing with the removal of bodies. We managed to kill a few of the attackers before they got away." There was an uncomfortable silence between us for what felt like an eternity. "You've changed, Nate," Francis said. "You never would have said that before. Whoever you used to be, it sounds like he was capable of a lot." He pointed to a small MP3 player on the floor. "They left you a message."

I turned on the player and selected track one, turning up the loud speaker. The voice was tinny and occasionally crackled, but it was easy to make out the words. "We have Dani and Samantha. They are both safe, for the moment. However, Jenny is now surplus to requirements. You have twelve hours to arrive, unarmed, at Mars Warfare, and we let her go. Fail, and she dies. I'll send you her body parts in the mail to prove that her death was neither quick nor pleasant. There will probably be film too…I like to document these things." Then the audio went dead.

Neither of us said anything for an age, and I started to walk away, lost in thought. Eventually, Francis broke the silence, "Do you have a plan, Nate?" he called after me.

I turned back to my friend. "I'm going to give myself up."

A lot of shouting had followed my announcement, even more so than when Francis had discovered I was going to blow up his car. I tried to explain that giving myself up was the only way to get my memories back and get Dani, Jenny, and Samantha to safety, but Francis hadn't wanted to listen.

I told Francis about the Fates and what they'd told me; he sat and listened, but still came to the same conclusion: that it was too dangerous to go alone. He mentioned how a person's future wasn't set in stone, but I'd already made my mind up.

"Francis, they have Samantha, Jenny, and now Dani, something the mystery woman on the phone had gone to great lengths to ensure didn't happen. I can't let them die without trying."

Francis eventually came around to my way of thinking, but insisted I take a weapon. That, however, wouldn't do me any good—I was, after all, trying to give myself up peacefully. Besides, the message had been explicit in the no weapons rule, and after my use of Jerry the last time, I knew that they'd be expecting me to do something.

So, I found myself standing before the ominous Mars Warfare building in Canary Wharf, trying to get my breathing under control. I was scared. I had no idea what was going to happen to me, but I was pretty certain it wasn't going to be fun.

Francis had said I'd changed, and he was right, I had. I was really, really angry. Not only was I okay with that, but I wanted to unleash that anger on the first person who pissed me off. If given the chance, I was going to find those responsible and make them regret their life decisions.

I took one last deep breath and walked through the rotating front entrance and into the building. The armed guards glanced over, but didn't recognize me, so I continued uninterrupted to the large reception area, where a young woman sat behind her desk. She wore a black headset and was hastily talking to someone as she typed on the keyboard in front of her.

"My name's—" I started.

The woman placed her hand over the headset's mouthpiece. "I'm busy here; please wait for a minute."

Well, that was unexpected. And I hadn't come all the way here to be told to wait. Instead, I walked over to a set of six identical chairs arranged near one of the doors, where two men sat talking in hushed tones. I nodded to one of them, picked up a chair, and, with a helping hand from some air magic, threw it through the nearest window.

The sound it made was deafening as glass exploded outward, but there wasn't a single noise from anyone around me. Utter silence descended, probably only for a few heartbeats, but it felt much longer. "My name is Nathan Garrett," I said loudly. "Tell your boss I'm here." I took another chair and sat as the armed guards all rushed toward me, guns out and ready to use what they deemed as necessary force.

No one touched me; there was no violent struggle. They just stood, glaring and pointing semiautomatic weapons in my general direction as the receptionist made a dozen phone calls to let people know I was here.

The two men who'd been sitting near the now-broken window had seen the writing on the wall and found a reason why they shouldn't be anywhere near me.

I was quite impressed with how soon someone came to get me. I'd expected Achilles, or maybe even the boss himself, but it was a woman of about thirty years of age. She was athletically built, with straight, shoulder-length dark hair. A small scar sat on her left cheek, and another on her chin. She wore no jewelry that I could see, and the knuckles on one hand had been broken at some point in her life. It was a fighter's injury, and combined with the scars meant she was the company's security, assassin, or mindless muscle.

"Come this way, please," she said, gesturing back to the lifts.

I immediately recognized the voice as the mystery woman from the phone calls. "Are you okay?" I asked once we were alone in the nondescript lift.

"Mister Garrett, I am here to escort you to my lord, not to make conversation." She opened a panel beside the door and placed a key inside a small hole, turning it once. This opened a second panel with the higher floors' numbers on it.

"That would have come in handy when I broke into the place," I said, but received no reply, and we rode the rest of the journey in silence. I found the small security camera in the corner of the lift, and it took all of my restraint not to flip it off.

Once at our destination, we stepped out of the lift and I glanced out the windows next to me. The orange numbers beside the lift doors confirmed that we were thirty-eight floors up. Anyone with an office this high up must have done something good. Or, as was more likely, something really bad.

The mystery woman led me down more corridors and through a set of double doors. I was amazed at the lack of security. We stopped outside a door with a numeric keypad next to card reader. My escort swiped her card and entered the code before opening the door and leading me inside.

Without a word, she stood still as the door clicked closed behind us and a hiss of air sounded above us. "What's happening?" I asked.

"Decontamination. We're going into a lab." She said nothing more as the hissing stopped and the door in front unlocked, allowing her to push it open.

The sounds that escaped from the room beyond were, compared to the silence a moment ago, immense. There were a dozen people inside, all wearing white suits and latex gloves. A pair, a man and woman, were hunched over a table at the far end, looking through a microscope and jotting things into a book. Others were mixing materials together and chatting amongst themselves.

We walked through without stopping and into another room. This one contained more tables and chairs, but was empty of people and smelled of disinfectant. A large window sat behind the table, allowing people to watch what was going on without having to go through the rigmarole of the decontamination process. The glass was tinted slightly, but I knew that people were inside watching me.

"Stay here," the woman said and vanished through the only door.

I took the time to wander around the room, opening the many drawers and cupboards, but found nothing of interest. There was a hissing noise again, coming from behind the cupboards. It grew louder and I started to feel dizzy, my vision turning dark. I rushed to the door, but it was locked, and a stream of fire thrown at the window did no damage. I fought whatever drugs were being pumped into the room for as long as possible, but eventually my body succumbed and the darkness took me.

The second the gas had hit me, I knew I wasn't going to wake up in anything resembling a good place. People don't gas you so they can give you something nice in return.

So, after opening my eyes, I wasn't exactly surprised to find myself in the same room I'd been knocked out in. I'd been shackled to a table. The table was made of wood and had two thick, silver manacles at each end, restraining my hands and feet. The feet weren't a problem, the fact that they'd left my shoes and socks on meant the manacles couldn't rub against my bare skin, but my hands were positioned up above my head, causing one of my arms to go to sleep. It wasn't the most comfortable position I'd ever been in, and I tried to rotate my shoulder a little to get some of the feeling back into it.

"Don't try to escape," a man said as he entered the room. He had my complete attention. He was about my height, but without my broad shoulders and chest, and wore a very expensive gray suit. He carried a walking stick, black wood with a chrome lion's head on top, but didn't use it to walk. Mordred's sword cane flashed in my head, this was probably something similar. Or maybe he was just a pretentious prick who carried a walking stick that he didn't need. The jury was still out.

The man moved a chair from the far wall and placed it just out of arm's reach beside me. "It's been a while. You look well."

"I'm sorry, do I know you?"

The man smiled—a thin evil smile that never reached his eyes. "You used to, yes."

"You're the man in charge of all this," I said. "'My lord,' as everyone seems to call you. Do you have a proper name?"

"'My lord' will do for now," he said with an air of smug satisfaction. "I'd almost given up searching for you. I assumed you'd been killed. And then I get a call saying some little thug is looking for information about you. It was like my birthday and Christmas all rolled into one."

"Must have been a busy day for you," I said. "You do know I came here voluntarily? Why the restraints?"

"Oh, those," he said as if he'd only just noticed them. "We didn't want you to try and leave, and you're only here to save people's lives. Did you think we'd just give you back all your memories and then you'd escape?" He moved closer to me. "You have no idea what's going on."

I turned my head and stared directly into his eyes; they were soulless, utterly without compassion or feeling. A shiver went down my spine. "You want the Fates," I said and enjoyed the twitch at the side of his mouth as my words annoyed him. "The whole bit about Welkin's research, well, that's important to you, but it's not what you really want. I took the Fates from you, and you want them back."

The man sat back in his chair. "I'm impressed. Although that's not entirely true. I want the Fates back, mostly to kill them as a way to show what happens to those who betray me. What you have in that brain of yours...is how to make more." He tapped the side of my head with the steel tip of his walking stick. "When you stole Welkin's notes on how to create Harbingers, you also stole my notes on how to create the Fates."

I laughed. I couldn't help it. "I think you're going to be disappointed. I burned those notes so you couldn't get them. So if you want what's in my head, you'll have to unlock my memories."

The man stood and whispered in my ear. "Not all of them, I won't."

I was about to tell him what he could do with himself, when Achilles entered the room, with Jenny in tow. She stood by the door, her arms crossed over her chest. Bruises covered her exposed shoulders, running up her neck, and she had one nasty-looking cut just above her eye where stitches had been applied to hold the wound closed.

"Bet you wished you'd never come here ten years ago," Achilles said. "Turns out you were a disappointment. The big bad wolf is just a scared little puppy."

I pulled at the restraints. The man in the gray suit smiled. "I am a man of my word," he said. "You have ten minutes, and then one of my psychic friends will rip the information I need from your mind. After which, you'll die. Slowly." He walked over to Jenny and touched her cheek, she flinched, but he grabbed her by the jaw, holding her for a second before pushing her over to me. "Say good-bye." And then he left, taking Achilles with him.

"Nate," Jenny whispered.

"Are you okay?" I asked. "I know, stupid question."

She lifted the bottom of her black top to show three cuts along her stomach. I'd seen something similar before, and knew exactly what they were. "How bad is the gargoyle venom?"

Jenny lowered her top and rubbed the back of one hand with the other. "About six hours before my organs start shutting down. I'll be dead in eight."

"They said you could go free."

She nodded. "Death *is* their version of setting me free. They only let me talk to you because they want to watch you suffer."

"Do you know how Dani and Samantha are?"

"Safe," she said. "They won't hurt either of them. But you'll never see them again."

I nodded. "I thought they would unlock my past. And since Mordred isn't about to come help me out, I'm stuffed."

Jenny shook her head and moved closer to me. "There's a third way."

That got my attention. "Why didn't the Fates mention it to me?"

"I don't know. But it's the only way you'll get your past back and get out of here with Dani and Samantha."

"So what is it?"

Jenny tenderly touched my cheek. "I want you to know something," she said. "I really liked our time together. It made me feel normal."

"Me too," I said. "What's the third way, Jenny?"

She walked over to the door, picked up a chair and smashed the metal leg into the door's control panel. "That should give us some time," she said and walked back toward me, kissing me gently on the mouth. A grating sound started, coming from the side of the table, but it didn't last for long as the kiss intensified and she grasped the sides of my head in her hands. I returned the passion, and suddenly, without warning, memories exploded in my head.

I tried to yell out, unaware of what was happening, as more and more memories came into the forefront of my mind. But the kiss intensified once more, unlocking chunks of my past with every heartbeat. I moved my head slightly, noticing dark marks on Jenny's wrist and forearm. Another memory exploded, giving me instant knowledge of what it meant.

The third way of unlocking memories was for a nonhuman to use their own life energy to break the Blood magic. The mass of runes on Jenny's wrists and forearms were there to help that along. Rudimentary magic used in one very specific way could remove a Blood magic curse by sacrificing someone who wasn't human.

I locked eyes with Jenny and screamed for her to stop, but it was muffled by her lips. I bucked and moved, trying to break the kiss, but her hands were now firmly planted on either side of my head. It was no use. More memories came and went, bringing every emotion with them. The births and deaths of people I cared about were relived over and over.

Tears fell from Jenny's eyes, landing on my face in a steady stream. I tried to break free, to stop her from sacrificing herself for my sake. There was banging and yelling from the other side of the broken door, and I wanted to tell her that we could get her the cure and that we could save her life, but it was useless. Jenny's strength began to wane and she sagged against me, the kiss finally breaking as her head dropped onto my chest. "You shouldn't have done that," I said breathlessly. "You didn't need to."

"I wanted...wanted my life to have meant something," she said. "Amongst all the death...death I caused. I needed to know you got those girls to safety."

I couldn't find the words to describe what Jenny had done. My mind was still processing everything I'd seen. And in the end only one thing came through. "I will never forget what you did."

Jenny released her hands and moved her head slowly, planting one last kiss on my lips. "I cut the table's runes."

Information flashed through my head. The runes had been blocking my use of magic. "Thank you."

Jenny whispered her final request into my ear, so quietly that I could barely make out the words. Then she slumped onto my chest and died as a half dozen people rushed toward us, dragging her off me.

"Fucking bitch," the gray-suited man said and delivered a swift kick to Jenny's lifeless body.

He turned his attention to me, his eyes full of fire and rage. I returned the stare dispassionately. "Hello, Mordred," I said. "It's been a while."

CHAPTER 35

1414, France.

Bodies lay at my feet as we walked through the largest building of the prison compound, mostly more French soldiers who Mordred had decreed were expendable. The walls were splattered with their blood. It didn't look like they'd fought back against their attackers. The soldiers hadn't expected to be betrayed.

Thomas, Ivy, and I made our way past the carnage to a large hall in the center of the building. At one time it had probably been awash with people, but the only reminder that it had ever been in use were the four banners that had been hung from the ceiling. The French flag hung on either side of the huge double doors, which were the entrance to the room. At the far end sat an orange flag with the picture of an ancient Greek warrior holding a large spear painted black. I'd never seen it before and certainly had no idea who might use it.

I ignored the décor and waited as Ivy and Thomas followed me into the hall. Thomas limped slightly on his right leg. He had taken a hard blow when the nightmare had hit him and broken it badly. He was lucky werewolves heal fast. In the meantime, Ivy walked beside the large werewolf allowing him to put less weight on his injury.

"Where do these doors lead?" I asked Ivy.

She looked around us, glancing back and forth from the two doors at opposite sides of the room. "The right leads up to the cells, the left to the experiment area. There's a corridor behind this room that goes between the two."

"Right, you two go up to the prisoners. Free anyone you find. I'm going to the experiment room. Mordred will want to remove evidence of what they've done; hopefully he's not had time to finish and escape."

Thomas grunted and set off toward the door with long, slow strides, but Ivy stayed behind, staring at me. "You promise you'll come back," she said.

"I'll finish this with Mordred and come back for you. Just keep Thomas out of trouble."

Ivy shook her head. "I meant that if anything happens, you'll come find me."

I looked down into the blue eyes of the girl who stood before me. They were filled with fear and concern. And a little hope. "No matter what happens, I *will* come find you."

Ivy maintained eye contact and then nodded once before running off to join Thomas. I watched them walk through the door together, an injured werewolf and a terrified girl. Two people I liked who'd had their lives destroyed by Mordred and his companions. One thing was certain—Mordred was not going to find me in a good mood.

I ran to the door, throwing it open and continuing my pace as I raced down one long, anonymous corridor. There were no windows or doors—the only decoration appeared to be the occasional smear of blood against the stone walls.

The corridor got steeper as I reached the end, where a huge iron door sat. I grabbed the looped metal handle and pulled it up with a click, pushing the door open. The room beyond was bigger than the hall upstairs had been; in fact, it was probably double the size. Cages, with runes carved into the metal, sat on one side of the room against the cold, thick walls. Apart from being made of iron instead of silver, the cages were identical to the one in Soissons where Mordred had kept Ivy, although these now contained only a collection of books and papers, which were furiously ablaze.

The rest of the room contained training equipment, dummies, sand bags, and thick wooden bull's-eyes. I realized that it wasn't just somewhere people were experimented on; it was where they trained.

At the far end of the room was another door, which was ajar. I quietly made my way toward it, getting almost halfway before Mordred stepped into my path. His eyes widened in shock for a split second before hardening like glass. "I assumed the nightmare would have finished you off."

"Then you're an idiot," I said. "Although I plan on making sure you don't make another mistake like it."

"Are you going to kill me, Nathan?" he mocked. "You've been trying for so long. I wonder if you've actually got it in you." He walked in a large arc around me, never dropping his gaze. He knew I only needed one chance, and he was too good to give it to me willingly. "Morgan still talks about you."

"Shut up," I seethed.

"No, she does. She wonders if you'll ever forgive her. A thousand years and she still won't let it go."

"She betrayed me."

"Betrayal?" Mordred snapped. "You *dare* talk to me about betrayal. Did Merlin betray you? Did he try to have you killed and to destroy everything you cared about? So I destroyed the thing that he cared for the most—his beautiful Arthur. I got Arthur to go to that little cabin and find you and Morgan in bed. The only reason she interjected herself in the fight was to save you."

I had no idea what Mordred was talking about. The words came out before I could stop myself. "Save me?"

"Does that twist inside you, knowing that Morgan saved your life that day?"

I shook my head. "You're lying. It's what you do best."

"Actually, killing people is what I do best," Mordred said. "Lying is sort of a...hobby. But right now I'm telling you the truth."

Mordred's speech allowed him to circle around me. "I'll give her your best," he said and sprinted across the room and through the open door.

It took only a moment to realize what his plan had been and to give chase, and by the time he reached the great hall I had made up most of the distance between us. He didn't even stop to open the door, just used his magic to blast it into tiny shards, which he gathered with more magic and threw at me a giant ball of deadly sharp pieces of wood and iron. It forced me to draw a shield of dense air to stop the thousands of projectiles from slamming into me. Instead, they bounced off, striking the surrounding stone and imbedding themselves deeply into the castle walls.

As the final shard vanished from view, I forced the air out in front of me like a powerful ram. It hit Mordred's back, throwing him through the air. He crashed down onto the throne in the center of the hall, pieces of wood scattering all around him. One flick of my hands and the wood burst into flame, causing Mordred to scramble away as the fire threatened to engulf him.

"Not a bad attempt, considering," he said once back to his feet.

He opened his mouth to say something else, but another wall of air slammed into him, driving him back against the side of the hall with vicious speed.

Mordred grinned. Even with the distance between us, I could see his eyes turn black, as if someone had poured tar into them. He flicked his hands and the wall of air holding him in place separated in two, crashing into the stone behind him as he dropped silently to the floor.

"Elemental magic that weak won't kill me, Nathan." Blood magic glyphs, black and terrible, glowed as they crossed his palms and up his naked forearms, mixing with white air glyphs. "You need to use something with a little more power." He suddenly raised his arms, palms toward me, and flicked his fingers.

The column of air was immense and slammed into me like a runaway horse. I raised my arms to protect myself, casting another sphere of air around me as the main door exploded behind me. This sphere needed much more powerful magic than the one I'd used to deflect the door shards. The noise in the hall was deafening and continued to echo as the black glyphs on my palms faded.

"I thought you'd forsaken Blood magic," Mordred said with a chuckle.

"Whatever works," I said through gritted teeth.

Mordred smiled. "This will be fun." He charged toward me, his right arm forming a dark blade, which arched up, aiming for my throat.

I blocked the blood sword with a hastily created guard of air on my forearm, but the vibration from the blow caused me to lose my footing and I staggered back. Mordred took the opportunity to stab at my eyes and I had to roll aside.

I shot a bolt of flame at Mordred's exposed side. He let out a cry of pain as it crashed into him, and the blade vanished, but he wasn't down for long. He threw a curve of Blood magic longer than my arm at me. I rolled aside again, but it caught my leg and pain erupted across it. Blood magic doesn't contain any force as such, but it does trigger emotions and pain when touched. Visions of Mordred's attack on Arthur flashed through my head.

"You never did learn how to control your emotions," Mordred said as he stalked toward me. "It's why you were never that great of a blood mage. You allowed petty feelings to enter the equation."

I fought against the feeling of helplessness that raged throughout me. It was all I'd felt when I'd witnessed Mordred plunge a Blood magic sword through Arthur's stomach. I hadn't been able to help my friend. Visions of Ivy replaced him. I would not fail her. Not now. Not ever.

As I tried to force myself back to my feet, Mordred placed one of his hands on my shoulder. Another wave of pain started through me as he pushed me back to the floor, turning me over onto my back. He wanted to look into my eyes when he killed me. I let him move me—I had little choice in the matter—but when he was close enough I blocked out the pain for a fraction of a second and rammed my fist into his throat. He staggered back, and I kicked him in the stomach with everything I had.

I'd bought myself a few seconds. I reached down inside me, allowing my own Blood magic to feed on the emotion wracking my body. When I'd gathered enough, I turned to look at Mordred.

Mordred's expression of pain and anger gave way to pure and unadulterated fear. "Your...eyes," he stammered.

Orange fire and black blood glyphs met across my body, and a torrent of fire released from my hands raced toward Mordred. The Blood magic had increased the fire's strength, turning it white hot. The stone floor scorched as flames touched it, moving too fast for him to avoid. He raised his hands, creating another shield of air, but the fire hit it with such ferocity that it turned the air into a wall of superheated agony, cooking whatever was closest to it.

I kept the fire coming, pumping more and more into the room, continuing the barrage against Mordred's shield as his screams echoed throughout the hall. By the time I stopped, he was kneeling on the floor, his hands a raw mess of boiled skin and flesh. They'd been against the edge of the sphere he'd created.

"You've crippled me," he shrieked.

I should have just killed him right there, but I couldn't. Maybe he wasn't the only one who needed to stare into his enemy's face. I stalked toward him as he tried to get back to his feet and escape, but a quick blast of air to the back of his legs removed that option.

He fell back to the floor with a crash, coupled with more shrieking. He slowly got himself upright, using his knees, and stood facing me. "You can kill me, but you'll never get to keep that girl. My employer will see to that."

The idea that Mordred was working for a mystery benefactor shocked me; he rarely did anything that was for someone else. "You're done, Mordred. At least die with some honor. Tell me who's funding all of this—who else wants these experiments?" My mind roared at me to use magic, and I had to force myself to draw my silver *jian* and step toward him, ready to deliver justice for all of those who'd died at his hands. But I stopped when a scream broke over me from Ivy's direction.

"You'd better pick," he said with an air of smugness as he began to edge away from me. "Me or the girl. You don't have time to do both." He used my distraction to blast the sword from my hand with a gust of air. It made him scream in pain, but it had the desired effect as the sword clattered onto the floor a dozen feet behind me.

Retrieving the sword would have only taken a moment, but another scream sounded, making my decision for me. I turned and ran in that direction, destroying the door before I was even halfway there and not stopping as I leapt over its remains.

The maze of corridors and rooms that lay beyond, including stairs both up and down, slowed me to a crawl. But a third scream, this one cut off, pinpointed the direction I needed to go.

I took a set of stone stairs two at a time running to the floor above, where I found Thomas, now in human form, lying on the bare floor. Blood tricked down the back of his neck and over his shoulder. I stopped beside him and hastily tried for a pulse, finding it weak but steady. I searched the rest of the floor, but found only broken furniture and blood.

By the time I'd returned to Thomas, dread had settled in my stomach like an anvil. "I couldn't stop them," Thomas said.

"Who did this? Where did they go?"

Thomas shook his head, wincing with the movement. "They attacked from behind as we looked through the rooms for prisoners. A man with long, dark hair took Ivy. I crawled from the next room over, but by the time I got here she was gone."

"They used silver. Hurt a werewolf with enough of it and he'll change back." I helped Thomas to a seated position against one of the doors. "Which way did they go?"

Thomas pointed down the hallway. "I blacked out just as they reached the door."

I took off down the hall and through the door, only to find a massive hole in the side of the empty room beyond. I scanned the rolling fields below me and saw nothing. No trace of Ivy or the man who had taken her. I'd failed, and that had allowed Mordred's companions to take her. "I will find you," I bellowed, allowing my magic to take the words as far as possible. The last words I said were a whisper. "I promise."

CHAPTER 36

London, England. Now.

Jenny's body was dragged from the room by two scientists, as everyone else ran around like headless chickens. Mordred stood and stared at me with an expression of rage. I winked at him. He'd be dead soon enough, so it wasn't like he would be able to hold his grudge for too much longer. Jenny's final request rang in my ears—*Make them pay.* I smiled. That was going to be my pleasure.

I'd been hoisted upright against the far wall so I could look down on everyone while they worked. "What are you actually doing?" I asked after one of the scientists took blood from me. She was shaking so hard that she missed the vein twice. I offered to do it for her if she wasn't competent enough.

"We want to make sure you survive the questioning process," Mordred said. "Don't want you to be allergic to something, or immune. We figured testing your blood first would be a good idea. And since whatever that bitch did seems to have restored your memories, this process should be much easier."

"Good luck with that," I said with a smile. "You do know I'm going to kill you?"

Mordred laughed, making everyone in the room stop what they were doing. They probably didn't hear his laugh too often. He had never had been the jovial type. "You're chained to a rune-covered table with silver manacles. You're not going anywhere except to an incinerator once we've discarded your useless body."

"Let me guess, you want to turn Dani and Samantha into Fates. Young ones too—though you'll need a third. A past Fate."

"We already have one." He clicked his fingers and the mystery woman from the phone calls entered the room. "She spent so much time trying to hide Dani and Samantha. We figured it'd be only right that they never be separated again."

"You're a psychic?" I asked her, but she looked away.

Mordred lifted her top to show the dark Blood magic marks on her stomach. "She's already undergone part of the process. And as Dani and Samantha are her daughters, it should be easier to convert them than it was with Cassandra and her granddaughter, Ivy."

I cursed myself for not figuring it out sooner, that the mystery woman was Dani and Samantha's mother.

"You're back to helping this asshole because he threatened your daughters." The memory of Ivy bringing Cassandra and me tea shot into the forefront of my mind. I'd been unable to keep Ivy from Mordred's clutches once, but now they were safe. And I would make sure they stayed that way.

Mordred took exception to my description of him and slammed his walking stick into my ribs. I winced, but forced through a smile, angering him even more. "You always were a shitty sorcerer," I said with a laugh and noticed that once again the room had gone silent. So, still a sore point.

"I don't need to be a great sorcerer to kill you," Mordred said with a smile. He turned to the scientist who had taken my blood. "The results. Now."

She fumbled with a piece of paper, almost dropping it. "Preliminary results suggest that he's perfectly healthy. But we need to test it with Blood magic. We started when he was unconscious, but it'll be a few hours yet."

Mordred sighed and backhanded the scientist as if striking a gnat in the air. She tumbled to the ground, knocking a second scientist over. "You have one hour," Mordred said. "If it's not done by then, I'll slit your throat."

The two scientists dusted themselves off and raced from the room.

"You have to be firm with people," he said to me before turning to one of his people. "Remove his shirt."

Almost immediately a white-coat-wearing Nazi cut through my t-shirt, ripping it from me.

"Impressed?" I asked Mordred.

He ignored the remark and stared at the six dark glyphs on my torso. "You have the same six that you've always had." He walked away and wrote on a piece of paper. "There's no residual mark from what I did to you. It appears that those marks you have protected you from further damage. It's something I wish I could have looked into a little further. But I have little time for fun these days."

"My lord, you need to see this," one of the scientists said as he continued to stare at my naked chest.

"You'd better buy me lunch," I told him, but he didn't even glance up at me. "At least put a fiver in my belt."

Mordred did as his crony asked, although it clearly pained him to do so, and raised an eyebrow as he examined the mark on my left pectoral. "It's fading," he said with an edge. "That bitch must have started a chain reaction." He spun back to the scientist, who had wisely started to edge away. "You will drag those fucking memories out of his head right now, or I will make you beg me to kill you."

"Scared, Mordred?" I taunted.

"Fuck you," he snapped, but his eyes remained on his subordinate.

"You're not even going to get the information yourself." I tutted. "I thought I meant something to you. I thought I was special."

Mordred stalked toward me until his face was an inch from mine. "My psychic over there is going to tear everything I need from your brain and then I'm going to fucking kill you."

I stared passed my old nemesis, toward one of the scientists, infuriating him even more. He'd started scratching his arm, raising his lab-coat to show off the unmistakable swirl of a Blood magic glyph. "You cursed him."

"Good help is hard to find," Mordred said. "If he betrays me, he dies. It's a nice little curse I've perfected over the years. I'd love to show you, but it has to be done willingly. Shame, really, I think that would have been fun."

"My lord, how long will it be before those marks vanish?" the scientist who'd examined me asked, his voice breaking slightly from nerves.

"It depends on just how intertwined these are with what was done to Nate all those centuries ago, and how much energy Jenny managed to expel. They could all vanish now, or take hundreds of years. Blood magic curses aren't exactly a science."

Mordred glared at me once again. "You've caused me no end of trouble in the past few hundred years. France, Holland, Istanbul, everywhere I go, you're right behind me, fucking up my plans as best as possible. I imagine screaming will be involved during your last few hours on earth. I might record it to play back on my iPod when I get bored. We'll use what information we drag out of you to make me more powerful."

The past ten years had done little for Mordred's sanity. "In all of your plotting and planning, you forgot something," I said.

"And what would that be?"

"Two things, actually. Firstly, you should have killed me when you had a chance. That was really stupid."

Mordred laughed. "And secondly?"

"Secondly, you should have remembered. Never piss off a sorcerer." Glyphs blared across my body, brilliant whites and oranges mixing as the table became engulfed in flame. In the blink of an eye the wood weakened to the point that I launched myself from it, the manacles still attached to my hands and feet as I landed a few feet away from a sprinting Mordred.

I looked around the room at the remaining scientists. Mordred had taken Dani's mum, bolted through the door, and locked it behind him, leaving five people in a room with me—a very angry and deadly sorcerer.

The first scientist tried to attack me with a scalpel. A stream of molten-hot fire the size of my finger hit him in the throat.

The female scientist who had taken my blood had started screaming almost immediately, intensifying as I killed two more of her colleagues who hadn't learned from their dead workmate and had tried the exact same attack with their scalpels. Two razor sharp blades of air appeared at the end of each of my hands. I cut through my attackers, drenching the surrounding floor and wall in blood. Three down, killed in a matter of seconds; two to go.

I turned to the still-screaming woman. "Will you please shut up?" My words had an effect as her screams transformed into a soft whimpering. "Now, before anymore of you have to die, would anyone like to tell me where I can find the keys for these things?" I raised the manacles. I could have used magic to remove them, but as they were silver, the amount it would take would have left me weak immediately afterward.

The scientist who had torn off my shirt fumbled in his pockets and tossed me the key, which I caught as it sailed over my head. Whether it was desperation to please his master or fear, the psychic ran at me, his palms toward me readying an attack, but I had plenty of time to weave invisible tendrils of air around his chest, before closing them like an anaconda, crushing his ribs. He stopped mid-stride and collapsed to the floor.

I unlocked the manacles from my wrists, dropping them to the floor with a satisfying bang, followed by the ones on my feet. The manacles were heavy and uncomfortable; I was grateful to have been able to remove them.

The scientist who'd taken my blood huddled in the nearest corner like a frightened rabbit. But before I asked her anything, the other scientist got back to his feet, holding one hand against his chest and breathing heavily. "You've probably got a few broken ribs," I said. "Maybe a punctured lung." As if on cue, he started coughing up blood.

"Last chance," I said.

He took a step toward me and I used a strong gust of wind to pick up one of the scalpels and flung it at him. He didn't notice it until it was too late, and then he fell to the floor. A thin trickle of blood fell between his eyes after the razor-sharp blade pieced his brain. Only the tip of the handle remained visible. "They're silver," I said to the remaining scientist, who nodded profusely.

"My lord wanted to kill you slowly. So he demanded we use silver on you."

I knelt in front of her. "His name is Mordred." I was utterly fed up of his people considering him better than he was. "And you have two choices. Help me, or die."

"What do you need?" she asked without pause.

"What's the best way out of here? The door or the window?"

"The air compression chamber outside will be locked," she said. "There's no way through it unless you rip the door apart. And that will take hours—it's silver laced."

"So, the window then," I said, glancing at the large glass portal.

"That window is a few inches thick. You'd need a bullet to get through it."

"Are you saying we're trapped in here?"

She nodded. "Are you going to kill me?" her voice was small.

"Why would I do that? Are you going to try to kill me?"

She shook her head.

"Then you're safe," I smiled. "I do have one question. How many people did you kill here?"

Her eyes darted around the room, searching for an escape that was unlikely to come. "I didn't kill anyone. I just did the work on their bodies."

I kept smiling. "How. Many?"

"A few dozen. But they were already dead," she pleaded. "I didn't kill anyone. I just did my job."

"So did the Nazis," I said, and with a wave of my hands I removed all of the oxygen from her lungs. Her eyes bulged in panic and she started to move, but within seconds she was unconscious on the floor. I had no intention of killing her, but that didn't mean I had to help her either.

I made my way to the viewing window and stared into the darkness beyond. People would have been running around trying to lock the building down—having a pissed off sixteen-hundred-year-old sorcerer wake up and kill a bunch of workers tended to cause people to panic. That meant only the most ardent of employees would have stayed behind, with a few inches of glass to separate them from me.

I concentrated, forcing as much heat as possible out of my glyph-covered hands and into the glass. The unconscious scientist had been right, the glass was thick, and it took a massive amount of force to melt all the way through to the other side. But once the initial hole had formed, the rest of the glass gave way like it was made of paper until the hole was large enough for me to climb through.

As I'd guessed, the room beyond, although dark and uninviting, was empty. It contained only chairs and tables, used while viewing whatever sick and twisted experiments Mordred's employees carried out at his request.

I was about to open the door and leave the room when a noise from behind it caused me to pause. After a few seconds of silence, and no repeat noise, I wondered if I was going mad. I'd just had a millennium and a half of memories dumped in my head, and I still felt a little groggy from it. Maybe I was hearing things, but just as I'd pushed the thought aside, I heard something else.

I placed my hand against the door and used my air magic to tell me of anyone living outside the room, much like I'd done to find Welkin a decade previously. I got three pings. Three people waited for me to come through the door, one directly behind the door and two more slightly down the corridor. A small smile creaked across my lips. If they were waiting for me, it would be rude not to oblige them.

The heavy door exploded outward in a tornado of howling wind. It hurtled into the armed guard who happened to be behind it, taking him off his feet and crashing into the nearest wall.

The other two guards were in shock. Their guns were still in holsters against their hips; instead, they held electric batons— a bit like a cattle prod—to use as weapons. However, unlike a cattle prod, everything beyond the handle is used to deliver a massive shock, easily the equivalent of a taser.

I darted for the closest guard, avoiding the humming baton as it swung toward me, and a blade of fire extended down from my hand. I sliced through his throat, and he crumpled to the ground, the immediately cauterized wound ensuring there was very little blood spray.

The second guard's eyes widened in panic and he dropped the baton, fumbling for the revolver in its holster. The gun fell to the ground as the blade tore through his Kevlar vest and into his heart, killing him instantly.

I picked up the thrown baton and went to check on the first guard, who'd been crushed by the flying door. It didn't take long to figure out he was dead—the massive piece of wood sticking out of his chest was a giveaway. I left the body alone and took a look at the baton. I'd not seen one in years, but I remembered that they hurt like a bitch. I touched the switch on the handle and the baton hummed to life, the small Tesla coil it contained made the baton turn slightly blue. I switched it off and tossed it to the floor. I didn't like using them, and the last time I'd heard about them they'd had some teething problems.

The one thing their use told me, though, was that Mordred wanted me alive. Otherwise, the guards would have opened fire and been done with it. That gave me the advantage, because I certainly wasn't about to show his guards the same level of stupidity.

No one else bothered me as I walked down the corridor, which surprised me as I'd expected a little resistance. I turned a corner toward the lifts and found the mystery lady from the phone standing in front of them. She held a katana in her hands, the tip pointing toward the floor in a casual way. The second she saw me, the sword was lifted and pointed directly at me. "This is where I have to stop you," she said.

I didn't move. "Do you have a name? Your real name, I mean?"

"Anne," she said. "My real name is Anne."

"So, Anne, I assume your daughters were taken from you long ago."

"Ten years," she said with more than a touch of anger and sadness. "Both have forgotten about me. But they are my daughters, and I will not let them come to harm."

"Mordred threatened to kill them if you didn't go back to working for him?"

She nodded.

"You really want to fight me? You do know what I used to do for a living, right?"

"You're a spy, assassin, basically whatever was needed. I know I can't beat you."

"I assumed Mordred would want to keep you out of harm's way."

"He's more concerned about saving his own skin." Her words were loaded with hate. "If I kill you, then he wins. If not, then he still gets away to safety. But if I don't try, he will kill my daughters."

"Did you say good-bye to them?"

A single tear fell from Anne's eye, but she didn't even flinch to wipe it away. "I've not seen them since they were brought here."

"I'll make you a deal then. You go say good-bye to your kids. And I'll wait here. Then you can come back and die."

Her eyes grew cold. "I'll put up more of a fight than you can imagine."

"No doubt," I said nonchalantly. "But I can see half a dozen weaknesses in your stance. Three of which would permit me to move through your attack and strike with impunity. You'll be dead within…thirty seconds." My returned memories and power had also given me back my experiences. It was a little overwhelming.

Anne looked shocked, and more than a little scared. "You can't know that."

"I can," I assured her. "Thirty seconds from your first attack, you'll be dead. How old are you?"

"A hundred and forty," she said.

"But you're only a psychic, yes? So you're still basically fighting at a human efficiency. Peak human, no doubt, but still human." I took a step toward her. "I'm not. I fight at a level no human can hope to match. I'm better than any human fighter you've ever met. Thirty seconds and you die. Or you leave and go try to save your daughters. Maybe you live, maybe you die, but at least your last act would be to do something for those you love."

"Jenny thought you were worth saving."

"I will not forget what she did for me. Nor will I allow her death to be wasted." I pushed anger from my voice. I wanted to save that rage and hatred at what had been done to Jenny for those responsible. I wanted it intact until I needed it. "And I will kill everyone involved. Including you, if you push me. Now decide. Stay and die a meaningless death, or for the first time do something with your life."

Anne held my stare, and a moment later lowered her sword. "Mordred will be heading to the roof to use his helicopter. Between there and here are maybe twenty men and Achilles. My daughters are two floors down. If I can't get them to safety, and if you survive, you must help them."

"I give you my word," I said. "Nothing on earth will keep me from them."

Anne pressed the lift call button before retrieving a card from her pocket and passing it to me. "This will get you access to the stairwell. They won't be expecting that."

I took the card and looked around. "Where's the stairwell?"

Anne pointed to a nearby door. "Go through there. It's designed to look like an office from the outside. But the stairs will take you where you need to go."

I took hold of the card but Anne refused to let go of her end. "You kill Achilles and Mordred. If you don't, my daughters will always be in danger."

I nodded. Anne released the card and stepped into the open lift. "I'll hold you to your word. If you've lied, and I live through this, we'll be seeing each other again."

I smiled. "I'd expect nothing less," I said before the lift doors closed.

CHAPTER 37

Anne hadn't been wrong about Mordred's men not expecting me to take the stairs. No one was waiting outside the door at the top of the stairs, not even a lone guard. The corridor was filled with plotted plants and office doors, the contents hidden by blind-covered windows. There was no natural sunlight—halogen lamps did the work of nature. The whole place felt sterile and claustrophobic.

"Hello," I shouted, hoping that at least someone might come investigate. My hope was answered when four guards appeared at the end of the corridor fifty feet away, each holding a baton. "Where's Mordred?" I asked.

One of them radioed to his friends whilst the other three rushed me.

They made it about five feet before a hurricane of fire slammed into them, tearing them off the ground and incinerating them as they flew through the nearest wall and into one of the offices next to me. I glanced inside the hole and saw the charred bodies of the guards—none of them were going to be getting back up.

Being fully aware of my limits was quite frankly liberating. I knew I couldn't just keep throwing huge amounts of magic around all the time. Somewhere out there Achilles and Mordred were waiting for me, and both of them would require a lot to defeat. But even so, it had been so long since I'd used my magic to fight that I'd spent the last ten years almost concerned it was going to consume me; it was nice to flex those muscles once again.

The fourth guard had finished on the radio and was obviously more intelligent than the first three combined as he stood back and watched with a mixture of shock and terror.

"Where's Mordred?" I demanded.

He opened his mouth but nothing came out. He had the fear of a man who had just seen his three armed friends decimated in a matter of seconds and who realized that he could end up the exact same way. I sighed and walked toward him, batting the baton aside and slapping him across the face hard enough to knock him to his knees with a split lip. "Mordred," I said again. "Where is he?"

"That's not your concern," said a voice from the end of the corridor, which got my immediate attention. "You won't get to see him."

"Achilles," I said and watched the frightened guard run over to the gargoyle. Unfortunately for him, it wasn't a warm welcome. The gargoyle grabbed the young guard and snapped his neck, throwing him aside like he was nothing. "I've had enough of incompetent guards. Mordred only hires humans because they're cheap, and he knows they won't try to take his power. But I say he could do better."

I walked backward down the corridor, and Achilles stalked toward me, never allowing the distance to grow between us. He was followed by a dozen guards, all of whom appeared rather pleased with themselves. Not one of them gave their dead comrades' bodies so much as a glance. It was as if they weren't even there. In some cases the new guards actually stepped onto their bodies as they walked toward me. It was one of the creepiest things I'd witnessed in a long time.

"Since when has a gargoyle needed a cheerleading squad?"

Achilles glanced behind him. "Who am I to turn away people who want to see me work?" The men jeered and howled with laughter and menace, attempting to put me off. In the confined space of the corridor, it made more sound than I'd have thought possible with such a small group.

"The real Achilles was the greatest warrior who ever lived, and you chose that name? Think pretty highly of yourself, don't you?"

Achilles smiled. "I *am* the greatest warrior who has ever lived. No one can beat me."

I chuckled and shook my head. "You're not fit to use Achilles' name—hell, you're not fit to be mentioned in the same breath as him." Achilles' face contorted with rage, so I continued. "You're a pale imitation of him. I've never even met the original—he died well before my time—but I still know he'd be ashamed to discover that his name was being used by a jumped-up little prick who thinks being able to bully and murder people entitles him to use the name of the world's greatest warrior. You're not the world's greatest anything. You're just a joke."

Achilles roared. None of his cheer squad made a sound. I was willing to bet that any noise they made might mean Achilles' rage would be turned on them. "I have never lost in battle!" he shouted.

"Battles? You beat up a bunch of human women, some children, and those who were unable to defend themselves against a gargoyle. You're just standing on the shoulders of greatness."

"I beat you," he said with a sadistic smile.

My laughter seemed to make him even angrier. "When? The first time, you got one of your thugs to shoot me, and the second you blew yourself up with a car bomb. Yeah, really good record you have against me."

A rumble started inside him "I. Am. Achilles," he roared.

I cracked my knuckles. "In that case, Achilles is about to get his ass kicked."

My intention had been to piss Achilles off so much that he screwed up. Considering his first action was to charge at me, head on, without even changing into his gargoyle form, it was fair to say I'd succeeded.

What I hadn't counted on was how fast he was without needing to change. He made the distance between us quicker than I'd ever imagined, and I only just managed to dodge aside at the last second. He continued to run, unable to slow in time to turn back on me.

Gargoyles can maintain a human shell, although it's really just for show. Their weight and strength don't change no matter what their outward appearance suggests. The real benefits of changing are the armor and killing weapons in his wings and claws. The fact that he thought he could take me without changing meant he was either really confident or *really* stupid.

I rolled back to my feet and for a brief moment was concerned that Achilles' cheer squad would try to attack me, but none of them had moved an inch. It was probably unwise for them to get involved when Achilles was fighting; he didn't strike me as caring about friendly fire.

Achilles roared once more and charged. I darted aside and wrapped thin columns of air around his arm, pulling them tight enough to take him off his feet and dump him headfirst into the nearest wall.

I continued to wrap the air around him, tighter and tighter, covering more and more of his body. Every time he breathed in, I constricted the air further. He yelled out in pain as something inside him crunched, and then I ignited the air. Achilles went up like a bonfire, the air only feeding the fire to make it even more powerful. It wasn't going to kill Achilles, but from the sounds of it, it hurt like a bitch.

He struggled and rolled, which only allowed me to wrap the air around him tighter as the inferno blazed away, but eventually he managed to grab a nearby plant pot and throw it at me, causing me to dodge aside as it smashed. A memory of an old friend flashed into my mind, distracting me and giving Achilles the chance to shake off the fire and get back to his feet, his skin blistered and burned.

"You still want to do this without changing?" I placed a little distance between us as he brushed the dirt off his arms. I hoped my brain hadn't decided to start playing games. I didn't need the extra trouble of having my memories flash before me when I was busy.

He smiled and threw a huge punch, which was easily avoided, but another memory, this one of Morded stabbing Arthur, snapped to the front of my mind, distracting me again, just enough that Achilles' follow-up jab to my ribs struck home, knocking the wind out of me. Instead of continuing, he backed off, grinning like an idiot. I rubbed my side and prepared for whatever game Achilles was trying to play.

He swung again, exactly the same as before, and once more hid his real punch behind the strength of the first. This time his left hand came up toward me as I avoided the first haymaker and tried to catch me on the jaw. But I anticipated it and stepped into the blow, grabbing his arm just above his elbow and headbutting him on the nose, using a dense pack of air on my forehead to cause maximum damage.

He swung his free hand at my head, but a second headbutt saw him drop the punch in midair and try to stagger away. I wasn't about to let him go that easily. I slammed my elbow into the bridge of his nose, and my knee into his stomach, giving him two more pieces of pain to consider.

Achilles bent forward slightly and I let go of his arm, dropped to a crouch, and smashed both of my hands into his solar plexus. I'd localized a tornado-like gale directly in front of my hands, and when it struck Achilles, the effect was more than a little dramatic. He lifted from the floor and soared a dozen feet back, hitting the nearest wall and going through it with ease, accompanied by the roar of the powerful gale.

It took him only moments to reappear, silhouetted in a cloud of dust and brick. "You're better than I'd imagined," Achilles said, his voice filled with rage and hatred. "I won't make that mistake again." There was a ripping sound, and a pair of wings unfurled from his back. He flicked them slightly before touching his face and ripping the skin from it, tearing off the pink, human shell and replacing it with hard stone. Red eyes burned from the darkness.

"I'm going to kill you!"

He launched himself toward me, destroying more of the wall with his thrashing wings, and landed only a few feet from me.

I looked up at the stone monster and smiled. "I've killed gargoyles before. One more won't make much difference."

While that was a true statement, it was also not the whole truth. Gargoyles couldn't use magic, but as long as their armor was around them, magic wouldn't do much to them either. The only way to kill them is to remove their armor, and the gargoyles I'd killed in the past were either in human form or I'd had help. Three or four sorcerers throwing everything they had at a gargoyle will eventually tear the armor like paper. But using that much magic would be like a bomb going off in the office. Besides, it was an all-or-nothing job, and I wasn't sure I had the magical endurance to carry it off. I might have my past back, but I was nowhere near full strength.

Any plans I might have had vanished as Achilles feinted with a punch and instead kicked out at me. It was so fast and precise that it was all I could do to raise a shield of air to absorb the force of the blow. And even then it was enough to lift me from my feet and dump me onto a weak wooden table, which collapsed beneath my weight. I rolled off and used air magic to whip the pieces of wood at Achilles, who reacted exactly as I'd expected him to. He did nothing. In fact, he laughed. Which meant he opened his mouth wide, allowing me to launch a thin stream of fire at his otherwise plated face.

He screamed as it torched the softest part of his body. Achilles dropped to his knees, and I rushed toward him, my fist wrapped so tightly in dense air that it was beginning to go numb. I hit the stricken gargoyle in his eye with everything I had, rocking him back. A second blow sent him to the ground, but the flat of one of his wings caught me in the chest and I flew back into the wall, knocking the wind out of me.

The momentary lapse gave Achilles enough time to get back to his feet. "You're like a fucking cockroach," he shouted, his voice raw and pained. "I'll just have to crush you like one."

He jumped into the air and I rolled away as he came down on the exact spot I'd been lying on. His foot destroyed the wooden floor, ripping it to shreds. If it had been me, I'd have been killed instantly. I kicked out at his knee, catching him behind the joint and forcing him to drop to one knee.

Time was something Achilles was in no mood to give. He dove for me again, his claws out, ready to gore and poison me. But I moved fast enough to avoid him. Unfortunately, he realized what I would do and had one of his wings moving to meet me. On instinct, I formed a blade of fire and cut upward at the same time as forming a second shield, trying to deflect the oncoming blow.

The wing hit the blade, and I felt more liquid on my face and neck. Fear bubbled inside me, *had he gotten through the second shield?* The sound of a wounded monster filled the air, and I knew that my blade had sliced through Achilles' wing, cutting off the last few feet.

Achilles roared with agony. "You've crippled me!"

Gargoyles needed all of their wings to become airborne. Achilles would never fly again.

I touched the severed stone wing with the tip of my shoe. It was thinner than the rest of the plates that covered a gargoyle's body, and thus the most likely part to be damaged in combat.

He gave me no time to think and ran at me. I raised a shield again, but another memory, one of pain and suffering flashed, and I dropped the shield, allowing him to grab me around the stomach and drive me into the wall, slamming his massive fists into my ribs and kidneys over and over again. A swift knee to my solar plexus and I was barely able to think, let alone stand and fight back. Achilles took hold of my jaw and lifted my face to his. "Mordred wants you alive. But fuck it. After all you've done, I'm going to tear you apart, and then I'm going to visit Holly. We have unfinished business." He headbutted me and allowed me to drop to the floor, kicking me twice in the ribs with enough force to lift me off the ground both times.

I tasted my own blood and felt more of it running down my torso. I needed space. I'd killed gargoyles before, so I knew how to kill Achilles, but I couldn't keep getting my ass kicked *and* have enough time to complete what I had to do.

Achilles stalked up and down beside me as the wound from his wing began to close. Once he reached my legs, and as he was about to turn, I forced as much air magic out of my hands as possible. More memories flickered to the front of my head, dozens of them all trying to force their way to the front, I ignored them and pushed the stone monster back with hurricane of magic. But the memories wouldn't fade, and my magic got weaker, so I did the only thing I could think of. I ran.

CHAPTER 38

Running may not have been the bravest course of action, but it kept me alive long enough to formulate a plan and allow my magic to start healing the injuries I'd received at Achilles' hands. I bolted back into the stairwell and up one flight, coming out in a maze of offices and corridors. I made my way through them until I reached a dead end.

A whip of air destroyed the dim lighting above me, casting the corridor into darkness. I didn't want to make things too easy for Achilles. I needed the time to prepare.

If my plan didn't work, I'd be a dead man. There was no way I wanted to continue going toe-to-toe with a pissed off gargoyle. Especially not after what I'd been through in the previous few hours. I was nowhere near full strength, and with my memories flickering to the front of my thoughts, reminding me of things I'd not thought of in a decade, and in some cases even longer. It was hard going, and not what I would have called a good place to fight for my life.

I cleared the thoughts out of my head as best as possible, knelt on the ground, closed my eyes, and concentrated on my breathing. I needed to get my shit together; I needed to make sure that my returning memories didn't fuck around with my magic. And for that I needed some time without distractions.

"Where the fuck are you?" Achilles roared, his voice accompanied by the sound of walls being destroyed as he searched for me. "Don't hide from me, you fucking coward."

I bit my tongue and continued concentrating, allowing myself to relax as I started to build the magic I needed.

"It's a shame your little friend Holly passed out when I started cutting her," he shouted after another wall was broken apart. "I wanted to have a ride."

I suppressed the rage that exploded inside me. It would do me no good. Besides, Achilles would soon learn the error of his ways.

"And that whore Jenny," he continued. "She refused me one time too many. It was so much fun to finally make sure she was going to die." He paused. "Shame she had to go ruin it by sacrificing herself."

Once more I remained silent, focused only on my breathing, remaining calm. The constant flashes of memory now happened without them interrupting me.

"Have you seen that werewolf whose heart I ripped out?" Achilles laughed. "His expression was priceless. And that asshole with the gun. I wanted to take his arm with me, but didn't have the chance."

"You're going to die," I whispered and allowed the words to carry on the air magic I pushed out onto the floor, filling every room and corridor as they searched out Achilles.

"Ah, you *are* here," he said. "I'm going to find you. Make it easy on yourself and just surrender."

"You have no idea who you've pissed off." The whispers once again carried to his ears. "And no idea what I will do to you." But he would soon learn.

"Come show me," Achilles screamed. "Stop these stupid fucking games." More explosions of brick sounded from nearby, continuing for a few minutes as Achilles let loose his rage on anything close to hand. It wasn't long before silence descended once more.

"I was a sorcerer," Achilles said, breaking the quiet. "I even went to see Merlin. And you know what he said? You know what that fucking old prick told me?" Achilles' voice rose with every word. "That I wasn't good enough to be an Acolyte. Well, fuck him. Not good enough? How *dare* he? I turned myself into *this*, and then I went after some of the Acolytes who had made it through his selection process. Killed three of them before Orestes offered me this job. So if I can kill Merlin's Acolytes, what hope in hell do you have?"

Merlin's Acolytes were the sorcerers he picked to work for him. They were always unwavering in their loyalty—and no pushover in the abilities stake either. Merlin always picked those that he deemed would become the best, people of exception. The fact that Achilles had murdered three of them showed he wasn't someone to underestimate, but it also showed that he really had no idea who I was. But as the magic I was preparing increased in power, I was pretty certain he'd soon have a very good idea.

It was a few minutes later when Achilles' shadow appeared at the end of the hallway I was in. "Are you in there? Hiding in the darkness?" he taunted as he stepped closer. "I see you, little man."

"I was never hiding," I said and stood up, brushing my trousers down. "I was waiting."

Achilles took a step closer. "So why remove the lights?" When I didn't immediately reply, he took a second, more tentative step toward me. The darkness consumed him, but the light from the corridor beyond gave me the tactical advantage of still being able to spot him. "What game is this?" he demanded.

"No game," I said, pushing open a nearby door with one hand, allowing daylight to flood through, into the corridor.

Achilles smiled and took another, more eager step. And then he stopped. "Why are you wearing a coat?"

I smiled. While making my way across the office floor, I'd grabbed a unattended coat. . I hadn't wanted the glyphs to give me away. "So you didn't see the glyphs as I used magic," I said. "The subtle stuff is always easier to conceal from someone, but the glyphs still light up." I breathed out, and my breath crystallized instantly.

Achilles' eyes opened in panic, as the realization of what the trap was hit him. He turned to run, but it was too late.

"Don't fight it," I said. "Do you know why gargoyles never go to cold places? It's because cold makes them sluggish—a dozen degrees below zero will freeze a gargoyle's limbs solid, like…well, like stone."

Achilles continued to struggle. "What have you done to me?"

I rolled up my sleeves, showing the white glyphs, which were so bright I could barely look at them. "The higher in the air one goes, the colder it becomes. The air I've created is the same as you'd find at about sixty thousand feet. It's frozen you pretty solid. But that's not everything. You see, as things cool they retract. That includes the plates of stone on your body."

Achilles' expression was one of horror as he stared at his chest. The plates, which normally interlocked over him, had moved apart. Not by a huge amount, but it was enough that the dark flesh underneath was exposed.

He glanced up in time to see me slam a blade of fire into his exposed stomach. "Die screaming, you son-of-a-bitch," I said and dragged the blade up, slicing open his stomach; his screams filled my ears, only stopping when I reached his chest. Black, tar-like, blood pumped out over the floor, covering my arm in the process. I removed the blade and Achilles fell to the floor with a crash. He whimpered slightly, the terror easy to see in his eyes. "You have about ten minutes before you bleed out," I said. "I believe I mentioned that this wasn't my first time."

I placed one knee on his chest and pushed down, causing Achilles to gasp in pain. His considerable strength had all but vanished. He could barely even raise his arms to defend himself.

"Now, if you're ready," I said and remade the blade of fire. "I think it's time to educate you as to exactly who I am." And then I set to work.

CHAPTER 39

It hadn't taken long for Achilles to die, but in the ten minutes between him collapsing to the floor and taking his last breath, I got what I needed out of him.

I'd tried asking about where Mordred might go if he did escape, but the sound of a dozen people running toward me distracted me, and by the time I'd realized I wasn't in immediate trouble, Achilles had died.

So I decided to use him for something more helpful.

I walked back along the corridor until I found the dozen armed guards who had been so keen on watching me and Achilles fight. They were standing in front of the stairwell, assault rifles at the ready. Apparently, keeping me alive was no longer a priority.

I stopped walking and threw the coat I'd stolen from a nearby room at them. It opened and Achilles' decapitated head fell out, rolling toward the group. As one they separated, all watching the stone-covered head bounce along the floor before coming to a stop by the wall just beyond their position. It took them a few moments to turn their attention back to me, following the trail of blood the head had created along the floor. Their complexions were considerably paler than a few seconds earlier.

I started forward and not a single man amongst the group stopped me from making my way through the passage they created. I reached the stairwell door and was about to open it when something came to mind. "I'm going to kill your boss," I said without looking back. "When I'm done, I'll be leaving this pisshole of a building. If I find any of you on the way out, I will kill you. My advice is to run and don't stop. You do not want to cross my path, as you will find me utterly devoid of mercy."

I opened the door and stepped into the stairwell beyond, letting the door swing shut behind me before I began up the stairs toward the roof, taking them three at a time. Using air magic to make me faster and more agile meant I made the few flights of stairs in under a minute.

At the very top of the stairwell was a short corridor with a fire exit door at one end. I tried the door, shoving my shoulder into it when it refused to budge. I ran one finger down the side and found that the metal had been melted. Mordred had sealed the door so that no one could get through. But he'd done a poor job. "You always were a shit sorcerer," I said and walked to the end of the corridor.

Air glyphs burst to life over me, and I ran forward, a vortex of air rushing all around me, ripping the walls apart as I moved. I hit the door at full speed, and the vortex did its job, ripping the door from its secured moorings and flinging it through the air. It impacted with a massive air conditioning unit on the roof, creating a bone-shuddering noise that got the attention of Mordred as he walked up a set of steps to a waiting helicopter.

He saw me and hurried up the metal stairs, but I'd closed the distance between us and threw fire magic at him before he reached their summit. He dove over the ball of fire, clearing the handrail of the stairs and landing on the concrete roof with a dull thud. Part of the fireball had caught his coat and he tapped the singed fabric, stopping more damage from occurring.

"I'd hoped Achilles would keep you busy longer," he shouted, his words almost drowned out by the sound of the helicopter rotors.

I was astounded. "You sacrificed him."

Mordred smiled. "I can always start over." He moved toward the foot of the stairs.

My glyphs shone and Mordred raised his hand, a remote control in it. "I'd lose those if I were you."

I glanced around me. "Is the roof wired with explosives or something?"

"Dani and Samantha are in a locked room on the thirty-seventh floor." He pushed one of several buttons on the remote. "I've now released a toxin into the room. In ten minutes they will both be dead."

I took a step forward as my only thoughts were how I had to get the girls free. I needed the remote. "Are you insane? You're not going to kill your only link to the Fates."

"It would be a disaster, true. But like I said, I'll make the sacrifice. Besides, that just means I'll have to double my efforts to find those you stole from me."

I stared at Mordred in shock, but knew he meant every word. He would kill those girls, along with anyone else whose death could help him escape.

"You want this?" He wiggled the remote at me before tossing it over the side of the building. "I believe you had to make this decision before, with Ivy. That didn't work out so well for you, now did it? So, you get a second chance. Either come take me, or save those girls. But I'd hurry up." He checked the watch on his wrist. "You have nine and a half minutes."

I turned and ran. Mordred's laughter followed me, and I prayed that I'd reach the girls in time.

A swath of dead bodies greeted me on my arrival at the thirty-seventh floor. I ran through them and eventually found Anne standing in a circle of bodies, blood-covered sword in hand, killing anyone who dared get close to her.

"Anne," I shouted, drawing the attention of the three remaining guards.

I kept running, dodging the knife that one of the guards held, darting around him and snapping his neck before he could turn on me. A second guard was within arm's reach. A blast of thick, heavy air the density of iron directly into his temple knocked him cold. Anne used the diversion to slam her katana into the stomach of the last guard, ripping it sideways with a shower of gore. She kept moving and plunged the sword into the unconscious guard's throat, twisting the blade and removing it with an accompanied spray. I wanted to say that she hadn't needed to kill him, but they were trying to keep her from her children. To be honest, I'd have considered a lot worse before I'd have told her she was in the wrong.

"The door's locked," she said. "I can't get through." Anne moved to the window next to the door, and then Dani's face appeared. She saw me and her eyes pleaded for help.

My air magic allowed me to see the gas as it swirled inside the room. They wouldn't have long before it overwhelmed them.

I motioned for her to take her sister and stand at the rear corner of the sizeable room and checked my watch. Three minutes left. The window was inscribed with several runes on both the inside and out. It would be almost impossible for me to get through in time. And the door was made of thick metal, probably titanium, and would be unaffected by any normal fire. I didn't have a lot of options.

Apart from asking Achilles questions, and removing his head, I'd spent the little time I'd had using his blood to charge my magic. It had been a long time since I'd used Blood magic, and I wasn't sure how much power I'd actually have left in me if I needed to use it.

I placed my hands near the metal door, ready to try the same trick that I'd used in the abandoned warehouse, and turned to Anne. "You need to back up."

"They're my daughters."

"And you'll be a lot safer a few feet back."

She nodded and, although she didn't like it, moved to the end of the corridor.

At first not much happened. Fire glyphs burned brightly across my body, mixing with the darkness of the blood glyphs, merging in places. And then, all at once, I released the magic inside me.

The fire burned so hot it was white. I had to close my eyes to keep myself from going blind as the door began to glow. Yet it still wasn't enough, so I pushed harder, willing the blood glyphs to give me the power I needed. The flame became more intense as a voice inside my head began to speak, wanting me to keep using magic. I gave into that voice. It was a familiar need, to allow myself to be totally enslaved in its power.

The titanium soon started to melt. Big chunks of it fell from the door and dropped hissing to the floor by my feet, forming a pool of molten metal. It was so hot that it burned right through the floor in some cases, but still I kept on, even when exhaustion began to take hold and that damn voice in my head grew louder. I didn't stop.

I channeled all of the hate and rage, the fear and hurt, from the past few days into more fuel for my magic. And eventually I made it all the way through. My watch had burned to a cinder long ago, so it was impossible to tell how long, but as the gas began to escape and the door began to fall apart, I switched magic and blew the toxic fumes along the corridor, away from anyone who could be hurt.

Inside, Dani and Samantha were huddled together in one corner, holding one another tightly. Dani looked up at me, tears streaming from her eyes. "Wait," I said and used more Blood magic to enhance my air magic and cool the metal, using a similar method to the one I'd done on Achilles.

When the door was cool enough, I helped the girls out.

"Go down there," I said shielding my eyes and pushing Dani away as she tried to hold me. "I won't be long." Dani looked hurt but did as she was asked, leaving the room free for me to enter.

I collapsed almost immediately, as the voice rose in volume. *Allow it to happen,* it said.

"I will not let you take me," I told it.

It's been so long. So long since you've used this much powerful magic. It felt good didn't it? To let loose. To live. I can make it all better. Make you more powerful, more capable.

"No," I snapped.

You should just let it happen. It's what you are. I can make you powerful. I can help you.

I caught my reflection in a nearby mirror. My eyes were jet black, the darkness spilling out from them beginning to crawl down to my nose and up to my hairline. The power the voice offered was immense. I wanted to accept it, but the price was too high. I would lose too much of myself. "You will not take me," I shouted and slammed my fists onto the floor as I forced the magic back down inside of me, cutting myself off from its seduction. I had to use every ounce of willpower to suppress the nightmare that wanted to consume me.

When I next caught sight of my reflection, the darkness had receded. The voice was still there, but it was a whisper. Something to ignore. It had been a long time since the darkness of a nightmare had first been allowed to enter me. And I knew that I was lucky to have fought it off once again.

I got up gingerly, my body protesting from the rigors it had been put through, and stepped out into the hallway. I found it empty, with no answer when I called the girls' names.

I looked around, frantic, and found the word "reception" written on the wall nearby. It had been done in blood, probably belonging to one of the many dead guards who had met Anne's wrath.

This time, I caught the lift down to the ground floor, where I found Anne, Dani, and Samantha sitting together nearby. Dani's smile brightened and she ran toward me, and this time I didn't push her away as she hugged me. "Thank you," she said and moved aside, as a younger version of her stepped forward. "This is Nate," Dani told her little sister.

Samantha waved, but there was a nervous edge to her.

"I've told them both who they are," Anne said, her voice almost breaking from the emotion. "That they're my daughters."

"Hi Samantha," I said. "How does it feel to have a big sister now?"

"Weird," Samantha said with a slight smile. "Nice though. Although I wish my dad were still here."

Anne's face clouded over. I hoped she wouldn't have to tell her newfound daughter that she was responsible for her dad's murder.

"What will happen to us now?" Samantha asked, suddenly tearful.

Dani hugged her little sister, and I knew that no matter what might happen next, these two sisters had found one another and they would never willingly let go. "Come with me back to Francis'," I said. "We'll sort out your next step from there." I looked at Anne. "That okay with you?"

She nodded and the four of us left the murder and death behind us, walking out into the crisp winter morning.

CHAPTER 40

I called on the way and spoke to Francis. He told me that he and Laurel were the only occupants in the subway as Jerry was with the rest of the vampires somewhere deep in the catacombs of ancient tunnels as his transformation started. Laurel was forbidden from going with him as she would constantly worry, and in Francis' eyes, that meant get in the way at any opportunity.

Samantha and Anne both eyed the entrance warily, but followed Dani and me down the stairs without complaint. Francis was in his shop, rehanging all of the items that had fallen off during the fighting. "So, you're alive," he said with a smile as Laurel appeared in the hallway and hugged Dani, a huge smile on her face.

"Apparently, I'm a bastard to kill," I said, and Laurel turned her attention to me hugging me so tightly I had to tell her to stop.

"Sorry," she said. "And thank you for talking to Jerry. He trusts you, and he let me turn him."

"I'm glad he's okay," I said, aware that he would be far from okay for some time to come. He'd always be a vampire with one arm, something he would have to compensate for. At some point another vampire would challenge him to a fight, sensing weakness. Jerry needed to be ready for it.

Dani and Laurel took Samantha and Anne further into the station, Dani introducing her mother and sister on the way. When I turned back to Francis, he'd recovered the box of my stuff and placed it on the table. "So, are you back to having full memories?" he asked.

"Sort of," I said. "They're all there, just jumbled up. I think it'll be a little while until everything gets put back in place." I told him about everything that had happened—Jenny's sacrifice, my returning memories, the death of Achilles, and Mordred's escape. As always, he just stood and listened until I'd finished.

"You know Blood magic?" he asked eventually. "Why not just use it to remove the curse yourself?"

"You can't use your own Blood magic to remove a curse. That would make the curse somewhat pointless. And Blood magic is different from normal magic. You have to actively want to use Blood magic. It's a conscious decision. As I had no idea I could use it, there was never a time when I thought to try. And without the experience, if I had tried, I'd have probably killed myself."

Francis nodded that he understood. "I'm sorry about Jenny."

"Thank you." I would miss her. Until I'd received my memories back, I hadn't remembered just how much she was like someone I'd known...Morgan. I shook my head free from the thought and picked up the sword cane. "Well, I know what this is," I said, unsheathing the sword. "They're given to all of Merlin's Acolytes. Mordred killed one and then stole this from them."

"Did he kill many?"

"Probably; it was a stupid fantasy amongst the Acolytes that anyone who killed Mordred would gain Merlin's favor. It got a few of them killed, and Mordred used to take the swords as a sort of trophy. I know of about five or six who crossed him and didn't come back, although the actual figure is probably double that."

"So you work for Avalon, then?" Francis asked, a concerned expression on his face. "You know, I told you they weren't to be trusted."

I hadn't decided how to broach the subject when it came up. Lying was pointless, as was trying to hide my past. But full disclosure may not have filled Francis with a lot of joy.

"I used to," I said deciding honesty was best. I liked Francis, and he'd helped me a lot. He deserved the truth. "I left just before the twentieth century. Merlin and I had a falling out of sorts, and I haven't worked for him since. And just so you know, I'm pretty certain they're still not to be trusted. What makes you so distrustful of them?"

"Experience," he said. "So, how did you get involved with this?"

"I'd been hunting Mordred for a long time and found out that he was conducting more experiments on kids and trying to create yet more crimes against magic. I decided to put a stop to it. I still had friends in Avalon, and I found Daniel through them. But be assured, I don't work for Merlin or Avalon anymore."

"So, how old are you anyway?"

I smiled. "Over sixteen hundred."

The shocked expression that crossed Francis' face caused me to smile.

"Yes, sixteen hundred," I said. "And I don't even moisturize."

Francis laughed at my poor attempt at humor. "Those blood curse marks, do you know what they are now?"

I shook my head. "I don't know what they do, or who put them there, or even why. But they've done me no harm, and no one who's examined them has ever been able to give me more information. Mordred suggested that Jenny's death has unlocked whatever they're meant to do. So, I guess we'll see what happens."

Anne soon joined us, a seriousness to her features. "Do you have a plan?"

"I'm going to take you to the Fates," I told her. "You should be with your family. Ivy is your sister, yes?"

Anne nodded. "Although she's much older than me, she doesn't look it."

"You'll be safe there," I said.

I wanted to say something else, but Dani and Samantha took that moment to join us, Laurel in tow, and I decided it could wait.

Dani told Francis and Laurel that she would stay in touch, and I explained to Francis that our deal still stood. Three jobs and then we were even. He told me he'd see me soon, and with that I departed the subway with Anne and her daughters, eager and nervous in equal measure, as we made our way to the Fates.

They were greeted by Cassandra and her two fellow Fates with hugs and kisses, and more than a few tears by all involved. After an hour of everyone talking at once, I took Cassandra aside to an unused room to speak alone. "You lied to me," I said. "You knew that Jenny would kill herself to save me. Dani's vision of me screaming for someone to stop, that's what she saw."

Cassandra took a deep breath and nodded. "I'm not happy about it. Nor am I proud, but if you had been told, if you knew the truth, you would have never gone to that place. Even after they took Dani, you would have thought of another way to get her back. And you'd have gotten both yourself and the girls killed."

As much as I understood why she'd lied, it didn't mean I had to like it. "Jenny wasn't related to you?"

Cassandra shook her head. "She was just a normal psychic girl. But an incredibly powerful one. After we escaped, she continued to work for Mordred, hoping that she'd be able to save more from within. She will be missed."

I looked away, pretending to stare at a painting on the wall next to me. "Yes, she will."

"I understand your anger at me, but my granddaughter would like to talk to you," Cassandra said as Ivy appeared in the doorway.

She looked the same as she had back in Soissons all those centuries ago. I started to say something, but she ran at me, flinging her arms around me and hugging me with all her might. "You came for me," she said, crying into my t-shirt.

"I'm sorry it took so long," I whispered.

Ivy pulled away and wiped at her puffy, red eyes. "Sorry, I don't normally do crying."

I wiped at my own eyes. "Not a problem."

Ivy smiled. "You need to tell Thomas where I am."

I nodded. Last I remembered, Thomas, or Tommy as he was now known, was a private investigator. "He'll be thrilled to hear from you."

"You've got to go see your friend," she said. "Do you want to know what I saw just then?" Ivy was more powerful than I'd ever imagined, being able to draw out my future without even a hint about what she was doing.

I shook my head. "No thanks, I'd rather it be a surprise."

"Just be careful, you've angered powerful people by destroying Mars Warfare." She took a piece of paper and a pen from a table next to me, writing on it and folding it in half twice. "In six weeks, open this paper. Not before."

I took the paper and put it in my pocket. "Six weeks."

Ivy gave me one last hug. "You need to go see your friend, the one in hospital."

I nodded. "Dani and Samantha will be safe here, yes?"

Ivy nodded. "And you can visit whenever you wish." She kissed me on the cheek and we left the room together, where I bumped into Anne.

"We need to talk," I said and took her back into the room.

"I want to thank you for your help," she said.

"You're welcome." I was aware that she wasn't going to like what I needed to say. "You're an assassin. Like me, you've killed people in the name of those you work for. Unlike me, your boss was a psychotic prick."

"Do you have a point?" Her eyes became hard, matching her tone.

"Dani and Samantha will call me every Sunday, without fail."

"Are you threatening me?"

"If they miss one call. If one Sunday goes by and I don't hear from them, you'll hear from me the following Monday. And it will be a meeting you're unlikely to forget in a hurry. Am I clear?"

"They are my daughters, what do you think I'll do to them?" Anne snapped.

"You're a murderer, and a cold one. And quite frankly, I don't trust you enough to leave them without checking up. Every Sunday. Without fail."

Anne stared at me in disbelief, but nodded her agreement. "I will never hurt those children."

"Good, because I'd hate to have gone through all this just to have to kill you." I took a step closer to her, and to Anne's credit she didn't move. "Thirty seconds, just remember that." And then I left her alone in the room as I said my good-byes to Dani and Samantha, promising to keep in touch.

Dani followed me out of the bookshop and stopped me as I hailed a taxi. "Thank you," she said. "For everything."

"You'll be okay. I'll call in a few days with a number I can be reached at. If you ever need me, just call."

She stared at the ground. I was about to ask if she was okay when she looked up and kissed me hard on the lips. Before the shock had vanished, she had pulled away and ran back to the shop, waving once before going back inside.

The taxi took me to the hospital, and it wasn't long before I was making my way along the corridor toward Holly's room with mixed emotions—fear of what I needed to say, and elation because Holly would be okay.

I found Lyn alone outside her daughter's room. She stood and embraced me. "I was just about to call and let you know. Mark had some work to do; he couldn't get away." I took that to mean he was tracking down his wayward son. "You go right on in."

I did as was asked, knocking on the door before entering Holly's room. The blinds were open, bathing the room in natural light as Holly sat up reading a book. "How are you?" I asked.

Holly beamed at me and placed her book on the cupboard beside her. "Considering everything that's happened, not too bad. Head feels a little fuzzy." She touched the new bandage on her head tentatively.

As I grabbed a chair and sat at the foot of the bed, Holly caught wind of my mood. "You need to talk, don't you?"

I nodded.

"Did you get your memories back?"

Another nod. "I have to leave. I have to go back to my old life."

It was Holly's turn to nod—her's was slow and filled with sadness. "I figured you would. Can you tell me if I was right about what you used to be?"

"I wasn't a cop, if that makes things easier."

She chuckled, although it was void of humor. "Well, that's something. So what are you? That monster who did this to me said you're a sorcerer. He took a long time telling me about the world I was too ignorant to know about—his words."

"You don't sound very concerned about it."

"A giant rock creature attacked and almost killed me. Magic isn't the worst thing I've seen in the last few days. Besides, who would believe me if I told them, and freaking out isn't going to help anyone. Are you going to answer my questions?"

"I'm sixteen hundred years old and a sorcerer, yes. And that monster is now dead."

"You say that like it's not a big deal. He wasn't your first kill, was he?"

"Not even close. I'm not the man you know, Holly. The life I've been leading for the past ten years wasn't mine. I need to reclaim what is."

She looked away from me, and when she spoke it was barely above a whisper, "I love you."

"I know and I'm sorry, I really am. I don't want to hurt you, but I can't let you believe that there's something more than there is, or that there's the possibility of more."

"Leaving is for the best then." She hurriedly turned away.

"I will always cherish your friendship. You helped me get through what would have otherwise killed me. I want you to know that I will always be grateful for that."

"That's okay, it was my pleasure. You need your old life back and I don't fit into that, being human and all."

"It's got nothing to do with you being human," I said softly. Part of me screamed to hold her and tell her that it would be okay, but that would make things worse, and there needed to be a clean break.

"Then what? As nice as it is that you want to spare my feelings, I'm a big girl and can make my own decisions."

I stood and walked to the end of the bed. "I need to get away from this life, from the people in it. I need to find out who I am again. Those ten years feel like someone else lived my life for me."

"So this is it?"

"It has to be."

"Will I see you again?"

"I don't know. Maybe one day, but not for a long time."

"I really do love you, you know," she said as my hand reached the door handle.

"I know, Holly," I said. "Take care of yourself." And then I left.

I walked through the hospital in a daze. Lyn hadn't been outside the room, so that was one awkward conversation I got to avoid.

I stepped out of the hospital, looked up at the cloud-covered sky and wondered what I was going to do next. There were a lot of people who were involved with Mars Warfare who hadn't been made accountable for what had happened there. At some point they would have to be found and forced to admit their guilt. And then there was Mordred. A loose end I intended to resolve as soon as possible.

When they discovered I was back, they were bound to send people after me. I decided then not to immediately reintroduce myself into a past that had been hidden from me. My enemies could discover that I was back in a time and place of my choosing. And I'd make sure that the day I chose would be the worst day of their lives.

EPILOGUE

New York City, New York.

It had been two months since Mars Warfare had been placed under siege and I'd rescued Dani and Samantha from the grip of Mordred. And two weeks since I'd opened the piece of paper Ivy had given me. All that was written on it was a time, date, and address.

That was why I found myself on top of a ten-story building, watching through the scope of an Accuracy International Arctic Warfare AWS covert. It was the exact same type of weapon Anne had left in the back of the Nissan GTR she'd gifted to me.

The tough security measures to get into the United States had been the hardest part of my plan. Once there, getting the rifle had been as easy as ordering pizza. A friend of Francis', an ex-army guy, got hold of a rifle for a few grand. For a country that had so many guns, stealing a few rifles wasn't very difficult. Even if those guns were from the military.

Finding a good spot to sit and wait had also been straightforward. The perfect vantage point was only down the block, but it was also full of office workers, and I didn't want anyone asking questions.

The solution had been fairly simple. I turned up with some fake identification and started telling the management that there was mold in the walls. Mold is deadly stuff in the best of circumstances, and after explaining that some companies had been sued when their employees had discovered that they'd been working in dangerous conditions, he was more than happy to evacuate the building for the next forty-eight hours.

Later that morning I walked through the abandoned building and found my perch on the rooftop. I'd been on the roof ever since, going on twelve hours, barely moving, my only company the giant stone gargoyles that loomed over me, and the occasional pigeon.

I kept one eye on the stone monstrosities for the first few hours; even though I was fully aware that they were never going to move, I still felt wary. Apparently, my run in with Achilles had left an impression on me.

I glanced down the scope again. The time on the piece of paper said one p.m.—I had just under an hour. I adjusted the sights so that I could see more of the front entrance to the lavish hotel a few hundred feet away and farther down the block on the opposite side of the street. It was the perfect position. The sun was directly behind me, giving me perfect visibility, and anyone looking up would see only the glare from the mass of polished glass all around the building. The silencer on the rifle meant that I was unlikely to be heard this high up. The sound of the bullets would be taken by the wind. And if there wasn't any, well, that wasn't going to be much of a problem either.

An hour later and the door to the hotel opened. One man stepped out into the crisp, sunny day. He held open the hotel entrance, allowing his charge to alight from the luxury within.

Mordred came into view, wearing an expensive suit and still looking like he didn't have a care in the world.

I steadied my breathing and placed my finger on the trigger, ready to finish what I'd started two months ago. And then the unthinkable happened. He stopped walking and starting talking to a mother and child. *Damn him.* I wasn't about to let a young boy see the man he was talking to get his head blown off. I moved my finger slightly, releasing the tension in the trigger, but ready to take the shot at a second's notice.

He kept talking for what felt like forever, blatantly flirting with the pretty, young mum. I wondered if she'd be so quick to smile and touch his arm if she knew what he was.

Eventually, the mother and son got into a taxi and set off, and Mordred said something to one of his bodyguards, who gave a lurid smile in response before moving away to get the car ready. Mordred was an arrogant bastard, too sure of his power and position to ever think that he was in danger. Without Ivy's help I'd never have found him, so his confidence was for good reason. He smiled at a few pretty women as they walked passed.

Then the sun rose behind me, and he raised his hand to shield his eyes. The same hand he'd grabbed Jenny with. I pulled the trigger.

The relatively small, subsonic silver bullet streaked through the air and hit Mordred in the wrist. It didn't so much make a hole, as remove his hand in its entirety, coming to a rest in the concrete beside him. It took Mordred a few seconds of shock to register what had happened, but once it did, and the fear crossed his eyes, he turned to run.

I'd only made one of the bullets with a small explosive charge, the rest were ordinary silver rifle ammo. I fired a second bullet, which took out his knee as he turned, dropping him down to a kneeling position.

Mordred stared up at the New York skyline, searching me out, as a third bullet struck him in his stomach. I watched him cry out. The absent bodyguard started to run toward his boss, and then Mordred mouthed something. I thought of Dani and Samantha, of Jenny and Anne and of Jerry and Robert. Of Holly.

"Fuck you too, Mordred." And I fired the fourth and final bullet through his eye, removing a large portion of his head.

The screams from below reached my ears as I edged back from my position and began dismantling the rifle, placing it all inside a backpack I'd brought the day before. When it was all tidied away, including the shell casings, I gave one last quick look around and, finding nothing, left the roof.

Once back at ground level, I walked away from the growing scene behind me and got into my parked Dodge Challenger SRT8, which I'd rented upon arriving in the country. It was big and a little ostentatious, but when in Rome.

I placed the backpack in front of the passenger seat and started the engine, pulling out into the heavy New York traffic as sirens wailed behind me. And I smiled.

ACKNOWLEDGEMENTS

The act of writing is a solitary endeavor, full of late nights and long days researching or staring at a computer screen as the story unfolds before you. But no book would be possible with a selection of amazing people who are both supportive and helpful.

I'd firstly like to thank my wife, Vanessa, for always believing in me, even when I didn't. And also my three lovely daughters. You four together are the reasons I write, and I love you more than I could ever say.

My parents, who never once thought I was incapable of achieving this goal, and who always taught me to strive to better myself, thank you for making me the man I am today.

My friends and family, who always asked me how the book was going and always sounded interested even when I discussed the dullest pieces of information regarding sentence structure, agent hunting, or what fifteenth-century people would have worn. It's finally written and I'll shut up about it now, I promise.

To Michelle Muto and D.B. Reynolds. Two of the finest writers I know, and two people I'm proud to call my friends. Without their help on this book, it would never have gotten where it has.

Speaking of writers, I'd like to thank everyone on Kelley Armstrong's forum, but especially those in OWG group 6. All fantastic writers, and each of them helped me craft this story. But a special mention goes out to Dianne, Chrissey, Danni, Teri, and

Angie, who took a lot of time to go through the book and tell me what did and didn't work.

All books also have a collection of readers—in my case, Howard, Alex, and Kerry. Thank you for your time and kind words.

It's probably cliché to thank your English teacher, but I don't care, I'm doing it anyway. Peter Pearcy (its weird calling my teacher by his first name) was not only the best English teacher I ever had, he was the best teacher. He allowed me to get away with murder, but he also ignited a spark inside me for writing that has burned for over twenty years. And for that I will always be grateful.

There are many people who helped in small ways with information that didn't make it into this book, but hopefully what I learnt will be used in a later one. Firstly, BMW Southampton, who explained how to steal a Z4 (short answer: you can't), and didn't call the cops when I asked. Hampshire Fire and Rescue for showing me how to start a fire to make it appear as an arson attack and also not calling the cops when I asked. Thank you both for not having me arrested.

The imperial war museum in London, who gracefully allowed me into the catacombs beneath the museum to see some of the items they have that aren't for public display. It was a day I will never forget, mostly because it was a day when I tried not to bump into anything explosive.

Last, but by no means least, to my friend Kev Burman, you are the wind beneath my wings (told you I'd put it).